PICKLED

by Ron Sellz

LOST AGE PUBLISHING

2017

Printed in the United States of America

Cover art and interior design by: Cyrusfiction Productions.

First Edition Paperback
ISBN: 978-1-946480-08-8

9018 Balboa Boulevard
Suite #562
Northridge, CA 91325

INTRODUCTION

Based on a true story, this book gets into the definition of someone being a prescription drug addict who has lost his control of his ability to discontinue the use of the powerful drug "Placydil"

The most interesting concept here is the narrative from the perspective of that main character, within which this true story is being told.

It is related in such a manner that the reader is brought into the life of someone who is desperately trying to get off the drugs that are ruining his writing career. He encounters one road block after another.

There are also some critical comments about the treatment that goes on inside of the rehab clinics.

PICKLED

RON SELLZ

CHAPTER ONE

Beads of sweat cascade down Rick's face as the station wagon comes to a stop. "Here we are," Valerie comments, looking over at her husband. Her stare focuses on Rick's trembling legs. Valerie has grown accustomed. to the tremors in his legs, but feels compelled to turn away hoping that Rick won't see the fear in her eyes. Rick could always look right through his wife's eyes. Valerie wishes it were daylight so she could hide behind her sunglasses.

"Why are you always turning away? Damn it! You know I can't help my legs." Rick throws his cigarette out of the car window, but the cigarette bounces off the rolled-up window and falls onto his lap. He jumps up. "Son of a bitch! I hate this fuckin' car. When are we gonna get rid of this thing?" Rick looks at his wife for her response. She's crying. Rick is enraged. "What are you crying about? I'm the one who should be crying!" He tenses. "You're always trying to steal my thunder. Aren't you?"

Valerie reaches into her cluttered purse and pulls out a tissue. "I'm sorry honey. I just can't stand to see you like this. It's tearing me up inside."

Valerie wipes her face with the Kleenex, then tries to discard it out her window. However, her window is also rolled up and the tissue falls into the back of the car.

Rick and Valerie are too nervous and upset to laugh. If

they were anywhere else, they would be in hysterics.

Rick looks around and wonders why Valerie stopped the car where she did.

"This is it," Valerie announces in an upbeat tone.

"Are you kidding? This can't be it," Rick firmly says, staring at the one-story building located at the end of a residential district.

The building looks cold and impersonal. Rick was brought up just a few miles from this ghastly place. He has passed the hospital many times on his way to the television studios in Hollywood. Rick tries to think of something funny to say about this place, but he draws a blank. Maybe if he wasn't in such a bad way, he would come up with a ball-buster. He loved to make Valerie laugh, but not this time. He decides to try anyway.

"This place looks like a library in Mayberry." Rick stares at his wife waiting for her to laugh, but she does not. "Mayberry! Damn it! From the TV show Andy Griffith was on."

Valerie nods her head.

"And you don't think that's funny?"

"I'm not in a laughing mood," she answers in a somber tone.

"I'll say you're not!" Rick looks around, hoping that someone will come out of the building and tell them that they'll have to come back another time due to a shortage of beds. Then he closes his eyes, hoping that when he opens them, he'll be back in his own home and his own bed. Unfortunately, it doesn't work. He's still in the car with his loving wife. Rick can easily see that this ordeal is deeply affecting Valerie. Because of her tears, her makeup is running down her perfect cheeks. Her big brown eyes aren't a pretty sight when they're swollen like this.

"The least you could do is laugh at my lousy joke. For all I know, this is a fuckin' 'Cuckoo's Nest' you're leaving me at.

And if it is, I'll be the one to fly over it!"

It was your idea to come here. I don't see why you have to make me feel guilty about bringing you here." Valerie's tone stiffens. "It was your decision!"

Valerie opens her door and steps out of the car. She walks around the back of the station wagon and approaches Rick's door. Valerie raises her voice assuming a commanding tone. "Are you coming?"

Rick sits silently in the car pretending to be deaf. He wishes he she'd disappear. Valerie stares at her husband for a moment, then takes her key and opens his door. Rick slowly gets out of the car and stares at the building. He can feel his wife's gaze. He doesn't want their eyes to meet, knowing they'll both break down.

Valerie's never seen him cry and he doesn't want to start now. It's not that he doesn't want to cry or never has. He just doesn't do it openly and he's never done it in front of his wife. The last time he cried was when his best friend caught a stray bullet in the head and died while they were climbing the rocks below the Palm Springs Tramway. The guy who shot the gun came running down the trail and found Rick, cradling his friend's head in his lap. The life had drained out and his friend was gone. Rick cried for days and never really got over it. He could not forgive the man who killed his friend even though he knew it was an accident.

Valerie takes Rick's grip, then takes her husband's arm. She kisses his cheek. "I just want you to know that I love you for what you're doing."

Rick looks at his wife and smiles. "I'm sorry about what I said before. I didn't mean to bite your head off. I'm just scared."

Valerie hugs him, wiping her tears on his shirt.

"Why don't you use Kleenex. I'm sure there's some more in your purse."

Valerie smiles. "You know I can never find anything in my purse when I need it. It's too cluttered."

Rick smiles. He's finally got her. "Ah ha! I finally got you to admit it. I knew all that junk in your purse would get to you sooner or later. Maybe you should check into this place with me. I'm sure the shrinks would like to know why you have a purse that weighs over a hundred pounds."

Valerie looks at her husband and laughs for a moment.

Rick is delighted. "It's about time I got you to laugh. I must be getting better."

Rick and Valerie stroll up the walkway arm in arm towards the hospital entrance. Rick looks back at their car. "That car's sicker than I am and look who's going into the shop."

Rick opens the door for his wife and they enter the reception room. The area is cold and quiet. There are a couple of vending machines next to the entrance. which probably support plenty of junk food junkies. There are no chairs to sit on. Instead, there's an old beat up couch with cigarette burns all over it.

Half of the lights on the ceiling are turned off to save energy and the walls are covered with certificates of appreciation issued by various civic groups.

The door to the admitting area opens as Rick approaches. A small Hawaiian man, Zulu, sticks his frail body into view. "I'll be with you in a moment."

Rick returns to his seat alongside Valerie on the couch.

"Now you won't forget to feed the dog that stuff in the kitchen and mix it with that stuff in the garage."

"I know, I know. And I'll remember to keep the porch light on at night even if I'm home and I'll remember to turn on the answering machine whenever I leave the house even if it's just to get the mail."

"And don't forget to…"

"C'mon honey. Don't worry. You just concentrate on getting better and let me worry about running the house. Please."

Rick mentions a couple of more chores that need attending to in spite of Valerie's pleads.

The double doors which lead into a corridor open slightly. Valerie calls this to Rick's attention.

"That's probably one of the inmates checking out the new bird," Rick comments.

"You make it sound like a prison camp. I think you've been, watching too much television."

The doors open a few more inches. Rick and Valerie spot a pair of brown eyes, dark greasy hair and a white tee-shirt.

"Wonderful," Rick sarcastically comments. "A god damn Mexican! I had to come all this way to see some god damn wetback! He'll probably cut my throat and take my cigarettes."

"I think you should change your attitude before you walk through those doors. That guy just might be your roommate."

"Thanks a lot!"

The Mexican continues peering into the waiting room. His eyes are riveted on the entrance. Rick and Valerie finally realize that the man isn't staring at them. He's staring at the entrance to the hospital. Then the Mexican flings open the doors and enters the waiting room. Rick and Valerie are shaken at first, but calm down as the man holds open the entrance for his wife and daughter.

The man embraces his wife and child. The man is about the same age as Rick, approximately twenty-five and his wife is a few years younger. His daughter looks to be at least three years old.

"*Hola* Papa," the little girl repeatedly shouts.

"I don't know about you, but I feel pretty silly about suspecting that guy of all sorts of vicious things," Rick tells his wife.

"I know what you mean. My prejudiced feelings must have been working overtime."

"He can't help being Mexican any more than I can help being Jewish. And you know how I feel when somebody calls me a dirty Jew."

"He probably feels the same way about being called a wet-back "

"Didn't I just say that?"

Valerie shrugs.

"But I did hear her call him Jose. That fits the stereotype anyway."

Valerie leers at her husband. Rick looks at his wife and tells her to be quiet. He wants to eavesdrop on the man's conversation with his wife.

It appears that Jose admitted himself to the hospital for an alcohol problem. He lost his job because of booze and he became withdrawn and sometimes violent towards those who tried helping him. He has been in the hospital for over three weeks and complains that the atmosphere in unit one is not conducive to bettering himself. He doesn't elaborate on this matter, choosing to change the subject. At this point, Rick and Valerie are disappointed that their conversation switches to Spanish. They can't understand one word, but it's interesting to listen and try and pick out certain words anyway.

It's easy to see the pain in Jose's wife's eyes when she realizes that her husband won't be coming home for at least another few weeks. Valerie is concerned and voices her opinion to Rick.

"There's a big difference between an alcoholic and me," Rick answers. "Our problems are totally different. I'm sure that guy's a heavy boozer. Just look at his belly. He's been putting away the booze for years. I'll bet his blood's eighty proof."

"Very funny!" Valerie comments sarcastically.

"It would be even funnier if I said eighty-six proof, but I don't want you to fall off the couch laughing."

The commotion from outside causes. Rick and Valerie's conversation to halt.

They turn to investigate the sounds and spot an elderly man being escorted by two policemen. They enter the building. Once inside, the first officer removes his handcuffs from the man's wrists.

"Now look Mr. Corlitz. We're doing you a favor. You can admit yourself or we can take you down to the station and book you. It's your choice."

The man scans the room. "Oh yeah! The only reason you brought me here was so that you wouldn't have all that paperwork at the station if you took me in for a five-o-two."

The second officer takes out his handcuffs and dangles them in front of the man's face. "Have it your own way," the officer says while opening up the handcuffs.

"All right. All right. I'll admit myself in. But only for one night. First thing in the morning I'm gonna call a cab and get the hell out of here."

"We don't care what you do tomorrow, Mr. Corlitz. We just want you to have a restful night, preferably not at the city's expense."

The officers escort Mr. Corlitz through the double doors marked," No Admittance."

Rick is growing concerned. "What kind of place is this? I'll bet everyone in here's on booze except me!" Rick tells Valerie in a panicked manner.

The door to the admitting room opens and Zulu appears. "Are you Mr. Brown?"

"That's me."

"Step this way please," Zulu says as he holds the door open for Rick and his wife.

Rick leans over and kisses Valerie. "This is it!" he says as he takes his wife's hand, escorting her into Zulu's office.

Zulu sits behind the main desk in the office. Rick looks around the office and spots a girl sitting behind an old-fashioned switchboard. It has switches, levers and an array of lights and plugs. The operator introduces herself as Linda. As she stands up and heads for the filling cabinet, Rick is stunned. Linda resembles the fat lady at the circus.

Rick glances at the chair behind the switchboard and wonders how in the world Linda could possibly fit on such a tiny seat.

Rick doesn't wish to embarrass Linda by his staring even though she catches his probing eyes. Rick smiles at Linda as she returns to her seat behind her switchboard. Rick also sits down at Zulu's desk. He knows that Linda's watching him.

Zulu begins the conversation, but Rick's making a conscious effort to ignore him. He knows that once the questions are answered, he'll be whisked off to some little corner of the hospital where he'll undoubtedly be surrounded by a bunch of drunks.

Rick puffs nervously on his cigarette, one time even swallowing the smoke he only meant to inhale. He's clearly growing more and more petrified.

Valerie looks at her husband, sensing what's wrong. She embraces him, planting a kiss on his neck. "I want you to know how proud I am of you," she whispers. kissing him again with her moist lips.

Rick works up a smile and faces Zulu. "Ask me no questions and I'll give you no answers," Rick says. His composure has returned.

"In case you couldn't tell, my husband's a writer.

Zulu is impressed. "Really! What kind of things do you write?"

"Television."

Zulu looks star struck. "No kidding! My cousin has a friend who knows a guy that writes for the TV. What shows have you written?

Rick's eyes light up. "Do you remember *Roots*?"

Zulu practically jumps out of his Hawaiian skin. "Are you kidding! Everybody's seen that."

Valerie is tempted to spoil Rick's gaming of Zulu, but decides to let him continue. After all, Rick seems more at ease!

"You wrote *Roots*?" Zulu asks incredulously, anxiously awaiting an affirmative answer from Rick.

"Of course, not," Rick replies in a casual manner.

Zulu's high hopes are dazed.

"But one of the actors on *Roots* acted on a show I wrote."

Zulu pumps himself up again. "What show was it?"

"It doesn't make any difference. The network decided not to air it.

Zulu seems mortally injured.

"Listen. I'm just kidding. I've written a lot of shows you've probably seen and I'd be delighted to talk with you about them." Rick squirms in his chair. "But for right now, can we get all this paperwork out of the way?"

Zulu nods his head and picks up a bevy of forms which must be filled out by all incoming patients. He informs Rick and Valerie that even though Rick's insurance company gave their unofficial permission for Rick to receive treatment, the hospital still needs a check for one thousand dollars from him. Zulu reminds them that the check will be held until the insurance company verifies that Rick is insured for drug detoxification treatment.

Rick and Valerie are hesitant about shelling out that much money, but Zulu assures them that their check will undoubtedly be returned the following morning.

They just have to make it official with the insurance company.

Valerie writes out a check and hands it to Zulu.

"It won't be good for a couple of days," Valerie says in an almost apologetic tone.

"That's all right," Zulu says reassuring them. "Don't even bother putting in money to cover the check unless I call you."

Most of Zulu's questions are simple and require only one word answers. "Let's see," Zulu comments as he brings out another form. "I'll need your drug history for, let's say, the past two years. What I mean is, tell me everything you've taken including all the drugs you got on the streets and from other sources."

Rick chortles. "You're gonna need another pencil."

Zulu shoots Rick a skeptical look. He's seen it all and nothing Rick says could possibly surprise him.

Rick could joke about anything at any time. It didn't matter that he was going to commit himself to a hospital. A joke was a joke and making someone laugh was a major and constant goal of his. Many of Rick's friends, as well as his family, frequently disbelieved Rick when he reported a news event to them which seemed slightly bizarre. They didn't know if he was joking or not.

Rick had a theory about making jokes. He believed that he should make a joke whenever the occasion arose. If he told one hundred jokes and only one of them was funny, then the ninety-nine bad jokes were worth telling. He'd remember the good joke and repeat it whenever he could, sometimes inserting it into his current script or monologue.

"I'm ready whenever you are," Zulu announces, reminding Rick to start relating his drug history.

Rick apologizes for daydreaming, but Zulu isn't paying any attention to him. Zulu's eyes are riveted on Rick's trembling legs. He is mesmerized by the sight of Rick's tremors.

Rick immediately grabs his legs, steadying them. "If they weren't shaking, I wouldn't be here," Rick says grinning.

Valerie isn't amused. She wants Rick to get on with it.

Rick has no qualms about naming all the drugs he's put into his system. He just doesn't want to do it in front of Valerie. She has no idea about the drugs he acquired on the streets and he wants to keep it that way. He's afraid of her reaction.

"Honey, would you do me a favor and get me a Coke from that machine in the waiting room?"

Valerie smiles at her husband, picks up her purse and leaves the room.

Rick's attention focuses on Zulu. "I hope you can write fast."

"I'm ready if you are." Zulu's pencil is poised.

Rick looks around making sure that Valerie's still in the other room. Then Rick takes in a deep breath. "I've taken Percodan, Codeine quarter grain, Codeine half grain, Codeine full grain, Codeine with Tylenol numbers three and four, Darvon, Darvocet N 100, and," Rick stops to catch his breath. He sees Zulu writing as fast as he can.

Zulu realizes that Rick has stopped. He picks up his head and looks at Rick. "Don't stop."

"Do you want me to slow down?" Rick inquires.

"That's all right. I'll correct the spelling after you're processed. Please continue."

"Let's see. Oh yes. Demerol, but I'm not sure what strength."

"That's okay. Keep going."

"Fiorinal, Talwin, Librium, Norgesic Forte, Nembutal, Placidyl, Dalmane, Parafon Forte, Seconal, Valium, Tuinal, Vistaril, Quaaludes, Phenergan and some other pills and injections I can't even think of. But if I think of them, I'll let you know. "Rick seems pleased that he was able to remember all of the names. He didn't think that he'd be able to do it because the pills he hospitalized himself for had affected his memory. That's why he practiced naming the pills on his way to the hospital.

Zulu finishes writing and slowly raises his head. He's aghast. "You mean there's more."

"Maybe two or three." Rick starts thinking. "Did I mention Phenobarbital?"

Zulu is amazed. He's never seen anyone who's taken so many pills and live to talk about the experience.

Valerie returns to the room handing Rick his drink. Rick consumes the entire bottle in a couple of gulps. Rick's built up a tremendous thirst jogging his memory for his drug history. It was like the proverbial rock being lifted off his shoulders. It frightened Rick to think that he had taken so many pills. He abused them all, frequently taking double doses and sometimes triple doses.

Valerie knows that Rick abused his medications and isn't surprised when she hears him telling Zulu about his drug history and why he came to taking so many pills.

Zulu doesn't need any more information, reminding Rick that he previously spoke with his personal doctor.

"The best thing we can do now is to get you a bed as fast as possible so treatment can begin."

Rick begins to sweat as Zulu presents him with the admission papers.

"Sign your life away on the dotted line," Zulu glibly states.

Rick takes the papers and stands up. "If you don't mind, I'd like to take the papers home and study them. You know, have my lawyer look them over and all that." Rick beams. "I figure it will take about two weeks." Rick heads for the door and opens it. "See you then."

Valerie's laughter makes Zulu realize that Rick is only joking. He's seen people have second thoughts before and really isn't surprised to see Rick heading for the door. Zulu feels silly that he didn't catch on sooner.

Rick returns to Zulu's desk. "Just kidding Zulu. I always turn chicken whenever I'm about to do something brave."

"Well, I'm glad you're here," Zulu says pleasantly.

"Are you kidding? I had to come here. Do you have any idea how hard it is to sit in bed all day killing dust particles with a rolled-up Playboy! "

Zulu thinks about Rick's statement for a moment, but decides not to ponder the issue. "I think you made a wise choice. You've definitely come to the right place."

Rick signs all the necessary papers and hands them to Zulu. Then Rick removes the gold chain from his neck and hands it to Valerie. "Remember, Valerie, when I get out of here I want my chain back."

"Of course, honey. Didn't I give it back to you the last time you were in the hospital?"

"Yeah! But I was home three weeks before I remembered that you were wearing it."

Valerie places the chain around her neck. She undoes the top button of her blouse enabling the chain to be seen better. Her chest looks sensual with the gold chain glimmering. The chain seems brighter against her sun-lamp tan. "You'll have to admit. It does look better on me." Valerie stands up and pirouettes.

"Real cute," Rick tells Valerie as he turns to address Zulu. "What's the policy here on valuables?"

"Well for your own protection, we suggest that you either send all valuables home, or we can lock them up in our safe." Zulu is anxious to see what Rick intends on doing with his fancy watch and wedding band.

Rick removes his watch and wedding band and hands them to Valerie along with his wallet.

Zulu prefers that all patients refrain from using the hospital safe. In the past, there have been some mysterious disappearances. Zulu knew nothing about them, except for those few times when he felt that he could get away with it. The people he steals from are usually junkies whose pockets are lined with ill gotten money. And since the money was usually gotten through unorthodox means, it would never be missed if he borrowed it. Besides, once released, the junkie usually fails to remember about any loot which he may have brought in with him. Without this fringe benefit, Zulu might have to quit his low paying job.

Zulu scans the admitting papers, making sure that Rick's signatures are in the right places. Zulu picks up the hospital files and searches for a bed to assign Rick to; After a moment, Zulu decides on unit three.

Naturally, Rick is curious about unit three as well as the other units in the hospital. His reasons are twofold. He wants to know about the general goings on in the unit and, more importantly, he's still stalling. He wants to put off the inevitable for as long as possible. He's still scared. His legs continue trembling and his speech is growing more erratic.

As the seconds pass, Rick grows more and more uncomfortable. He begins complaining about severe back pain associated with sitting in the chair. Rick stands up telling Zulu that if he moves around while he talks, he'll be fine.

Zulu is curious about Rick's condition. "You sure you're okay?" Zulu asks compassionately.

"I'll be fine. Really!"

"How'd you hurt yourself anyway?"

"I had back surgery about two years ago for a ruptured herniated disc. I screwed up my back lifting a typewriter and

I've been paying for it ever since."

"I guess the operation wasn't a success."

"I'll never know if it was because a few months after the operation, I was in a car accident. It slowed up the healing process and all that. That's why I'm in here. I went cold turkey from all the pain pills six months ago, but I couldn't stop taking the Placidyls. I tried to cold turkey them too, but I started going through withdrawals. That's when my doctor told me about this place."

"Placidyls, huh? Aren't those sleeping pills? I never heard of them before. About the only thing I know about are Quaaludes. Aren't they just about the same?"

"Placidyls are ten times better. I used to trade them with my friends. I'd give them Quaaludes for Placidyls."

"Where'd you get the Quaaludes?"

"From my doctor. He didn't want me to keep taking Placidyl so he kept switching me to other stuff. He's a real good doctor. He's legit and all that. Not like some Dr. Feelgoods who only care about making some extra money. They don't give a shit about their patients."

"I know what you mean. There are a lot of Dr. Feelgoods' patients in this place. I've got a whole unit full of them."

"Which unit?"

"Unit three," replies Zulu.

Hearing this, Rick begins quizzing Zulu about unit three. Zulu realizes that Rick's stalling for time, but feels that Rick has a right to know about the other units. He informs Rick and Valerie that every patient in the hospital is admitted into the facility at that person's own choosing. Any patient is free to leave whenever he wishes. However, some insurance companies frown on those patients who leave against medical advice or "AMA." If a patient does leave "AMA," the insurance company usually refuses to pay the bill.

"Unit one is solely for alcoholics. There are padded rooms for the worst types, as well as semi-private rooms for the typical alcoholic who just has a slight problem and recognizes it in time. We try to keep the same age groups together and usually don't have any problems. Some of the patients participate in group therapy sessions with unit three. And any patient who wishes to remain in his unit is free to do so. Unless of course, we feel that it would be in their best interest to join the group.

You might say that unit one is the dullest unit in the whole place. Most of the time, the patients just stand around in the corridors doing nothing.

They don't especially like conversing with the other patients on their unit. I guess it has a lot to do with their problem. I'd rather be around drug addicts than alcoholics. Guys on drugs are usually more fun. The only problems we ever encounter is when they start..." Zulu stops abruptly. He doesn't want to scare Rick into leaving. He can see the fear in Rick's eyes.

Valerie notices that her husband is biting his nails. Something he only does when he becomes unnerved. Valerie takes hold of Rick's hand and caresses it.

"When can I visit?" Valerie asks Zulu.

"Well, when I'm on duty you can see him anytime. Otherwise, they're pretty strict about visitors. Twelve to four are the normal visiting hours, but you'll have to check with your husband first. It's not a good idea to just come over. You know. In case he's in therapy or something."

"What about television? I suppose all the rooms have TVs?"

Zulu chuckles to himself. "No. Not quite. Units one and three have one set located in a television room. We're supposed to be getting new sets in each unit soon. Maybe even while you're here."

Rick seems disturbed. "You mean there is only one television set in each unit and everybody has to share it?"

"You make it sound pretty morbid. It's not that bad. Really!" Zulu knows that the television issue is very important to Rick. "I'm sure you won't have any problem with the others in your unit. The TV's always on, but hardly anyone watches it. You can watch whatever you want." Zulu makes an 'X' over his chest. "Cross my heart."

"Which unit are you talking about?" Valerie asks.

"Unit three." Zulu looks through some papers on his desk. "As a matter of fact, I can sign you up for the best room in the whole unit."

Valerie gives Zulu a puzzled look. "Why is it the best?"

"Because they get their meals first. That way they're always hot."

"I hate to keep asking questions, but what kind of people are in this unit?"

"People like your husband. As a matter of fact, most of the patients in this place are under thirty." Zulu pats Rick on his shoulder. "Relax Rick. You're here to get better. Just leave everything to us. Your case is routine."

Rick looks slightly relieved. "What kind of cases are in unit three"?

"Mostly drug patients. There are a few depression cases and there's at least one 'dust' case."

Rick looks blankly at Valerie. She returns his perplexed look.

"Angel Dust?"

"Yes."

"Aren't those people dangerous? I mean, don't they always have violent flashbacks and all that?"

"Don't look so worried. The staff is trained for that. You haven't tried Angel Dust have you?"

"Are you kidding? I've taken a lot of stuff, but I'd never put an animal tranquilizer in my body. Those people are crazy."

Rick continues talking about Angel Dust as Zulu slips a small piece of paper into his typewriter. He begins typing.

"I don't think I've ever seen the stuff," Rick tells Zulu. "I never even met anyone who's smoked it."

Zulu removes the slip of paper from his typewriter and inserts it into a wrist band which he places around Rick's wrist.

"You'd know the stuff all right. It has a strong medicinal smell."

"Have you ever smoked it?"

"Are you kidding? I can't handle cigarettes." Zulu tightens the wrist band and brings out a pair of scissors. "Is this too tight?" Zulu asks as he adjusts the band.

Rick feels the wrist band. It's fine."

Zulu snips off the slack.

"What about unit two?" Rick asks, making sure that Zulu doesn't forget.

"That's our medical unit. It's the only unit with a full-time nursing staff and three doctors. There's an operating room in there, but it's hardly ever used. All of the patients in there have some sort of medical problems. Most of the guys are alcoholics with shot livers and believe me you wouldn't like it."

Rick perks up. "How about TVs?"

"I thought you'd ask that," Zulu says smiling. Each bed has its own color set which…"

Rick interrupts. "Can I get into unit two?"

Valerie studies her husband's face. She knows that he's deep in thought.

"I should be in there anyway. I need a doctor or a nurse around me all the time because of my back."

Zulu believes he is being gamed, but suddenly remembers that Rick did mention his back problem earlier. "Is it very painful?"

"I should be in bed most of the time. It doesn't hurt as

much when I'm in bed" Rick suddenly remembers something else. Something more important. "Besides, I should be in unit two because of the television. There are certain shows I have to watch because I may have to write a script for them. And if I miss seeing even one show, it might make the difference between working and not working. I can't afford to fall behind even one week."

Zulu nods his head in agreement. He sets down the file belonging to unit three and picks up the unit two file.

Rick shoots Valerie his sly glance. She knows that Rick will get his way. He usually does.

"There's a bed in unit two, but it doesn't have a TV," Zulu tells Rick in an apologetic manner.

"That's okay." Rick's wheels are turning. Then," Do you think you can get me one?"

"Well, I could have it taken from another patient's bed."

"I'd really appreciate it."

"I'll see what I can do."

Rick looks at his wife, with the look of a gambler who bluffed his way to a winning hand. Rick loves getting his way, especially when he doesn't deserve it.

Rick is glad he's going into unit two. He could kiss Zulu for that. He senses that Zulu probably wouldn't even mind. After all, Rick and Valerie agree that Zulu looks slightly effeminate.

"Is that it?" Rick wants to know, examining his wristband. "No more questions?"

"No more questions," Zulu answers as he picks up the telephone and calls someone in the hospital. He requests that an attendant be sent to the admitting office to escort a new patient to unit two. Zulu sets down the phone. "That's it."

"Does that mean I won't see you again until I leave? I mean, you're the only person in this place I know."

"Don't worry. I'll be by your room to visit. I'm always

walking around the units. Maybe I'll see you tomorrow with your check in my hand."

"As long as you don't come to see me because you want another check." Everyone in the admitting office laughs as the attendant enters the room.

"Don't worry about a thing," Zulu says, handing the attendant the admitting papers.

Rick looks at the male attendant. He's dressed in white. Rick immediately becomes uneasy. The attendant looks like the typical male nurse. George is a black man about six feet two with a peculiar look in his eye. Rick shoots a look at Valerie. "It figures," Rick whispers to Valerie.

Valerie doesn't have to say a word, but turns away keeping her expression out of George's view. She remembers that on their way to the hospital, Rick told her that the attendants would probably be a bunch of homosexuals. Valerie can't help noticing the look in George's eyes. It's kind of a dazed look. His eyes are open as far as they can be, almost stretching his face. The other features on his face are as perfect as they can be. It's as if he uses make-up.

George approaches Rick and takes his grip from the floor, flinging it around his shoulder like a purse. Rick is surprised that George doesn't lisp.

"If you'll just follow me. My name is George. I work in all three units and you'll probably see me from time to time."

Rick ignores George for a moment as he turns towards his wife. He wants to say something noble, but the words elude him. He has a hard time looking at his wife straight on. Rick nervously scans the room. He's obviously looking for the right words. "Are you sure you can get along without me?" Rick takes in a quick breath. "I can come back tomorrow."

Valerie throws her arms around Rick. She begins to cry. "Honey, I love you. I love you for what you're doing." She wipes her tears on Rick's shoulder. "Sometimes I thought that you just wouldn't wake up in the morning because of those pills. I've prayed for this day. And now that you're here, I know that I'm not going to lose you. Ever! She kisses him again. "I love you so much!" Valerie kisses Rick again and again, each kiss more passionate than the last. She knows that when she's finished, her husband will leave her. Finally, their embrace ends.

"How about it, Zulu. Can you fix it so my wife can sleep over?"

"Afraid not, but the doctors sometimes give their best patients passes to go home. You know, to read their mail and things," Zulu winks at Rick.

"Think you could swing an overnight pass for me tonight?"

"I'll let you answer that."

Rick shrugs. "Oh well. Can't say I didn't try."

Valerie removes a Kleenex from her purse and blows her nose. "How long do you think Rick will have to be here? What I mean is, how long does it usually take?"

"That all depends on Rick. Every patient's different. He might be out of here in a couple of weeks. Who knows. Maybe even sooner."

Rick gives Valerie a last and longing kiss. He walks her to the door where George is waiting. Rick reaches out and cups the chain on Valerie's neck.

"I still say it looks better on me," Rick says forcing himself to smile. Valerie tries not to cry, but her eyes swell up from holding her tears back.

"Don't worry honey, I'll call you tonight. "Rick takes a step into the corridor, then returns to Zulu's office for one more look at his wife. She's crying. He knows why she's crying. Zulu didn't fool her. His problem can't be solved as fast as Zulu might like them to believe. Rick and Valerie know that he'll be in the hospital for a long time. His ordeal has just begun.

CHAPTER TWO

The corridors are cold and sterile. Because of the late hour, Rick and George fail to pass anyone as they walk down the long corridor. George falls a few steps behind Rick. Rick has an uncomfortable feeling that George is checking him out as they walk. This is making Rick extremely uneasy. He wouldn't mind it if George was a woman, but the thought of George staring at his body makes him sick. Rick slows down his pace until they are walking abreast. George grins at Rick and puts his arm on top of Rick's shoulder, directing him to make a left turn as they reach the end of the corridor. Rick becomes unnerved and doesn't quite know how to handle George's friendliness. He finally decides to quicken his pace and once again walks ahead of George.

"Wait a second," George calls out.

Rick stops and looks back as George approaches.

"I didn't get a chance to introduce myself," he says, extending his hand.

"My name is George. I'm the main orderly in this place. Sort of an assistant to anyone who needs me."

Rick shakes hands with George, making a conscious effort to squeeze George's hand using practically all of his strength. Rick wants George to know that his hand shake is manly and strictly heterosexual.

"I'm Rick Brown," he says releasing George's hand.

George rubs the pain out of his hand and winces from the discomfort. "That's some grip you've got there."

Rick leers at George. He's made his point. "Really!" he comments innocently. "I hadn't noticed."

George and Rick continue down the corridor. Rick sees an open door and walks toward it.

"You'd better not go in there," George warns.

"Why?" Rick says stopping in his tracks. He looks into the unit, but is hesitant about stepping inside.

"That's the alcoholic ward, unit one. Those guys are pretty unstable. I don't even like going in there. No telling what's likely to happen. And I work here. Why, you'd be fresh meat to them."

Rick isn't too thrilled with George's choice of words. "What's that supposed to mean?" Rick asks suspiciously.

"Forget it. If you stay here long enough, you'll find out."

"Can we go inside?"

"What for? You're on unit two. You'll be allowed to visit the other units anytime you want." George is growing impatient. "C'mon man! I think you're stalling me."

"No, really I almost ended up in there myself and I'd really like to see it. I'm just curious, that's all."

George throws up his arms. "Go ahead, but it's your behind."

Rick shoots George a resentful look. "Thanks." Rick slowly walks down the corridor of unit one. Every ten feet or so, there is a closed door with a pane of glass in the center. Rick stops to peer through the glass. Inside the first room, a man is lying in his bed, crying. Rick looks around the room and sees no furniture or any loose objects. Just a man in his bed Then it dawns on him. The room is padded. Suddenly, the man cries out in pain and begins running around the room screaming. Rick is horrified, and turns away.

Rick decides to take a second look and sees the man staring out at him, pounding his fist against the shatter proof glass. The patient begins screaming like a wild man.

"Get me the fuck out of here!" the man cries out. "Open this fuckin' door, I wanna go home."

Rick sees that the man's fists are turning black and blue from the terrible beating he's inflicting on them.

"Open the fucking door!" the man demands.

Rick quickly steps away from the door and sees George staring at him. Rick decides to continue his tour, thereby putting off the inevitable for a few more minutes.

Rick sees a few people milling about at the end of the corridor and decides to stroll down in their direction. He approaches the first man, who quickly sizes him up. The man steps in front of Rick, blocking his path.

"How much money you got man?" he asks in a demanding tone.

Rick is visibly shaken. "Just a couple of bucks. Why?"

The man shakes his head as he adjusts his hospital gown. "Sorry man, that's not enough." The man opens the door to his room and disappears inside.

Rick shakes his head, deciding that he's had enough of unit one. He pivots around and walks out of the unit. George is impatiently waiting.

"Are you ready to go to your unit now?"

"Lead the way."

Rick and George continue through the maze of corridors. George points out the hospital's kitchen as they pass, explaining that the patients are given only three meals a day and that the kitchen is off limits to all patients. Fortunately, there are vending machines in the lobby for the patients to use. Patients are also allowed to have food brought in from the outside, provided that a visitor supplies it.

Suddenly, Rick and George hear an alarm going off. George instinctively tells Rick to be quiet as the P.A. blurts out, "Code blue, unit one, code blue, unit one."

George tells Rick to stay put while he attends to the alert. Naturally, Rick is curious about the code, but George runs down the corridor and out of sight.

Rick stands quietly for a few moments as different hospital personnel race past him then Rick lights a cigarette, picks up his grip, and decides to go back to unit one to see what's going on. Suddenly, he hears an ear shattering scream coming from the corridor closest to his position. Throwing down his cigarette, Rick runs down the corridor figuring that someone's in serious trouble. But by the time he reaches the end of the corridor, the screaming stops. Rick doesn't know what to do, and decides to wait for George to return. Hopefully, George will explain the alarm signal.

Five minutes later, George appears but refuses to discuss the code blue and the screaming. "You're asking too many questions man. Why don't you just kick back and relax, and stop trying to clutter your mind with things you don't need to know. Now let's just get to your unit, okay? I've got a lot of work to do."

Rick's feet are beginning to hurt. Rick's tired of walking through the maze of corridors. He's glad to finally reach the corridor which leads to unit two. Rick studies the corridor, counting eight rooms, four nurses and no doctors. George informs him that only one doctor is present during the night shift. After all, they don't need a bunch of doctors running around the hospital at night. Nothing ever happens that one doctor can't handle.

"What if somebody needed a doctor during that code blue thing? He'd be all tied up and you wouldn't be able to get another doctor here in time."

George looks at Rick without answering. He doesn't wish to discuss the hospital's functions with a patient. After all, there's no reason why he should.

Rick senses that George is fed up with all of his questions. He doesn't like imposing on George, but he's really curious about this place.

Rick and George reach the nurse's station and George hands the head nurse Rick's file. George looks back at Rick. "I'll be seeing you man," George says as he heads down the corridor. Then George turns around. "Don't do anything I wouldn't do," George says laughing as he continues down the corridor and out of sight.

The nurse looks through Rick's file, then introduces herself as Maggie. Rick notices that Maggie seems to be the epitome of a nurse. Her nurse's cap is even positioned on her head like it's part of her hair style. She is about fortyish and is most pleasant looking, with a sort of calming smile. uses it to assure her most flustered patients that because she is attending to them everything will be all right. Maggie is only a few inches shorter than Rick, but her professionalism towers over even the tallest of trouble makers. Rick knows that he's in good hands, the best of hands. He feels good about Maggie.

Rick follows Maggie into the room across from the nurse's station. Rick scans the room and is surprised how pleasant it looks. It's nothing like the images he had conjured up in his head. He expected to see shackles next to each bed to tie down the patients. It is simply like any other hospital room he had ever seen. There are four beds in the room. Two of the beds are partitioned off so that Rick can't see if they are occupied. Maggie directs Rick to the bed in the corner of the room. Rick immediately spots the small color television over the bed and turns it on, making sure that it works. Maggie races over to the bed and shuts off the television.

"C'mon Rick. We've got a lot to do before you can lie back and soak up TV rays."

Rick knows she is right and decides to do whatever Maggie wants. Maggie smiles at Rick, handing him a set of towels and a hospital gown. Rick looks at the gown and moans. Maggie is used to this reaction.

"Listen buster. If you brought your own pajamas, you don't have to wear that thing. But you can't very well wear nothing around here. I can't have my nurses drooling all over the place while you're prancing around in your birthday suit."

Rick reaches into his grip and pulls out his pajamas. He holds them up, enabling Maggie to see that they will cover his entire body. "At least my pajamas aren't tied with a string in the back."

Maggie smiles and pulls the curtain around his bed. "Now you just get into bed and a nurse will be here in a few minutes."

"What! Where are you going?"

Maggie looks at her watch. "Honey, I went off duty ten minutes ago, I just wanted to stick around till you got here. I always wait around whenever we get a new arrival with sexy pajamas. "Maggie grins at Rick. "Now you just lie there and the nurse will be in with your medication. Okay doctor?"

"Doctor!"

"Surely you must be a doctor," Maggie replies. "How could anyone take so many pills and not be a doctor. You're at least a pharmacist." Maggie smiles and exits the room.

Rick lights a cigarette, but is unable to find an ashtray. After a few puffs, Rick notices the large ash on the end of his cigarette. Fearing that ashes on the floor will be frowned upon, Rick decides to find a receptacle for his ashes. Studying the room carefully, Rick spots an ashtray on a table across from him, it belongs to his roommate. Rick notices that the man is staring at him with a glazed expression.

"Do you mind if I borrow your ashtray?" Rick asks.

The man remains silent and closes his eyes.

Deciding to take matters into his own hands, Rick gets out of his bed and walks over to his roommate's bed. Rick picks up the ashtray as his roommate's eyes pop open.

"Is it time for another shot?" Rick's roommate asks, slurring his words.

Rick is confused. "What?"

"Do you want me to turn over or do you want to inject it into my arm?"

"I just came over to borrow your ashtray"

Rick's roommate closes his eyes. "That's okay. I'd rather not have another needle hole in my arm."

Rick realizes that his roommate was talking in his sleep. He returns to his bed with his ashtray as his roommate begins snoring.

Rick sits on his bed listening to the nurses. Because of all the commotion, he figures that they're changing shifts. He wishes they'd hurry up and begin his treatment.

Rick begins thinking about his treatment. He desperately wants to get better. He feels that he shouldn't be made to wait like this. It's unfair. Don't these people know what he's been through, he thought. He wants to get cured. Immediately.

All of a sudden, Rick realizes that it is exactly twenty-four hours since he had taken his last sleeping pill. He begins to crave its sweet taste. His body has adjusted to the routine of taking a Placidyl every night. He hasn't deprived himself of the pill for more than two months. And now, his body is telling him what it wants. He can actually taste the pill in the back of his throat even though he hasn't taken anything. The taste teases his taste buds. His body clock is just reminding him what it wants. Nothing but a Placidyl will make this taste go away.

Suddenly, Rick hears that terrible scream he heard before. It scares him at first, but he keeps listening trying to discern the man's words. He is definitely saying something. But what?

"*Et me out of ere!*" the man cries out.

Hearing this, Rick gets out of bed to investigate. He opens the door and is met by two nurses. Both nurses are Korean and Rick notices that the other nurses at the station are also Korean.

"You supposed to be in bed," the first nurse says as the other nurse pushes in the medication cart.

"But what about that guy who's screaming?" Rick demands to know.

"You not mind about other patients. That none your business! "Now go over to bed so we take blood pressure."

Wonderful, Rick tells himself. How in the hell is he going to get better when he has to take orders from nurses who can hardly understand English?

Rick sits on his bed as the nurses take his vital signs. All the while, the man continues crying out like a wounded animal whose foot has been caught in a steel bear trap. The nurses simply choose to ignore his cries for help. Rick forgets about his need for a Placidyl until the medication nurse hands him a cup containing an assortment of pills. Rick looks into the cup and notices six different pills of all shapes and sizes. Some of the pills look familiar, but he doesn't quite recognize them.

"What are these?" he nonchalantly asks.

The nurse hands him a cup of juice, and with her other hand pushes the medication cup towards Rick's face. "You take pills. No ask questions."

Rick begins struggling with the nurse. She keeps pushing the cup towards his face and he continues refusing them. The struggle ensues and the nurse finally relents.

The other nurse approaches the side of Rick's bed. Then

one nurse pushes Rick's head back while the other nurse empties the medication cup down his throat

Rick begins choking profusely as the nurse tries pouring water into his partially open mouth. She digs her fingers between his teeth and forces his mouth to open even more.

"You drink water," she pleads.

Rick's choking attack subsides and he gulps down the water. "From now on, you take pill and that not happen. You scare us."

"Thanks a lot!" Rick sarcastically retorts. "The next time I start choking, I'll wake up one of my roommates. At least they won't just stand there and do nothing!" Rick knows that he's being overly harsh, but he feels that the whole incident shouldn't have occurred.

Both nurses exchange confused looks. "What you mean?"

"Never mind," Rick says, giving both nurses a disgusted look.

The door to Rick's room opens and another Korean nurse enters. The three nurses begin chatting amongst themselves in Korean. Rick can't understand a word of their conversation, but is able to tell from their looks that he is the topic of discussion. It doesn't bother Rick to hear them speaking a foreign language, but their frequent giggling is enough to make his skin crawl. Why don't they just laugh like normal people, he thought. Then the third nurse looks his way.

"You bad boy," she says, as if she is addressing a nine-year-old. "You take pills like other patients and no ask questions."

Rick is appalled. How dare these idiots treat him like some kid. And why didn't they want to tell him what kind of pills they wanted him to take. As far as he knows, they have to tell him what kind of medication he is being given if he asks. Don't they know this? Don't they think he has any rights as a patient? What kind of place is this?

The nurses leave the room as Rick reclines. He laughs to himself about the last few minutes. He thinks it would be amusing to swear at the nurses. They wouldn't know that he was telling them profanities. They'd probably just giggle after being told to fuck off. After a few minutes of silent thought, Rick realizes that for the first time in his life, he had been forced to take a pill. And six pills no less. He never turned down a pill in his life. He knows that if the nurses had told him what the pills were, he would have taken the medication right away. It makes no difference to him. But that's not what happened and he did try to refuse taking them. At last, he thought, I'm on the road to recovery.

Rick hears the death scream again and springs out of bed to investigate. Rick's delighted that the corridor outside his room is void of any nurses who might prevent him from sneaking a look. As he peers into the corridors, the screaming stops. Then, Rick spots a couple of Korean nurses standing by the nurse's station. He's able to hear them talking in Korean and every few seconds they giggle. Suddenly, the screaming starts up again. Rick looks across the corridor and into the room at the end of the hall. All he can see is the corner of a bed.

"*Et me ot ah ere,*" the voice pleads.

Rick takes a couple of steps into the corridor and edges his way towards the man's room. Rick gets to the point where he sees a pair of feet in the bed. The feet are tied down with bed sheets. Then the bed begins crashing up and down as the man continues screaming.

Rick is horrified. Is this guy some kind of prisoner, he thought. Is he a drug addict who went insane? Rick really doesn't want to forge ahead and find out. It's too frightening.

His eyes are transfixed on the bed as it bounces up and down and sometimes side to side. Rick doesn't know that one of the nurses has crept up behind him.

"What you doing?"

Rick whirls around. He is obviously startled by her sudden appearance. "Why don't you help that guy? Can't you hear him calling you?"

"That not your business. You get back in bed and go sleep or I tell doctor."

"But what about him?" Rick wants to know. "How can you just stand here and talk to me when that man's screaming for help?"

"We take care of him. He our patient, not yours."

Rick heads back to his room, deciding to get in the last word. He turns around and faces the nurse. "I suppose you're going to calm him down by dazzling him with your command of the English language."

The nurse shoots Rick a nasty glance, and says something in Korean to the nurse down the hall. Rick doesn't feel like standing, and returns to his room.

As Rick closes the door, he can hear the nurses giggling: he knows they're talking about him.

Rick sits down on his bed and glances around the room. He wonders if the other two beds are occupied and, if they are, what kind of problems his roommates have. Surely their problems have to be more interesting than his.

Rick lights another cigarette as he heads for the bathroom which connects to the next room. Rick tries the door knob, but it is locked. A voice inside informs him that the bathroom is being used. Rick apologizes and heads back to his bed.

Once back in bed, Rick hears the toilet flush and the sound of the bathroom door being unlocked. He prepares to get up as his phone begins to ring. Rick knows who it is and answers the phone accordingly.

"Hi Valerie. I love you."

"Hi Rick," the male voice answers, "It's Steve."

Rick is shocked. No one is supposed to know where he is except his family. "Steve! What the fuck are you doing calling me? I told you I was going out of town for a couple of weeks. How'd you find out where I was?"

"Valerie told me. I told her it was an emergency."

"So, what's so important?" Rick wants to know as he feels a pain in his gut. Rick remembers why he wouldn't even tell his writing partner where he was going. He hates Steve with a passion and whenever he talks to him or sees him, he gets a pain in his stomach. Rick figures that if Steve knew where he was, then he would call him for every little thing. Rick wanted Steve to carry on with their work, especially since Rick has carried their partnership since its inception.

"You know that show we pitched last week? You Know. The one which doesn't have a title?"

"Yeah," Rick suspiciously answers.

"Well, they want us to write the script."

"That's great! But what's the problem? Go ahead and write it."

"Valerie said that you'd be in there for a couple of weeks so I thought I'd come down there and we could work on the script together."

Rick can't believe his ears. "Are you serious? I can't write a script while I'm in here."

"But they have to have it in two weeks. I promised."

"So, write it. I don't see what the problem is. I've written plenty of scripts without you. That's what a partner is supposed to do. Whenever you weren't around and we had an assignment, I wrote the script and put your name on it. I don't know why you're so worried. Just write the damn script by yourself."

"But..."

Rick interrupts, not giving Steve a chance to finish his

thought. "Don't you understand where I am? I'm in a hospital. If I sit around writing scripts, I'll never get out of here."

"Can't you check back into the hospital after we write the script?"

"I don't believe you!" Rick could feel the pain in his stomach growing more intense. "You're a fucking idiot! Don't you realize where I am and what I'm in here for?"

"I understand what you're doing, but I thought you said when we started that nothing would interfere with our work."

"You're right, Steve. Why don't I meet you at your parents' house and we can work on the script while I'm going through withdrawals."

Steve grows silent for the moment, but Rick isn't finished.

"You know what my problem is, and now that I'm finally doing something about it you want to be selfish." Rick pauses to catch his breath. "I'll tell you what. Why don't you just write the script by yourself and leave my name off of it. You'll make twice the money and you won't have to share the credit."

"You know I wouldn't do that. we're partners."

"Don't feed me that shit. You can't do it!" Why don't you just admit it. You're afraid to write it by yourself because you've never written more than one page of dialogue without my help. Maybe you can get your parents to help you write it. They've done it before and they'll do it again. For the sake of me, I'll never figure it out. They must feel guilty about the way they brought you up or something."

"They only do it because they're professionals and they've been at it for a long time."

"Fine! Let 'em write the script for you and put their names on it. As a matter of fact, why don't you just write with them from now on. Or are you afraid they'd refuse because they know that you can't even spell your own name without help."

"That's a real nice thing to say partner," Steve says

resentfully. "I really appreciate it."

"I'm sorry Steve, but how can I make you understand what's going on. Don't you realize the gravity of the situation? I almost died a couple of times.

"Don't you think I value my life more than some television script? And even if I worked on the script instead of checking myself in here, I might not be alive to see the show produced." Rick is at his wits' end. "Don't you understand? Valerie was afraid that I just wouldn't wake up one morning. I have to get better. And I have to get better now!

"All right, all right," he says relenting. "I'll talk to you later."

"Wait a second Steve," Rick shouts into the phone. "Maybe I can help with a couple of scenes or … Hello … Hello …"

Steve had already hung up the phone. Rick is glad that he did because he really doesn't want to work on the script.

The pain in Rick's stomach is gone. Rick attributes it to the pills taking effect, and the fact that he's no longer on the phone with his imbecilic, no-talent partner.

The medicine he was given seems to be doing its job. He will simply relax in bed and let the pills take effect. He knows from his research on Placidyls that lower doses of that drug or something similar are administered as part of the withdrawal program. He only hopes that he can enjoy the effects.

Rick starts to doze as the phone begins ringing. His eyes pop open as he picks up the receiver. "God damn it, Steve!" Rick yells into the phone.

"Rick, it's me," the feminine voice says.

"Thank god. I thought it was that ass hole again."

"He told me you got the assignment."

"Yeah, and the son of a bitch wants me to write the script too."

"You're kidding! Boy! That jerk has got a lot of nerve. I think you'd be better without him."

"Believe me, I'm planning on it. And soon. I just need a few more credits before I tell him to drop dead. If he was a good writer I wouldn't mind so much. But the only contribution he makes is getting his parents to arrange appointments for us. And I'm sick of putting his name on my scripts."

"Well, you knew this would happen."

Rick remains silent. He prefers not addressing this issue. "Forget about Steve. How are you doing?"

"Fine. How's my little boy?"

"He's okay. He asked me where you were so I told him. He told me to tell you that he really loves you and that he's proud of his daddy for what he's doing."

"That's wonderful. I've only been away for a few hours and he's suddenly talking. Not bad for a twelve-month-old baby."

"Have they started treating you yet?" Valerie asks, her voice cracking.

Rick is concerned. "Have you been crying?"

"Just a little," Valerie says, trying not to break down again. She pauses for a moment, then begins crying. "It's just that I love you so much and I want you to get better and come home."

"Don't worry about me," Rick says, in a soothing tone. "I'm fine." Rick pauses for a moment, deciding to come up with an excuse to end their conversation. "Honey, I'd better get off the phone. The nurse just walked in. I'll talk to you tomorrow. I love you." Rick puts down the phone and closes his eyes. The nurse didn't enter the room. He just wanted to get off the phone. He's tired and needs to relax. Besides, the pills are beginning to work and Rick is feeling pretty groggy.

As Rick starts drifting off, he begins thinking about the

ordeal he has put his wife through. Any other woman would have left him, but not Valerie. She is truly something special. He's glad she called. He needed the encouragement. And above all, he has to get better. He will do it for her.

CHAPTER THREE

The next morning, Rick wakes up in a daze. He tries remembering the events of the previous night, but he draws a blank. However, one thing is certain. He feels great, his back isn't bothering him and, above all, he's gotten a good night's sleep without taking a Placidyl. Now Rick thinks he can look at his problem objectively. What events led him to taking the final plunge? Why didn't he do this earlier? Rick knows the answer to his own question. It is quite simple. He had become physically dependent on Placidyls. And it wasn't simply a case of being hooked on taking just one pill at bed time. Sure, it started out innocently enough. But he never dreamed something like this would happen, especially when he was under his doctor's supervision.

Rick knows that the events of the past week were the main reasons he ended up in this drug hospital. At the beginning of the week, he took two Placidyls at once, (In the past he had frequently taken a second pill when one pill wasn't doing its job.) The following night, Rick again took two pills, but they didn't seem to work, so he added a third. The next evening, he decided to take three pills. He remembered that two pills weren't sufficient the night before. It never occurred to him that, at some point, he might not wake up because he was dipping too heavily into his pill bottle.

Maggie enters the room, interrupting Rick's train of

thought. "Hi Rick, daydreaming?"

Rick is startled at first, but realizes that there is no reason for him to be so jumpy. After all, Maggie's presence is the only ray of sunshine in this place. "Oh, I was just thinking about how I got here."

"I would have been in to see you earlier, but I wanted to familiarize myself with your case."

"What'd you find out?"

"That you're lucky to be alive …. What finally made you decide to commit yourself?"

"I was scared to death, that's what. I really thought I could handle taking the sleeping pills until a couple of nights ago."

Maggie looks concerned. Rick can tell that she really does care. "What happened?" she compassionately asks.

"Well, I got used to taking two at a time, but they didn't always work, so once in a while I took three. But the other night, after two pills didn't work, I took two more for the first time. I could have taken one more, but I wanted to try four. I guess I really wanted to get loaded, or maybe I was subconsciously committing suicide. I don't really know, but I did get to sleep that night."

"How'd you feel when you woke up?"

"Pretty out of it. I was getting kind of scared. I really didn't want to take four sleeping pills, but that night I wanted them."

Maggie draws an obvious conclusion. "You knew where you were heading didn't you?"

"I guess I did-, but I just wouldn't admit it to myself. I even tried to cold-turkey the pills about a month ago, but I couldn't handle it."

"Not many people can."

"Yeah, well, I thought I was doing pretty good job until one day when I was in the back yard killing ants. Valerie came out to see what I was doing. That's my wife. When I told her that I was killing a colony of ants, she told me that there weren't any ants. I was really pissed. The ants were all over the place. I saw them."

"Were there any ants?"

"No. I was hallucinating. It was pretty scary and I realized that I wasn't handling it like I thought I was."

"What'd you do then?"

"I went back on the pills and everything was okay until I started increasing the dosage."

"You know, usually something happens before someone commits himself to a place like this. What broke your camel's back?"

Rick takes in a deep breath as he stares around the room. He doesn't mind telling Maggie his story, but it's easier to remember if he doesn't look at her directly. "Well, the night I took four pills, I first decided that I would just take three. But when the three pills began working, I got out of bed and took a fourth pill. When I woke up the next day, I was really worried why did I take a fourth pill when the three pills were working? Obviously, I was getting worse and I knew it. I figured that if I didn't do something quick, I'd end up in a box. That's when I came here."

"Well, I'm glad you're here. A lot of people wait until they've overdosed."

"I know what you mean. I never thought I'd end up in a place like this."

"This place isn't half bad," she says cheerfully. "You should see some of the other rehab centers. They're really atrocious. "Maggie looks at-her watch.

"What's this place like anyway?"

"I'm sorry Rick. I have to run, but I'll see you later." Maggie whirls around and heads for the door.

"What about my medication?" Rick inquires.

Maggie turns around. She's astonished. "You mean you don't remember?"

Rick shakes his head, in embarrassment. "What did I forget this time? "Rick mumbles under his breath. Am I still having memory-lapses? he wonders, "Remember what?"

"You got your medication almost an hour ago, I saw you take it myself."

"Oh yeah! I guess I forgot," Rick sheepishly admits. "I was just testing you. And I must say, you're on the ball. Keep up the good work."

"Sure Rick," Maggie sarcastically comments as she exits the room.

It bothers Rick to think about his memory lapses. They have been more frequent the past few weeks. On countless occasions, he and Valerie had argued about important events he had forgotten about. He sometimes had trouble remembering names of people he knew. This infuriated Valerie. She couldn't understand it. Especially since some of the names he forgot belonged to her relatives. Valerie's family often laughed at Rick when he asked them what their names were.

They knew that Rick was a joker, and was only trying to game them. They had no idea that Rick's memory was deteriorating. Valerie had no idea that the problem went much deeper. Along with forgetting names, Rick had also forgotten many words in his vocabulary. He frequently stuttered as he tried remembering the words. He knew he was falling apart, but refused to admit it to himself. But now he can look at his problem objectively, as if it was happening to someone else.

Rick wasn't trying to fool Maggie. He really didn't remember that he had already received his medication. However, he does feel the taste of orange juice in his mouth, so he knows that Maggie wasn't trying to put one over on him.

Rick desperately wants to catch a few more minutes of

sleep, but his bladder wins out. Rick doesn't know why, but the decision whether or not to get up and go to the bathroom seems like a hard one. That's awfully silly, he thought. It is obvious what he has to do, so why is he having a mental argument with himself. Rick chuckles out loud as he swings his body around and dangles his legs over the bed. Rick looks down to the floor and sees that his slippers are a few inches from his feet. Leaning forward, Rick eases his feet towards the slippers. Suddenly, Rick loses his equilibrium and falls with a thud, onto the floor. Rick quickly surveys the room hoping no one saw his blunder. Fortunately, no one had.

Rick tries getting up, but continues falling back on his ass. He ultimately realizes what the problem is. He's loaded. And it isn't just a slightly loaded sensation he's feeling, but rather, a major high. It has to be part of his treatment, he thinks. Or maybe it's a withdrawal symptom. In any event, it sure feels great and he isn't about to complain. Why should he? They obviously know what they're doing.

The problem still remains. Rick can't stand up. Both legs are now trembling and, if that isn't bad enough, he's lightheaded too. Extremely lightheaded. "What am I going to do?" he says softly, hoping that no one hears him talking to himself. He just can't lie there and pee in his pants, but there's no one around to help him. Then Rick sees the nurse call button dangling off his bed and reaches for it, depressing the button.

Five minutes pass before the nurse enters. She sees Rick sprawled on the floor and shrugs. "Didn't they tell you the rules and regulations before you checked in. All patients are forbidden to get drunk when I'm on duty," she says joshing, helping Rick back into his bed.

"Thanks for the lift."

"Now don't you try that again. You're supposed to stay in

bed," she says as she leaves Rick's room.

"But I don't want to stay in bed," he shouts. "I have to go to the bathroom," he adds in a frustrated tone. He knows that she didn't hear him.

Rick fumes and prepares to leave his bed again as the nurse returns, pushing a wheelchair into the room. She parks it by Rick's bedside.

"From now on and until further notice, all your traveling will be done by wheels."

Rick doesn't react.

"Well, say something. Hey, I know, why don't you take it for a spin around your room."

"No thanks," Rick says dejectedly.

The nurse decides to leave Rick alone and exits. She knows he'll eventually try his wheelchair. After all, it's now a necessity.

Rick is apprehensive at first. The sight of a wheelchair conjures up images of paraplegics and amputees. Rick knows that if he wasn't under the medication's spell, he'd probably panic.

Rick hesitantly gazes at the wheelchair for a moment, then begins smiling. He finally realizes that he needs it, but only on a temporary basis. As a matter of fact, it might even be fun.

The wheelchair is a perfect fit. Rick rides around the room testing the chair's endurance and his own agility. He is glad to be loaded. This way, the wheelchair seems to be more of a toy than a necessity.

Rick makes his way towards the bathroom, but is told by a voice inside that it is being used. The voice belongs to the same person who occupied the bathroom the previous night. Because his bladder is ready to burst, Rick decides to wait by the door and make his presence known. Every few seconds, Rick purposely coughs and makes noises with his throat. He wants to make the guy in the bathroom feel guilty about taking so long. After several minutes of throat noises and coughs.

Rick finally hears the bathroom door being unlocked from the inside.

"That's funny," Rick mumbles," I didn't hear the toilet flush. I hope he doesn't expect me to do it," he says, maneuvering his wheelchair into the bathroom for much needed relief.

Much to Rick's dismay, the door leading into the next room has been left open. Rick moves across the bathroom to the open door and sees a man sitting on the edge of a bed. As Rick starts to close the door, the man looks his way.

"Hey man, you got an extra cigarette on you?" he slovenly asks.

Rick resents this strange looking man. He hates people who mooch cigarettes, especially people like this guy. He looks like a typical drug addict. His torso is all shriveled up and his arms and legs resemble toothpicks.

He looks like he's just been in a fight, and the brown color of his Latin face has white blotches covering it. The least this guy can do, Rick thought, is to comb his greasy hair.

"You got a cigarette man?" he sluggishly asks again.

"Sorry, but I'm all out," Rick replies as he closes the bathroom door.

Rick eases his body off the wheelchair and onto the toilet, but notices something very peculiar. There are several cigarette filters on the bathroom floor. There are no signs of tobacco, used or otherwise. Just a few filters strewn about.

Rick makes it back into his bed as a voice calls out to him from the bed across from his.

"How ya doing? I'm Mark. What are ya in here for?" he says, firing off questions like someone who is stricken with a case of diarrhea of the mouth. "You're not contagious or anything, are you? Which are you, an alcoholic or a drug addict? Maybe you have a disease or something. Do you?"

Rick immediately puts Mark's fears to rest, briefly explaining why he's there.

Mark feels at ease and the two begin talking freely. Both men hit it off right away. They have a lot in common. They're both the same age and have a mutual hatred for the Korean nurses.

"Well, I came into this place because I was really depressed. It started out to be no big thing, but it got pretty heavy. You know, I broke up with my lady and I was doing really shitty in school. Most people are in here because of money, but not me. That stuff screws up a lot of people. If you don't have it then you're depressed because you know that you'll never have it. And if you have money, you get depressed because you don't know what the hell to do with all that shit…. In my case, money's got nothing to do with it. I've got plenty of money. Through a couple of wise investments, I've made more money than most people make in a lifetime."

Rick's affection for his new friend quickly diminishes. He hates to hear people bragging about themselves and how much money they have. He knows that part of his ill feelings about Mark stem from his own jealously of him.

Rick's tired of listening to Mark. He wants to tell him off, until … he realizes how lucky he is to get a guy like Mark for his roommate. I'd better be nice to this guy, Rick thought, or they might transfer me into the next room with the cigarette moocher. "What are you in for?" Rick inquires.

"Well, like I was saying, I'm in here for depression, I can handle my girl leaving me and the fact that I wasn't going to make it to law school, but I couldn't handle my parents splitting up. I just couldn't take it."

"How come you're in this unit?"

Mark removes his leg from under the blanket and shows Rick a two-foot cast wrapped around his leg. "This is gonna sound pretty stupid, but I broke my leg the day I got here. They put me in unit three first and after they gave me my medication for being depressed, I tripped on my meal tray and broke my leg. "Mark takes a drink of water, but he misses his mouth and the water dribbles down his face. "Shit! That's the second time this morning."

"Why don't you ask the nurse for help? I'm sure they'd do it."

Mark leers at Rick. He obviously resents his helpful hint. "No way man! If they knew how loaded I really am, they'd cut down on my shots.... Anyway, it's not that I'm glad I broke my leg, it's just that I'm glad because they put me in this unit. The other unit wasn't helping my depression one bit. They put me in there with a bunch of ass holes who were more depressed than I was."

Mark raises his voice hoping that the staff will hear him and perhaps extend his time in unit two. "If they knew what they were doing, they'd leave me in this unit! "Mark looks towards their door expecting someone to enter, but no one does. Mark lowers his voice. "This unit's really great! They bring you all your meals and we have our own TVs. Why, we can even stay in bed all day if we want. And if we get bored, we can run around the hospital and terrorize the other units." Mark pauses for a brief moment of reflection. "They treat you like you were a god damn prisoner in the other units, but they can't do nothing to you if you're from unit two."

"Why do you need to cruise the hospital?"

"Are you kidding? That's the best part. Those freaks in the other units aren't allowed to leave their units for anything. But patients like us can go anywhere we please. Didn't you hear me before? I thought I just got done telling you that."

"I guess I didn't hear you."

"You'll see. Pretty soon you'll be all over this place like a fly on shit."

This guy's really got a lot of class, Rick thought as he watched his roommate picking his nose while he continues talking.

"You'll probably spend all your time in unit three like I do."

"No way man!" Rick says shaking his head. "I'm staying right here. There's not one ounce of gypsy blood in my veins. The next time I see the other units will be on my way out the door."

"I've seen tougher nuts crack easier, man! You can put 'em off for a couple of days, but you'll have to go to unit three sooner or later. It's part of the therapy."

"What are you talking about? What therapy?" Rick demands to know. He feels his heart rate increasing.

"Group therapy. You know. Everybody from the unit sits around with a couple of shrinks and discusses problems."

"No way!" Rick adamantly tells his roommate. "I'll do anything they want, but I won't go to any group therapy. It's not for me. I'm not that far gone."

"It doesn't matter, man. You have to go even if you don't want to. It's not up to you. What do you think they hold discussions trying to figure out who gets to go and who doesn't get to go? If they say you go, then you go!"

"Forget that shit! My problem's strictly a physical addiction thing. If it were mental addiction I might go, but like I said, my problem's strictly physical." Rick sits up on his bed and lights a cigarette.

"I forget what you were on?"

"Placidyls."

Mark immediately perks up. "You mean "pickles"? God! I haven't seen one of those for at least a year. You wouldn't by any chance have any to sell. You know, as long as you're kicking them anyway. I thought you could use the cash instead of flushing 'em." Mark's face beams with delight as he anticipates Rick's answer.

"Sorry, I ran out before I came here."

Mark's hopes are dashed. "That's too bad." Mark says mournfully. "I'd rather have a "pickle" than just about anything else. Even Quaaludes." Mark lights a cigarette, then reclines on his bed.

The room is silent for a few moments as Rick leans over to put out his cigarette. Then a partition on the other side of the room opens.

Rick calls out an introduction to the man in the corner of the room, but his words fall on deaf ears. Rick watches in amazement as the man meticulously makes his bed. Rick decides that staring at the man is not very well mannered, so he turns away.

"Watch this guy Rick. He doesn't mind," Mark whispers.

Rick turns back and focuses his attention on the strange man. After his bed is made, the man, who moves like a robot, disappears into the bathroom. A few seconds later, the man returns and begins dressing. Rick is amazed. He's never seen anyone dress as quickly as this fellow. It must have taken him thirty seconds to get completely dressed. Rick never saw anybody move that fast who wasn't being chased by a cop. It's simply an incredible sight.

A nurse brings four breakfast trays into the room. Rick, Mark and the fast dresser in the corner each get a meal. The nurse sets the fourth tray in front of a closed partition and leaves the room.

"Who's that tray for?"

"You'll find out later. Alexander won't be up for another hour," Mark says, directing Rick's attention back to the guy in the corner of their room.

Rick and Mark can't help laughing as they watch their

roommate literally inhale his food. He eats his entire breakfast faster than he had dressed. Then the man picks up his tray and exits the room.

"He won't be back until lunchtime," Mark comments.

"What's with that guy anyway?" Rick wants to know, chuckling like a ten-year-old.

"I'm not really sure. About all I know is that his name is Bob and that he's in here for depression. He never says one word to anybody and he acts like a god damned mechanical man. I don't even know what they're giving him, but I wish I had some. Just think of all that good dope they're wasting on him." Mark's obviously disgusted.

"I'll bet he's getting speed," Rick comically adds.

Mark laughs. "I wouldn't doubt it. He's one weird dude."

"I wonder where he went?"

"He's over in three and he fits right in, too. He walks around the place like some zombie and just stares at the clock waiting for his next meal."

"What's he doing in our unit?"

"Hell if I know. I wish they'd move him over to three. I've been having nightmares about him. I keep dreaming that I open my eyes and he's standing over my bed with a knife and fork. I'm sure you can figure out the rest."

"Sounds wonderful," Rick sarcastically comments as his phone rings.

"Hello," Rick says into the receiver as Mark continues talking to him.

"Hi honey, it's me," Valerie says in her low-keyed voice.

Rick doesn't feel like talking to his wife right now. He doesn't know why, but he thinks it's related to the drugs he's been given. At any rate, he doesn't want to tell her that he doesn't want to talk on the phone because he's loaded, so he makes up another reason. "Listen Valerie, you caught me at a really bad time. I'm surprised they didn't tell you when you called, but I'm going to be tied up all day with a bunch of tests and stuff like that. I'm on a five-minute break right now and I'm not supposed to exert myself in any manner. I guess they mean that I shouldn't even talk on the phone."

Valerie interrupts. Naturally, she is more than understanding. "That's okay honey. I just called to see how you're doing, but I'll call you tomorrow if you want. Just tell me the best time for you."

"That's all right honey, we can talk," Rick says, anticipating her answer.

"No Rick. You get back to what you were doing and I'll talk to you tomorrow. Okay honey, I love you."

"I love you too Valerie. Bye."

Rick hangs up the phone realizing that Mark has not stopped talking to him. Rick figures that Mark's medication, like his, has begun working and that Mark is probably feeling pretty loaded.

Rick tries listening to Mark, but he can't understand his babbling. Rick can't really tell if Mark's conversation is muttled because he's loaded, or because Rick is coming on to his own medication. At any rate, about the only thing Rick can relate to is the fact that he feels great. As a matter of fact, he hasn't been this loaded since he first started taking Placidyls. And that was over three years ago. What a great feeling, he thought. The cure is actually better than the illness.

The only thought in Rick's mind as he begins dozing is that he will not, under any circumstances, attend group therapy. Little does he know that group therapy will be the most interesting part of his recovery.

CHAPTER FOUR

"*Et me ot of ere'*" the voice cries out.

Rick spots Mark getting dressed and decides to ask him about the strange plead. Surely, he must know why that guy keeps screaming, Rick thought. After all, Mark acts oblivious to the man's cries for help. He must have his reasons for ignoring them.

Rick raises the head of his bed as Mark places a crutch under each arm. The man from across the corridor continues screaming.

"Did you hear that?" Rick asks in a somewhat more than curious tone.

Mark looks at Rick without emotion. "Yeah, I heard it. So what? It's no big thing. You'll get used to it."

"Your attitude's pretty blasé," Rick incredulously answers. "How come everybody in this place ignores that guy? What Is wrong with him anyway?"

Mark takes a couple of steps away from his bed, aided by his crutches.

"Forget it man," Mark says sternly. "He's just got problems like the rest of us. Don't concern yourself with him because he's a lost cause."

Mark's uncaring attitude begins eroding any good feelings which Rick had harbored for his roommate.

"What an asshole," Rick mumbles to himself as Mark eases

his way toward the door.

Rick glances at Mark's empty bed and spots a tongue depressor taped on the wall above it. Rick looks above Bob's bed and sees another tongue depressor. He hesitantly turns around and notices that there is also one above his bed. He cringes. "Wait a second Mark," Rick calls out, stopping Mark in the doorway. "What are tongue depressors doing over our beds? Don't they usually keep them in jars or something?"

Mark seems a bit perturbed at Rick's naivete'. "Don't you know anything, man! When they're over a bed like that, they're called anything but tongue depressors."

"Well, what are they then?"

"They're for seizures, man!"

Rick is horrified. "Seizures!"

"You got it. As a matter of fact, you might even have one while you're here." Mark is obviously enjoying this. He can see the fear in Rick's face growing. "That's probably one of the withdrawal symptoms they didn't want to tell you about, but don't sweat it man. It goes with the territory. Odds are, you'll either see someone having a seizure or you'll have one yourself. And if that happens, they'll rip one of those sticks off the wall and jam it in your mouth so you won't swallow your tongue."

Mark turns to leave, but decides he's not finished. He turns back around and faces Rick. "Seizures are a fact of life around here so you might as well get used to it. I think you're a pretty good candidate for a seizure. You might have one in the next few seconds or you might have one tomorrow. There's just no telling. Who knows," he adds philosophically, "that tongue depressor over your bed just might end up saving your life. That is of course, unless there's no one around to jam it down your throat." Mark laughs. "If anybody wants me, I'll be over in unit three."

Rick knows that if he wasn't feeling the effects of his

medication, he'd really be shaken by Mark's remarks. Instead, Rick simply dismisses the thought of having a seizure. "If you see Bob, say hello for me," Rick yells, as Mark disappears from the doorway.

Cries for help permeate the corridors of unit two as Rick tries to find an interesting program on his color television. His efforts quickly prove futile and he shuts off the set, deciding to watch the traffic passing by his open door.

Rick loves girl watching and can't possibly imagine anything as beautiful as a sharp looking woman. He only wishes, as he stares out into the corridor, that at least one of the nurses was worthy of his attention. He could look at a beautiful woman for hours on end without tiring, but unfortunately, the nurses on unit two are all too plain.

He continues staring out his open door as a strange shadow appears on the corridor wall. The shadow moves ever so close in the direction of Rick's room. He recognizes that the shadow belongs to a wheelchair. Rick continues watching, his eyes transfixed on the edge of his doorway, as the wheelchair passes slowly by his room. The occupant of the chair is the man in the adjoining room. Rick feels eerie as he glances at this all but shriveled up human being. The strange man catches Rick staring at him and wheels his chair into Rick's room. Rick immediately looks away and lights a cigarette, hoping that the man will go away. Instead of leaving, the man eases his way over to Rick. The man introduces himself as Nick and immediately asks Rick for a cigarette. Rick pretends that he doesn't hear the man's question.

"You got an extra cigarette?" Nick asks in a slightly clearer voice.

Rick feels that he should comply, having been caught with his carton of cigarettes m plain view. Rick hands Nick a cigarette from a freshly opened pack. Then Rick spots a plastic bag resting on Nick's lap. It appears to be a bag of Nick's urine. As Rick stares, the bag fills up slightly. This sickens Rick, but at the same time, he's fascinated. Rick's eyes follow the protruding tubes from the bag of urine until they disappear behind Nick's hospital gown. Rick knows that they are somehow connected to Nick's body, but he has no desire to inquire about them. Instead, Rick doesn't say a word to Nick, hoping that he'll simply leave.

Nick sets the borrowed cigarette on his lap and begins gazing at his host. Rick doesn't know what to say to this intruder.

"How long have you been in this place? Rick says, hoping to break the tension.

Nick remains silent, preferring to stare off into $pace.

Rick points at the tongue depressor taped over his bed. "You know, I just found out about these tongue depressor things. I sure hope they don't have to use one of them on me."

Nick doesn't respond.

"About ten years ago, I saw a guy having a seizure at my Dad's office. It was pretty scary. He was just standing in front of the coffee machine, then he fell on the floor and began spinning around like a top or something. It was like his brain exploded. I got the hell out of there and wouldn't go back to my Dad's office for over a month."

Nick surreptitiously removes a book of matches from Rick's nightstand. He hasn't heard one word of Rick's story.

"I sure hope that doesn't happen to me," Rick adds, as Nick maneuvers his wheelchair out of the room.

Rick waits a few minutes before heading into the bathroom. He suspects that Nick might return and try to mooch a pack of cigarettes. After all, Rick thought, Nick saw that he had a carton of cigarettes. He'll probably be back when he finishes the cigarette Rick gave him.

The bathroom door is again locked. Rick could see, through the crack in the door, that the lights were off. Obviously, those idiots in the next room forgot to unlock the door after they used the bathroom, Rick thought, as he removes a cartridge from his pen and slips it into the door knob. Suddenly, the door opens a few inches.

"I'm using the toilet man," the eerie voice informs Rick.

Rick is startled. He didn't expect to find anyone in the bathroom, especially Nick. But what the hell was he doing in there with the lights off, Rick thought.

"Is anyone in here?" the medication nurse calls out as she wheels in her drug cart.

Rick leaves his position by the bathroom door and steps into view of the medication nurse. After confirming his identity, the nurse hands Rick a cup containing his medication. Rick takes a pill out of the cup and holds it in front of his face. "What's this one for?" Rick curiously asks.

"That's Mag Sulfate," replies the nurse.

Rick puts the pill back into the cup. "I've never heard of it."

"That's because it doesn't get you loaded. It's just used to flush out your system."

"You mean like 'Drano' or something?"

The nurse grins. "Yeah," she says pleasantly. "I guess you could say that."

Rick pours the contents of the cup into his hands and holds them up to the nurse "How about these, what are they for?"

"They're just different chemicals for your withdrawal symptoms."

"Like what?"

"You know," she slyly says. "It's the same stuff that you've been taking. Just in lower doses."

Rick is satisfied with her answers, and takes his medication while she watches. Why didn't those Korean nurses tell him about his medication like this nurse just did, he thought, as he climbs back into his bed.

In a matter of minutes, Rick is, once again, high as a kite. He doesn't know what to do with his nervous energy. Then he remembers what Mark told him about having the run of the hospital. He's genuinely curious about the rest of the place and decides to investigate.

Rick puts on his bathrobe and slippers and climbs into his wheelchair. He doesn't know how he'll find the other units, but he sure is going to try.

Unit two's corridors are void of any hospital personnel. Rick exits his room and speeds down the first corridor.

Approaching the next corridor, Rick freezes as he spots a trio of nurses coming his way. He knows they'll spot him if he tries hiding, so he decides to proceed like he has urgent business.

The three nurses greet him with friendly smiles as he wheels past. Rick looks back and sees the nurses disappearing into another corridor. He turns back around and is shocked to find a woman standing directly in front of him. She is the best-looking thing Rick has seen in the hospital. Her petite figure is only enhanced by her blond hair. She looks out of place in this hospital and she's obviously not a patient. She can't be, Rick thinks. She's too perfect. Even her fingernails have fresh polish on them.

"I'm in charge of patient relations at this hospital," Judy informs Rick.

Rick is skeptical at first, but is simply too loaded to challenge her.

She doesn't have on a uniform and isn't wearing a hospital badge like the rest of the staff.

"If your stay here is to be a pleasant one, I think there are some things you should know."

Rick beams with delight as Judy takes control of his wheelchair and pushes him down the corridor.

"I've been here over six months and believe me, there's a lot that goes on here that only I know about."

Rick's grin increases as he thinks of the sexual connotations of Judy's statement.

Judy directs the wheelchair down another corridor stopping it in front of the operating room. "We can talk better in here," Judy says as she pushes the wheelchair through the double doors.

Rick scans the room and is pleasantly surprised to discover that they are its sole occupants. Judy pushes Rick to a corner of the room and stops his wheelchair next to a gurney. Judy keeps her position behind Rick and places her hands on his shoulders.

"I think you'll do just fine here," Judy tells Rick as she massages his shoulders vigorously.

Rick is in ecstasy. He loves having his body massaged, especially his back and shoulders. "Don't stop," Rick tells her, as he moans with delight.

Rick closes his eyes and lets his thoughts wander as Judy's hands scurry down his back. Rick leans forward as Judy's hands reach the bottom of his back approaching his backside. Suddenly she removes her hands, much to his displeasure.

"What's the matter? "Rick asks in his little boy tone.

Judy steps around the wheelchair and stands directly in front of Rick. "I just thought the rest of your body should get equal time," she comments as she undoes Rick's bathrobe and slips her hands inside his pajama top. Judy begins massaging Rick's chest, tugging gently on his chest hairs. He can tell she's getting excited.

"How does that feel?" she sensuously asks, her voice trembling.

"Terrific!" Rick comments as he slumps down in his wheelchair and reaches out with his hands, touching ever so gently, Judy's chest. "Do you mind?" Rick inquires as he strokes Judy's breasts through her blouse.

Judy answers with a sly smile. Then Judy takes Rick's hands and maneuvers them past the open buttons of her blouse. "I like this way better," Judy comments as Rick's fingers make tiny circles around her erected pink nipples.

Then, much to his surprise, Judy backs away from Rick, withdrawing his hands from her blouse. Judy removes Rick's bathrobe and tosses it onto the sterile floor of the operating room. Judy gazes at Rick's body in the wheelchair as she removes her blouse. Rick knows that she isn't wearing a bra, and is surprised that her luscious breasts have no tan lines on them.

Judy leans forward, giving Rick a closer look at her breasts as he unzips her pants. Judy backs away.

"Careful sugar," she tells him as her pants come tumbling down. "Let's not rush things. I want our encounter to be just per-fuck." Judy laughs. "Get it?"

Rick nods his head, realizing that Judy isn't wearing any underwear. What a wonderful sight, Rick thought, as he admires Judy's beautiful body. Rick only wishes that he wasn't so loaded. He remembers what he had read in various drug books that told of a person's diminished sex drive when drugs had been taken. On the other hand, Rick thought, he might last longer with Judy because his body won't know enough to get excited. At any rate, he isn't about to blow this opportunity, loaded or not.

Judy wheels a gurney alongside Rick's wheelchair. She hops onto the gurney and beckons him with her nude body. "Let's not waste any time sugar," she tells him as she stretches out her hand.

Rick is determined to get onto that gurney and stands up, bracing himself against his wheelchair. Then Rick lunges at Judy's open hand, but he misses. Instead, he hits the side of the gurney and sends it across the room.

Rick wheels himself over to the gurney for another try. He can tell that Judy is amused, but she's also growing impatient. Surely, she must know that his perception is off, he thought.

"Let's do it right this time, sugar. I don't want you to use up all your precious energy on that silly wheelchair. And believe me, when we're through, you're gonna need that thing because you're gonna be all tuckered out."

"You're gonna need a wheelchair honey," retorts Rick. because I'm not gonna quit until you collapse from exhaustion."

Once again, Judy extends her hand. And this time, Rick is determined not to miss. Then Rick leans forward and grabs her hand with both of his. He puts all of his weight into his hands and pulls, trying to get that one precious step he needs.

"Let go! Damn it! You're pulling too hard," Judy tells Rick as the gurney tilts causing two of the gurney's wheels to lift off the floor.

Suddenly, the gurney topples over sending Judy crashing to the floor. Fortunately, Rick falls back into his wheelchair.

"Sorry about that," Rick tells Judy as she stares at him with a vitriolic look. "I guess I'm more loaded than I thought."

Judy grabs her pants and blouse and hurriedly puts them on. "You schmuck! I'll bet you woke up this whole fucking place," she says as she scurries out of the operating room, leaving a very flustered and horny patient behind.

"I don't think she really works here," Rick says, directing his wheelchair out of the room. He isn't really bothered by the fact that he can't add another notch to his belt, but it would have been nice.

Pushing with all his might, Rick manages to get through

the operating room's double doors. Rick anxiously looks down the corridors trying to get his bearings, but one corridor looks like another. He doesn't really care whether he winds up back in his room or ends up in unit three. The optimum thing, of course, would be to bump into Judy in the store room or something. Rick feels bad about knocking her off the gurney and desperately wants to find her again and do it right. He's never missed the brass ring before and he wants a second chance.

Rick opts for the corridor on his right. He knows that he's heading away from his unit because he doesn't remember passing by the employee's coffee room before. The odor of cigarette smoke permeates the hallway adjoining the room. Even though he's a smoker, Rick finds the odor unbearable, and decides to hold his breath until he safely passes the room. Rick knows that if he weren't so loaded, he wouldn't really be as bothered by the smoke, but for now he'll just hold his breath.

His chest tightens as he approaches the end of the corridor. He decides that he'll hold his breath until he reaches the end of the corridor. Rick fails to notice the curious stares by the hospital personnel as he wheels past them. His only concern right now is reaching his goal. His heart's beating faster and faster. Rick decides to think about something else, remembering how he always held his breath whenever he passed by a cemetery. He was always told by his parents that he was supposed to hold his breath while passing a cemetery. It was supposedly showing respect for the dead. He had always complied with their request, but he thought of that chore in a different way. It always worked fine when the cemetery was a small one, but if it went on and on like the one off the Santa Monica freeway, then it would be literally impossible to hold one's breath for such a long time. He told his friends about the breathing ritual, adding that if it was a big cemetery and they held their breath, they'd end up in it themselves. Rick could always count on getting his friends to laugh at his post script.

Reaching the end of the corridor, Rick lets out a deep sigh as his head sinks into his lap. He decides not to move for a couple of minutes hoping to regain his composure. He can feel his body returning to normal as an attendant comes by, asking if he's all right. Rick assures the man that he's fine and the attendant goes about his business.

Rick continues down the next corridor until he arrives at unit one. He semi remembers that he was there the previous night, but beyond that he remembers nothing.

As he stares through the open door, afraid to enter, an attendant inside spots him and races over to his position. Rick tenses.

"What the hell are you doing out here?" the attendant demands to know as he pushes Rick into unit one.

"Wait a minute," Rick shouts in a flustered tone. "What the fuck are you doing? I don't belong here! I'm on unit two!"

The attendant gives Rick a suspicious look. "Sure man," he sarcastically tells Rick. "Now look," he says in a commanding voice," If I see you out of this unit again, I'm gonna put you in shackles and lock your god damn ass in a padded room! You got that?" he adds, threatening.

Rick remains motionless as the attendant stares at him. Rick is afraid to move, fearing that this maniac might really hurt him if he continues disagreeing with him. He decides to simply wait until the guy goes about his normal duties, then he'll get the hell out of there.

Rick watches as the attendant takes a few steps away from his wheelchair and enters a patient's room. Rick places his hands on his wheels and pivots around as the attendant races out of the room and heads for the nurse's station. The attendant whispers something to the head nurse and she picks up the telephone.

Rick watches her for a moment before deciding to leave. He exits unit one as the paging system announces a "code blue" alert in unit one. Rick experiences Déjà vu as he tries remembering where he heard those words before. While he's contemplating, several hospital personnel race past him down unit one's corridor, disappearing into a patient's room.

Rick stares down the unit's corridor as a nurse, sitting at the nurse's station, spots him. She promptly gets up and hurries over to Rick.

"I'm sorry, but patients are not allowed out of this unit. You must stay within these confines if you want our help," she says dictatorially. "We can't be held responsible if you leave this unit."

"But I'm not on this unit. I'm on unit two."

"That's what they all say around here when things get too uncomfortable."

"I tell you I don't belong here," he says adamantly. Rick inches his wheelchair towards the door.

"Don't even think about leaving," she says, grabbing the wheelchair and pulling it back a few feet. Then she returns to her station, keeping an eye on Rick as she moves.

Rick decides to wait until she has forgotten about him before making his escape. Unfortunately, the nurse is determined not to let Rick get that chance, and instructs the staff around her to keep a sharp eye on him. Rick knows that he's the topic of her conversation because she keeps pointing at him and the nursing staff is making a mental note of his appearance.

Rick is beginning to feel more like a prisoner than a patient. If only they'd look away for a minute. he thought. He'd show them.

He could demand that they check with his unit, but on the

other hand, they might decide to lock him up for a while and check out his story at their convenience. He isn't about to take that chance.

Rick sits silently contemplating his next move, as four hospital personnel slowly exit the patient's room. They're all talking in sotto voices and shaking their heads. Two of the attendants walk a few feet down the corridor and return with a gurney which they bring into the room. Moments later, they exit the room with the gurney and its cargo. Rick knows that the man under the bed sheet is dead. Why else would the sheet be over his head, he thought.

Like most people, Rick is afraid of death. He copes with it by not thinking about it. But he is also curious about it and subconsciously hopes that the bed sheet falls off, enabling him to get a look at the body. Fortunately, the sheet doesn't fall off, but Rick catches a glimpse of the patient's feet sticking out, as the attendants wheel the gurney in his direction. As the gurney comes closer, Rick decides to scrutinize the feet and try and guess the cadaver's age.

Suddenly, the doors to the unit open and the hospital supervisor enters. He scans the corridors and eyes a number of patients standing around, watching the gurney and its cargo. The supervisor spots Rick in his wheelchair and pushes him aside as the gurney approaches.

"All right people, this isn't a social event. Let's clear the halls please," he says gruffly as the patients begin to scatter. "Let's get with it," he says, clapping his hands together for a more forceful and authoritarian look.

The supervisor sees that Rick hasn't moved. He takes a step in Rick's direction tapping him on his shoulder. "I said let's move it. Clear the corridor."

Rick looks up and smiles. "Yes sir, right away sir," he insipidly replies.

Rick turns his wheelchair around and leaves unit one.

The gurney pushes open the doors as Rick watches, huddled next to the water fountain. There are only two corridors to choose from and Rick doesn't want to take the wrong turn and possibly end up in the hospital morgue. He'll simply see where the cadaver is taken and he'll head in the opposite direction.

The gurney travels down the right corridor and Rick proceeds down the left one.

"This hospital has too many corridors," Rick tells himself as he approaches the end of another corridor. He feels lost in a crazy maze of white walls as he finally approaches two double doors which are marked in bold lettering: Unit Three. "It Is about time. I finally made it!"

Not knowing what to expect, Rick feels hesitant about just busting in. He's afraid that the staff might think he belongs there and lock him up in a padded room.

Rick notices that the doors are slightly ajar and sneaks a peek, inching his wheelchair up to the doors. He leans over, almost falling out of the chair, and catches a glimpse of people walking about. As he studies the situation, an attendant comes up behind him.

"These doors are a bitch to get through, especially when you're in a wheelchair," he states as he grabs onto the wheelchair and pushes it through the double doors and into unit three.

Rick looks up at the attendant informing him that he wasn't having trouble with the doors, but the attendant interrupts.

"No need to thank me. It's just part of my job," the smiling attendant tells Rick as he saunters out of unit three.

The main thing on Rick's mind is blending in. He doesn't want to be noticed by the staff or the patients.

Sizing up the situation, Rick realizes that he's the only one in a wheelchair. Surely, they'll spot him. "I'm nothing but a square peg in a round hole," he mumbles, maneuvering his wheelchair away from the doors.

Rick feels his medication wearing off and thinks about returning to his unit, hoping that by the time he gets there the medication nurse should be waiting for him with his usual cup of pills. But he's come this far, so he might as well stay and observe the unit for at least a few minutes. "But what if I don't get my pills in time and I have a seizure or something," he wonders in a sotto voice. Rick realizes that he's talking to himself. "Wonderful. Now I'm talking to myself. Maybe I belong here after all."

Rick looks for tongue depressors, but doesn't see any. He's ready to panic, He doesn't want to have a seizure in a unit void of tongue depressors, so he hurriedly turns his wheelchair around and heads for the door. Then he hears someone crying. Turning his attentions toward the pay phone, Rick sees a girl, about seventeen, crying into the phone.

"When can I come home mommy?" she affably asks as tears stream down her face, extinguishing the cigarette in her hand.

Her conversation touches Rick. She promised her parents that she'd stay at the hospital for at least thirty days, but that was only three days ago. And now, she wants to go. Home.

Her actions are more interesting than her conversation, as Rick watches her repeatedly trying to smoke a tear-drenched cigarette. It strikes Rick funny that she keeps trying to light it with used matches. If anyone belongs in this place, Rick thought, she surely does.

Rick ponders the girl's predicament, wondering if he'd be, on the phone to Valerie in a few days begging to come home. "Nonsense!" he tells himself. "Not me. And not in three days or even three weeks. I'm gonna stick it out until I've got Placidyls licked. I'm here to get off pills and get my life back together. I've got too much to lose if I screw up. I'll never end up like her. Never!"

Rick attributes his ramblings to the fact that his drugged state is subsiding.

He figures that he'll stop talking to himself when he gets his medication, but he'll stay in unit three for just a few more minutes.

The nurse's station is situated in the middle of unit three. The two corridors on each side of the station both seem to dead end, but there is a sign at the end of one hallway which reads: Exit. Being naturally curious, Rick places his hands on the oversized wheels of his wheelchair and pushes on them, causing him to move. Then, with a violent jerk, the wheelchair comes to an abrupt halt. Rick is terrified as he looks around for the cause. For a brief moment, Rick theorizes that the attendant from unit one has come to drag him back to the booze unit. Fortunately, the man behind his wheelchair is a patient in the drug unit. Rick is overwhelmed by the tremendous physique of this twenty-year-old who now stands before him with a large grin.

"Hi! My name's Charlie," he says grabbing onto Rick's right hand, and begins shaking it vigorously with a mechanical motion. He chortles as his grip on Rick's hand tightens.

Rick immediately guesses that this guy is some kind of psycho. Charlie has this scary, dazed look about him, like he's trying to scare a little kid on Halloween night. The more Rick stares at Charlie, the more he comes to believe that he's just a harmless giant, not unlike Lenny in, *Of Mice and Men*.

Finally, Rick gets Charlie to release his hand. Rick wants to rub the pain out of his hand but thinks better of it, deciding to do it when Charlie isn't around. He thinks that Charlie might want to kiss his hand to make it better, or something equally as childish. Rick immediately surmises that Charlie is the type who desperately seeks the approval of others.

Charlie begins telling Rick that he's in the hospital because of his severe psychological problems. Rick's thoughts drift on to other matters as Charlie talks incessantly about his depression and paranoia problems.

"Do you like me?" Charlie asks, interrupting Rick's train of thought.

Rick is a bit confused by Charlie's question. "What? Why ah," Rick hesitates for a moment while he digests the tone and content of Charlie's question. Rick's face lights up. "Sure, I like you."

Charlie is relieved and it shows.

"You seem like a real nice guy," Rick adds.

"Good! I'm glad you don't hate me," Charlie says, wiping his brow with his hand. "Most people are against me."

"Why do you say that? You know that's not true," Rick tells Charlie in a compassionate and affable tone.

"Oh, I know that's not really true, but most of the time I feel like it is. I really have a lot of friends, except they sometimes get mad at me and then they're not my friends anymore." Charlie pauses to catch his breath. He's pretty worked up. "Are you really sure that you like me and aren't just saying that because if you are, I don't really blame you. Most people Don't like me." Charlie chuckles. "I bet you think I'm paranoid. That's okay if you do because everyone says I am." Charlie looks down at his feet. "I guess I am a little bit."

Rick is taken aback. What the hell did Charlie just say, he thinks as he addresses Charlie. "C'mon Charlie. I don't say things I don't mean."

"Does that mean you don't hate me?" he says backing away from Rick.

Rick chooses his words carefully, realizing that the wrong thing might set Charlie off. "I really like you Charlie! You're one of the nicest guys I've ever met. Really! I mean it!"

Hearing this, Charlie breaks out with a broad, gaping smile

that goes from ear to ear. He grabs Rick's hand and begins shaking it profusely. "I'm glad, most people hate me," he says as he releases Rick's hand.

Charlie strolls down the corridor and out the exit. Rick plans on going down the corridor himself, but thinks better of it figuring he'd probably run into Charlie again. His ears and his hand just couldn't take it. Not for a while, anyway.

Rick sits quietly for a few minutes, content to watch the goings on in unit two. There is a television room a few feet away from him which connects to a conference room. The corridor is solid except for the door and a giant pane glass window which looks into the conference room.

Rick makes his way over to the window and peers in. There are about twenty chairs in the room arranged in a circle. Behind the chairs are a couple of small tables and a coffee maker, which serves only decaffeinated coffee. The room is empty until an attendant comes in, carrying an armful of ashtrays which he puts on the table.

Rick looks at the ceiling and notices that the room is void of any air vents or outlets for the smoke. There has to be some place for smoke to go when people start smoking in there, Rick thought, as the attendant places an ashtray in front of each chair."

"Maybe they're going to use this room to entice non-smokers to smoke," Rick tells himself, making a mental note to use this experience in one of his comedy scripts.

Patients begin entering the room, taking their seats as the attendant finishes doling out the ashtrays. Rick enjoys watching the patients. Each one comes in, sits down, takes an ashtray and lights a cigarette. And if that isn1 t funny enough, each patient opens and then closes the door to the room as if it's some sort of ritual.

The room fills up with people, mostly young and plain

looking, but Rick notices something peculiar. He doesn't see any familiar faces in the room, or for that matter, in the whole unit. Where are his roommates, Mark and Bob? Mark told him that he was going to unit three and that Bob spends all of his non-eating time in unit three. And what about Charlie? Where did he go?

Rick travels down unit three's corridors looking for his roommates. He speeds down the corridors with ease. He's delighted that he finally gets to race his wheelchair. He quickly forgets that he's looking for Mark and Bob, choosing to race up and down the hallways instead.

Dr. Iris Whitehead enters the unit carrying her clipboard. She shouts down both corridors that group therapy is now going to be held and that everyone in the unit is compelled to attend.

Rick brings his wheelchair to an abrupt halt at the end of the corridor, as Dr. Whitehead disappears into the conference room. He has no intentions of attending group therapy and decides to leave unit three, thus avoiding any unpleasant confrontations.

Rick guides his wheelchair towards the doors of the unit, as a patient saunters out of his room and stops directly in front of Rick's wheelchair. For a moment, Rick thinks about running over this little tyke, but wisely chooses against it.

"Excuse me," Rick says, but the strange little patient doesn't even look up, preferring to stare at his shoes. Rick sits patiently for a few moments, then nudges the patient with his wheelchair.

The patient seems oblivious to Rick and ominously giggles. Rick feels creepy as he looks at the patient standing before him. This guy's obviously a psychopath, Rick thinks, as he maneuvers his wheelchair around the strange patient.

Rick opens the door to leave and takes a look over his shoulder. The guy that had blocked his path is still standing in the same exact spot and he's still giggling.

Rick starts to push through the doors, when he spots a pack of cigarettes on the floor by the television room. Checking his pockets, he realizes that the cigarettes are his. Rick goes over and picks them up.

Heading back for the exit, Rick passes by the conference room window and decides to look in, spotting a familiar face. Her appearance has changed since the last time he saw her, but it is definitely Judy. Only this time, she is wearing a hospital identification bracelet and is clad in a hospital gown. Rick feels like a sucker., having believed her story that she works at the hospital.

Judy spots Rick staring in at the session and she immediately smiles, beckoning him inside. She alerts the other patients to Rick's presence and everyone stares out at him. Rick is sure that everyone in the room is privy about their little get together in the operating room.

Making a hasty retreat, Rick leaves the drug-psycho unit and heads back to the comfortable confines of his own unit.

"I'm sure glad to get out of that place," Rick tells himself, as he negotiates the turns of the corridors approaching his unit. "It1s a good thing I'm in this unit. That therapy crap is fine for them, but not for me. My problem's just a ripple in the ocean compared to the rest of the nuts in this place.

Rick is glad to get back to his own unit, especially when he finds the medication nurse waiting for him with his usual cup of six pills.

Without asking any questions, Rick pours the pills into the back of his throat and washes them down with orange juice. "I'm sure glad I'm not in unit three," he tells the nurse. "This is where I belong."

Rick lies down on his bed, waiting for his medication to begin working its Wonders.

CHAPTER FIVE

Rick tries tuning out the sounds of the hospital, but finds it an impossible task. The screaming man's cries for help deeply concern him even though he's finally gotten used to it. It saddens him to think that he has become oblivious to the man's cries for help, but that seems to be the attitude of everyone at the hospital. Perhaps if he wasn't so loaded, he might just do something to help that poor guy, he thought, squirming around in his bed trying to get comfortable.

Rick wants to lie down on his back and stretch out, but there is a rather large obstacle pressing against his feet. Rick pushes the object with his foot, thinking it's an extra blanket or a pillow. But it isn't. The object feels too big and heavy. His eyes shoot open to see that the problem is a well-built, dirty-blond sitting on the edge of his bed. She stares at him displaying a large smile. She begins stroking his leg through the sheets.

"Hi. I hope you don't mind sharing your bed with me," she says with a smirk on her face. She obviously knows the sexual connotations of her statement. "I'm Carla. I saw you in my unit a while ago and I followed you over here. They almost caught me leaving three and if I don't get back before group is over, they'll come looking for me."

Rick enjoys listening to Carla's manner of speech. She doesn't stop to catch her breath, let alone give him a chance to add his two cents. She just rambles on.

"Boy, I really hate those group sessions. You know, they make us go to them twice a day and they don't accept any excuse for missing them. That is, of course, unless you're not there when they start. They're not very good at taking attendance. Most of the psychos are too loaded to answer them anyway and there are too many of them for the staff to know by name."

While she continues babbling, Rick can't help but notice that her dynamite figure has a small roll of fat slightly beneath her navel. As Carla takes one of Rick's cigarettes out of the pack and lights it, Rick notices that her spare tire is protruding out of the bottom of her blouse. It bounces up and down as she speaks.

Carla catches Rick staring at her blob of fat, and immediately sucks in her gut as she tucks her blouse into her pants. "I only go to group when I want my medication changed," she continues. "I hate sitting there and listening to a bunch of addicts and psychos. I've got my own problems. Why the hell should I listen to theirs."

"What are you in here for?" Rick interrupts.

"Pills. But it's not what you think. I've only been here for six days, but before that I didn't take anything for over two weeks."

Rick is obviously confused. Apparently, he didn't hear her correctly. "I don't get it! Didn't you just say that you're in here because of pills?"

"You'll catch on," she says omnisciently. "There are lots of guys in here doing the same thing. The system lets you."

"What are you talking about? What do you mean, the system lets you?" Rick shakes his head, hoping to gather his thoughts. "Maybe my medication is working too well," Rick says under his breath.

"Just what I said," replies Carla as she puffs on the borrowed cigarette.

"Are you saying that you're not addicted to pills and you really don't belong here?"

"Oh, I've got a problem with pills all right, but it's not what you think. My problem is scoring. All my Placidyl connections dried up so I checked in here."

Rick sits up, astonished. He's pleased to find someone with a similar problem. Surely, she must know what he's going through. "That's what I'm here for," he proudly announces, anticipating a compassionate remark from Carla. "I needed help to get off 'em too."

"Well, don't look at me. I'm not here to kick I 'em. I'm here to get more."

Rick shoots Carla a confused look as she takes a fresh cigarette from his pack and lights it. "Lighten up man. I'm not the only one in here doing this. They just make it easy for us, and as long as they do, why shouldn't we take advantage of it. It's not all fun and games you know. And if you can put up with the bullshit they give you, it's worth it. It's even kind-of fun if you know what I mean."

"I don't mean to sound naive or anything, but are you saying that You're in here to make drug connections?"

Carla seems a bit perturbed. Her patience is wearing thin. The last thing, she expected to do in his room was to answer a lot of stupid questions. "This place is my connection.... Don't you understand what I've been telling you?" she says in a slightly hostile manner, her speech becoming more slurred. Carla drops her cigarette into the ashtray and stands up. "I don't understand how someone so good looking can be so ignorant!" she spouts as she takes another cigarette from Rick's pack and places it behind her ear.

"Wait a second," Rick pleads, fearing that she'll leave without explaining what she's been telling him. "How can you get away with it without your insurance company getting wise?"

Carla removes another cigarette from the pack and lights it. She inhales the first whiff of smoke and answers as the smoke pours out of her mouth. "Insurance company," she cackles. "I'm on Medi-Cal."

"Medi-Cal! I never heard of that. Is that some sort of welfare or something?"

Carla doesn't seem to mind his question. "Yeah, I guess you might say that. It's for us poor souls who don't have any money and shit like that." Carla laughs out loud. "You could say Medi-Cal is my very own personal dope pusher."

"Huh!"

"That's right. They pick up my tab for two weeks with no questions asked. All I have to do is walk in and tell them that I'm a drug addict and that I want to get help."

"So, they give you dope even though you aren't really addicted?"

"Now you're catching on." Carla is pleased that Rick finally got it right.

Rick digests all that he's heard. "That sounds like an addict's vacation. What do ya do when your two weeks are up?"

"That's why you have to play their game. You just keep telling the shrinks that you're depressed and they'll see that Medi-Cal extends your hospital time. It's foolproof."

"How many times have you been in here?"

"Oh, I've only been here twice before. But back in Sacramento I was always checking myself into drug clinics whenever the streets dried up or when I ran out of money."

"They must be pretty dumb around here not to catch on."

"Don't kid yourself. They know what's going on, but why should they destroy their gravy train." Carla sees the blank expression on Rick's face. "Let me put it to you this way. This place is run by a bunch of doctors who also happen to be the owners." Carla takes Rick's arm and examines the band around his wrist. "This says that you're Dr. Berger's patient. Have you seen him yet?"

"No I haven't, but I've only been here for a little while."

"That doesn't matter. You'll probably never see him. He's one of the owners. They never come into the units unless it's an emergency, like if you owe them money or something. This place is just a business to them. They're in it for the money and they'll take anybody who can pay, and especially Medi-Cal patients like me. They keep padding the bill and Medi-Cal keeps paying them, no questions asked. And if you have private insurance, forget it! They'll keep you here forever and they'll juice up the bill even more."

"C'mon Carla. That sounds a little far-fetched. I can leave anytime I want."

"Sure, you can, but Medi-Cal takes a dim view of their patients who leave AMA."

"Well, I'm on private insurance."

"Then you'd better forget about splitting AMA because your insurance company could come after you for the money they spent. If I were you, I'd call the post office and tell them to forward all your mail to this place because you're gonna be here for a long time."

Rick stops paying attention to Carla and starts giggling to himself. Carla is annoyed at Rick's rudeness.

"What the hell's so funny?" Carla demands to know.

"I was just thinking. We're both in here for the same thing, except I'm trying to get off Placidyls and you're trying to stay on them."

"You think that's funny?" she says incredulously.

"Sure I do. If I weren't in here I could get them, but I wouldn't want them. And if you were out on the streets, you'd want them, but you couldn't get them."

Carla's bewildered. "Yeah, and who's on first! … Change the subject, will ya."

"Sure. What do you want to talk about?" Rick ponders for a moment. "I know, let's talk about something that we can both relate to."

"Like what?"

"Like how many Placidyls you were taking at once."

"Never mind me. How about you?" she says, evidently tired of reciting her own story.

"Oh, I got up to taking four at a time," Rick says, proudly. Carla is dumbfounded. "That's all! Just four!"

Rick feels slighted. "What do you mean, just four? They were seven-fifties!"

Rick expects Carla to be impressed with the dosage.

"Big fuckin' deal, I was taking seven seven-fifties, twice a day," she casually remarks.

Rick is aghast. He remains silent for a moment while he multiplies in his head. "That's over five thousand milligrams! How in the hell did you swallow all those?"

"You're living in the dark ages. Nobody swallows 'Pickles' anymore. That's a waste of good dope."

"You mean you shoot 'em?" he asks skeptically.

Carla pulls up her pant leg and exposes needle marks in her vein. She quickly covers it up in embarrassment because she knows that her legs look better without them. "What else! You get a better rush when you shoot. The high doesn't last as long, but it goes right into your system. It's ten times better." Carla is getting fed up with Rick's lack of knowledge. "Don't you know anything?"

Rick's thoughts wander as he contemplates what it would be like to inject himself with a syringe. "My wife would flip if she caught me shooting up." Rick laughs.

Carla is shocked with this bit of information. "What do

you mean your wife! You didn't tell me you're married!"

"Over three years. I have a little boy who's almost one. That's why. I'm here. I'm getting off the pills for them."

Carla removes the last cigarette from Rick's pack and places it behind her other ear. "I'd better get back to my unit," she says, exiting Rick's room.

§

Rick removes a fresh pack of cigarettes from his grip and opens it. He lights a cigarette and reclines in bed as Bob returns to the room carrying his lunch tray. Rick watches in astonishment as Bob seats himself on the edge of his bed, then pulls over the table and sets down his tray. He positions the table right up to his belly and begins consuming his meal in record pace.

In a matter of moments, Bob's tray is void of any food, except for a scoop of cottage cheese which he plops into his mouth. From Rick's point of view, Bob looks like he's contracted rabies because of the apparent frothing at the mouth from the cottage cheese.

After licking his fingers clean, Bob pops up holding his tray and mechanically exits the room passing Mark who is returning from unit three.

"You missed a great show," Rick says as he watches Mark place his crutches against his bed.

"You mean Bob?"

"Yeah. You should have seen him. I'll bet he set a new indoor record for eating."

Mark doesn't react to Rick's joke.

"How come he gets. his lunch before anyone else?"

"You'd get it early too if you stood outside the kitchen at lunch time."

Rick shakes his head as he nervously puffs on his cigarette.

Mark studies Rick for a moment.

"You know, if you think this place is getting to you, you'd better go to therapy and tell them you're depressed. They'll give you tranquilizers and you'll be fine. Really! It's better than chicken soup."

Rick silently thinks over Mark's suggestion, but shrugs off the idea. "I've heard some interesting things about this place."

Mark perks up. He's very interested in anything about the hospital. "Like what?"

"Well, this girl from unit three came in here a few minutes ago, and told me all sorts of wild things. She said that there are some drug addicts in here who only admit themselves to get free dope. Can that be true?"

Mark seems amused, but doesn't answer.

"If it is true, what the hell am I doing here? How am I supposed to get better in a place like this?"

"Hey man, don't sweat it. You're taking all this too personal."

Rick is growing impatient. "What about it Mark? Please tell me!" he pleads. "C'mon Rick. It's no big secret. Probably half the addicts in three only checked in there to get loaded. They come here once, maybe twice a year, stay for two weeks and move on. When you think about it, it's kind of funny. They get room, board, and drugs for two weeks and it doesn't cost them one cent."

"How can this place keep going?"

"Simple," Mark replies philosophically. "Nobody complains. The patients love it here and the doctors love the money. Can you think of a better set up?" Mark chuckles. "It's kind of like a marriage."

Rick turns his head in disgust and flips on his television as three lunch trays are brought into the room. Rick and Mark are each given a tray and the third one is placed alongside a closed partition which encloses another patient.

"Lunch is here Alexander," the female attendant says, informing the patient behind the partition.

"Oh, all right," the voice from inside sluggishly answers. "I'm coming."

Rick focuses his attention on the partition as it opens and the patient emerges. Alexander is about thirty-five and is probably the only person in the hospital who prefers wearing a hospital gown. His appearance is disheveled, and a terrible stench accompanies his presence as he passes by Rick and Mark on his way to the bathroom. Rick stares at Alexander's feet, noticing that they are not inside his slippers, but are on top of them, sliding them on the floor as he walks.

"What the hell is that?" Rick asks Mark as Alexander disappears into the bathroom.

"I knew you'd like him," Mark sarcastically tells his roommate.

"God! I hope he cleans up or something. He smells awful!"

"You'd better get used to it. Alexander is what he is and that's that! I've complained to the head nurse for three days and they haven't done anything about him … I don't think they can force somebody to take a bath, but I could be wrong. Anyway, just do what I do and spend as little time in this room as possible.

Unit three's safe. Alexander's never been in there.

"Well, I won't stand for it. His stench infringes on our wellbeing, especially mine. I can't believe they'd let him get that bad. It's unhealthy. Why doesn't he take care of himself? What the hell's his problem?"

"From what I hear, Alexander was living alone in his house when his neighbors called the cops. They hadn't seen him for a few days, and there was a terrible smell coming from his house. He wouldn't answer the door so the cops busted it down." Mark pauses for a moment to catch his breath. "You sure you want to hear the rest of this? It's pretty sickening."

Rick nods his head affirmatively.

"Anyway, the cops found him living in a bunch of garbage and bugs. Man, there were roaches all over the place and they weren't the kind that you smoke either."

"Sounds like a delightful atmosphere," Rick comments.

"Yeah, but the worst thing was that he wasn't even using the bathroom. He shits all over the house and I heard one of the nurses say that he was even lying in the stuff," Mark says cringing.

"Yuck! Rick says in a sickening tone. Why the hell did they bring him here?"

"This place always gets the overflow when the nut houses run out of room."

"I wish they'd put him somewhere else."

"I guess the smell's worse where you are, but if you can put up with it, it won't be so bad. He doesn't make any noise and he only talks to the nurses. He tells them "no" all the time. He's the closest thing to death you'll ever see. He's totally given up living and all he does is eat, sleep and shit. I wish he'd do all three in the toilet."

Alexander exits the bathroom and heads back to his bed. Rick notices urine stains on his hospital gown as he walks past. Rick turns away, having no desire to see Alexander's backside protruding from his open gown.

Mark prefers coping with Alexander by simply ignoring his presence.

Rick amuses himself by watching Alexander eat his lunch. Alexander doesn't look up from his food and he doesn't use his silverware. Rick thinks to himself that maybe Bob and Alexander are related.

The nurse enters the room, responding to Mark's request.

She approaches Mark is bed and shuts off the nurse call button.

Alexander interrupts from across the room. "Nurse," he says, whining. "Could I get some more mashed potatoes please. A double portion."

The nurse shoots Alexander a stern look. "You just eat what's on your plate Alexander and I'll see if there are any leftovers for you," she says in a motherly fashion.

Mark feels slighted. After all, he called the nurse in and resents her for answering Alexander first "Nurse, could I have my medication now, please. It's already fifteen minutes late and I really feel lousy," Mark says, hoping to stir a compassionate response.

"I'm sorry Mark, but your doctor's taken you off all medication."

Mark is aghast. "What!" he cries out. "He can't do that! I've never even seen the son of a bitch. How the hell does he know if I'm better or not. I'm gonna sue this whole fuckin' place unless you give me something." Mark becomes more adamant. "And I mean now! Right now!"

"I'm sorry Mark, but those are your doctor's orders. Besides, you're scheduled to be released today. You're going home," she cheerfully adds.

Mark is taken aback. "I'm going home!" he says not believing his ears.

"That's right. You can go to the admitting room any time. Your parents should be there shortly," she says heading for the door.

"But what about my medication? They can't just cut me off like this! What am I supposed to do?"

The nurse turns around. "Oh, don't worry about that. They're sending some medication home with you. You can pick it up on your way out, after you sign the release forms."

"Can't I get something now?" he pleads.

The nurse ignores his question.

"At least give me one Valium. Please! That's like candy. Surely you can give me just one Valium."

"I'm sorry."

"Please! I'll do anything. I swear, I won't tell anyone."

"It's against hospital policy to medicate patients who are checking out. I'm sorry, but I just can't do it," she coldly adds. "Besides," all the medication that was allocated to you was sent back to the pharmacy. Even if I wanted to, there's no place for me to get you what you want."

Mark thinks to himself for a moment. "What about Rick's medication. If it all right with him, can you give me one of his pills?"

"I'm sorry Mark," she replies shaking her head. The medication nurse is the only one who has the key to the drug cart and she's not due back in this unit for another two hours." The nurse exits the room.

Mark screams at the top of his lungs, "You're all a bunch of fucking incompetent nurses. You don't give a shit about your patients and you're a bunch of incompetent whores!" Mark feels better, having let off a little steam.

Rick is afraid to say anything to his roommate, not knowing what to expect.

Mark looks at Rick. He can tell that Rick is a bit apprehensive about speaking. Mark catches Rick looking his way and he smiles at him, easing the tension. "I'm all right Rick. Really! I just thought I'd leave this place with a bang."

"You didn't mention the male nurses. You're not going to ignore them are you," Rick facetiously adds.

"You're right. I wouldn't want them to feel left out," he says, placing a crutch under each arm. He stands up and faces the open door of their room. "And all you male nurses out there are a bunch of douche bag faggots!" he screams, loud enough for the whole hospital to hear. Mark picks up his grip and slings it over his shoulder. "I guess that takes care of business," he tells Rick as he makes his way out the door. Then, Mark turns around and leers at Rick. "Don't take offense, but I hope I never see your face again," Mark leaves the room for the last time.

Rick's glad that Mark is gone. "He's too unstable," Rick mumbles, turning up the volume on his television.

Raising the head of his bed, Rick decides to watch the afternoon news. The top story of the day concerns the Pope's visit to Washington. The story keeps dragging on, so Rick flips off the set having no desire to hear about the Pope or his visit.

Rick senses that his medication is wearing off and wonders when his supply will be replenished. He feels kind of tired and decides that if he takes a short snooze, he'd be awakened by the nurse when it's time for his pills.

Rick shuts his eyes and lets his thoughts wander, but something is keeping him awake. Rick opens his eyes and realizes that the strange sounds that bothered him while he watched the news, now were emanating from behind Alexander's partition. It sounds like a church choir or something similar. Rick tunes out all other sounds and focuses his attention on the people singing. After a few moments, Rick hears a clicking sound and the singing stops. He surmises that Alexander is watching the news reports concerning the Pope's visit. That's strange, Rick thought, remembering what Mark told him about Alexander's lack of concern for anything. Perhaps Alexander is some kind of religious zealot, Rick theorizes. At any rate, Rick is glad that Alexander's set is now off. Now he can get some rest.

Closing his eyes once again, Rick feels himself drifting into a light sleep. Unfortunately, something else seems to be bothering him. He feels someone's presence next to his bed. Rick opens his eyes and sees Zulu standing over his bed sporting a broad smile.

"How ya doing Rick? I told you I'd see you again."

Rick and Zulu shake hands while Zulu removes a piece of paper from his pocket, giving it to Rick. Rick holds the paper in front of his eyes and studies it.

"I'll bet you thought I was handing you a line when I told you that I'd probably be returning your check."

"Well, to be perfectly frank, I didn't count on getting it back before it got cashed."

"You surprised?"

"Flabbergasted is more like it," Rick says, tearing up the check and dropping the pieces into his ashtray. "Can you stay for a minute?"

"Not right now, but don't worry. I'll see you later. I just came by to give you back your check and to offer some friendly advice."

"What?"

"You know that attendant who took you to this unit after I admitted you?"

"Yeah, what about him?"

Zulu is hesitant. He doesn't want to come out and tell Rick the real truth about the attendant, but he does want to make sure that he's properly warned.

"Well, just try and stay away from him, that's all."

"Wait a second Zulu. What's that supposed to mean?"

"Well, he kind of said something about You didn't care for."

"Like what?" Rick asks, fearing the worst.

"He said things like, how he'd like to give you a sponge bath and he said that he'd really like to..." Zulu interrupts himself. "C'mon Rick, you know what I mean. Just stay away from him and if he gives you any trouble, complain to his supervisor."

"How about if I punch him in his face first and then call the supervisor."

"Only if I'm there to see it. I'd like to see somebody put George in his place."

"What'd he do to you?"

"Well, we were kind of real close a while ago, but I couldn't take him for long. He just comes on too strong, always trying to prove how tough he is."

"All right Zulu. If I have to hit him I'll call you, but on one condition."

"Name it?"

"That you'll come by and visit me once in a while. You're the only person I know in this place who seems to have his head screwed on straight."

"Don't worry about it. I'll see you around. I'm always running around the units." Zulu heads for the door. "See you later Rick," he says as he leaves.

Rick stares at the torn-up check in his ashtray as the medication nurse pushes her cart into the room. She reaches into her pocket for the key, but comes up empty. Rick shuts his eyes, pretending to be asleep as the nurse looks through all her pockets. Then, when she's confident that no one's watching her, she surreptitiously bends down and removes a spare key from underneath the medicine cart. She opens it.

The nurse fills Rick's cup with an array of pills and approaches his bed, carrying the pills and a cup of juice. Rick opens his eyes, pretending to have just awakened.

"Here's your medication Mr. Brown," she says, examining his wrist band. "You are Mr. Brown, I trust? she says in a joking manner.

"The one and only," Rick replies as he takes the cup. Rick stares into the cup for a moment, then empties the contents into his mouth, washing them down with the juice. Then, something clicks in Rick's head. He looks at the nurse askance. "How many pills did I just take?"

"Why, six," she nonchalantly replies. "Why?" she inquires in a slightly skittish tone.

"I could have sworn that there were only five pills in this cup. I only saw one capsule in there and I've been getting two," Rick says suspiciously.

"I can assure you that there were six pills. I ought to know. I counted them myself," she defensively states closing up her medication cart.

"Don't forget to have another key made," Rick tells her as she pushes the cart out of the room.

Rick knows that she heard his remark and is probably too embarrassed to acknowledge it. Nevertheless, Rick can't get the image of the pills out of his head. He's sure that he only saw five pills in his cup, but why would she purposely abscond with one of hits pills. After all, pills that detox patients aren't worth anything to anyone. He must have counted wrong, he thought, dismissing the notion from his mind. But he'll count his pills from now on.

Rick begins feeling lightheaded as the pills begin taking effect. Everything is kind of hazy and he feels very weary. He decides that he won't let himself fall asleep. This way, he can enjoy the sensation.

Rick tries thinking of some stimulus that will keep him from dozing, when a woman, apparently an attendant, enters his room and approaches his bed. She checks his wristband before talking.

"Hi Rick," she says in a nauseatingly pleasant tone "I'm Sherri from unit three. I came in to see why you didn't attend our group session. We all missed you, you know."

Rick feels that the medication is enabling him to say what's on his mind without holding back. "Listen Sherri, you might as well know right now that I have no intention of going to any therapy sessions."

"I'm sorry to hear you say that, because the sessions are for your benefit. And by going, you could shorten your stay here. Really! It's for your own good. Just give it a chance and come to one session. You'll see. You'll probably even like it," she says smiling, anticipating a positive answer.

Rick dwells on his answer as he stares at Sherri's physique. He's sure that her brown hair must be at least two feet long, but how does she wrap it around her head like that, he wonders. It's almost a perfect circle. She'd be a real knockout if her ass wasn't so big, he thinks as Sherri waits for his answer.

"Well, can I count on you then?" I'll even come and get you if you want. Come on," she pleads. "What do you say?"

"Maybe tomorrow."

Sherri is ecstatic. "Terrific! I'll pick you up after breakfast and you'll be back in time for lunch."

"Only on one condition," Rick stipulates.

"What?"

"That you'll wear your hair down so I can see if it touches your ass."

Sherri isn't the least bit shocked, having heard worse things from patients on medication. "See you tomorrow!" She shoots Rick a sexy smile and then saunters out of the room shaking her behind for Rick's benefit.

"Zulu ought to take walking lessons from you," Rick shouts, but Sherri is gone.

The telephone rings, waking Rick from a deep sleep. "Hello," he yells into the phone, realizing that he's speaking into the ear piece. He turns the phone around. "Hello."

"Rick, is that you?" the female voice asks.

"Who's this?" Rick groggily wants to know.

"It's your sister, Marsha. Valerie just told me what you are doing and I was really shocked. I never knew you were that bad off."

"Well, now you know," he tells his sister in a perturbed tone.

"I'm really proud of you. I didn't think you were that smart."

Marsha's statement upsets Rick. "What the hell's that supposed to mean?" he demands.

"Don't get so defensive. I'm on your side, remember? Anyway, I'd better get off. I have to go to work. I'll call you later, bye." She hangs up.

Rick slams down the phone, then picks it up again and dials. "Hello Valerie, it's me. Did you know that Marsha was going to call me?"

"She asked me where you were so I told her. I assumed that it was okay to let your family know where you are, but I didn't know she was going to call you. Why? Is something wrong? Are you all right?"

"Everything's fine. I just don't want to get a lot of calls. I don't care who it is. Just tell everyone to leave me alone. And if my parents ask any questions, you just tell them the hospital won't allow me to take any calls."

"What about me?" Valerie wearily asks anticipating the answer.

Rick knows that Valerie is on the verge of breaking down. He can tell that his ordeal is even harder on her. "Honey, I love you and I want you to call me whenever you feel like talking and I'll call you too whenever I can."

Their conversation continues as Valerie pauses to blow her nose. Rick knows that Valerie isn't listening to his calming remarks because she's crying, but he continues talking anyway.

"This place is really weird. I could write a book about this hospital, or even a movie."

"Is it really that bad?" she hesitantly asks.

"Not really. It's kind of interesting. At night, it's like being in a M*A*S*H unit." Rick pauses, hoping to hear her laugh, but she doesn't. "During the day it's like a soap opera. If it was on television, you'd stay home and watch it."

"It sounds like you're having a nice time," Valerie comments as the man from across the corridor screams out.

Valerie is horrified. "What was that terrible noise?"

"Oh that," he says, trying to act casual. "He's just some wild banshee they've got chained to his bed. We even set our watches by his screams."

"Charming place," she comments sarcastically. "What's going on with you? Are you feeling any better? You haven't seen any ants or bugs flying around have you?"

"I haven't seen one insect since I've been here, but there are a few squirrels in unit three."

"I know," Valerie says interrupting, "And they're all nuts."

Rick laughs. "That's pretty funny. Remind me to write that down."

"Never mind the jokes. Tell me the truth and Don't make up any fancy stories."

"Really honey, everything's fine. I don't crave Placidyls anymore and I'm just doing whatever they tell me."

"When do you think they'll let you come home?"

"I can't say for sure, but they want me to go to group therapy tomorrow. The girl said something about it speeding up my release date."

"You mean like psychotherapy?"

"Hell if I know. I don't think I'll go there even though I told her that I would."

"Honey, if they want you to go then I think you should. Didn't you just get through telling me that you were going to do whatever they told you?"

Rick resents being told what to do, especially when Valerie knows that he'll do whatever he wants despite her opinion.

"Hold on a second," Rick says as he puts down the phone and lights up a cigarette. He doesn't really feel like picking up the phone and continuing his conversation with his wife. For some reason, he doesn't care to communicate with her while he's in the hospital. He could just leave the phone on the bed and she'd figure that he fell asleep or something, but on the other hand, she might suspect the worst and become frantic. Rick picks up the phone. "Valerie, I'm sorry honey, but the nurse just came in to take my vitals again."

"That's all right, I'll hold on," she says affably.

"I'd better call you later. I have to go into the hallway so they can weigh me, okay honey?" Rick says smiling. He knows that she'll have to comply with his wishes.

"All right honey, but don't forget to call me later, even if it's late. I love you."

"I love you too, bye," Rick hangs up the phone. He's glad to be off the phone. He knows he should feel bad about fibbing to Valerie, but he really isn't too concerned. He knows that if positions were reversed, she'd probably do the same thing to him. Anyway, he didn't want to argue with her about his decision not to attend group therapy. His mind's made up. He has no intentions of going, to therapy. Not tomorrow and not the day after that.

Rick has one problem to ponder. Sherri is coming for him the next morning to escort him to the session. He remembers that he told her that he'd go with her tomorrow. Rick thinks for a moment, then smiles. All he has to do when Sherri arrives is remind her that he promised to go with her tomorrow. Then he'll simply remind her that tomorrow never comes....

CHAPTER SIX

The medication nurse wheels her cart into Rick's room and approaches his bed. Rick is fast asleep. The nurse puts her hand on Rick's head and shakes it.

"Wake up Rick. It's time for your medication."

Rick doesn't respond.

The nurse shakes him more vigorously. "C'mon Rick, just wake up to take your pills and then you can go back to sleep," she says as she uses her other hand to uncover him.

Rick opens his eyes and sees the nurse standing next to his bed. "Oh hi," he says groggily. Rick scratches his head and looks around the room. "What time is it?"

"It's time for your medication," she informs him as she prepares his cup of pills.

"That's good." Rick rubs his eyes. "I was having trouble sleeping."

"I could see that. That's why you woke up right away," she sarcastically replies, handing Rick the cup of pills and a glass of orange juice.

Rick looks into the cup and counts six pills. He looks at the nurse and smiles. "They're all here. All six of them." He gulps down the pills and turns over on his stomach.

The nurse discards the empty cup and wheels her cart out of the room. She looks back responding to Rick's snoring. She smiles. "Sleep tight."

A few minutes later, George pushes the meal cart into Rick's room. George picks up a tray and places it in front of Alexander's bed. George doesn't seem to mind that Alexander is ignoring his presence.

"C'mon Alexander, time to eat your dinner so you can grow up to be big and strong like your cute roommate." George looks over at Rick and notices him sleeping.

"Oh, go away!" Alexander sluggishly says. "I'm not hungry."

George is amused. "Well, that's a first for you Alexander. I never thought I'd hear you say that. As long as you're not hungry, I'll just take your tray back to the kitchen." George slowly picks up Alexander's tray as Alexander sits up.

"Oh, all right. I'll eat it."

George sets the tray down. "I knew you'd come through Alexander."

Alexander studies his tray. "Could I have another carton of milk?"

"Sure Alex, I'll see what I can scrounge up."

"Alexander'"

"What?"

"Not Alex! The name's Alexander, not Alex," he tells George in a hostile tone.

George smiles affably. "Sorry man, I mean Alexander, it won't happen again. Okay Alex?"

"Alexander!"

"Oh yeah. I guess I forgot," he slyly says, returning to the cart for another tray.

George approaches Rick's bed carrying his dinner tray. George notices that Rick is still sleeping and decides to wake him up. He sets the tray on the table and reaches for Rick's blanket which he removes from the bed. George admires Rick's body as he sleeps. "It's a pity you brought your own pajamas. You'd look mighty fine in a hospital gown," he says loudly enough for Rick to hear, but Rick doesn't react. George reaches out and gently slaps Ricks rump. "1ets go sugar. George has your dinner for you."

Rick squirms in his bed and reaches out for his blanket, but is unable to find it. George steps closer to the bed hoping that Rick will grab a piece of him instead. George is delighted that Rick's hand has landed on his thigh. Rick moves his hand up and down George's leg, then Rick's eyes pop open and he hurriedly sits up. He quickly realizes what he's been touching.

"Sorry," Rick tells George as he rubs his hand across his tired eyes. "I didn't know that you were there."

George smiles. "That's okay, it felt scrumptious. I only wish you didn't stop when you did."

Rick's thoughts clear and he realizes what George is talking about. Rick's affable manner turns into anger and embarrassment. "What the hell are you standing around for? You waiting for a tip?"

George licks his lips. "That sounds wonderful. What'd you have in mind?"

"How about a punch in the mouth," he says holding up his closed fist.

"That's a bit drastic, don't you think? I should have told you that I'm not into a pain trip."

Rick isn't sure what George means by his remark, but he's sure that it's something he doesn't want George to explain. "Considering where I am and what you're thinking, I think a fist in your face is more than proper."

"All right, darling. I can take a hint." George casually walks towards the door. Then he turns to address Rick. "You'll break down sooner or later. They all do," he adds confidently.

"You can cut out that darling crap too!"

"Anything you say, Rick honey."

"Go fuck yourself George!"

"Aren't we crude today."

"In case you haven't noticed, I'm only interested in women. Period."

"Don't knock something you haven't tried. I bet you'd love it!"

"Listen George, I think you've said enough. I'd hate to throw up and ruin my clean sheets."

George smiles at Rick one last time as he walks out of the room, making sure to shake his ass for Rick.

"Fucking faggot!" Rick comments to himself, as he turns over hoping to fall back to sleep.

Rick sleeps through the nurses changing their shifts. Normally he'd wake up because of all the noise the nurses make, especially the Korean nurses. His medication's working better than ever and he doesn't even hear Alexander knocking his meal tray off the table and onto the floor. A Korean nurse enters and looks at the mess on the floor.

"You sloppy eater, Alexander," the Korean nurse exclaims, but instead of cleaning up the mess, she just turns around and exits.

"Can I have another carton of milk?" Alexander calls out to the nurse.

She pops her head into the room and stares at Alexander, "What you want now?" she impatiently asks.

"Another milk."

"Another milk?" she asks.

"Yes please."

"You funny man," she says giggling, heading out the door. Alexander turns over on his side and stares at the wall.

Nick is on the prowl again. He maneuvers his wheelchair down the corridor and passes Rick's room, looking in as he goes by. A moment later, Nick returns and again peers into the room. He sees that Rick is sound asleep and that his dinner tray hasn't been touched. Nick studies the food on the tray from a distance and notices Rick's pack of cigarettes next to it. Nick starts to enter Rick's room as a Korean nurse approaches him.

"You no go in other patient's room. You only can go in own room."

Instead of answering, Nick backs his wheelchair out of the doorway and goes quietly back to his room. He looks over his shoulder as he enters his room and sees the Korean nurse staring at him with her hands on her hips. Nick snickers at her for a few moments before entering his room.

Rick's room is silent. Rick is fast asleep and Alexander is also resting quietly. Suddenly, their bathroom door creaks open. Nick slowly wheels himself into the room. He sits. quietly, surveying the situation before acting. He studies Rick making sure that he really is sleeping. Once satisfied, he turns his attention to Alexander and notices that he's facing the wall. Nick remains motionless in his chair as he works up enough guts to proceed with his plan. Then Nick moves toward Rick's bed and stops in front of his table. Nick reaches up and grabs Rick's dinner tray, placing it on his lap. Then Nick takes Rick's pack of cigarettes and stuffs it underneath his urine pouch. Nick pivots around and hurriedly makes his way back to the bathroom. He closes the door behind him, but forgets to do it quietly and the sound of the door slamming shut awakens Rick.

Rick doesn't know why he awoke so suddenly, but he's really only interested in one thing. He's starving. He sees Alexander's dinner tray, but he doesn't see a tray on his own table. He figures that he probably ate his dinner when it was brought in and George probably came by and took the empty tray back to the kitchen.

Minutes later, a Korean nurse enters, responding to Rick's call button.

"Could I have something to eat please. I'm starving!"

The nurse shoots Rick a puzzled look. "Where your tray? You not eat it too!" She giggles.

Rick isn't in the mood for her games. "Hay! Just get me something to eat. I'm really hungry."

"You already get dinner. You not allowed to get dinner after dinner," she says as she scurries out of the room."

"What's the matter with you people," Rick calls out. "This isn't a weight clinic. What the hell is so terrible about getting me something to eat if I'm hungry." Rick is steamed.

The nurse comes back with a carton of orange juice which she sets on Rick's table. "You drink this," she says, placing a straw into the carton.

Rick is growing more and more flustered. "Don't you people listen to anything your patients tell you? I distinctly said that I'm hungry. You got that! Hungry!"

"You feel better after you take juice."

"What the fuck's the matter with you?" he shouts, dropping his juice into the trash can.

"Maybe you try prune juice," she says heading for the door. "It make you go to bathroom and you feel better and stop yelling."

"Just bring me something to eat or stay the fuck out of my room!" he yells, pressing the nurse call button again and again.

A moment later, two Korean nurses enter Rick's room and stand in the doorway. Rick stares at them expecting them to approach his bed, but they don't. Instead they look around the room deciding that no one wanted them.

"You no press button unless you want something," the first nurse tells Rick.

"I do want something."

"What you want? You no look sick."

"I just want something to eat." "How come you no eat dinner?"

"What the hall difference does it make? I'm starving and I want something to eat!" Rick is ready to burst his seams.

The two nurses begin chatting in Korean and they exit Rick's room. Rick feels that he finally got his message across even though they didn't acknowledge his request.

Rick relaxes in his bed, preferring to just stare at the ceiling. Suddenly, the man from across the corridor screams out. Rick is frightened, but quickly calms down. He knows he'll never get used to it.

Rick senses a certain shallowness in his room and notices that Bob's bed is empty. He first thinks that Bob's probably in unit three roaming around, but he also sees that all of Bob's belongings are gone. It's as if he was never there. Rick turns his attentions to the empty bed across from him and realizes that Mark is also gone. He knows that Mark went home, but as far as Bob is concerned, Rick theorizes that he was probably transferred to a mental institution.

Rick looks to his left and sees Alexander lying in his bed. Rick wishes that Mark or even Bob were there instead of Alexander. Even though Alexander's about fifteen feet away, Rick can still catch a whiff of Alexander's body odor.

Rick can't tell if Alexander's asleep, but he would like to know about Bob's whereabouts. "Hey Alex," Rick calls out.

"The name is Alexander," he answers harshly, still facing the wall.

"okay, okay," Rick answers, deciding not to play games with him. "Listen Alexander, what do you know about Bob. What I mean is, where did he go? Did he check out or did he just move to another unit."

Alexander doesn't respond. Rick sits up in his bed waiting for Alexander's answer. Rick can see that he is too busy cleaning out his nose with his finger.

"Did you hear what I said?"

"Leave me alone," he says with a whine.

"Sorry I bothered you. I should know better than to ask you anything when you're working on such an important excavation. I hope you don't lose a fingernail in there." Rick is confident that Alexander will at least give him a dirty look, but he doesn't do anything. "We'll talk again Alex. Real soon."

Alexander turns over and faces Rick. His finger is still in his nose.

"I'm not Alex," he sternly tells Rick. "It's Alexander!"

"Is that all you can say?" Rick hopes to stir Alexander.

"Leave me alone!" Alexander pleads, turning back around.

"Tell you what. I'll leave you alone if you'll just take a bath."

"No!"

"Well, how about if the nurses wash you. That way, you won't have to touch a wash rag or a bar of soap."

"Just leave me alone!"

"Not until you clean up. You smell like a damn sewer!"

Alexander pulls a blanket over his head and reaches out, closing the partition around his bed.

Rick looks away from Alexander's side of the room and silently wishes Alexander would also leave. He wouldn't mind being the only one in the room. After all, he likes his privacy.

Rick flips on his television, but doesn't find any program worthy or his attention. As he changes the channels for the second time, he notices several nurses scurrying past his open door. Rick shuts off his television and focuses his attention on the commotion coming from down the corridor. Rick hears the sounds growing louder. His eyes are riveted on his door.

A nurse races into Rick's room carrying an IV unit. She hurriedly hooks it onto an IV stand. Then she lowers the guardrails on the bed which once belonged to Bob. The nurse stands by the bed as a gurney is wheeled into the room. The two Korean nurses handling the gurney are being helped by two tiny Oriental doctors. Dr. Wang and his associate.

Rick can't help noticing that everyone seems kind of panicked. Rick scrutinizes his new roommate and doesn't notice anything odd about him. He seems perfectly normal except for the fact that he's sleeping. His new-roommate is a good looking Latin man with dark hair and a dark complexion who is about the same size as Rick and probably about the same age, Rick guesses.

Rick can't figure why all these doctors and nurses seem so worried. He theorizes that he probably missed something and he focuses his attention on the gurney and its cargo. Then Rick spots it. The patient is tied to the gurney with strips of bed sheets. His arms and legs are tied to the guardrails on the gurney and his shoes have peculiar metal straps on them.

"All right nurse. Let's lower one rail at a time." Dr. Wang says as he unties Jose's bonds. "And be sure that he doesn't choke on that depressor." he tells the other nurse who's standing at the head of the gurney.

Rick sits up in his bed and stares at his new roommate as Dr. Wang and a nurse lower the guardrail on one side of the gurney. Wang moves to the other side and unties the sheets around Jose's left leg and arm. Dr. Wang throws the bed sheets onto the floor and then puts his hands under Jose's body ready to lift him off the gurney and onto the bed.

"On the count of three. Ready. One, two..."

Everyone prepares to lift Jose, but suddenly his entire body tenses and begins shaking.

"Quick Put him down now! He's having another seizure. We'll just have to wait till it's over. Nurse, get the IV ready and let him have ten milligrams Valium. Stat!"

"Yes doctor," the nurse says heading out of the room.

It finally dawns on Rick what's going on. He's petrified at first, never before having seen a seizure like this. Oh sure, he remembers the guy at his father's office who had a seizure, but that was nothing compared to this. Besides, Rick thought, those doctors and nurses look pretty concerned. Obviously, Jose's not just having a simple every day seizure, but a grand mal seizure.

Rick watches the doctors and nurses as they stand around the gurney, staring at Jose.

"Excuse me please," Rick calls out.

One nurse approaches Rick, "You no ask questions now. You go to sleep," she says as she closes the partition around Rick's bed.

Rick is furious. For all the nurse knew, he might have said that there was a rattlesnake under his bed. Anyway, what's so terrible about asking a simple question, Rick thinks as he opens the partition a few inches.

The nurse inserts the IV into Jose's arm and Loads it with Valium. Dr. Wang looks at his watch.

"He should be coming out of his seizure any minute," he confidently tells the people around him. Dr. Wang rubs Jose's head with his hand. "Jose," he shouts," Wake up Jose. C'mon Jose, open your eyes and tell us you're fine." Dr. Wang claps his hands together hoping to stir a response from Jose. "C'mon Jose, wake up. Tell us we can go home." Dr. Wang places his thumb on Jose's closed eye lid and forces it open. Jose's eyeball is riveted to the top of the socket. Suddenly, Jose's eyeball drops down to the center of the socket. Dr. Wang seems pleased.

"C'mon Jose, wake up. It's Dr. Wang, your friend."

Jose's arm swings out, hitting Dr. Wang in the stomach. Dr. Wang isn't hurt. He grabs onto Jose's arm and holds it against the rail. "Nurse," he commands," Take his other arm and hold it down until I tell you differently."

The nurse grabs Jose's arm as he relaxes and opens his eyes. Dr. Wang sees that Jose is all right. He releases his grip on Jose's arm.

"It's okay to let go now, nurse."

The nurse obliges.

"Well Jose, it's about time you opened your eyes," Dr. Wang says smiling. He's obviously relieved. "You gave us quite a scare for a while."

Jose tries talking, but he is only able to make strange noises with his voice.

"Don't try talking Jose. You almost swallowed your tongue back there on the street. It's a lucky thing we got to you in time. Otherwise you wouldn't be alive at this very moment. It's a small price to pay, but you won't have your voice back for probably a few weeks."

Jose lifts his hand up a few inches, grabbing onto Dr. Wang's hand. Jose shakes hands with his doctor. He tries thanking him, but his voice doesn't work even though he's trying as hard as he can. The only sound he can manage is a kind of squeaking.

"Don't try and talk Jose. I know how happy you are that I'm here with you, but I don't want you to talk, okay?"

Jose smiles at his doctor as he nods his head up and down.

"Now just relax and we'll lift you off this thing and put you in bed where you belong," Dr. Wang's tone helps to reassure his patient.

Jose nods his head while Dr. Wang and the nurses lift him off the gurney and onto the bed, Dr. Wang, his associate and the nurses begin tying the bed sheets around Jose's legs and hands.

"We're doing this for your own protection Jose. we don't want you to hurt yourself in the event you have another seizure. And you know yourself that you'll probably have another one.

We just want you in restraints until your body has a chance to get back to normal."

Jose looks worried and he begins moaning. Dr. Wang can easily see that Jose's trying to use all his strength to break his bonds. Jose flexes his arms, but is unable to break the sheets holding his hands against the guard rails. Then Jose tries to maneuver his chest around hoping to at least loosen his restraints, but to no avail.

Rick is watching Jose's struggle and is kind of perplexed. Why doesn't Jose try and free his legs, Rick asks himself, as he watches Jose trying to break the bonds around his hands once again. From Rick's point of view, Jose resembles a rodeo bull who's been roped and is now being tied up. It hurts Rick to see the pain in Jose's face. Rick wishes there were something he could do for his roommate, but he knows that if he says anything, the nurse would probably come over to his bed and staple his partition shut.

Just when it seems that Jose is calm, he begins crying.

"What's the matter my friend?" Dr. Wang inquires.

Jose reluctantly points to his pants.

Dr. Wang smiles at Jose. "What are you crying about my friend. We all have bodily functions. You know you can't help it. It's just one of those things," Dr. Wang says compassionately.

Dr. Wang holds Jose's hand in response to his crying. Then a nurse enters holding a box of Pampers which she opens and hands to Dr. Wang. He takes out a diaper and opens it up.

"Here we go Jose. We'll put this thing on and you'll feel as good as new."

Dr. Wang's associate and one, of the nurses take off Jose's pants and remove his soiled diaper. Then the nurses lift Jose's buttocks and Dr. Wang places the new diaper in place. He sprinkles some baby power liberally over the diaper and then wraps it into place. The nurses pull Jose's pants back on him.

"You can sleep in your clothes tonight my friend and tomorrow I'll have your own pajamas brought in. Okay?"

Jose works up a grin and shakes his head affirmatively.

Dr. Wang turns his attentions to the people around him. He indicates Jose's smiling face. "What a terrific smile he has. I bet you never saw anybody with a smile like that," he says cheerfully. Dr. Wang pats Jose on his head. "That a boy Jose. Now you just listen to the nurses and do whatever they tell you and I'll be back to check on you tomorrow."

Dr. Wang turns to leave, but Jose moans loud enough to catch his attention. Jose tries talking, but he can only manage to make a few faint sounds which no one can understand.

"What's wrong my friend? Tell me."

Jose tries talking again, but he can't make himself understood. Then he begins crying as Dr. Wang tries to help him.

"C'mon my friend, tell me what's bothering you. Are you hungry or thirsty?"

Jose doesn't respond to his doctor's question. Then Jose points to the restraints on his legs.

Dr. Wang catches on. "Oh, you don't like having your legs and hands tied is that it?"

Jose smiles and nods his head up and down.

"Don 't worry my friend. They'll be off before you know it. When I come here tomorrow I'll probably have them removed, but you have to have them for at least one night. Okay?"

Jose doesn't respond to his doctor's question. Instead, he tries reaching into his pocket for his cigarettes, but the restraints hold his hand firmly in place a few inches from his goal.

Dr. Wang removes the cigarettes from Jose's pocket. "I'm sorry my friend, but no smoking tonight." he tells Jose as he places his pack of cigarettes in the drawer next to his bed.

Suddenly, Jose tenses and his eyes roll back. He's having another seizure. Rick watches as Dr. Wang rips a tongue depressor off the wall and sticks it into Jose's mouth. Dr. Wang, his associate and the nurses stand quietly by as the seizure subsides. Dr. Wang repeatedly slaps Jose's arm.

"C'mon Jose. Wake up my friend. Do you hear me Jose?" Dr. Wang stares at his patient for a few moments. "Say something," he pleads.

Jose opens his eyes and smiles. Dr. Wang can tell that Jose is tired.

"You'll be fine my friend," he tells Jose as he covers him with a blanket. Dr. Wang makes some notes on Jose's chart and hands it to the head nurse. "Just follow my instructions and call me if anything happens."

"You want him go sleep now?"

"Well, why don't you just give h.im the five milligrams Valium I ordered on his chart and let him take it from there. There's no urgency for him to sleep even though it would probably help. He's had a hard day." Dr. Wang faces Jose. "And don't try to make any dates with these nurses."

Rick just about throws up as he listens to Dr. Wang.

"I'll see you tomorrow my friend," Dr. Wang tells his patient as he pats his head.

Jose smiles at his doctor and nods his head.

"So long Jose," Dr. Wang says as he exits with his associate.

The nurses check the IV connections and leave the room.

Jose lifts up his head and looks around the room. He catches Rick looking his way and breaks out with a large smile. Rick smiles back, but doesn't know what to say to his roommate. Jose lifts up his hand and moves his fingers back and forth. Rick surmises that Jose is waving at him.

"How ya doing?" Rick says, initiating the conversation. Jose tries talking, but all he can make is faint sounds.

"Don't try talking. I heard what they said about your vocal cords being all screwed up. Anyway, you look like you could use some rest. I'll talk to you tomorrow."

Jose smiles at Rick and lays his head down on his pillow.

The nurse enters and approaches Jose's IV. She injects five milligrams of Valium into the unit and discards the syringe into the trash. As she leaves, Rick calls out to her.

"Excuse me, but I'm supposed to be getting something to eat."

"You not bother me with that. I not your nurse. She be here when she not busy," she says on her way out the door.

Then Rick's nurse enters and approaches his bed. She's holding a syringe.

"Where's my dinner?"

"You no get two dinners in one night," she says motioning for Rick to turn over.

"I don't need a shot," Rick sternly tells her, refusing to turn over.

The nurse prepares her syringe and pushes Rick over jamming the syringe into his cheek.

"Ouch!" Rick cries out. "That hurts. Who taught you how to give shots?"

"What you mean? I no give painful shots," she says indignantly.

"Just tell me who your teacher was," Rick asks as he rubs his rear.

"My father taught me how give shots. He very famous man," she adds trying to impress him.

"What'd your father do for a living besides putting shoes on horses?" Rick tries to keep from laughing, but he breaks out grinning.

"What so funny?"

"My butt feels funny from the shot," he says trying to get

back on the track. "Why'd you give me a shot anyway? I didn't ask for it. All I want is something to eat. I'm starving."

"You eat tomorrow. Right now, you go sleep."

"But I'm not tired," Rick protests. "I wanna watch television," he tells her forcefully.

Rick continues arguing with the nurse, but his words become slurred. He doesn't realize it, but the injection is making him tired. The nurse begins giggling at Rick's slurred speech.

Rick's eyes start closing as the nurse heads out of the room. Rick is too loaded to notice that the nurse has left and he just rambles on.

"Why should I go to sleep if I'm not tired. All I want to do is get something to sleep and go to eat." Rick dozes off into a deep sleep.

CHAPTER SEVEN

A female attendant brings the breakfast trays into the room. Rick takes the cover off his tray and discovers a box of corn flakes and a banana. This isn't Rick's idea of a good breakfast, but he's hungry enough to eat anything.

Rick forces himself to swallow the first spoonful of corn flakes. He's determined to eat them even though they're stale. His banana isn't much better, having attained its ripeness a few days before.

Alexander eats his breakfast without complaining. In fact, he calls the nurse into the room hoping she'll bring him another banana or two.

Rick can't bear to eat another bite. He knows that even if he finishes his meal, he'll still be hungry. So why should he eat any more when there's a chance that if he complains, he might be given something else. Rick depresses the call button and pushes his breakfast aside.

Are you going to eat any more?" Alexander calls out in a sotto voice.

Forget it Alexander. Even if I don't eat this slop, it still belongs to me."

"What about your banana? You didn't take any bites out of it."

Rick glares at Alexander, but Alexander stares at the banana undaunted.

Rick finally relents and throws his rotten banana at Alexander. Unfortunately, Alexander doesn't make an effort to catch it and the banana hits the side of his bed and lands inside the trash can alongside Alexander's bed.

"Sorry about that," Rick tells his roommate in an almost apologetic tone.

Alexander stares into the trash can and then to Rick's surprise picks the banana out of the trash and eats it. Rick can't bear to watch and turns away.

Jose's bed is empty. Rick remembers seeing Jose the night before in Bob's bed, but now he's not there. Maybe he dreamed it, Rick thinks as he hears the buzzing sound of a motor. Rick looks across from his bed and sees Jose in the bed that once belonged to Mark. The head of the bed rises and Rick sees Jose's smiling face.

"How ya doing?" Rick asks his new roommate. Rick is happy to see him again.

Jose points into his mouth reminding Rick that he is still unable to utter a word.

"I'm sorry, I forgot you can't talk," Rick says in an affable tone. Rick spots the breakfast tray next to Jose's bed. It hasn't been touched. "I'm not eating my breakfast either. They've got a lot of nerve giving us that shit! They charge us an arm and a leg for this place and they only spend a few pennies for our food."

Jose shrugs his shoulders and lifts his fingers up and down. At first, Rick thinks that Jose is waving at him, so he waves back. Jose continues moving his fingers, giving Rick the impression that Jose wants him to come over to his bedside.

"You want me to come over there?"

Jose smiles and nods his head up and down.

Rick slides off his bed and into his wheelchair. He maneuvers his wheelchair over to Jose's bed. "What do you need?"

Jose makes a strange sound with his throat and points his fingers towards his mouth.

"Are you hungry?"

Jose nods his head up and down while trying to speak, but Rick can't understand him.

"No problem," Rick says as he lifts the cover off the breakfast tray, exposing a package of corn flakes and a rotten banana. "I know this isn't much of a breakfast and if you were watching me you know that I didn't eat it. Don't worry though. If you don't wanna eat this shit we have a living garbage disposal in our room." Rick indicates Alexander who's consuming Rick's banana. "That guy will eat anything," Rick tells Jose as he empties the corn flakes into a bowl and then pours the milk onto the corn flakes.

Jose gets Rick's attention by moaning and shaking his head from side to side. Rick pushes the tray closer to Jose and sees that Jose is trying to communicate with him.

"I'm not very good at interpreting what you want," Rick says as an idea pops into his head. "Wait a second." Rick returns to his bedside and picks up his grip removing a pad of paper and a pen. He returns to Jose and hands him the items. Rick feels silly because Jose can't very well write with his hands bound to the guardrails. Rick looks around the room and then decides to untie Jose's hands. "I'll have to tie them up again when you're finished writing," Rick tells his smiling roommate.

Rick unties Jose's hands and places the pen and paper on his stomach. "Do you want me to untie your legs too?"

Jose shakes his head from side to side as he lifts his left hand over to his stomach. Then Jose takes his left hand and moves it over to his other hand, lifting it onto his stomach.

"What's the matter with your right hand?" Rick inquisitively asks.

Jose holds out his left hand as if to say wait a minute. Then Jose tries writing on the pad, but he can't grip the pen properly and gives up in disgust.

"Would a pencil be easier?"

Jose smiles and nods his head up and down.

Rick opens the dresser next to Jose's bed and finds a pencil which he hands his roommate. Jose takes the pencil and scribbles out his message. Rick watches Jose writing and notices how childish his style is. Jose prints out his message and makes a noise with his throat indicating that he's finished. Rick takes the pad and reads it aloud.

"My right hand does is not working so good." Rick pauses for a moment to digest the words he just read. "Is it paralyzed?"

Jose shakes his head back and forth and motions with his left hand for the paper and pencil. Jose scribbles an answer to Rick's question.

Rick bends over Jose's bed and reads Jose's latest message, ONLY THREE FINGERS DO NOT WORK SO GOOD.

"It's no big thing," Rick says philosophically. "Most women I've met only care about one finger working and I can see that that finger Is fine.

Jose smiles as Rick takes the banana off his tray and begins to peel it. Jose sees what Rick's doing and immediately begins writing out another message. Jose looks at Rick every few seconds and moans trying to stop Rick from what he's doing.

"What's the matter?" Rick asks noticing that Jose's writing again. Rick sets the banana down and patiently waits for Jose to finish. A moment later, Jose sets down his pencil and Rick takes the pad and reads it to himself.

I CAN NOT EAT ANYTHING BECAUSE MY TONGUE IS IN THE WAY. THEY ARE GOING TO BE MAKING ME A SPECIAL BREAKFAST WHICH

THEY WILL FEED ME BECAUSE I NEED THEM TO HELP ME EAT MY FOOD BECAUSE I CAN NOT AND I MIGHT HAVE A SEIZURE WHEN I AM EATING AND I COULD DIE FROM CHOKING.

"Why the hell did they send this stuff in here if they know that you can't eat it?"

Jose shrugs his shoulders.

Rick returns to his side of the room and returns with his pack of cigarettes. Jose watches him light his cigarette and motions for Rick to let him have one also. Rick is only too happy to oblige and puts one of his cigarettes into Jose's left hand. Jose tries putting the cigarette into his mouth, but he's fighting a losing battle and the cigarette falls onto his chest. Rick surmises what the problem is.

"Do you want me to light it for you?"

Jose smiles and nods his head up and down. Rick lights the cigarette as Jose scribbles another message on his pad. Rick sees Jose writing and decides to wait for him to finish before handing him the cigarette. Jose sees that Rick is waiting for him with his cigarette and motions for him to be patient. Finally, Jose turns the pad around enabling Rick to read it.

YOU HAVE TO STAY WITH ME WHILE I SMOKE OR THEY WILL NOT LET ME DO IT AND THEN THEY WOULD YELL AT ME AND BE MAD. I ALSO CAN NOT HOLD IT BY MYSELF AND YOU HAVE TO PUT IT INTO MY MOUTH FOR ME SO I CAN SMOKE IT BECAUSE I NEED YOU TO DO IT FOR ME.

"No problem. "Rick says as he places the cigarette into Jose's mouth. Jose inhales the smoke and pulls his head back. Rick removes the cigarette and puffs on his own as he watches Jose enjoying the first puff he's had since he checked in.

Jose takes a second puff on the cigarette as a nurse enters

and sees what's going on. She places her hands on her hips and takes an authoritarian stance.

"What's going on here?" she demands to know. "You're not allowed to visit with the other patients, especially him," she says, approaching Jose's bed.

"I was only helping him smoke a cigarette," Rick sheepishly tells the nurse.

"He's not allowed to smoke," she sternly says realizing that Jose's hands are not in their restraints. "And who untied his hands?" She glares at Rick.

"A nurse did. She brought in his breakfast and untied his hands so he could eat. She probably didn't know that Jose needs help to eat his meals."

"I see," she says suspiciously. Then she turns to leave.

"Wait a second," Rick calls out. "When's he gonna get his breakfast?" There's no way he can eat this stuff. He has to have a special meal prepared for him and he has to have someone who'll help him eat it."

"Special orders take longer," she says as she disappears from sight.

"She bluffs pretty easy," Rick tells Jose. "I guess now I don't have to tie up your hands again because she thinks that another nurse okayed it."

Jose smiles at his roommate as the same nurse enters and storms over to Jose's side of the room. She has a bone to pick with Rick.

"No one untied him so you must have done it!" she tells Rick in a belligerent tone as she grabs onto his wheelchair and pushes him back to his side of the room. "Now you get back in your own bed and stay there or I'll put you in restraints too!" She closes the partition around Rick's bed.

The nurse returns to Jose's bed and extinguishes his cigarette in the ashtray. "No more smoking for you'" she tells

Jose as she ties his hands to the guardrails.

"What about my food? "Rick calls out from behind his partition.

"You1ll have to wait until lunch like everyone else. No one gets special favors around here. We treat every patient equally."

"In that case, we're all doomed!" Rick calls out, but the nurse doesn't respond.

Rick cautiously opens his partition and discovers that the nurse has left. Rick looks around his room and sees Jose crying. Rick doesn't know what to say but he doesn't think that Jose has a legitimate reason for crying.

"C'mon Jose. I'll come over there pretty soon and we can have another cigarette together."

Rick's words cheer up Jose and he stops crying. Rick can see the tears streaming down Jose's face. He knows what a nuisance they can be.

"Can I get you a Kleenex or something?"

Jose nods his head.

Rick lights up a cigarette and climbs into his wheelchair for the journey over to Jose's bedside. Rick takes a Kleenex off of Jose's dresser and wipes the tears from Jose's face. Then Rick takes the cigarette out of his mouth and places it into Jose's mouth. Jose takes a long drag off Rick's cigarette and smiles at his friend.

"I'd better get back into my bed," Rick tells his roommate as he lets him have one more puff of his cigarette. "Sorry I can't untie your hands, but you know how it is."

Jose smiles at Rick as if to say, thank you for caring.

Rick heads back to his bed as Jose watches his new friend.

Rick climbs into his bed as he takes one last puff on his cigarette. Rick drops his cigarette into the ashtray when he notices a peculiar silence in the room. Rick looks across at Jose and notices that his body is quivering. Rick stares at his roommate for a moment then sees that Jose's hands have broken their bonds. Jose flings his arms wildly, crashing them into the guardrails. Not knowing what else to do, Rick presses the nurse call button and keeps his finger on the button hoping that someone will respond immediately.

"Somebody help! HELP!" Rick shouts at the top of his lungs, but no one comes. "Somebody help! He's having a seizure. Come quick, help!"

Rick turns his head from side to side, trying to keep an eye on the door while at the same time, watching Jose. Rick wishes there were something he could do, but he knows that he's not versed in the treatment of someone who's having an attack. Rick watches Jose's arms waving about sporadically and every few seconds, his legs move and tremble. Suddenly, Jose's body grows ominously silent and his head rolls off his pillow and against the guardrails of his bed.

"Help!" Rick again shouts, but no one responds to his plea. Rick presses the call button again and again, even though he's beginning to think that it's broken. Then Rick remembers what Mark told him about the tongue depressors and how they're used for seizures. Rick realizes that if he doesn't do something and quick, his roommate might expire before his very eyes.

Rick jumps out of his bed and falls into his wheelchair. He maneuvers himself over to Jose's bedside and grabs his arm to steady it. Then Rick sits up, putting his weight on Jose's bed and he grabs the tongue depressor off the wall. Rick holds the depressor over Jose's mouth, but he discovers that Jose's teeth are clenched. With all his strength, Rick pries open Jose's teeth and he jams the depressor into his mouth. Rick is relieved until he realizes that the stick is at the bottom of Jose's tongue and not on top of it where it should be. He remembers how Mark explained that the depressor is used to keep the person from swallowing his tongue. Rick reaches for the tongue depressor and pulls it out of Jose's mouth. Just as he prepares to jam it into the right place, two nurses enter and see Rick leaning over Jose with the tongue depressor in his hand.

"What do you think you're doing?" the first nurse yells out as she races over to Rick. She grabs the tongue depressor from his hand, dropping it into the trash. "Get away from him this instant," she commands indignantly, pushing Rick back into his wheelchair.

"What the hell do you think you're doing?" Rick asks vitriolically. "Can't you see he's having a seizure?"

Both nurses ignore Rick's remark.

"Do something!" he insists as Jose's arms crash into the guardrails.

The first nurse realizes what's going on and she rummages through the trash until she finds the tongue depressor she just discarded. She wipes it off with a Kleenex and jams it into Jose's mouth as the second nurse wheels Rick back to his side of the room.

Rick leers at the nurse as she returns to Jose's bedside, closing the partition around his bed.

Maggie enters the room and spots Rick in his wheelchair fuming. "What's going on?"

"Jose's having a seizure or something and those bitches just stopped me from putting a tongue depressor in his mouth like you're supposed to do."

Instead of discussing the matter, Maggie goes behind the closed partition to lend her nurses a hand.

A few minutes later, Maggie exits the partition and approaches Rick.

"I don't believe how they treated me. They acted like I was standing over him with a dagger in my hand. All I was trying to do was save him from choking to death on his tongue."

"I understand what you did Rick, but they had no way of knowing what you were doing. Their first concern was the patient. They didn't have time to size up the situation and ask you what you were doing."

"Any dummy could see what I was doing. And if they were so concerned with their patient, why did it take them so long to answer the buzzer? I kept screaming for help!"

Maggie smiles affably. "Well, it's nice to know you're such a watch dog."

"Maggie, I'm here to get better, not to worry about other patients. Suppose I was having a seizure, do you think Alexander would lift one smelly finger to call for help." Rick shakes his head. "Hell no! I'd probably die! And what if I didn't see Jose having a seizure. Who would call the nurse in? And don't tell me that they're always checking in to make sure that everything's okay, because they're not."

"You paint a pretty grim picture of the goings on around here, but believe me, it's not really that bad. Now I'm not trying to make any excuses for the length of time it took them to respond to your call, but we were changing shifts and things are particularly hectic around here when we do."

"You can't expect patients like Jose to wait for the shifts to change before having a seizure, can you?"

"C'mon Rick, this place isn't perfect, but believe me, if I didn't think this hospital was a good one, I wouldn't want to work here. What happened just now with Jose was just one of those things. You know we're spread pretty thin around here and there just isn't enough personnel to take care of every problem that arises. Now before you jump all over me about the short staff I think it's only fair to tell you that all hospitals are understaffed and it's not because they don't get paid enough. There just aren't enough people interested in nursing like there used to be."

"I think you're a hell of a lady and one good talker, but just guarantee me one thing," Rick says letting his harsh attitude subside.

"What's that?"

"The next time you see my buzzer flashing, don't send anyone in here but yourself,"

Maggie laughs, "I'll try to keep an eye on you whenever I can," She winks at him.

"No, I really mean it. You weren't here a little while ago, I don't like the way I'm being treated, especially at night, Those Korean nurses are really the pits, all they do is giggle and they never get me what I want. Last night I didn't get any dinner and when I complained, they giggled and told me that I'm not allowed to get two dinners in one night, if they could understand English, they'd know that I wasn't given dinner the first time. And instead of taking an interest in my complaint, they did the only thing they knew to do. They gave me a shot that knocked me out."

Maggie understands Rick's complaint, "I can't blame you for being upset. We've had a lot of problems with that shift."

"If they have to hire a bunch of nurses who can't speak English, why can't they split them up so they're not always working together. They should put a few on each shift and they should have to answer to an English-speaking nurse."

"That would solve a lot of problems around here, but you have to understand that no one but those nurses are willing to work the grave yard shift. I've spoken to the administrator about just that several times and they always tell me that they'll take it under consideration."

"Well, at least you know what the problem is and you're trying to do something about it."

"I guess you're kind of like me in a way. Tough! You've only been here a little while and you're trying to institute changes.

Why, I've been here for a long time and I'm still trying to get them to do things the right way. And when I say the right way, I'm not trying to get them to do what I want, but my way happens to be the proper way to run a nursing staff. I should know. I've been a nurse for almost twenty-five years and I've learned a lot about what patients need and how they should be treated."

"Why don't you leave me your telephone number and I'll call you if I need something. I'm sure you'd get here before the Korean's answer my buzzer."

Maggie laughs. "I bet you try and get all the nurses numbers."

"Just the professionals. And the cute ones."

"Which category do I fall under?"

"A little of both, but more of one."

"Which one?" Maggie asks anticipating the answer.

"Let's just say that you're my favorite nurse in this whole place and I refuse to say any more on the grounds that you might slap my face." Rick thinks to himself for a moment. "Actually, I can say anything I want to you and you can't get mad at me because you wouldn't know if it was me talking or my medication."

"You want to bet?" Maggie says slyly.

The partition around Jose's bed opens and the nurses head for the door. Maggie looks on and is surprised that the nurses aren't saying one thing to her.

"They must be mad at you because they know you're my favorite patient," she tells Rick.

Rick is confused. "I don't get it."

"They only like patients who just lay in their beds and don't call them. It makes their jobs easier and they can spend more time gabbing away with their friends,"

"You mean they don't like me because I ask questions about my medication?"

"That's part of it, but it goes beyond that."

"What about Jose? They must rely hate him."

"Let's just say they'll be happy when he's gone."

"Why?"

"A patient like Jose makes them uncomfortable. They're not used to dealing with someone who has a problem like he does."

"How do you feel about him?"

"Sad, mostly. I just wish there was something that I could do for him. You know, most of the people that come in here are really bad off. We get to see them at the worst possible time in their life, but we also get to be around them as they get better. That's the nice part about this job. But somebody like Jose isn't your typical patient. He came in here with his problem and when he leaves here, he'll still have his same problem. That's why most of the nurses don't like coming in here. They're afraid they'll have to change his diaper or something."

"You mean like feeding him?"

"Oh, you saw them feeding him?"

"No. He's still waiting for his breakfast. I don't know why they brought him corn flakes and a banana when they know that he can't eat anything solid."

Maggie looks at her watch. "You mean he hasn't eaten anything yet?" Maggie can't believe her ears.

Rick nods his head. "The only thing he's had so far is a few drags on a cigarette and I got yelled at for letting him have it."

Maggie gets up. "Well I'll check with the kitchen and see what's taking them so long with his breakfast."

"There's one thing I don't understand. There's a sign on the door outside that says that this place doesn't take emergency cases. As far as I know, Jose's an emergency case so why did they bring him here?"

"He is not exactly your typical emergency patient. "Maggie

looks at her watch again, then comments to herself," I guess I can tell you about Jose's condition."

Rick presses the bed control and the head of his bed rises. He doesn't want to miss one word of Maggie's story, figuring she'll probably whisper so that no one will know what she's about to tell him.

Maggie looks around the room making sure that no one else is listening. "About ten years ago, Jose and his family were flying across the country. Jose's father was a pilot with the airlines and every summer they would rent a small plane and fly somewhere. Jose's dad wanted his son to take an interest in planes, so he gave him responsibilities. Each time they flew, Jose had more and more things to take care of. His dad sometimes even let him fly the plane which is a great thrill for anyone, especially when the teacher is an airline pilot. Anyway, Jose was in charge of making sure the tanks had enough gas in them, especially on this trip because the gas gauge in the plane was broken. To make a long story short, Jose forgot to have fuel put into the plane while his parents were visiting their friends at one of their stops and the plane ran out of fuel over a residential area and crashed. Jose was the only survivor of the crash and he paid for his mistake dearly. He not only lost his whole family, but he's paralyzed from the waist down and he suffered brain damage which restricts his hand movements, and he also suffers from frequent epileptic seizures."

Rick is horrified to hear this and stares over at his roommate who's now resting comfortably.

"Last night, he tried to kill himself the simplest way he could think of. He has to take his medicine all the time and if it works, he won't have seizures all the time. He knew that if he stopped taking it, he'd probably have a seizure and die, provided that no one was around to help him. Anyway, he snuck out of his friends! house, where he was living and when he got down the street, he had a seizure. They were going to take him over to the county hospital, but there wasn't any room for him so his doctor, who's on our staff, brought him here."

"Are they gonna send him to county when there's enough room?"

"I doubt it. We'll probably just take care of him until he's well enough to leave and then we'll find a place to send him."

"You mean back to his friends' house?"

"Not there. His friends don't want him back. He's too much trouble for them and I can't really blame them. Jose's quite a handful.

It's a good thing he has someone like you in the same room"

"I can't just ignore him."

"Why not? Alexander does," she says glancing at Alexander with a contemptuous look.

"He wouldn't know it if his pants were on fire."

Maggie tries not to laugh. After all, that wouldn't be the professional thing to do.

"What's the matter with Jose's voice? How come he can't talk?"

"Well, that's what sometimes happens with a seizure. You sometimes try to swallow your tongue. In Jose's case, he almost choked on it and would have too if help hadn't arrived in time. They literally pulled his tongue out of his throat, but not before it injured his vocal cords. His voice should come back in a few weeks, then he'll be talking up a storm. He's really a nice guy from what I hear, but he still has the mentality of a ten-year-old."

"That explains his writing."

Maggie is happily surprised. "Oh, so you gave him the paper to write on."

"I had to do something. I couldn't understand his moans."

Maggie smiles at Rick. "I'm glad they put Jose in your room. Maybe you can even talk to him and convince him that he should stop blaming himself. for the plane crash. He might end up a productive human being if only he'd get on with his life and stop blaming himself for something that happened ten years ago."

"Maggie, I'm a patient, remember? Not a psychiatrist."

"Your head seems to be screwed on better than most of the shrinks I've known," she says as she heads for the door. "I'll see you later. And don't give my nurses to hard a time," she adds, sporting a broad smile.

Maggie passes Sherri in the doorway.

"Hi Sherri. Did you come.to take Rick to group therapy?"

"I sure did," Sherri says confidently.

"I bet he'll liven things up over there. Even teach them a thing or two."

Sherri gives Maggie a perplexed smile as she walks past her and over to Rick's bed. Rick pushes the button on his bed control causing the head of his bed to recline.

"You better not be going to sleep because I came to take you over to group."

Rick looks at Sherri with a forced look of astonishment. "Group therapy! Today?" Rick is certain that his tone should convince Sherri that he really did forget about his promise to accompany her to unit three.

"C'mon Rick don't feed me that," she says looking at Rick askance. "Don't pretend you forgot."

Rick realizes that he isn't doing too good a job at faking a memory lapse. "Oh yeah. I remember, didn't you say that you'd just take me to the afternoon session and kind of ease my way into the group. I am a first timer you know."

"Don't put words in my mouth Rick, and don't try to get out of going either. It's part of your therapy C'mon and get out of bed," she says positioning his wheelchair alongside his bed. "I'll bet once you get in there, you'll want to hang around for the afternoon session too."

Rick sits up and dangles his legs over the side of the bed. "Don't count on it," he says as his legs touch the floor. He stands up, supporting himself for the first time since he's been in the hospital.

Sherri grabs Rick's arm fearing that he might fall.

"Let go," Rick tells her as he pulls himself free and walks, ever so carefully, into the bathroom. "If I don't come out in ten minutes, start the therapy without me," he yells from inside the bathroom.

"Don't start yet Rick," Sherri shouts as the medication nurse enters the room. "The nurse is here with your medication."

"Okay, okay I'm coming," Rick says as he exits the bathroom and approaches the medication cart. Rick looks at the nurse's watch. "What time is it?" he asks as he takes the pills from her and swallows them with his cup of juice.

"It's nine thirty," she tells Rick checking her watch.

"Back to the bathroom Rick. Group starts pretty soon."

"Just a second," Rick tells Sherri turning his attention back to the nurse. "How come you're an hour late with my medication?"

"One of the nurses from the other shift accidently took the key to the cart home with her. We had to wait for her before we could begin dispensing the medication, I'm sorry if you experienced any discomfort."

"That's okay, but why didn't you use the spare key under the cart?" Rick realizes that he's said enough and he quickly clams up.

"What spare key?" she asks staring at Rick blankly. What are you talking about?"

Sharri and the nurse exchange confused looks.

"Well, I mean, I just thought that they1.d have a spare for this cart. You know, like, well, just what I said. A spare key. Just like a spare tire."

The screaming from down the corridor interrupts Rick. He's glad to hear any sound other than his own because he knows that he isn't doing such a terrific job erasing what he just told the nurse about the key under the medicine cart.

The nurse turns her cart around and pushes it out the door. "I should have given him his medication first then I wouldn't have to listen to his horrible screaming," she tells Rick and Sherri as she exits the room.

"Back to the bathroom," Rick tells Sherri as he gingerly takes tiny steps back into the bathroom.

Rick takes his place on the toilet and silently contemplates what's likely to happen in group therapy. He knows that he can't get out of going, so he might as well make the best of an uncomfortable situation. He decides to simply remain silent and if they ask any questions, he'll just tell them that he has a sore throat and it hurts to talk. He figures that he can get away with it for a few days and hopefully he'll be released before his sore throat has time to properly clear up.

Rick looks around the bathroom and notices more cigarette butts on the floor. He's puzzled as to why anyone would smoke the cigarettes that far down, but figures that in a place like this, anything's possible.

Rick catches himself talking out loud and wonders why he's doing it. "I don't talk to myself when I'm in the bathroom at home, so why am I suddenly doing it in here. There I go again, talking to myself. Oh well," he says philosophically, "At least I don't have to use that stupid wheelchair anymore. I'm sick of those assholes staring at me like I'm some sort of a cripple or something," he tells himself as he gets up from the toilet. Then Rick loses his balance and falls back onto the toilet with a thud. "Oh shit! I can't stand up again and everything looks funny in here. At least I feel great!" Rick tells himself in a loud voice as he leans over and opens the bathroom door. "Sherri!" he yells out. "I'm sort of having a problem standing up. Could you please push in my wheelchair?" Rick asks hesitantly.

"Sorry to hear that," Sherri says as she scoots the wheelchair into the bathroom, making sure that she doesn't step into view of Rick. "You were walking so well a couple of seconds ago, but I guess it's a start anyway," she says, hoping that Rick won't feel bad about returning to his wheelchair.

Rick gets into his wheelchair and moves to the end of the bathroom, opening up the door into the next room so that the patients in there will know that the bathroom is vacant. Rick sees Nick sitting in his wheelchair with a pack of cigarettes on his lap. Nick sees Rick staring at him and pushes the cigarettes aside hoping that Rick didn't see them. Rick stares at Nick for a moment, but it doesn't dawn on him that those are his cigarettes.

"How you doing in here?" Rick asks pleasantly.

Nick nervously nods his head up and down. "I'm all right, but I'm supposed to have lots of privacy. My doctor told me so," Nick adds hoping that Rick will take a hint and leave.

Rick gets the message and whirls his wheelchair around, heading out of the bathroom and over to Sherri who's waiting for him. She grabs hold of his chair.

"Shall we go?" she says starting for the door as Rick checks his bathrobe pockets.

"Take me back to my table for a minute to get my cigarettes."

Sherri obliges and turns the chair around so that Rick can easily reach the table.

Rick scans the table, but doesn't see his cigarettes. His lighter is right where he left it, but his cigarettes aren't next to it like he remembers. Then it dawns on him. "That son of a bitch stole my cigarettes," he says vitriolically. "I don't know how he did it, but I know it's that bastard! He probably did it when I was sleeping. That dirty bastard! I knew he acted funny when he saw me. Those were probably my cigarettes on his lap. I'll bet that pack was full just like mine. What am I saying, that was my pack!" Rick contemplates his next move in silence then, "Take me back into his room. I'm gonna ring that bastard's neck and get my stuff back," he says in an authoritarian tone.

"Don't you have any more cigarettes?"

"Yeah, I've got a whole carton in my bag."

"Why don't you just get another pack and forget about what he did. No sense causing trouble and making an enemy in this place.

"I know you're right, but it really pisses me off."

"Well, why don't you just forget about it this time. He probably knows you're on to him anyway if you saw him with your cigarettes. He'll probably watch his step from now on. Anyway, if you did start something, there's no telling what a guy like that is likely to do and I'll bet you've got a lot more to lose than he does."

Rick grins at Sherri. "All right," he says relenting. "I'll do it your way, but he'd better watch out because I'll be waiting for him the next time."

"Enough chit chat," Sherri tells Rick as she pushes his wheelchair out of the room and down the corridor.

They leave unit two's corridor and head down another corridor. As they pass the kitchen, George emerges and sees Rick coming his way. George smiles effeminately as Rick approaches, standing in front of the wheelchair's path forcing Sherri to stop.

"Hi Ricky," George says in an overly friendly tone. "Would

you like to come into the break room with me for something sweet to eat?"

"Cut out that sweet talk crap!" Rick warns him in a demonstrative tone.

"Don't you have some toilets to clean up or something?"

George is taken aback. But, in a way, he likes Rick's spunk. "My, oh

my. Such horrid words from such a cute person."

"And knock off that Ricky shit!" Rick turns around and faces Sherri. "Let's go," he barks as he maneuvers his wheelchair around George and heads down the corridor with Sherri in close pursuit."

Sherri looks back at George as he stands in the same spot. "He didn't mean it George," she says. "He's pretty loaded right now and he doesn't know what he's saying."

George smiles at Sherri as she turns around and notices that Rick is at the end of the corridor and is turning down the next one. She scurries after him as George looks on.

"You shouldn't have said those things to George," Sherri tells Rick as she grabs hold of his wheelchair and pushes it down the corridor.

"I don't care for his kind and there's no reason why I have to take any crap from some fucking fag! That son of a bitch even said some things about me to someone else which I didn't care for."

"Like what?" Sherri inquisitively asks.

"Forget it. It's not worth repeating, but if you see him again you can tell him that he'd better stay away from me if he knows what's good for him."

"I think you already told him that, but not in those exact words."

"Just the same, tell him again because if I see him one more time and he comes on to me, I'll make sure that he ends up in the medical ward."

"He might like that. Especially if he ends up in your room." She grins. "Very funny," Rick sarcastically comments.

"Not to change the subject or anything, but is it true that you write scripts for television?"

"It's true," Rick nonchalantly replies as they head down another corridor.

"Do you get to meet a lot of movie stars?" she anxiously asks.

"Don't get so excited. They're just people like us, only with swelled heads and a lot of money."

"I guess you don't like them."

"That's not true. There are a few that I really like, but that's not a very good percentage. It's just that it's easy for them to get the way they are because of all the money and the attention. It just goes to their heads. Especially the ones who didn't have to struggle. I really hate those bastards!"

"I guess it's not like that in your end of the business."

"Are you kidding? I's probably ten times worse. One of the reasons it's so bad is because of nepotism. I hardly watch any television anymore because it's so bad. Parents who make it as writers and producers are always hiring their families and friends to write scripts and most of those people can't even construct a simple sentence."

"I watch a lot of TV and I think it's pretty good."

"Oh yeah!" Rick says in a perturbed tone. "How many times do you see the same plot on different shows?" Rick is obviously building up to a point.

"I don't know. I never paid much attention."

"Well, like this year for instance, there were at least ten different comedies that locked their cast in a room for thirty minutes. A couple of shows locked their people in a basement, one show locked its star in the bathroom and another show was about being snowed in, in a mountain cabin. I could keep going, but it makes me sick to think about it."

"Why do they keep using the same ideas over and over?"

"Because these no-talent bastards refuse to see freelance writers to get fresh ideas. Some of them figure that if they can't think of any new ideas then there aren't any. So, they keep using the same old tired stories again and again. Oh sure, they try to disguise them, but they can't really hide it. They think the public is stupid and doesn't notice it, but they do."

"I don't think I want to hear any more," she says in a depressed tone.

"It's hard for me to stop once I start spewing my venom."

"If you're looking for new ideas, pay attention to some of the patients in group therapy. I bet you could write a book about their problems and it would be a best seller."

"I don't mean to put down your idea or anything, but whenever someone finds out that I'm a writer, they always tell me about something that I should write a book about."

"Sorry I opened my mouth."

"Hey, don't take it that way. I didn't mean anything by it. It's just that if I wanted to write a book, I'd rather pick out a topic that I thought of."

Sherri realizes that she was too hard on Rick. "Yeah, I guess I know what you mean. You probably have a bunch of ideas for books," she says as she remembers what she wanted to tell him. Her spirits rise once again.

"But I'll bet that you'll want to write a book about some of the nuts in here. You could never make up some of these people. They're real bizarre."

"Well, I'll keep an open mind and if I decide to write a book about these patients, or nuts as you probably call them, then I'll put your name in my book."

Sherri is over whelmed by Rick's generosity. "Oh, that

would be really nice of you. Thank you,"

"No sweat. I'll use your name for one of the patients," Rick says with a smirk on his face."

Sherri shoots Rick a suspicious look as she stops the wheelchair in front of unit three's doors.

"I guess it wouldn't do any good to try and get out of going in?" Rick asks already knowing her answer.

"Not this time," Sherri comments as she gets ready to push the wheelchair through the doors and into unit three.

Rick knows that if he wasn't so loaded, he'd give Sherri a better fight about not attending the therapy session. But the way he feels right now, he doesn't really mind going. As a matter of fact, he's kind of looking forward to it. After all, maybe he will write a book about this place someday.

CHAPTER EIGHT

Sherri pushes Ricks wheelchair through unit three's doors and into the drug unit. Rick is hesitant about staying, remembering a few of the details from his earlier visit to this unit. He's afraid that Charlie will see him and run over to him and shake his hand vigorously. Rick remembers the pain from Charlie's last visit and doesn't particularly care to repeat the incident. Besides, in Charlie's state of mind, there's no telling what he's likely to do he thinks that Rick really doesn't like him.

"I didn't realize what time it was," Sherri says checking her watch. "You don't need me anymore. Just go into the therapy room when the doctor starts the session and I'll come back for you when it's over." Sherri heads for the exit. "If I'm not here when you're finished, don't worry. Just wait for me and I'll find you." Sherri pauses by the door waiting for Rick to acknowledge what she just said.

Rick feels uncomfortable about being left alone in unit three, especially now, when therapy is about to begin.

Rick really needed someone to hold his hand the first time therapy was to begin. "Can't you just stay with me for this one session?" Rick pleads. "I'm not chicken or anything. I just feel uncomfortable with a group of people I don't know." Rick knows that he sounds paranoid, but he doesn't care. After all, this isn't just any group of strangers, it's a group of strangers with serious problems.

"C'mon Rick," Sherri says affably. "Everyone in this place goes through the same things you're feeling now and they have to deal with it same way you have to." She pushes the doors open. "Don't worry. If anyone can deal with it, you can," she says positively as he leaves unit three.

Rick's first thought is to follow Sherri out of unit three and head back to the comfortable confines of his own unit. Rick quickly dismisses this notion, realizing that if doesn't attend therapy he just might not be released on time.

"Hi Rick," a voice calls out from behind his wheelchair.

Rick turns around and sees George standing next to him. Rick knows that unit three is George's main base of operations and decides that he'd better not mouth off to him.

"How ya doing George?" Rick hopes that George will be equally polite.

George is surprised to hear Rick spouting off pleasantries and decides to act in the same manner. "Fine, thank you. I see you're here for the therapy session."

"That's right."

"I wish I could join the group. I'd love to hear you open yourself up. Especially to me," he adds knowing that Rick will certainly react to his homosexual statement.

Rick chooses to remain silent."

"See you later doll," George says slyly as he heads out of unit three.

"Fucking faggot!" Rick mumbles to himself as he stares at the doors.

"Were you talking to me?" Norma says as she passes by Rick's position.

"No I wasn't," Rick says, instinctively looking up in the direction of feminine voice.

Norma is a petite beauty in her late teens. She has a beautiful smile which is partially covered by her jet-black hair that gently caresses her shoulders. She still has a few freckles which probably bother her and she has a cute little pug nose. "I'm sorry," she says apologetically, wishing to herself that she never said anything to Rick in the first place. "I guess it was my imagination or something."

"I was just talking to myself," Rick informs her.

"I know what you mean. Sometimes I find myself talking to myself too." She admits sheepishly as she crosses her shapely legs.

Rick stares at Norma's legs wondering what it would be like to touch them then he notices her legs are covered with stubbles. He finds himself wishing that she'd shave her legs, then remembers that female patients aren't allowed to handle razors unless supervised.

Rick s gaping is making Norma uncomfortable and she instinctively tries taking a step back, but because her legs are crossed she almost loses her balance.

"You'd better be careful or you'll wind up in my unit with a broken leg."

"You're on unit two?" She's obviously surprised that Rick isn't from the alcoholic unit.

"Don't tell me I look like an alcoholic."

"I guess your wheelchair should have told me that you're from two. How come you're in it anyway?"

"because I can't stand up, but I think I'm getting better."

"You have an accident or something?" Norma says catching herself. "Oh, I'm sorry. I guess I'm being too nosey. I shouldn't be asking you personal questions like this."

"That's okay. I don't mind. You can ask me anything you want, but I think the first thing you should know is that my name's Rick."

Norma smiles, realizing that she's made a positive acquaintance. I'm Norma. Are you coming to group?"

"Are you going?"

"I don't have any choice. This is my unit," she says in a. surrendering tone.

"Well, if you're going then I'll go, but I was just going to split back to my unit as soon as the group started."

Norma seems a bit surprised. "How come? I mean I have my own reasons for not wanting to go, but you haven't even been in there yet."

"Well, why don't you want to go?"

"I don't know. I guess you could say that I'm just a shy person and I don't like having a lot of people staring at me, waiting for me to say something. I know that talking and stuff is part of group therapy, but I still feel silly about it and I'd rather avoid it than be a part of it. Besides, if you don't go then they come down on you and say things like you're exhibiting anti-social behavior.

"I don't know how shy I am, but I don't care to tell my whole life story to a bunch of drug addicts and psychos."

"I know what you mean, but most of the people there are too doped up to hear anything, let alone your story!"

"Thanks a lot!" Rick tells her in a slightly depressed tone.

"You know what I mean." Norma says, realizing that Rick's only kidding her.

"What time's it supposed to start?"

"Oh, whenever Dr. Whitehead decides to show up. She is usually pretty good about getting it started on time because we all have to take our medication at a certain time and she doesn't want to screw up our equilibrium."

"I hope the session doesn't take too long because I have to get back to room for medication I don't know how it is over here, but in my unit, if you miss your medication time then you have to wait till she finishes with everybody before she comes back."

"Don't worry about that. They're pretty good about ending the group in plenty of time for the patients from the other units to go back for their pills. "Oh shit!" Norma says as she checks through the pockets of her shorts. "I left my cigarettes in my room."

"No problem," Rick says, offering his cigarettes to her. I've got plenty, as long as you'll sit next to me in group so some psycho doesn't."

Norma smiles at Rick. "I'd accept your invitation, but I only smoke menthol."

Norma heads down the corridor then turns around. "Be right back," she says as she disappears into her room.

"I'll save you a seat," Rick calls out hoping that Norma can hear him.

Rick sits quietly for a few minutes content to watch the goings on in this unit. He stares down the main corridor and notices a familiar figure slowly walking back and forth. He recognizes the patient as the one who bumped into his wheel chair when he first visited the unit. Rick can hear the patient giggling to himself as he moves and he can see that the man is smiling ominously, but for no apparent reason. Several patients walk past this strange man, but no one pays any attention to him.

Rick spots several patients entering the doorway, which he assumes leads into the group therapy room. He moves his wheelchair a few feet down the corridor until he comes to the window which looks into the therapy room. He peers in and is surprised at what he sees. There is only one person in the room. Rick shakes his head in disgust figuring that maybe he imagined seeing all those people entering the room, but for now there's only one person in there and he's just placing a bunch of ashtrays on each chair in the room. Rick can't figure out where all those people went, but he suddenly remembers that he is very loaded and probably hallucinating. Then Rick sees another patient enter the doorway next to his position and he instinctively looks into the therapy room, but the patient doesn't enter. Rick stares at the closed door in the room, but it doesn't open. Rick finally puts two and two together figuring that since the therapy room door is located at the side of the room and because the doorway from the corridor is immediately next to the therapy room window, there must be a second room next to the therapy room which is where all those patients must be.

Rick maneuvers his wheelchair a few feet down the corridor stopping it in front of the doorway where all the patients entered moments before. Rick looks into the room and sees about ten patients. Some are standing and the rest are sitting on the chairs in the room. Their attention is focused on the television set which is tuned to a program on religion. Rick can't help noticing that no one pays any attention to him. He scans the room and doesn't see anyone talking. He figures that the program must be extremely captivating because everyone is glued to it. Rick decides to listen to the program also, but after a few minutes he is at a loss to explain why a bunch of people, especially these patients, would want to watch some religious zealot explain the meaning of the Bible.

Charlie enters the room but doesn't acknowledge Rick, even though he stares squarely at him. Charlie moves over to the television and changes the channel, stopping it at cartoons. Rick looks around figuring that everyone in the room will react, but no one does. They remain glued to their positions, intent on watching the television regardless of the program. It takes Rick a few moments before he realizes that these people are so loaded that they don't know, or care what's on the television. For right now, it's just something for them to do.

Charlie looks around for a place to sit and decides that

there's room for him between two people on the couch. Charlie walks over to the couch and plops himself down. He wedges himself between two patients and when the patients realize that Charlie is sitting next to them, they quickly get up preferring to stand in the corner of the room. Charlie doesn't seem to mind what's more, everybody seems content with the arrangement.

Charlie is the only one in the room making any sounds whatsoever. Like everyone else, he just stares at the television, but he constantly laughs at the cartoons.

Another patient enters the room and takes a seat next to Charlie on the couch. The patient doesn't seem to mind Charlie's laughing, until Charlie slaps him on his back as he reacts to the cartoon. The patient is almost knocked off the couch and he wisely chooses to stand up rather than endure another slap from Charlie.

Rick can't help noticing that everyone in the room is smoking. There are only a few ashtrays in the room and everyone is sharing them. Then the attendant from the therapy room enters and gathers up a few more ashtrays from the patients which he takes into the therapy room. No one seems to notice that their ashtrays nave disappeared and several patients dump their ashes into the spot where their ashtrays had been moments before. Only now, their ashes fall onto the floor and in some cases, some ashes are flicked onto other patients who are unaware of their smoldering Garments.

Rick directs his attention to another patient who was holding an ashtray on his lap until the attendant took it away. Several patients were dumping their ashes into the ashtray on the man's lap, but now, they are just reaching over without looking and flicking their cigarettes on his lap. Then one of the patients, who's finished with his cigarette, instinctively reaches over to extinguish it unfortunately, he mashes his cigarette into another patient's leg thinking that he's still in possession of the ashtray. Rick can't help being amused as neither patient reacts.

Dr. Iris Whitehead enters the television room and quietly scans the room without making her presence known. Then, "All right people," she says loud enough for the entire unit to hear, "We have a lot of work to do today so let's get started." Dr. Whitehead heads into the therapy room.

Charlie is the first one up and practically knocks down two patients so that he can be the first patient into the therapy room. Rick is even pushed out of the way as Charlie makes a beeline past him. Apparently, Charlie has forgotten his conversation with Rick because he looked at Rick squarely and acted as if he didn't know him. Rick isn't bothered by this, but he realized that Charlie will probably introduce himself to him all over again and he doesn't think that he's physically up to it. At least his hand and back aren't.

All the patients from the television room slowly enter the therapy room before Rick enters. He wheels himself into the room and takes a position in the far corner of the room next to an unoccupied chair. Rick sees several more patients enter as he waits for Norma, hoping that she'll sit in the chair next to him.

The room fills up quickly as Dr. Whitehead glances at her clipboard. Rick looks around nervously, hoping that Norma will come in before someone else takes the seat he's been saving. Unfortunately, Rick's hopes are dashed when Bessy enters the room and plops down her fat body in the chair he reserved for Norma. Rick resents Bessy immediately. Not because she's fat and ugly which would normally be enough of a reason for him to dislike her, but because she smells from not bathing. Rick doesn't have any animosity towards the black race, but one look at her and he knows what he feels: hatred and contempt. Rick feels justified with his feelings because instead of returning his smile like most people, Bessy snickers at him. She looks more like a fat male truck driver with a hormone problem, Rick tells himself as Bessy shoots him a nasty glance.

Norma enters the room and looks around for a place to sit. She sees Rick, but all he can do is shrug his shoulders because he was unable to hold a seat for her. Rick hopes Norma understands.

Each patient enters the room making sure that the door is closed behind him. It's more of a ritual than anything else. Rick wonders why they don't just keep the door open until everyone arrives, but he realizes that they're probably instructed to do it so that they have some semblance of order in this place.

Dr. Whitehead counts the people in the room and seems satisfied to start the session. She motions for the attendant to wait outside making sure that no one enters while the session is in progress.

"All right people," Dr. Whitehead says as she scans her clipboard. "Why don't we just start on one side of the room and see how we're all doing today. Let's see, yesterday we started on my left so today we'll start on my right," she says turning her attention to the patient next to her. "How are you doing today?" she asks the thirty-year-old alcoholic.

"I'm still pretty depressed you know. I can't get used to not drinking and I know that if they let me out of here tomorrow, I'd go to the first bar I see and get me a bottle."

"I'm sorry to hear you say that, but at least you're being honest with yourself," Dr. Whitehead comments as she makes some notes on her clipboard.

Dr. Whitehead. turns her attentions to the next person as Rick looks around the room. The only familiar faces he sees belong to Charlie and Norma. Everyone else in the room is watching. Dr. Whitehead and the patient she's talking to. Then Rick spots Judy sitting next to Dr. Whitehead. Judy isn't paying any attention to the goings on, but rather, she's watching Rick. Their eyes meet for an instant and Judy winks at Rick. Rick hastily looks away from Judy's piercing eyes and notices that her legs are spread for his benefit. Suddenly it dawns on Rick that Judy isn't wearing any underwear. Naturally, Rick is embarrassed and turns away hoping that Judy didn't see his probing eyes, but she is very much aware of what he was looking at. A moment later, Rick looks over at Judy and is relieved that her legs are now together, but as soon as she spots him looking at her legs, she quickly spreads them again exposing herself to him. Rick takes in an eyeful, but he doesn't look up knowing that Judy is waiting for their eyes to meet once again.

How about you Denise. Do you feel any better today?" Dr. Whitehead asks.

"I don't know," Denise replies softly. "I'm still pretty depressed and I'm still crying a lot. I don't know why and I can't help it," she adds as she breaks down in tears.

Dr. Whitehead makes a note on her clipboard to change Denise's medication to something stronger. "Don't worry Denise," Dr. Whitehead says compassionately as she looks up from her clipboard. "We'll give you something stronger that should deter your feelings of inadequacy and I'll expect you to see me half an hour earlier for our private session. Okay?"

Denise nods her head up and down as she puts a Kleenex to her nose and blows.

Dr. Whitehead turns her attentions to the patient sitting next to Denise. "How about you Chad? Do you feel like talking today?" she asks skeptically.

"Not today," he insipidly replies. "Maybe tomorrow though," be adds in a sotto voice.

"I see," Dr. Whitehead comments as she makes a note to herself. "Maybe you shouldn't come to these sessions if you aren't willing to share your thoughts with us."

"Yeah," comments one of the other patients. "You can't always just sit there and not say nothing. We don't do that to you. You get to hear what's bugging us and you never tell us what's going on in your head. If you can't open up to us then we don't want to have your ass in here," he says, chiding his fellow patient.

"Right on!" shouts another patient.

"I think what your peers are saying is that we're all in this together and if they allow themselves to be open and accept criticism about their problems, then you should at least be honest with them and let yourself open up too. We're not here to make fun of you or your problems and I think you know that. You also know that we're all interested in helping each other, but we can't do that unless everyone's sincere about getting better and that's what it's all about. We can't help you if you don't let us."

"I just don't feel like talking damn it!"

"Okay," Dr. Whitehead says relenting. "But I don't think it's fair of you to show up to any more sessions unless you have something to contribute."

"You people don't give a fuck about my problems! You're just going through the motions so you can keep us here forever and get more money for doing it."

Dr. Whitehead is disappointed to hear this, but at the same time, she's glad that he's unloading his ill feelings to the group. "You know that's not true. Just look around you. Half the people in this group weren't here last week, but you were. And do you know what happened to those people who were here last week?" Dr. Whitehead waits for him to answer, but he doesn't. "I'll tell you what happened to them. They got better and went home to continue living healthy lives. And if they need us again, they can always come back because they know that we care and aren't just interested in the monetary rewards of this place."

"That's a bunch of shit and you know it! Sure, you'd let 'em come back, but if their insurance ran out you'd tell 1em to fuck off!"

"You're full of shit!" shouts one of the patients. "I've been here before and the only reason I came back is because I fucked up. The last time I was here I got better and the only reason why I'm back is because of myself. They did a fucking good job on my head, but I guess I wasn't a good candidate for getting better because I had a screwed attitude like you and if you ever plan on getting cured then you'd better stop fucking around and let yourself get help or you'll never get better and you'll be an asshole the rest of your life like you are now!"

"All right gentlemen," Dr. Whitehead interrupts. "Let's go on to someone else. "She chuckles slightly hoping to break the tension. "We can continue with this when cooler heads prevail."

"That's great I You finally got me to talk and now you're going on to someone else's problems." Chad gets up and heads for the door. "This place is really fucked!" he says heading out the door.

"At least he's not shy anymore, Dr. Whitehead says breaking the tension in the room.

Everyone feels slightly relieved and some of the patients giggle openly as Dr. Whitehead flips through her notes.

"I see we have a new patient who's decided to join our little group. Dr. Whitehead directs her attention to Rick. "You must be Rick Brown."

Rick nods his head 1n acknowledgement.

"Would you care to enlighten us with a brief history as to why you've joined our little group?

"No thanks. I' like to go through my stay here anonymously."

Dr. Whitehead seems pleased to have someone in the group with a sense of humor. "That's fine Mr. Brown, but I'd like to hear more from you if you don't mind. "She obviously wants to get some serious work done.

"I really don't feel like talking if you don't mind. I'd just like to observe tor today."

"Not another one," she facetiously comments causing a few people to chuckle.

Rick laughs too, but he remains steadfast, refusing to contribute to his first session. "It's just that I feel pretty uncomfortable right now about talking."

"C'mon man," comments one of the patients. "You're no different than the rest of us and we opened up as soon as we got here. At least I did."

"Good for you," Rick tells the patient in a contemptuous voice.

"All right Mr. Brown, I'll respect your wish not to contribute to our group, but tomorrow I expect you to make your feelings known."

"Excuse me Rick," Carol calls out. She is a young, voluptuous, seventeen-year-old blonde who should be a center-fold model. "Can I ask you something before you take a vow of silence?"

Rick is amused by this beautiful girl and would submit himself to anything she wants, reasonable or out of the question. "Sure. Ask away."

"Well, when I saw you the other night when you were checking in, you seemed perfectly normal. What I mean is, you were walking and standing up fine without any obvious problem. I don't know what your problem is and what you're doing here, but now that see you I was just wondering why you're in a wheelchair now when you weren't in one when you checked in?" Carol looks around feeling slightly embarrassed due to the fact that in her current loaded state, she made a simple question seem like a complicated one.

"That's a good question, but a rather long one," Rick comments as he ponders his response. "As a matter of fact, that's one hell of a question," Rick says aloud as he further contemplates his answer. Suddenly, the answer pops into Rick's head and he's totally shocked at what he realizes. "I know this is gonna sound really stupid," he admits as he looks around and sees that everyone, especially Dr. Whitehead, is listening intently to him. "I don't know what I'm doing in this wheelchair. About all I remember is that when I admitted myself, I was walking fine and I didn't have any trouble getting from place to place until they started treating me for Placidyl addiction and ever since I took those six pills, I can't even see straight, let alone stand up on my feet without falling on my ass. About all I know is that I'm really feeling great and don't give two shits about anything. Hell! As long as they keep giving me my withdrawal pills, I don't mind being confined to this thing," he says slapping at his wheelchair.

Hearing this, Dr. Whitehead scans through her papers and writes something on Rick's file. Then she opens the door and summons the attendant inside, whispering in his ear. Then Dr. Whitehead writes out a message and hands it to the attendant who races out of the room and out of unit three.

Dr. Whitehead decides that she should focus the session on someone else's problem, but she has a hard time interrupting Rick's drug history.

"So, I got used to taking two seven placidyls at a time and then I started taking three Placidyls at a time and then a few nights ago, I took two Placidyls and when they didn't work, I took two more."

"Excuse me Rick," Dr. Whitehead interrupts, but I think you've said enough for one session, especially when I agreed that you could just be an observer for today. I think you should give someone else a chance, don't you?"

Everyone in the room can tell that one of the reasons Rick keeps rambling on is due to the fact that he is extremely loaded.

"I'm sorry. What did you say?" Rick asks, looking at Dr. Whitehead. Dr. Whitehead isn't too pleased with Rick, preferring not to answer him. "Let's move along to the next person," she informs the group, continuing to ignore Rick's question.

The next person to speak is Carmen. She is a young, married, chubby Mexican woman with two children. She is in the hospital for severe depression and it shows. She's a picture of despair. "I'm doing okay," she says dejectedly.

"Have you made any progress since our morning session?" Dr. Whitehead inquires as affably as she can.

"Not really," replies Carmen, as she stares at the floor. "I know what I have to do, but I'm kind of scared of my old man. He wants me to take him back and I know that I should do it for my kids."

"Carmen, you should do whatever you want, but you should do it because it's right for you. Don't use your kids as your excuse. If you want to go back to your husband, then do it because you want to and for no other reason. Remember, it's your life we're talking about here. Your kids will go along with anything you want especially if it's in your best interest."

"I know that he'll beat me and my kids again if I go back, but he promised that he wouldn't do it anymore if I come home."

"Is it okay if I say something that might help her," Rick asks Dr. Whitehead.

Dr. Whitehead seems pleased that someone is willing to take the initiative and help another patient. "Sure Rick, go ahead. We're all here to help one another."

"Well, I don't know the whole story, but it sounds to me like Carmen's really unhappy with her husband and if he's been beating her and her kids then she ought to get the hell out of there and go someplace where she can start living again. Even some other city where she can start fresh without worrying about her husband finding her and beating her up." Rick feels embarrassed for the moment. "Whoops! I already said that, didn't I? I mean the part about being beat up. I guess it's the drugs they gave me. I feel pretty loaded right now."

"Don't worry about it Rick," Dr. Whitehead says in a sincere tone. "Believe me, we all understand. Now please continue. I'm sure we'd all like to hear what point you're 1eading up to."

Rick stares at Dr. Whitehead with a blank expression on his face. "I thought I already made my point."

"Oh, I'm sorry," she says looking up from her notes. "I guess I didn't hear it. I hope you won't mind repeating it. I'm sure it was a good point."

"Well, I basically agree with what you said and I told her to get the hell away from her husband and get a divorce."

"But he'd find me and beat me and my kids good!" Carmen cries out. "He has friends in his gang that'll do anything he wants and they'll find out where I am and tell him and then he'll find out and beat on me like he always does." Carmen is noticeably shaking as she nervously puffs on her cigarette.

Rick looks around hoping that someone else will contribute to the discussion, but no one does. "Sounds like you're scared to death to do what's right even though you know what you have to do. Don't you think you should concentrate on getting better so you can take care of your kids? I'm sure they miss you and can't wait for you to get out of this place."

"I just don't want to leave here until I'm not scared anymore!"

"All right, Rick. I think you've said enough to Carmen for

today, why don't you talk to her further after we're finished here and maybe you can help her overcome her inability to make the proper decision. Is that all right with you Carmen?"

"I guess so," Carmen answers as she continues staring at the floor.

"Very well then," Dr. Whitehead says as she prepares to address the person sitting next to Carmen. "You seem to be much better today Carol. From what you said earlier to Rick about his not being in a wheelchair when he arrived, I think you've overcome your shyness with the surroundings here. Now if only you could keep yourself as open in front of your parents, you might find that they're as willing to communicate with you as the rest of us are."

Carol seems perturbed that she is being discussed openly. "Couldn't we talk about something else?"

"I thought we agreed that we'd share your problems with the rest of the group and that you'd listen to suggestions that anyone might have."

Carol remains silent. It's obvious that she resents Dr. Whitehead for wanting her to talk about her problems. If Carol's dirty looks could kill, Dr. Whitehead would be history.

"Is it all right it I ask a question?" Rick inquires as Carol nervously looks at him.

"Certainly Rick Dr. Whitehead answers," just as long as it pertains to someone else and not you."

"Yeah, right," Rick answers insipidly. He pauses for a moment while he thinks about the proper way to phrase his question to Carol. Then he maneuvers his wheelchair enabling him to face her. "Don't get pissed a me if I don't say this right, because I feel pretty lightheaded right now, but if we're supposed to help each other I think I should know something about you."

Carol looks at Rick askance. "I'm sorry, but I have a

boyfriend who's a karate expert," she says breaking the tension she's built up around herself."

Rick laughs too, but he wants to continue with his statement. "We can discuss our sex problems later, but I was wondering if you wouldn't mind informing me as to what you're doing in here."

Carol seems relieved. "That's it? That's all you want to know?"

"Well, after I know why you're here then maybe I can help you with a solution."

"I knew there had to be a catch," she says omnisciently.

"Carol," Dr. Whitehead interrupts, "Would you mind not bantering with Rick and kindly answer his question before I move on to someone else?"

Carol gives Dr. Whitehead another venomous glance before turning her attention back to Rick. Carol begins to giggle which only shows Rick and everyone else how nervous she is about discussing her problem. Nevertheless, she begins. "I came here because it was the only place where I could go without running away again."

"Did you run away a lot?" Rick interrupts.

"Excuse me Rick, but please let Carol finish before you offer any suggestions."

Rick slumps back into his wheelchair. "Sorry," he sheepishly says, apologizing to both Dr. Whitehead and Carol.

Carol smiles at Rick as she continues. "My mom and I always got along even though we argued a lot, but whenever my dad was around, he always sided with my mom no matter who was right. Then I'd fight with him and he'd get pissed because I said he was afraid to go against my mom and he'd blow his top at me." She pauses for a moment as she lights a cigarette, her hands shaking. "I know I love my dad, but sometimes I wish he'd hit my mom and straighten her out.

I know he'd only have to do it one time and that would be it. I guess some families are run by the wife, but I really hate that. My mom tries to do both jobs and sometimes I get the feeling that she wishes that my dad would leave for good so she could totally take over my life. I really hate my dad for letting her do that to him and I wish he'd belt her and maybe she'd straighten out and get better. Carol extinguishes her cigarette in the ashtray even though she's only taken a couple of puffs. "I know everything would be all right if he'd hit her in the mouth just once. She'd back down for sure and I bet it would even save their marriage."

Dr. Whitehead hears something that she wasn't aware of before. "Well Carol, that's the first time you've mentioned that your parents aren't happy in their current situation."

"What do you mean?" Carol asks unaware that she's disclosed something important.

In all the times we've talked, you failed to bring out the fact that your parents might be headed for a divorce."

"Did I say that, because if I did, I really didn't mean to."

"Nevertheless, you said it. Now I need to know if that's true and you're the only one here who knows whether or not it is."

"Well," Carol says, beginning to open herself up, "I have a feeling that my dad's been seeing someone else. and I think my mom knows it too. But I think my dad's doing it to, you know, sort of put my mom on notice that if she doesn't change, he's ready to split for good."

"If they do get a divorce, who would you want to live with?"

"I don't, know. I've thought about it a few times, but I guess it's something I really don't want to confront. No kid wants their parents to split up."

"Even if they're making their child miserable because they really don't belong together? Don't answer that till you've answered this question. If you were married and had a couple of kids, but you realized that you've made a mistake and now want a divorce, would you stay together because of your kids?"

"Well, I guess I would Because I wouldn't want to ruin my kid's lives."

"So, what you 're saying is, that despite your own happiness, you'd stay married to someone you don't like anymore because of your children. Don't you think you're entitled to be happy yourself?"

"Sure I do, but I'd have to think of my children."

"Exactly. But would you like your children to be as miserable as you are right now?"

The message finally gets through to Carol. "I see what you're saying."

"Do you agree?"

"I guess I do, but I still don't know what to do about it."

"You don't have to do anything. Just don't expect too much from your parents, especially your father. It's obvious that they're staying together because they want to and if they want a divorce they'll get one. Take your parents for what they are. If they're unhappy with each other, don't let yourself feel guilty. It appears that you've let their problems fall onto your shoulders. You can't let that happen. You've got your own life and it's a lonely road, but it's one that has to be traveled by yourself."

As Dr. Whitehead. continues, Carol nods her head up and down to show her that she is listening. The other patients are also listening, or at least they appear to be paying attention.

"Can I say something?" Rick interrupts again.

Dr. Whitehead seems miffed that Rick is interrupting her for the second time. "I think we should let someone else have the opportunity to contribute to this matter," she says turning her attention away from Rick and directing her eyes towards the rest of the group.

Dr. Whitehead seems perturbed that no one besides Rick is willing to say anything. "All right Rick, but you've been saying an awful lot for someone who wanted to just be an observer." Dr. Whitehead is beginning to resent Rick.

Rick pays little mind to the doctor's remark and directs his statement to Carol. "You said something before that I don't think anyone caught besides myself." Rick can sense that Carol is paying close attention to him and is interested in what he has to say.

"A few minutes ago, when I guess I came off kind of threatening, you told me to watch out because you had a boyfriend who's a karate expert."

Carol smiles as she silently beckons Rick to continue.

Anyway, it kind of hit me, after listening to you about your father and how you wish he'd become forceful and put you mother in her place, that you chose a boyfriend that's not afraid to defend you, not unlike the kind of person you'd like your father to become. I don't really know what my point is, but I think it's kind of interesting."

Carol is pleased with Rick's observation as is Dr. Whitehead.

"How do you feel about what Rick just said Carol?"

"I think he knows me pretty well," she replies sheepishly.

Dr. Whitehead seems pleased. "Good! We're getting a lot accomplished today, thanks to someone who wanted to spend his time here in the shadows of silence. "She directs her attention to Rick.

Rick and Carol exchange more than friendly glances as Dr. Whitehead continues with the next patient, who's suffering from an advanced case of depression. Rick pretends to be listening to the black girl sitting next to him, but every chance he gets, he looks away from the depressed patient and catches an eyeful of Carol who's also taking fleeting glances at him.

"I told you I don't feel like talking!" Bessy adamantly yells across the room to Dr. Whitehead. "Just leave me alone!" she pleads.

"I think. You'd better change her medication," Neil yells out enabling everyone to hear his recommendation. Neil is a thirty-year-old professional bird trainer and a former drug addict. He readily admits to having taken just about every drug in existence and he's not afraid to speak his mind on the subject, especially when he thinks his experiences can benefit someone else who's having a drug problem.

Rick quietly listens to Neil offering his opinions to the depressed girl and is impressed with Neil's knowledge of depression and how it leads to drug use and abuse. He can tell that Neil truly does care about his fellow patients.

Rick has a feeling that he and Neil will become good friends, but he knows that once he leaves this place, he probably won't carry their friendship beyond these walls! If he did, it would always remind him of how he was and where he had been. He'd just like to get cured of his Placidyl addiction and forget about this place, but while he's here, he wants to make the best of it knowing that the more friends he makes in this place, the less boring it will be.

"I don't want no white boy telling me what to do with my life!" Bessy yells to Neil.

Rick wishes that Bessy wasn't sitting next to him fearing that she might take out her hostility on the closest person which would be him. Rick scoots his wheelchair back as Bessy continues screaming at Neil.

"I ain't listening to no heroin addict Especially no honky heroin drug addict!"

"Please Bessy," Dr. Whitehead says trying to intervene. "We're on your side. Neil's only trying to help the same way you tried to help Carmen yesterday."

"Don't be giving me no jive ass shit! And don't be talking to me no more. I wanna be left alone, you got that!"

"Hey, I'm sorry I said anything," Neil says trying to calm her ruffled feathers. "I just thought I could help. You know, I was where you are at and I remember how shitty I felt. Man, when I kicked all the shit I was taking, no one would come near me because I'd bite their head off if they did." Neil stands up, enabling everyone to look at his frail body. "Before I started shooting, I weighed almost two hundred pounds and I wasn't fat. Now look at me," he says as he pivots around. "I bet all that shit I was doing took me down almost ninety pounds. I almost died man! Do you hear me?" he yells at the top of his lungs. "Died! Dead! All because I wouldn't let Dr. Whitehead help me. And when I finally came to my stupid senses, I realized that she was right all along and that lady saved my life. Now all I'm trying to do is to give you a little of what she gave me before you come as close to meeting your maker as I did." Neil takes his seat as Dr. Whitehead gives him an appreciative glance.

"That's fine and dandy for you man, but I don't need no help from you. I just wanna be left alone and that's that! Don't be talking to me no more and don't think I ain't meaning it!" she says making sure that she gives everyone in the room a long and hard look with her threatening eyes.

"How are you today Sue?" Dr. Whitehead says directing her question to the lesbian on the other side of Rick.

Sue may be a female, but she's anything but feminine. She's about thirty years old and she's probably never sought out any affection from the opposite sex. She's been shaving ever since she discovered that she wasn't interested in boys which was almost fifteen years ago, when all her friends talked about their fleeting romances with the male of the species. She has a man's haircut complete with an obvious part on the side of her short hair and there's even a trace of hair next to her ears which she hopes will be mistaken for sideburns. She has a nasty habit of biting her nails and doesn't mind doing just that as she prepares to answer Dr. Whitehead's question.

"Can't we talk about this in your office," she answers in a husky voice. "I don't see why you always have to pick on me."

Dr. Whitehead is taken aback. "C'mon Sue. I thought we agreed that you'd at least listen to what your friends have to say."

"What makes you think these assholes are my friends. I don't have any friends here," she says adamantly.

"I don't think you're being fair to the people in this room," Neil comments, getting his two cents in.

"Shut the fuck up Red!" she yells at Neil hoping to dissuade him in the future.

"That's good sue. Let out all of your troubles and say what you're feeling."

"Don't give me any of that psychology shit, bitch! And don't try and pick apart everything I say because if you do I'll leave."

"That's it Sue. Just let it all out and don't hold anything back. Now what do you want to do right now that you're feeling?"

Sue holds up her fist and waves it around in a threatening motion. "I feel like going back to my room and hitting the wall with my fist until it's broken."

"Why should you do that? What do you want to punish yourself for?"

"I don't know. I just feel like busting my hand that's all," Sue slumps back into her chair and she begins to cry, burying her face behind the chair next to her so that no one can see her in this state.

Dr. Whitehead seems pleased with today's session and is

busy scribbling in her note pad.

The next few patients don't have anything of interest to contribute to the session and Dr. Whitehead decides to end the group as soon as Judy has a turn. Dr. Whitehead addresses Judy, but she fails to answer. She's too busy spreading her legs for all the male patients to view. Then Dr. Whitehead notices why she isn't paying any attention to her.

"Judy, I'm talking to you," she says in her usual authoritarian manner. Judy remains silent as Dr. Whitehead decides on a solution of her own.

Dr. Whitehead leans forward in her chair and grabs onto Judy's bare legs, forcing them together.

"Hey, what do you think you're doing?" Judy protests.

"This is my show young lady, not yours. That sort of behavior belongs in the gutter and this place is no gutter."

"That's your opinion," Judy says glibly.

"Don't you think you owe the people in this group an apology for wasting their time and disrupting this session?" she asks expecting Judy to answer, but Judy remains silent contemplating her next move.

"I'd like to say something to everyone in this group all right."

Dr. Whitehead seems pleased. "Go right on ahead please."

Judy stands up and faces the whole group, favoring the side where Rick is. "I'd just like to let every guy in here know that I'm going to fuck every one of you," she announces in a most serious and affable fashion.

Dr. Whitehead is stunned as are all the males in the room, including Rick. Then several patients applaud and stamp their feet while one of the patients begins making cat calls.

"You'll all be just another notch on my bed by the time the week is out." Judy adds. Then she faces Sue. "All except you Sue. You're not a pretty enough dyke for my taste buds," Judy adds blowing everyone in the room a moist kiss.

Dr. Whitehead grabs Judy's arm and tries wrestling her back into her chair.

"Sit down this instant!" Dr. Whitehead forcefully says as she tugs on Judy's arm. "I refuse to put up with this obstinate and vulgar behavior." She tugs on her arm even harder.

Judy grabs onto Dr. Whitehead's arm, forcing her to release her grip. Judy heads for the door. "Don't you ever touch me again you bitch!" she yells out as she opens the door and exits, leaving the door ajar.

One of the patients gets up and instinctively closes the door and then returns to his seat.

"Are you going to let Judy get away with that?" one of the patients inquires as Dr. Whitehead gets up and opens the door.

"Don't forget to be here for this afternoon's session," she informs the group as she exits the room and races after Judy.

Rick decides to wait until everyone has left the therapy room before he exits. He doesn't want some crazed patient to topple his wheelchair in the mad rush to be one of the first out of the room.

As Rick makes his way across the room and towards the door, he estimates that he has about fifteen minutes before the medication nurse is due back in his room to replenish his medication. He doesn't need to know the time because his own body clock has been telling him that he's almost ready for more pills to keep up his loaded state.

Rick exits the therapy room and enters the television room. He looks around and notices that no one is paying any attention to him despite his openness during the session. He spots Neil sitting on the couch smoking a cigarette and talking at a fast pace to one of the depressed patients.

"You can't give up on yourself just because you've been

getting shitty breaks," he tells a seventeen-year-old girl with an advanced case of acne. "If I did what you've been telling me then I'd probably be six feet under by now. You're lucky you have friends who give a shit about you and a mother who's interested in your welfare. Shit I never had any of that!" he adds disgustedly.

Rick turns his attentions away from Neil and studies the other people in the room. Then Rick notices that Bob is sitting in the corner of the room with his hands covering his face. At first, Rick wants to go over and greet him, after all, he's curious as to why Bob moved out of his room. Rick prepares to approach Bob, but he suddenly remembers that Bob wasn't very friendly in the past and he's probably the same now. Rick pushes his wheelchair back a few feet deciding that if he sees Bob in the future, he'll just greet him like anyone else and if Bob makes a friendly gesture towards him, then he'll reciprocate.

Rick checks the clock above the nurse's station and notices that he has only ten minutes to go before he's due to get re-medicated. He decides to hang around the television room for another five minutes, hoping to see something interesting. He doesn't know what he's likely to see, but just knowing that the unexpected can happen at any moment is enough to keep Rick there.

"Hey buddy, how you doing?" a voice calls out from behind Rick's wheelchair.

As Rick turns around, he is greeted by a hard slap on his back. Rick turns his head, but he knows that Charlie is the one responsible for this back-slapping greeting. Rick stares at this grinning giant and decides that he'd better smile too. Rick decides that it he slaps Charlie with equal force, then Charlie might possibly get the message to stop doing that.

Charlie approaches the front of Rick's wheelchair as Rick

firms up his arm ready to get even. Then Rick lashes out with his right arm, fist clenched, and he delivers a hard slap on Charlie's back.

Rick is surprised that Charlie doesn't mind. He simply smiles at Charlie as they again shake hands. Unfortunately, Rick had forgotten how hard Charlie's grip is until Charlie begins squeezing. Rick knows that Charlie isn't hurting him deliberately, but just the same, Rick pulls his hand away and as before, he doesn't want to rub the pain out of his hand in front of Charlie.

Rick's hand throbs and he places it against his leg and begins rubbing it, hoping that Charlie won't see what he's doing.

"I didn't think you'd remember me." Rick tells him in the most likeable tone he can muster.

"Are you kidding?" Charlie tells Rick as he slaps his back for a second time. "I never forget my friends." he says taking a step away from Rick. "You're still my friend, aren't you?" he asks, expecting to hear something negative. He's no longer smiling.

"Of course I am," Rick says affectionately.

"That's good." Charlie is now smiling from ear to ear. "Most people are against me because they don't like me," he informs Rick as he walks out of the television room.

Rick looks around bewildered, but no one seems interested in him or his conversation with Charlie.

Rick moves his wheelchair out into the corridor, but he's unable to find any trace of Charlie. Rick figures that when he left the TV room, he probably ran down the corridor and into his room. Rick doesn't know where Charlie's room is, but he has a feeling that he'll find out before he's discharged from the hospital.

Rick takes another look at the clock and notices that he's

not alone. Several patients are gathering near him and they too are very interested in staring at the clock. Whenever someone new joins the group, they take a look at the clock and then they stand by a closed door next to the nurse's station. After a few minutes pass, there are several people standing in line in front of the closed door. Then a nurse exits a room located behind the nurse's station and approaches Rick. Rick backs away from her expecting that she'll tell him that he's not supposed to be hanging around unit three. As the nurse comes closer, Rick pivots around in his wheelchair, deciding to head back to his unit before the nurse confronts him.

"Excuse me," the nurse tells Rick as she walks past him and goes into the television room. "It's medication time," she informs the group.

Rick looks into the room and sees everyone getting up. In a matter of a few seconds, everyone scampers out of the room and takes their place in the line with the other patients.

Rick knows he should be getting back to his own unit, but he wants to wait around and see what's so damn interesting about that door. Then the door opens and two nurses begin handing out medication to each patient in line. Each patient is handed a cup of juice and a pill or two which is taken in front of both nurses. After their medication is taken, each patient goes back to whatever he was doing, but how the patient seems to be in an elevated mood.

Rick panics when he notices that he's one minute away from getting his medication. He knows that his medication nurse won't wait in his room until he returns.

Rick wheels himself out of unit three. He plans on coming back after he's eaten his lunch, but the main reason he's returning to his unit is because he wants to be medicated. He knows he'll feel better once he swallows his six pills.

Rick races dawn unit two's corridor and enters his room,

hoping to find the medication nurse waiting for him. Rick looks around in disappointment, figuring that she already came in and when she didn't find him in his bed, she left. Rick wheels himself over to the nurse's station to find out if the medication nurse came into his room while he was in unit three. Unfortunately, there's no one at the station to answer his question.

Dejected, Rick returns to his room and prepares to get into bed when he realizes that Alexander probably knows. whether or not the nurse had come in while he was out. Rick approaches Alexander's bedside, holding his breath. Alexander is on his side and he appears to be sleeping, but Rick is intent on waking him. Rick turns away from Alexander long enough to take in enough air to talk to him without inhaling any of his dreadful fumes. Rick taps Alexander on his shoulder.

"Did the medication nurse come in yet?" Rick asks as he turns his head to take in another breath of unpolluted air.

Alexander remains on his side as he flings his arm out, pushing away Rick's hand. "Leave me alone," he pleads, sounding like a little boy who's being picked on by the neighborhood bully.

"Just answer yes or no," Rick pursues the matter, refusing to give up.

"Leave me alone," he pleads for a second time, sounding even more childlike.

Rick makes the mistake of breathing normally again and accidentally inhales Alexander's terrible odor. Rick instinctively backs away and decides to head back to his bed. He pivots his wheelchair around when he spots Alexander's trash can next to his bed. Rick knows that the trash is emptied sometime in the middle of the night, so he figures that by checking the discarded packets of medication in the trash, he can figure out of the medication nurse has made two trips to his room today.

Rick guides his wheelchair over to Alexander's trash can. He looks inside and sees what appears to be Alexander's discarded breakfast of oatmeal. Rick shakes his head in disgust as he rummages through the trash can trying not to get any oatmeal on his hands. Why doesn't that son of a bitch just keep his damn breakfast on his tray like everyone else, Rick wonders as he pulls out two empty pill packets.

Alexander begins coughing profusely as Rick continues looking through his trash. Then Alexander tums over and sees what Rick is doing. Instead of saying anything, Alexander pulls the can away from Rick and lifts it closer to the side of his bed. Alexander's cough is growing worse as he hangs his head over the side of his bed. Then Alexander vomits into the trash can as Rick looks on.

Rick senses something peculiar and finally realizes that Alexander got the same breakfast of corn flakes and a banana. Rick is ready to puke himself when he realizes that he mistook Alexander's vomit for oatmeal. Rick grabs Alexander's bed sheets and wipes the vomit off his hands as Alexander continues vomiting into the trash can.

Rick returns to his bed carrying the vomit drenched medicine packets. When Rick put the packets in his pocket, he didn't mind that they had a little bit of oatmeal on them, but now that he knows what's really on the packets, he'd rather just take off his pajama top and burn it. Instead, Rick takes a tissue and reaches into his pocket removing the packets. He wipes them off, hoping to read the labels. The first packet contained one-two milligram tablet of Ativan. Rick knows this to be a powerful tranquilizer. The second packet contained one-two hundred milligram tablet of Mellaril, which is also a powerful tranquilizer. Rick remembers taking these pills himself. He realizes how powerful they were for him, but he was only taking the minimum doses of the medication and Alexander is being given the maximum doses. When Rick was on this medication, his doctor expressly told him not to combine the two different drugs because of possible severe complications which might arise. Rick wonders why Alexander would be given these pills at the same time, but figures that every case is different. God knows, Rick thought, Alexander probably needs all the help he can get and if he gets it from combining different pills, more power to him.

Because both pill packets were in the same place in the trash, Rick believes that the nurse hasn't come into the room for her afternoon pill dispensing.

As Rick gets back into his bed, he glances over to Jose's side of the room and sees Jose sleeping quietly. Rick notices that Jose's hands and feet are no longer tied to the guard rails of the bed. He's glad to see this, figuring that Jose is getting better and he'll probably stop having seizures. Rick turns back towards his own bed, but something catches his eye. He looks on the floor next to Jose's bed and sees his baby bottle resting next to one of the legs on his bed. Rick gets back into his wheelchair and makes his way over to Jose's side of the room. As Rick travels the short distance, he realizes that he probably didn't need to use his wheelchair remembering that he felt the same way when he got up and walked around before. He'd get out of his wheelchair and walk the rest of the distance, but that would be silly. He plans on giving up his wheelchair eventually, he tells himself as he picks up Jose's bottle and places it next to Jose's mouth. Rick stares at his room mate for a moment and wonders what Jose's reaction to the bottle would be if he put it against Jose's lips. Rick looks around making sure he's alone. Then Rick nudges the bottle with his hand until the nipple is against Jose's closed mouth. Suddenly, Jose's lips open, ever so slightly, and suck in the nipple. Rick can't get over the fact that Jose takes the nipple between his lips and sucks on it just like a little baby.

Rick decides to try another experiment. Then he removes the nipple from Jose's lips to see if he'll wake up.

As soon as he removes the bottle, Jose's lips begin searching for the nipple. His lips protrude from his mouth like a fish trying to snatch a piece of bait. Rick is amused at Jose's behavior, but decides to stop teasing him.

Rick puts the nipple next to Jose's lips and they close around it. His lips wrap tightly around the nipple and Jose continues sucking.

Rick returns to his bed as the medication nurse pushes in her cart. She positions the cart in the middle of the room and prepares some medication which she gives to Alexander. The nurse makes sure that Alexander takes both of his pills before she returns to her cart to prepare Rick's medication.

"How" come you're late?" Rick inquires as he tries to see the potpourri of pills in one of the cart's drawers.

"I had to go back to the pharmacy to get more medication."

"Oh," Rick replies, as the nurse approaches.

The nurse hands Rick the cup of pills and Rick instinctively takes a gander inside. Rick is taken aback and the nurse sense that something is troubling him.

"What's the matter?"

"There are only three pills in here and I've always gotten six. These aren't even the same ones I've been taking. It's obviously someone else's. It's a good thing I looked because if I took it then I'd probably get hooked on whatever it is and I sure as hell don't need to get hooked on any more shit."

"You have a pretty positive attitude. Most patients in here for addiction aren't as interested in their health as you are," she says noticing that Rick is smiling at her," but I didn't make a mistake."

Rick's smile quickly fades. "What are you talking about?" he shrieks. "I ought to know what I've been taking and it sure isn't this stuff." Rick stares at the pills in the cup and tries handing it back to the nurse.

"You'd better take them," she tells him in a slightly threatening manner.

"What's the matter with you?" I just told you that these aren't mine and I should know. I've been taking six pills every four hours, not three Look at my chart. You'll see."

The nurse takes out Rick's chart and scans it for a few moments as Rick reclines in his bed. He's confident she'll discover her error. Then the nurse replaces the chart in its. slot.

"You're on new medication as of now. Your doctor ordered these pills." She picks up the cup of pills from Rick's tray and hands it back to him.

Rick takes the cup, but he isn't happy about it. "I don't even know what this stuff is and I'm not taking anything unless I know what It is."

"I can understand that," she says as she takes the cup from Rick and examines each pill one at a time. "One seizure pill and two vitamin pills," she informs him handing him back his medication.

"Now I know there's been a mistake," he says confidently. "You'd better check with my doctor. The stuff I've been getting is a bunch of powerful pills which are for my addiction to Placidyls. Boy, they really knock me for a loop and I'm not gonna take any of that shit because I'm not ready to yet. I just know it."

"Look Mr. Brown," she says looking through his chart for a second time. "I don't know what you're talking about because you never got any strong drugs. You've just been taking anti-itch pills, seizure pills and vitamin pills."

"Don't give me that shit!" Rick is turning hostile. None of this makes any sense to him. "One of the pills was Demerol. I ought to know what Demerol look like so don't try and con me with any shit about vitamin pills. I know what I was taking."

Rick doesn't know why the nurse is lying to him, but he's determined to keep fighting until he gets what he wants.

As the argument ensues, Rick realizes that he's rambling at a very fast pace. The nurse keeps asking him to repeat what he's saying because he's talking too fast for her to comprehend. Rick is 'Surprised when the nurse asks him to talk in softer tones because he doesn't have to yell to be understood. Rick had no idea he was yelling, attributing it to the fact that he's going through normal withdrawal. It seems to be getting worse as the minute's pass. He's sure that he's going through the withdrawal because he's now craving his medication. He knows that it's partly in his head because his body clock isn't getting the medicine on time, but now he can even taste something strange in the back of his throat. He hasn't had this feeling for a long time, but he recognizes it from before as his body telling him what it wants and it's telling him that it wants a Placidyl. Rick tries explaining this to the nurse, but she doesn't seem to care about anything except the two vitamin pills and the seizure pill.

"Just take your medication and you'll be fine," she instructs him.

"What the fuck's the matter with you?" he yells as he grabs his chart from the nurse.

Rick scans the chart as the nurse tries to grab it from his clutches. She is successful, but Rick saw what he wanted.

"Must I call in an attendant?"

"Look! I don't know who's doing what, but I'll just assume for the moment that you really believe what you're telling me. I've never seen you before and I don't think you'd lie to me."

"Thanks a lot," she sarcastically answers.

This is the first time in a few minutes that Rick can think

and talk rationally, and now he's determined to say what's on his mind because he thinks that he's found the evidence to make the nurse believe him.

"Now that's my chart and I won't argue the point with you about what they've been giving me so far, but I want you to look at the chart objectively."

The nurse looks at Rick askance as she opens up his chart.

"Now that contains everything I've been given since I've been here, but if you'll notice, all my medication information over the past couple of days was written with the same pen."

"So what?"

"What do you mean, so what? Don't you think that's a little bit strange that every person who's written in my chart used the same pen?' Every person except you. You're the only one who used a different pen because you probably don't know what's going on so I guess you probably just think I'm crazy or something.

The nurse closes the chart and places it back on the side of the medication cart. She's heard enough. "Listen Mr. Brown. If you choose not to take the medication that your doctor prescribed for you, then I'll be forced to call in an attendant and he'll make sure that you take it!"

"Why won't you listen to me?"

The nurse has heard enough and she's at the end of her rope. "Look you checked in here voluntarily for help because of your problem, whatever it may be, and if you won't listen to us and let us help you, then you might as well check out of here and go home because there are a lot of people who want our help."

Rick hears what she's saying, but he feels he has to remind her once again that the pills he was given before were six in number and not three, adding that they consisted of tranquilizers, sleeping pills in low doses and pain pills.

And as far as he knows, all these pills were part of his treatment for Placidyl addiction.

"You're obviously not familiar with detoxification procedures Mr. Brown.

Why would we give you all those pills if you were only addicted to one sleeping pill? Tranquilizers and pain medication aren't used in treating patients such as yourself."

"Then how come they kept giving them to me?"

"C'mon," she says shaking her head. "I wasn't born yesterday." She looks towards the open door of Rick's room. "Should I call in an attendant now?"

Rick relents and takes the pills. The nurse smiles and pushes her cart out of his room.

Rick is positive that the six pills he was given the whole time were for withdrawal from Placidyls. However, it does strike him odd that he would be given Demerol and depressants for a sleeping pill addiction, but it never occurred to him that someone had made a mistake somewhere down the line. And now, they weren't willing to admit to their mistake. Rick remembers what Carol asked him in the session about being fine when he admitted himself, but that he was now in a wheelchair because he couldn't walk. Now he knows why, but he doesn't have any proof and even if he did, what good would it do.

Rick leans over his bed and picks up his trash can which he empties on his bed. In the back of his mind he feels that if he can prove that he was taking heavy narcotics they might admit their mistake and commence giving him the same medication.

After looking through the trash, Rick is surprised that he can't find even one discarded pill packet. He knows that the nurse from this morning threw six packets in his trash, but now they aren't here. He's beginning to smell a conspiracy and he knows that he won't find any evidence to support his theory.

"Maggie!" Rick yells out as he sees Maggie passing by his open door.

Maggie pops her head into Rick's room," How you doing slugger?" she asks cheerfully.

"I've got to talk to you," he says, beckoning her into the room. There's a certain sense of urgency in his tone.

Maggie approaches Rick's bed with her usual smiling glow.

"There's something going on here that isn't exactly kosher."

"Gripe away," Maggie replies as she anxiously awaits Rick's explanation.

"You remember any of the stuff I was being given?"

"Not really," she replies as she dawns her thinking cap. "That's no problem because patients with your symptoms are usually treated the same with slight deviations, depending on the addiction. Do you want me to get your chart and tell you?"

"That wouldn't do any good, because someone's tampered with it."

"What?" she responds incredulously.

"They screwed up and gave me a bunch of powerful pills and now they just cut me off because they discovered their mistake and now I'm going through withdrawal because of it."

"Sounds a little farfetched."

"Get my chart then. I remember you told me something about one of my pills. You said it was Mag Sulfate or something which was supposed to clean out my system or something."

"That's standard stuff, not a narcotic."

"I'm not saying it is, but just take a look at my chart, okay?"

"All right," she replies as she heads for the door. "But I don't see what good it'll do."

Rick doesn't know if Maggie is also part of the conspiracy, but he's going to find out depending on what she says when she returns. As far as he's concerned, if Maggie doesn't return with his chart, or says something like she couldn't find it, then

Rick will feel pretty certain that she's also part of the cover up and he'll treat her like any other nurse in this place.

Rick reclines in bed with his eyes closed, hoping that Maggie will be on his side. He doesn't believe that she's like the rest of the personnel in this place.

Maggie enters Rick's room carrying his chart. She approaches his bed sporting a confused look. Rick can easily tell that something's bothering her.

"What's wrong?"

Maggie opens up his chart and studies it carefully before speaking. "I know you were given Mag Sulfate and I know that I saw it in your chart, but now it's not in here," she says indicating the chart.

"What about the Demerol and the tranquilizers I was getting?" Rick asks with heightened anticipation.

"I don't know about that, but I was sure that you were given Mag Sulfate."

Rick seems pleased. "That does it! Now I have proof and now I want satisfaction from those bastards. I'm not gonna lay here and suffer and go through withdrawal because they don't want to get into trouble. They got me addicted to stuff I haven't taken for over a year and now they'd better treat me for it. Rick is confident that Maggie will take his side.

"I don't know how far l can back you up on this love because I only remember the Mag sulfate and that's all I remember."

Maggie notices that Rick is sweating profusely and she instinctively puts her hand on his forehead.

"You're burning up!" she informs him as she takes his pulse.

"I'm really thirsty, can I have something to drink?" Rick indicates a cup of water on his table.

Maggie picks up the cup and hands it to Rick. "Stick out your tongue first."

Rick opens his mouth and sticks his tongue out. Maggie looks at his tongue and notices how dry it appears.

"Is your mouth really dry?"

Rick nods his head as he sips the water.

"What else are you feeling other than normal aches and pains?"

Rick leans over and takes the pitcher of water from the table. He pours himself another cup of water and drinks it before answering. "Every once in a while, I feel like throwing up and I'm always constipated."

Maggie is concerned. "Is that all?" she asks sticking a thermometer into his mouth.

"I get dizzy a lot. Especially when I get up and I'm always scratching myself because I itch, and every once in a while, my leg pops up and down from the pain."

"Is it like a muscle twitching or something?"

"Yeah, something like that. What do you think it is?"

"Sounds like withdrawal."

Rick is delighted to hear this. "See I told you. I'm going through withdrawal thanks to all that stuff they gave me."

"I don't doubt that they gave you some of the wrong medication, but withdrawal symptoms are to be expected in your condition."

Rick isn't satisfied with Maggie's answer and he becomes slightly belligerent. "Then how come I've gotten worse in the last couple of hours? And don't tell me it's all in my head."

"Look Rick. You knew that you'd go through withdrawal when you came in here and you also knew that when they medicated you, your symptoms wouldn't show. Now I know you're a bright fellow and expect you to act accordingly and face facts. You're not on a vacation here and coming off something as powerful as Placidyls is a rough thing to do for anybody. If I were you, I'd forget what happened and just concentrate on getting better and if you'll put your mind on that, then I'll make sure that the rest is taken care of."

Rick knows that Maggie is looking out for his best interest and he doesn't want to be on the outs with her. "I'll do whatever you want, but I won't forget what happened."

Maggie seems satisfied. "And if you have to spew more venom, push the call button and wait for me. You just dish it out and I'll take it, okay?"

"I'll be fine," he says affably.

"You bet your ass you will! All my patients make it. Especially the good-looking ones."

Rick's embarrassed to hear this. He could never take a compliment gracefully, even though he's had plenty of practice.

"There's something I'd better warn you about before I go off duty," Maggie tells Rick as she glances at her watch. "I don't know whether you've had a chance to bump heads with her yet, but if I were you, I'd try to avoid the head nurse of the next shift. She's really a hardnosed biddy."

"Why don't you just stay here? There's an extra bed over there." Rick indicates Bob's vacant bed.

"What's the matter with your bed?" she asks slyly.

Rick scoots over making room for Maggie. Then he lifts up his sheets tempting her.

Maggie shakes her head. "Maybe if you were a few years younger, I'd take you up on that."

"Very funny," Rick retorts as Maggie heads for the door.

"Remember what I said about the head nurse. Her name's Rayburn and she's one old goat of a nurse so keep away from her. And if you rub her the wrong way, she'll have you sedated for eight hours to keep you out of her hair."

"What if I play up to her and she ends up liking me?"

"Then she'll have you sedated for two shifts. She's never

met a patient she didn't hate." Maggie grins at Rick and exits.

Rick feels tired enough to sleep, but there are too many things going on in his mind. On one hand, he's upset because the hospital realized their mistake concerning his medication and on the other hand, he's glad to finally get down to the process of being cured. He's mad that he's a wasted all this time and he feels like he's back at square one. He knows that it's partly his fault because he should have let the staff know that he shouldn't be prescribed Demerol and tranquilizers for a sleeping pill addiction. He figures that subconsciously, he knew of their mistake, but because he wanted to get loaded he didn't say anything. He knew these pills weren't part of his cure, but he pushed his feelings of right and wrong to the back of his mind. And now that he's no longer getting any powerful medication, he wishes that he hadn't taken those other pills in the first place because that just delayed his recovery process and he'll probably be in this place for a couple of days longer than he was originally scheduled.

The taste of Placidyls is overwhelming. He knows that if he had saved just one pill and brought it with him, all he'd have to do is take it now and in a few minutes, he'd feel great and he could finally get the rest he so desperately needs. But he doesn't have a Placidyl and even if he did, he doesn't know if he's strong enough to avoid taking it. Oh sure, he wonders, it's easy to say that he wouldn't take it, but if he had one in front of him, he doesn't think he could stop himself from popping it into his mouth. He tried that in the past and he always procrastinated. He'd fool himself saying that he'd take the pills now and he'd quit tomorrow, but the following day, he'd give himself the same argument knowing damn well that he'd probably never stop taking them. But now, things are different. He doesn't have that precious pill in front of him and there's nothing he can do, and no decision to make.

Rick presses the call button, hoping that he can explain his symptoms to the nurse on duty and she might take pity on him and somehow provide him with some relief in the form of an injection or a powerful pill.

He knows it's a long shot, but he has to do something. He feels awful and the only solution seems to be another drug. If they would only just give him a mild sleeping pill, like a Dalmane, he'd be fine and it wouldn't impede his recovery process. Rick knows that's not likely to happen, but nevertheless, it's worth a try.

Rick's body is crying out for something to ease his suffering and at this point, he'll even take the simplest medication so long as it has some effect on him.

Maybe he can con the nurse when she arrives. He must try because he needs something and he needs it now. He'll get down on his hands and knees if necessary, but he must take some kind of action. He knows that he just can't lie in his bed and suffer. He'll do anything to get a pill. Anything! He needs it...!

CHAPTER NINE

Nurse Doris Rayburn stands over Rick's bed like a conquering hero. Rick has no idea that she's there and if he had known that she'd be the one to answer his call for a nurse, he probably would have thought twice about pressing the button.

Doris stares at Rick's curled up body and watches him squirm about in his bed trying to get comfortable. Rick turns over quickly, but still doesn't see Doris standing next to his bed. He's too busy trying to make peace with himself concerning the medication he's craving. Rick closes his eyes to help his concentration. He's trying to put himself asleep by imagining that he's just taken two Placidyls, and now they're just beginning to work. As Rick's imagination begins to work, the sweet taste in his throat gradually subsides. He knows that this is a sign that the Placidyls are working and in a matter of minutes, he'll be fast asleep without having taken a single sleeping pill.

Doris Rayburn is becoming flustered. She has been staring at Rick for a few minutes and he seems like any other patient, but why is he now smiling, she asks herself.

Doris stares at Rick's smiling face for a few more moments before deciding to intrude on his thoughts. Doris begins making noises in her throat like she's clearing the phlegm out. Doris frequently uses this device to gain her patients' attention. She knows that she could just call out that person's name, but that would be too subtle and it simply isn't her style. This way, she can get the patient's attention and he'll be slightly off balance. Several people have told her that they think it's rude of her to initiate a conversation by first getting their attention by making vulgar noises, but she doesn't really care for other people's opinions. Especially when it concerns her views on how patients should be handled. After all, she's been doing it for more than thirty years and she's not about to start changing now. She's even suspicious of new medications which the doctors sometimes order administered. Before she'll dispense anything new, she always argues with the doctors claiming that the old medications are more in tune to their patient's needs. She always relents but not before ruffling a few of the doctors' feathers.

Rick reacts to Doris' throat noises and is startled. His eyes pop open, disturbing his self-induced Placidyl adventure.

"What do you want?" Doris asks harshly.

"Uh?" Rick replies as he remembers why he pressed the call button. "Oh yeah."

"Well, what is it?" she hurriedly asks, as if she was late for a pressing engagement.

Rick realizes that he isn't going to get what he wants from Doris in his present state, so he decides to act out the part of a poor unfortunate person who doesn't know what's happening to him in terms of his withdrawal. Rick slumps back down on his bed and props his head up with his pillow. If there's any affection in this stone-faced monster, he'll do his best to bring it out.

"I feel really sick and I don't know what's wrong with me." he tells Doris. letting his voice grow faint as he speaks.

Doris stares at Rick coldly, almost as if she knows what he's leading up to. "I've just looked at your chart and there's no reason for you to be feeling this way."

"I don't know what it is either, but I'm beginning to think that it's withdrawal."

"That could be."

"Can't you do anything about it? I feel really nauseous and I feel like I'm going to faint and I itch a lot," he recites to Doris as he remembers the side effects of some drugs. He recalls reading about them in one of his doctor's drug books. Surely, she'll have to take action. How can she avoid the issue, he tells himself as he decides to add more symptoms to the list. "And I'm always really tired too, but I can't go to sleep and when I try to look at something I get dizzy."

"Sounds like you're going through withdrawal all right and the best thing for it is to just hang in there. You'll make it!"

"Isn't there something you can do? Couldn't you just give me a lower dosage of something to counteract what I'm going through? I feel like tearing my hair out!" he adds dramatically.

"Why don't you just try getting some sleep?"

"But I can't sleep. I told you."

"Nonsense! The body needs sleep and if you can't get it then your body just isn't ready. No use trying to sleep if your body isn't ready. In all my years, I never knew anybody who died from lack of sleep.

I don't like giving sleeping pills at night and I do my best to keep my patients off them unless the doctor insists."

Rick knows he's fighting a losing battle and he decides to change his tactics to something more drastic. Rick sits up in his bed and grabs a knife from his open drawer. Nurse Rayburn is horrified, not knowing what to expect. She instinctively backs away as Rick takes the knife and scrapes it across his back.

"What are you doing?"

Rick finishes scratching his back and then begins scratching his arms and legs with the knife. "I told you! This itch is driving me crazy! "Rick begins blinking his eyes wildly as he falls back onto his bed.

"You all right?" she asks compassionately.

Rick's glad to hear her voice her concern for him. He knows she's weakening. "I'll be all right in a few minutes. I'm just really dizzy that's all."

"As long as you don't have a seizure," she comments as she wipes her brow. "I hate those damn tongue depressors. They always split apart whenever I have to use them and I don't like getting bit either."

Rick realizes that he isn't going to win this battle like he thought. He knows that the only withdrawal symptom she cares about is an epileptic seizure. He knows that it's just possible that he might have one, and if he does he doesn't want her around to jam a depressor into his mouth. But if that unfortunate event does happen to him, he'll do his best to bite her if she tries putting her fingers into his mouth.

Doris heads for the door. "Don't call for a nurse unless it's important," she says coldly as she prepares to close the door.

Rick shoots Doris a dirty look as he sits up in bed preparing to get off and pay a visit to the bathroom. Doris sees what Rick's about to do and races over to him pushing the wheelchair next to his bed.

"Here you go," she says as she positions the wheelchair in front of him.

"I don't need that anymore," Rick informs her as he pushes the wheelchair out of his way.

Doris gives Rick a stern look as she retrieves the wheelchair. "You mustn't make so much noise," she says harshly, indicating Jose in his bed. "You'll wake up your roommate."

Rick pushes the wheelchair away from him as Nurse Rayburn looks on. Then Rick gets out of his bed and stands up, holding himself up by leaning on his bed's guardrails. "I don't care," he tells her in a dejected tone. "I have to go to the bathroom," he informs her, making his way across the room swaying as he goes almost to the point of falling down.

For a third time, the nurse takes the wheelchair and pushes it in front of Rick. "I insist you use this! The hospital is not responsible if you should fall down and injure yourself because you refused to use the wheelchair that was prescribed for you."

Rick pushes the wheelchair away again. This time, it crashes into Alexander's bed. Alexander wakes up and sees Doris standing next to the Bathroom door with Rick.

"Nurse," Alexander calls out. "Can I have some Jello? A double portion with a banana?"

"I'll tell your nurse Alexander," Nurse Rayburn yells out, loud enough to awaken Jose.

Rick disappears into the bathroom and takes his place on the toilet seat as Nurse Rayburn opens the bathroom door, sticking her head in.

When you're through in here I expect you to use your wheelchair and I won't take no for an answer!"

"How about negative?" Rick asks glibly.

Doris is beside herself with rage.

"Look! In case you didn't know it, the only reason I needed that wheelchair is because someone screwed up and gave me a bunch of drugs which kept me from walking on my own two feet. Now that I'm not taking them anymore, I don't need that damn chair."

"What are you talking about? Your chart didn't show any medication like that. You're on normal detox."

"Why don't you get them to show you the first chart?"

"I don't know what you mean," she says indignantly.

"I figured that," Rick says. He's beginning to think that she's one of the people who helped prepare his new chart. "Just for the sake of argument, let's suppose that you do know what

I'm talking about. If you do, then you know that all the stuff I was taking made me constipated. If you have good ears, then you know that I haven't accomplished anything sitting here. And I'm not about to get anything done in here unless you let me have my privacy. My bowels work much better when there's no bullshit around if you get my drift." Rick begins to chuckle as he sees that Nurse Rayburn is pretty insulted.

Rick isn't able to perform in the bathroom even though he was left alone to conduct his business.

Rick returns to his bed, hoping to come up with another plan. He lights up a cigarette, but after one puff he begins feeling faint and he quickly puts his cigarette out hoping that the dizziness he is feeling will go away. Then without warning, Rick vomits all over himself. He immediately gets up and heads for the bathroom. He feels the urge to vomit again and he'd rather do it in the toilet.

The bathroom door is locked. Rick fidgets with the handle hoping that it will somehow unlock and he can get in before he vomits on himself or the floor. At any rate, he doesn't wish to preoccupy himself with the decision of where to throw up, he just wants to get inside and throw up in the toilet like any other sick person. Suddenly, Rick feels the urge to vomit. He can feel a certain queasy warmth in his chest. It rises to his mouth and he gags. Rick crouches on his knees ready for the inevitable, but nothing happens. Rick's relieved, but at the same time, he's disappointed. He knows that once he does throw up, he'll probably feel better and maybe he can get some rest. Rick tries throwing up again as he hears the bathroom door being unlocked. Again, it's a false alarm. Rick bolts into the bathroom and takes his position in front of the toilet. It disgusts him to have his head in a community toilet bowl, but at this point, it's as welcome as a cup of pills.

Rick feels a warm sensation on his knees and he looks

down to see what it is. Rick jumps up when he realizes that his pajama bottoms are smoking due to a cigarette filter smoldering on the floor. Then Rick feels the urge again and he positions himself in front of the toilet. He figures that it would be sheer poetry if he threw up on the cigarette filter extinguishing it. After all, smoking makes some people sick and what better way to get rid of a cigarette, he thought, his head buried in the toilet bowl. Suddenly, the toilet seat falls and hits the top of Rick's head causing him to get alarmingly close to the water in the commode. Rick flips the lid back into position, but it hits the toilet lever hard enough to force it to bounce back hitting Rick's head even harder.

Rick is flustered. He no longer feels nauseous, but he might as well make the most of the toilet while he's in the bathroom and he takes his place on the toilet seat. As Rick tries accomplishing what would otherwise be a simple bodily function, he thinks to himself that a toilet seat is only safe when you're sitting on it. Unfortunately, Rick's bit of levity doesn't help his efforts to perform. and he returns to his bed in his constipated state.

As Rick makes himself comfortable in his bed, he realizes that he's so constipated because of all the medication he's been given. Not only that, but it's further compounded by his normal withdrawal symptoms. He knows better than to play games with himself and blame the hospital for his problems. He feels that they're partly responsible, but he wouldn't be there in the first place if he didn't abuse the drugs he was given. However, there is one question that keeps running through his mind. Why is he now going through withdrawal? Why didn't he have these terrible feelings earlier, he wonders as he pulls the blankets into place. He realizes that the medication they mistakenly gave him kept him from having withdrawal symptoms, but now that they're giving him the right medication for his particular problem, why is he now experiencing the symptoms?

Rick doesn't have the answer to his questions and he'd prefer to wrestle with this dilemma when he's not so exhausted. Right now, he needs some rest if only he could get some sleep he'd feel better. "I'm sure I'll be all right, but I sure wish I had a Placidyl," he mumbles to himself as he forces his eyes to close.

Moments later, Rick opens his eyes. He scans the room for an instant making sure that no one's standing over his bed. He shuts his eyes again, only this time, they stay closed by themselves.

CHAPTER TEN

Rick wakes up in a cold sweat. He looks around for a towel to wipe his face, but he can't seem to find one. -He decides to use his sheet instead, figuring that it will be changed later that day.

Rick is extremely thirsty. As he looks around his room he realizes that the dizziness he felt earlier is still with him. He takes a sip of water, but he doesn't think all the water in the world will satisfy his parched mouth. He knows that It's part of the withdrawal symptoms and he'll just have to get used to it.

Hoping he'll fall back to sleep, Rick closes his eyes as he rests his head on the pillow. Suddenly, his eyes pop open reacting to Jose's pounding on his guardrails. Rick hurriedly looks around for the nurse call button, fearing that Jose's having another seizure. Rick gets ready to press the button as he stares at Jose and notices that he's not having a seizure. He's only pounding on the guardrails to get Rick's attention.

Jose motions for Rick to come over to his side of the room and Rick obliges.

Jose motions towards his mouth and then points," indicating his dresser drawer.

"You want something in here?" Rick asks as he places his hand on the drawer.

Jose motions towards his mouth and nods his head smiling. He tries saying "Yes," but the only, sound he is able to make is a sotto squeak.

Rick opens the drawer and finds a couple of packs of cigarettes, assorted change and a few family pictures along with various toiletries. Rick stares blankly in the drawer as Jose moans trying to get his attention.

"I don't know what you want," Rick tells Jose as he hands him his writing pad. "You'd better write it down," Rick says, looking around for a pencil.

Jose pats Rick on the back with the writing pad and points to his mouth again. Only this time, he does his best to imitate a person smoking a cigarette.

"Oh! You want your cigarettes." Rick is happy that he is able to communicate with him.

Rick takes Jose's pack of cigarettes and opens it. He removes a cigarette which he places between Jose's eager lips. Rick lights the cigarette, but Jose isn't inhaling the cigarette as the flame confronts the end of the cigarette.

"It's not catching," Rick informs Jose as he tries placing the lighter closer to the cigarette.

Jose waves his hands wildly, convincing Rick to take the cigarette out of his mouth. Then Jose picks up his writing pad and retrieves his pencil which fell to the side of his blanket. Jose hurriedly scribbles down a few words and hands the pad to Rick.

YOU HAVE TO HELP ME SMOKE THE CIGARETTE AND YOU HAVE TO STAY WITH ME BECAUSE I AM NOT ALLOWED TO SMOKE IT BY MYSELF BECAUSE MY HAND DOES NOT WORK SO WELL AND I AM AFRAID THAT I WILL BURN MYSELF AND I WILL HURT BECAUSE IT DOES NOT FEEL VERY GOOD.

"No problem," Rick says with a deliberate smile. Rick lights Jose's cigarette and places it between his lips.

Jose inhales deeply as Rick looks on. He feels strange

about having to help someone else smoke, especially when that person could easily quit due to the fact that most of the time, no one's around to help him. It's not like someone who's addicted to cigarettes. After all, those people have to have a cigarette all the time and for a person like Jose, he is only able to smoke when he is being helped by someone else. Jose wouldn't have to exercise very much will power if he wanted to quit smoking, Rick wonders, as he helps Jose take one last puff on the cigarette.

Rick wishes he could have a normal conversation with Jose, but under the circumstances all he can do is silently wonder what they might talk about if Jose were well.

"I'd better get back to bed," Rick tells Jose as he turns away holding Jose's cigarette.

Jose moans and begins making motions with his bands, conveying to Rick that he just wants one more puff.

"C'mon Jose," Rick a s sluggishly. "I'll help you smoke a cigarette later. If I don't get back in bed I think I might faint or something," Rick takes the cigarette and prepares to mash it into Jose's ashtray, but Jose isn't satisfied with Rick's statement and he begins moaning and waving his hands indicating that he desperately wants another puff.

"Forget it!" Rick tells Jose sternly as he puts out the cigarette. "I'm going back to bed. Okay?"

Rick looks at Jose hoping to find him in agreement, but Jose isn't moving. Jose just stares at the ceiling with a blank expression on his face. Suddenly, Jose's eyes roll back and his body tenses.

"What's the matter?" Rick asks in a panicked tone not realizing what Is going on.

Jose's body is totally rigid for a moment, then one of his arms begins to quiver and twitch. Suddenly, Jose's left arm swings out almost hitting Rick. Rick instinctively backs away as Jose's other arm crashes into the guardrail with a force that shakes the bed.

Panic stricken, Rick doesn't know what to do and for a few moments he stares at Jose, afraid to move. Suddenly, Rick snaps out of his transfixed state and he presses the nurses call button as he screams. "Help!" he shouts. "Somebody please help! He's having a seizure! Help!"

Rick turns around and faces the open door expecting to see a bevy of nurses race into the room, but no one is there. Rick-knows that he just can't stand there and do nothing, but what can he do. Then he realizes what he should be doing and he rushes to the head of Jose's bed hoping to take the tongue depressor off the wall and jam it into Jose's mouth. Unfortunately, the tongue depressor was not replaced from the last time Jose had a seizure, so Rick races to the other side of the room where he rips the tongue depressor off the wall. He returns to Jose's side and pries open his mouth with one hand and stuffs the tongue depressor into his mouth with the other hand making sure that It's placed between Jose's tongue and the roof of his mouth. Rick lets out a sigh as he watches the seizure continue.

Nurse Doris Rayburn casually enters the room and spots Rick standing over Jose.

"What are you doing out of your bed?" she snaps as she approaches Jose's bed.

"What the hell does it look like?" he angrily replies. "No one bothered coming in so I did your job for you."

"You get back in your bed this instant!" she demands pointing to Rick's bed.

"I don't know what you're so pissed about. If I didn't put that thing in his mouth, he might have choked to death by the time you decided to make your rounds." Rick heads back to his side or the room, convinced that he put Doris in her place.

"You just stay in your bed and let my staff handle the patients. And I won't tell you again," she says in her typical vitriolic fashion.

Rick doesn't like letting anyone get in the last word, especially, Doris. "I just hope that the next time he has a seizure, your staff isn't on a coffee break."

Doris whirls around and looks caustically at Rick, declining to say a word.

Dr. Wang enters the room and politely smiles at Rick before he spots Doris standing over Jose. Doris is staring at her watch.

"Another seizure?" he asks, approaching Jose's bedside.

"Going on four minutes. I think it's a grand mal this time."

"How about the five minutes before you bothered coming in?" Rick shouts from his bed.

"I think it would be a good idea to move your patient as soon as his seizure ends. "Nurse Rayburn indicates Rick. "That detox patient seems to be bothering poor Mario."

"His name's Jose," Rick shouts, hoping that Doris will react and Dr. Wang will see how unreasonable she really is."

Another nurse enters the room and races over to Jose's bed.

"Ten milligrams Valium, stat!" Dr. Wang tells the nurse.

The nurse runs out of the room as Dr. Wang takes Jose's wrist in his hand to check his pulse. Dr. Wang seems concerned. "Have you been charting his seizures?"

"Yes Doctor," Doris answers, "this his third one today."

"You did send for his chart?" Dr. Wang asks as he scans the room looking for Jose's chart.

Dr. Wang's question catches Doris off her guard and she nervously looks around the room even though. she's just going through the motions, pretending that someone accidentally took Jose's chart. "It must have been taken out by mistake, she tells him as she picks up the call button.

"Get with it nurse!" he tells her harshly with a sense of urgency. "Go get it yourself. I don't need you standing over my shoulder when there's a whole wing of patients who probably need you."

Suddenly Jose begins gagging. Dr. Wang figures out the problem and checks the tongue depressor in Jose's mouth. "Damn!" he yells as he adjusts it. "Which one of your nurses put this thing in his mouth? It was so far down his throat, he could have choked on it."

"None or my nurses," she answers sarcastically looking at Rick askance. "He took it upon himself to perform our duties before we had a chance to answer his yelling," She quickly catches herself. "I mean the buzzer," she blurts out, hoping that Dr. Wang didn't hear what she let slip out.

"I heard you the first time," he replies vitriolically. "And I also heard him yelling for help while I was tending one of my patients down the hall. And when I looked up, I saw you walking away from this room instead of running the other way to lend your assistance."

"What are you saying Doctor?" she asks innocently.

"Look nurse, let's not play games here. First go get me his chart and we'll discuss the way you're running this unit another time, preferably after your shift."

"Yes Doctor," she replies indignantly. Nurse Rayburn does an about face and exits the room, silently cussing out Dr. Wang as she goes.

Jose's arm crashes into the guardrail once again. Dr. Wang reacts by holding it down. Rick can see what's going on and it's quite amusing. After all, Dr. Wang is a frail little man who probably weighs in the area of one hundred and ten pounds and he's trying to hold down a man's arm that is as big as his own waist. Rick can tell that Dr. Wang is growing tired by the pained expression on his face.

Dr. Wang breathes a sigh of relief when he sees the nurse entering, holding a syringe which she puts into Jose's IV. A few moments pass before Dr. Wang lets go of Jose's arm. "He'll probably go right to sleep as soon as his seizure's over," he tells the nurse hoping to reassure her. "Sometimes they fall right to sleep and don't even wake up when the seizure's over."

"Will he be all right, Doctor?"

"He'll be fine, but when he wakes up his hand and arm will probably be sore from the beating they took."

"That's good," she replies as she turns to leave, then suddenly remembers something she wants to tell Dr. Wang. "I couldn't help overhearing you and Nurse Rayburn. She's been riding us pretty hard lately and we all appreciate what you told her."

"Well, I can't very well discipline the nurses for fouling up when the head nurse is mainly responsible. There's no room for slow response time, especially when we're dealing with someone like Jose here." Dr. Wang pats Jose's arm affectionately.

"Yes Doctor," the nurse tells him as she exits the room.

"Excuse me Doctor," Rick calls out, interrupting Dr. Wang's silent thoughts as he looks at Jose.

Dr. Wang looks up and sees that Rick's addressing him. "Yes, what is it?"

Rick is hesitant about what he's about to say. "I'd kind of like to talk to you private."

Without giving it a second thought, Dr. Wang approaches Rick's side of the room. He takes a seat next to Rick's bed.

Rick knows that his story had better be good if Dr. Wang's going to be cooperative. "Well, I'm kind of having really bad withdrawal symptoms and I don't know what to do. I feel like I'm coming apart at the seams. I'm real uncomfortable and I'm having a lot of pain, but if you could just give me something mild like a Demerol or something, in a low dosage of course, I know I'd feel better."

Dr. Wang looks at Rick with a curious expression on his face. Rick reads this look with a certain amount of reservation. He knows he isn't going to get anything from Dr. Wang even though he tried his best. Nevertheless, it's just possible that the next words from Dr. Wang might be that he agrees with Rick and he'll give him something to ease his predicament.

"I'm familiar with your chart and I know what you must be going through and I sympathize with your plight. However, you'll just have to do the best you can under the circumstances and in no time at all you'll feel better."

Rick's heart is breaking. He knows that his plan failed and as far as he's concerned, Dr. Wang told him what he really wanted to hear, but at the same time, he wishes he'd reconsider. "Can't you give me anything?" Rick asks almost pleading.

"Just take the medication they're giving you and you'll be fine." Dr. Wang is becoming slightly agitated at Rick's persistence.

"But they're just vitamin pills! They were giving me six pills before and I had to use a wheelchair because I couldn't walk."

Dr. Wang seems surprised to hear this. "Wait a minute. Don't go so fast. Slow down and tell me what you're talking about?"

"They were giving me pain pills and tranquilizers ever since I got here and when they found out that they screwed up, they stopped giving them to me and they changed my chart to cover up their mistake."

Dr. Wang looks at Rick skeptically. "That sounds pretty farfetched."

"Then how come I'm going through such heavy withdrawal? Huh?"

"Listen my friend. You came here because you were addicted to a sleeping pill and from studying your chart, you've progressed normally and the symptoms you're experiencing now are simply normal withdrawal. You knew when you made the decision to get help that you'd experience withdrawal and now you want to blame them on something that's more palatable for you to cope with." Dr. Wang stands up. "You really shouldn't play games with yourself like this and just concentrate on getting better. That's what you came in here for." Dr. Wang heads for the door, but turns around sporting a smile. "Thanks for taking care of Jose. I hope you won't have to do it again, but if you do then just make sure that the tongue depressor isn't so far down, okay?"

Rick is pleased that Dr. Wang isn't mad at him. "Can I just ask one question?" Rick asks, forgetting about his exaggerated withdrawal symptoms.

Dr. Wang nods his head as he checks his watch. "Make it a fast one."

"When I put that thing in Jose's mouth, did I save his life?"

"Let's just say that Jose's lucky to have you for his roommate." Dr. Wang smiles affectionately at Rick and then exits. "Could I have a word with you Miss Rayburn," Dr. Wang yells down the corridor.

A loud scream permeates the corridors, once again scaring Rick. He still can't get used to it like the other patients and he still doesn't know why the man keeps screaming. Rick is extremely uncomfortable and screaming might help him get a little relief, but he doesn't want to do anything that barbaric figuring that if he does, a trio of nurses would probably rush into his room and tie his hands and arms to the guardrails like that screaming banshee down the corridor.

A hospital volunteer enters Rick's room. He stands in the center of the room making some notes on a pad. "Can I get you anything?"

"What?"

"You know, like a hamburger or candy bars. Stuff like that. I go down the street for food, magazines and sometimes even booze," he adds kiddingly.

Rick fakes a laugh. "Could you get me a milk shake? Vanilla."

"No problem," he affably replies.

"Wait a minute," Rick tells the volunteer as he reaches into his grip and retrieves his wallet. Rick opens his wallet, but something appears to be wrong. Rick peers in the money compartment expecting to see his money appear out of thin air. He feels slightly embarrassed. "I guess I forgot to put my money in my wallet." Rick laughs nervously.

"That's too bad," the volunteer says shaking his head. He takes a couple of steps towards the door. "I'll be back tomorrow in case you get some money."

"Can't you just get it for me today and I'll give you the money tomorrow?"

"Sorry, I never extend credit. I used to do it, but not anymore. Too many patients got better and left before I could get my money," There is an obvious trace of resentment in his voice which leads Rick to believe that this guy's probably a former patient and not just a friendly volunteer?"

Rick remembers putting two dollars in his wallet when he was admitted, but how could it disappear. He doesn't remember spending it, so it still must be in his wallet. He decides to tear his wallet apart thinking that he hid the two dollars. He doesn't know why he'd hide his money from himself, but at any rate, he knows that his money must still be in his wallet.

Rick spots something peculiar. There is a bulge in the corner of his wallet which he believes is from his two dollars. He figures that he probably crumbled his money and stuffed it into his wallet. Rick reaches into the corner of his wallet and removes the bulging object.

"What the hell's this?" Rick mumbles, almost as if he were expecting someone to answer his question. Rick stares at the plastic packet he retrieved from his wallet. The packet contains one green pill. A Placidyl 750 milligram. Rick feels like a little boy who put his tooth under his pillow and when he lifted his pillow the following day, there was money where the tooth once was. This is surely a gift from the drug fairy, Rick thinks to himself as he salivates at the prospect of taking the pill.

After a moment of thought, Rick figures that this pill probably came from the hospital due to the fact that it's encased in plastic as are all their pills. But why, he wonders. Why would someone take a pill and put it in his wallet? Could this be some kind of test to see if he wanted to be cured? Were there hidden cameras in the room to monitor what he does with the pill? Then Rick remembers that his money is gone. Obviously, someone knew that he wanted a Placidyl so they gave him one and took his two dollars as payment.

Rick removes the Placidyl from the packet and carefully studies it. He wishes that he had another one too because one pill probably won't do anything even though it's been a few days since he's taken any Placidyls.

Rick picks up his cup of juice, but he feels kind of peculiar and uncomfortable about what he's about to do. He knows that if he takes the Placidyl, he'll probably feel great for a few hours, but what will he do after that. He doesn't have any more money to buy another pill and even if he did he doesn't know how to get in touch with the mysterious drug supplier. He also knows that if he takes the pill, he'll be the epitome of a drug addict and that's not an easy thing to admit to one's self. Besides, he admitted himself to this place because he wanted to get off Placidyls. He could have stayed home and continued taking them until he died, but he made a decision to get better. He's here to get off them and not here to score more, he tells himself as he decides on a course of action.

In spite of everything he's been telling himself, Rick prepares to take the pill. He places the Placidyl on his tongue as he brings the cup of juice up to his mouth. Then Rick suddenly stops and he reaches into his mouth. removing the pill, which he then drops into his juice. He sets his cup on the table next to his bed and he plops his head on his pillow. He just had a mental tug of war with himself and the devil side of him was suppressed. He knows he can still save the pill or even wait until it dissolves and drink the juice, but he's going to be strong. After all, he's not going to let one stupid little pill ruin his recovery process. With his luck, he'd have such a setback because of the pill that the hospital would want to keep him there an extra week and he's not about to let that happen. He's there to get better and he's determined to succeed at any cost. He's made up his mind, but just to make sure, Rick spills his cup of juice containing the Placidyl into the trash.

CHAPTER ELEVEN

Rick heads for unit three, leaving his wheelchair behind. He's not used to walking, but he isn't about to use his wheelchair anymore. After all, he's no cripple and he's tired of all those curious looks by the staff and the patients. This way, at least he can move about freely without drawing attention to himself.

Rick had no intention of returning to unit three so soon, especially for the afternoon therapy session, but he had to get out of his room. Alexander is just too hard to be around. Alexander's stench is bad enough, but his constant changing of the channels on his television was driving Rick crazy. He tried to get Alexander to just leave his TV on one channel, but Alexander paid no attention to him. After all, if the Pope hadn't chosen this particular time to visit the United States, Alexander wouldn't have anything on TV to watch. At any rate, he keeps changing the channels so he doesn't miss one minute of the Pope's visit.

Rick stops outside unit three's doors. He's having second thoughts about entering, partially due to the fact that he isn't feeling quite himself. He's also aware that part of his problem is the withdrawal symptoms he's experiencing. He's also still hostile concerning his treatment which forced him to use a wheelchair. Rick knows that he should put this unfortunate experience behind him and forge ahead, but he can't help being bitter. As far as he's concerned, the normal withdrawal symptoms from Placidyl addiction would already be over and he'd just need the psychological treatment for his addiction instead of the medical treatment he's now receiving.

"Glad to see you've decided to come to another session," Dr. Whitehead greets Rick as she holds the unit's doors open for him.

Rick forces a smile and slowly walks into unit three. He resents Dr. Whitehead for sneaking up on him from behind, feeling that she may have been spying on him as he was deciding whether or not to go through the door's. In a way, he's kind of glad Dr. Whitehead prompted him. He really needed help in making up his mind, even though he probably would have entered the unit anyway. As far as Rick's concerned, anything is better than returning to Alexander and the racket he's been making with his television set.

Dr. Whitehead scurries past Rick and heads towards the therapy room. "Coming?" She holds open the door to the therapy room.

"Aren't you going to let everyone know that you're here?"

"I did that five minutes ago. I just went to the admitting room to attend to an urgent matter. Should I hold the door open for you?"

"Yeah, sure," Rick tells her as he enters the therapy room.

Dr. Whitehead looks around for any stragglers before closing the door.

Rick has no trouble finding a seat. There are probably thirty chairs in the room and only ten of them are occupied. Rick takes a seat in the corner of the room. He studies the patients and notices that Carol is the only female in attendance. Carol looks bored to tears. but she perks up when she spots Rick.

The only other people Rick recognizes are Charlie and Neil. Rick watches them for a few moments as Charlie tries to shake hands with Neil. Neil doesn't want to shake Charlie's hand, insisting that they can be friends without having to touch each other.

"All right everyone. What do you say we start?"

"Excuse me Dr. Whitehead, but shouldn't we wait for the rest of the group to show up?"

"This is the entire group Mr. Brown," Dr. Whitehead snaps as she makes some notes on one of her charts. "And as long as you spoke up first today, why don't we start with you."

Rick cringes. "What do you mean?"

Dr. Whitehead shakes her head as she sets her patient files on the floor. "Never mind, I've got a different idea. Since I detect a certain amount of tension in here, why don't we try and let our defenses down for a few minutes."

Several patients look around, bewildered. Rick has no idea what Dr. Whitehead's talking about, but he nervously listens figuring that it's something that he'll try and get out of before it begins.

"Now some of you have done touch therapy before and I'm sure you agree with me that it's an interesting experience."

A few patients moan with disgust. Carol raises her hand deciding to speak up without being recognized by Dr. Whitehead.

"Is this for volunteers or don't we have any choice?"

"I realize that new experiences are hard and sometimes scary things to try, but if we are to grow within ourselves, we should welcome new things with an open mind." Dr. Whitehead gets up and pulls down the shade on the window which looks out into the unit. Then she moves back to her position by the door and places her hand on the light switch. "Now when I turn off the lights, I want everyone to approach the center of the room. You won't know whose hand you're shaking or who you're hugging. By the way I do encourage hugging and embracing. The object of this exercise is to get you to lower your barriers so that you can see that the other people in this room are exactly like you. People sometimes are afraid to show emotions when the eyes of others are upon them, but you won't have that problem because the lights will be off and no one will be watching you. Remember when the lights go off, everyone just be yourselves and do whatever comes natural. You'll see that even though our problems are all different, it really doesn't matter so much when you realize that the next guy has the same feelings and desires as you."

"How long will the lights be off?" one of the patients asks as he stares at Carol.

"You just leave that to me and don't worry about it," Dr. Whitehead chides.

Carol glances around at the other patients. She can't help noticing that practically every patient has his eyes riveted on her.

Rick has no desire to participate in this charade. He's convinced that it's only one of Dr. Whitehead's ploys at wasting time because she didn't get a full group to work with. "Excuse me Dr. Whitehead," Rick begins to get up.

Dr. Whitehead folds her arms together in disgust. "Just where do you think you're going?"

"To the bathroom. I'll be right back."

"Just wait until touch therapy's over. I'm sure your bladder won't burst."

Dejected, Rick sinks back to his chair. He didn't think he could get away with leaving, but he had to try. And as long as Rick must participate in touch therapy, he decides that it won't be too bad if the only person he touches is Carol. It's kind of intriguing that he can touch Carol anywhere and she won't know who to get mad at because the lights will be off.

Rick shoots a glance at Carol, but she isn't reciprocating. She's too busy trying to ignore the prying eyes of the other patients who probably have the same idea about touching her.

Darkness fills the room as the lights go off.

"Everyone to the center of the room and Don't be afraid to touch your neighbor," Dr. Whitehead instructs the group from the safe confines of her position by the door.

Rick sits quietly in his seat, afraid to venture out and meet his fellow patients.

"How ya doing, I'm Fred," one of the patients says, addressing another patient in the center of the room.

"I'm Roger," the other patient replies. "Glad to meet you."

The room is ominously silent for a few moments. Rick decides he'd better join the group before Dr. Whitehead turns on the lights and discovers he hasn't left his chair.

Moving cautiously, Rick proceeds a few steps away from the corner of the room. Then he bumps into another person. "Oh, excuse me."

"That Is okay," the female voice answers. "My name's Carol, who are you?"

Rick instinctively reaches out to shake hands with Carol, but he accidently puts his hand between her legs. Rick quickly realizes his blunder and abruptly pulls his hand back as Carol begins screaming.

"I'm sorry Carol."

Carol continues to scream. "Leave me alone I"

"I didn't mean it, but it's so dark in here I couldn't see where I was putting my hand."

"Dirty fucking bastards!" Carol shrieks.

Rick fails to understand why Carol would say those things to him for his slight error. "I said I was sorry. What else do you want me to say?"

Carol screams again. Dr. Whitehead flips the lights back on and is horrified at the sight she beholds. All of the patients are crawling about on the floor, save Rick who's still standing.

Carol is in the middle of this apparent orgy and her clothes have all but been torn off. A couple of patients have their heads buried in Carol's crotch while other patients hold down her arms, enabling them to caress her breasts.

"Help me Rick!" Dr. Whitehead commands as she rushes over to lend Carol her assistance. She doesn't have a hard time ending her patient's little excursion into their sexual fiesta because the lights cause them to have a quick change of heart concerning their activities with Carol.

Carol gathers her clothes together and dashes out of the room crying as Dr. Whitehead scolds her group for their criminal behavior.

"I didn't do anything," Rick complains. He obviously resents Dr. Whitehead's implications that he was also responsible for what happened to Carol. "You didn't do anything to stop it!"

"What the hell did you want me to do. I couldn't see anything, remember? You had the lights off."

"Be that as it may, I distinctly heard Carol scream out when she approached you."

"What are you talking about?" Rick answers in a flustered tone. "I couldn't see where my hand was because it was so damn dark in here. Didn't you hear me apologize?"

"Screaming's all I heard Mr. Brown," she snottily answers as Dr. Murray Schwartz enters the room.

Dr. Schwartz is a small man who'd like to think of himself as a miniature Freud. His appearance is the only thing about him that resembles Freud, with his moustache and neatly trimmed beard. Dr. Schwartz introduces himself to the group using his soft professional voice. He feels that a soft-spoken person can easily command the respect of the people in his surroundings without yelling. Dr. Schwartz chews on his pipe stem as Dr. Whitehead ushers him over to her side for a quiet discussion. Then Dr. Whitehead leaves the room, explaining that Dr. Schwartz will carry on with the session.

"I'm Dr. Schwartz, for those of you who are new to this group. And even though we haven't talked on a one to one basis yet, I'd just like you to know that I'm familiar with everyone's case. I know everything that goes on inside this hospital and I know what every person's problem is so don't think you can get away with anything just because we haven't met yet." Dr. Schwartz jams the pipe stem into his mouth.

Everyone in the room exchanges curious and suspicious looks as they await Dr. Schwartz's next statement.

"I don't particularly like the numbers in this room so I suggest that we disband for today and, hopefully, tomorrow's sessions will produce a better turnout."

"We normally don't leave here for another fifteen minutes," one of the patients reminds him. "And I'd kind of like to discuss my feelings today."

"We'll take up that matter tomorrow first thing, but for now, why don't you all retire to your normal activities until your medication time." Dr. Schwartz gets up and opens the door to leave. "I'll see you all here tomorrow," he says as he walks through the door and exits the unit.

The patients don't know just quite how to react to Dr. Schwartz's action of ending their session early. Slowly, each person gets up and exits the room until Rick is the only one left. Rick is glad that the session is over. He had his reservations about attending, fearing that he'd be asked to speak about his personal problems and at this point of his treatment, he's just too uncomfortable with his recovery process to start sharing his inner feelings with a new doctor and a different group of patients. He might have felt different if the same people who showed up to the first session had shown up for this session.

Rick slowly gets up and heads for the door, but he stops for a moment, hoping that the dizziness he's experiencing will be short-lived. He begins feeling faint as he stands alone in the room, then he begins sweating. Rick doesn't know why he should suddenly feel so bad when a few moments ago, he was fine.

Rick takes a seat on the floor, burying his head between his legs. After a few moments, the only discomfort he feels comes from his full bladder. Rick stands up and heads for the door. He decides to find a bathroom on this unit, fearing that he'll never make it back to his own room in time.

Rick heads down the corridor deciding to go into the first open door he sees. Hopefully, the room won't be occupied. Unfortunately, the only room that seems to be open is full of people. The sign on the door reads: Arts and Crafts Room. Rick peers into the room and scrutinizes its occupants. He spots several people sitting around a long table, but no one seems concerned that he's even there. They're all too busy working on their various paintings and clay projects.

"Excuse me, but is there a bathroom in here someplace?"

"Just go down that way and make a quick left," one of the patients tells Rick, pointing to the comer of the room.

After five minutes in the bathroom, Rick is totally disgusted. He realizes that his medication is responsible for his bladder not responding, but just knowing the cause does not effect a solution. He figures that sooner or later his problem will be solved and he'll just have to wait for that time to come. Otherwise, his only choice would be a catheter and he'll never go through with something as distasteful as that.

Rick opens the bathroom door to leave and is startled to find someone standing directly in front of him. Rick smiles at Judy as he tries making his way past her, but she has other ideas. She returns Rick's smile as she slides her body over, obstructing Rick's escape path. Then she holds Rick in place while she removes her blouse with her free hand.

"The bathroom Is all yours," Rick nervously tells her.

"Don't rush away in such a hurry sugar! I've got to let you make amends before you go so you'll feel like a real man again." Judy wiggles off her blouse and unzips her pants.

Rick would love to continue his affair with Judy, but he's aware that if he goes through with her request, she'll probably never leave him alone and anything he does with her will certainly spread throughout the hospital like a contagious disease.

Rick pushes Judy aside and he scurries past her. "I 1ve got to get back to my unit for my medication," Rick tells a flustered Judy as he disappears from view.

"Don't worry sugar, Judy calls out. "I'll stay here and wait for you."

Rick races down the corridor for the exit. As he passes the therapy room, he looks through the large window and notices his writing partner, Steve, patiently sitting in one of the chairs. At first, Rick believes that he's seeing things. He can't possibly imagine why Steve would be there.

Steve sees Rick glaring at him and he beckons him inside.

Rick enters the therapy room in a most cautious state. While he's glad to see a familiar face from the outside world, the last person he thought would visit him was his partner.

"Hi Rick," Steve says smiling.

"It's nice to see someone who isn't wearing hospital fatigues," Rick quips. "You should have let me know you were coming so I could brush up on my hospital jokes."

Steve laughs politely as he opens his briefcase and removes a script along with some other material. "When you getting out of this boobie hatch?"

"I really don't know, but it shouldn't be too long."

"That's good Because I wanna go to Vegas for a couple of weeks."

"What's that have to do with me?"

"Well, I just thought you could carry the ball for me while I'm gone, just like I'm doing your work for you now."

"I find that hard to swallow Steve. Especially when this is the first time you've had to pinch-hit for me, when I've done it for you whenever you decided to disappear when we were on assignment. I must admit though, you're always punctual when they're shooting the script we write whether you contributed to it or not."

Steve is fast becoming distressed with his partner's attitude. "That's real gratitude! You're forgetting that if it wasn't for me, you'd probably still be working for your father wishing that you could sell at least one script. Just remember, you're where you are today because of me."

Rick is running out of patience. "Don't tell me you're taking credit for me being in this hospital too?"

"Don't give me any of your bullshit Rick. I remember when you begged me to write with you because you couldn't sell a script and if you keep up this bullshit we might as well split up and I'll go it alone."

"Who you gonna get to write scripts for you, your parents?"

"You're really an asshole!"

"The truth does hurt, doesn't it? And talk about assholes, I can't believe what you said to me over the phone about how I should leave here and work on the script with you. Don't you give one shit about me getting better? Wait. Don't answer that because I don't need the aggravation. You obviously didn't come here because you're genuinely concerned about my health so it must have something to do with the script in your hand." Rick takes the script from Steve and skims through it.

"What do you think?" Steve asks anxiously, forgetting his hostility for the moment.

Rick tosses the script across the room and folds his arms glaring at Steve.

"What the fuck Is the matter with you Rick? If that gets messed up, I'll have to start all over because it's my only copy."

"There's just one thing wrong with that script."

"Well, just tell me what it is and I'll fix it." Steve crosses to the other side of the room to retrieve the script. He returns to his seat and gets his pen ready to take down Rick's remarks.

"The first thing you can do is discard the first act totally and after you're done with that you can make up a new title page without my name."

Steve is astonished. "What's eating you?"

"Those jokes you did in act one were very funny, but I thought they were funny when I wrote them for another show and now I see that you decided to use them in this script instead of thinking up new material."

"Boy, that's appreciation for you," he sarcastically tells his partner. "I thought since you weren't helping me I had a free hand to make this one damn good script. I even used some of your old material so your touch would be in the show."

"Don't feed me that! You only used those jokes because you couldn't come up with anything by yourself. I'm surprised you didn't rob your parents' joke file. At least that way, I probably wouldn't know, but this kind of shit is too obvious and I won't stand for it. I'd hate to see what act two looks like. Where is it?"

"I haven't written it yet," Steve sheepishly admits. "I thought we could work on it together. I have to split the money with you anyway."

"Forget it Steve," he says with conviction. "You can't work on the second act until act one's finished and you'd better forget about what you already wrote and start from scratch."

"Do you have any ideas?"

"Yeah. Leave me out I told you before that I'm here to get better and I'm in no mood to write jokes."

Steve stuffs the script back into his briefcase and closes it.

Rick tilts his head, hoping to get a glimpse inside Steve's briefcase. "Wait a second. What's that stuff underneath the script with my name on it?" Rick reaches over, opens up the briefcase and removes three pages of typed material. He scans the first two pages and seems most pleased. Then he flips to the third page, but Steve grabs the material away from him.

"It's just our Hawaiian material for that guy's show," he says, hoping that Rick won't study the material too closely.

"Well, it looks pretty good, but you didn't add anything to the first two pages I wrote. I was pretty pissed at you when you didn't show up to help me write it, but I see that you added a third page on your own. If you had shown up in the first place, we could have written the whole thing together."

Do you want to hear the third page?"

"Sure I do. Maybe you can even make me laugh and I'll forget about this place."

Steve stands up and holds the material in front of him. He's about to begin when he realizes that the door to the room is open. Steve closes the door and he takes his place in the center of the room. Then he begins reading. "Good evening ladies and gentlemen and welcome to beautiful Hawaii, the towel capital of the world. Now for those of you who are lucky enough to live here, let me explain what I just said. All you tourists know what I'm talking about because the first thing you do when you arrive in our hotel room is figure out how you're going to steal your hotel towels when you leave without your maid calling Hawaii 5-0. But what you don't understand is, that your maid could care less how many towels you steal so long as you don't discover her hidden video camera which she hid behind your dresser mirror that faces the bed." Steve chuckles.

Rick seems pleased. "I'm glad you like it, but why don't you read me the stuff you came up with. I already know what I wrote."

Steve flips to the third page. "And you should see my sister. She Is the only girl I know who squeezes her pimples before she goes to the dermatologist." Steve forces a laugh.

Rick is distressed. "What the hell are you laughing at? That's not even a Hawaiian joke!"

"Sure it is. His sister's Hawaiian, isn't she?"

"Let's just say that it wouldn't withstand a court challenge. And I don't even think it's very funny either. It's just another way of saying that old joke about the woman who always cleans up her house before the maid arrives."

"Well, I didn't expect you'd like every joke I wrote."

"I'm not going to lie to you and say something is funny that isn't. Just keep reading."

Steve finds his place. "Oh yeah," he says as he prepares to pick up where he left off. "Anyway, me and my two friends rented a boat from the 'Up the Ocean Without a Paddle' boat company for some Hawaiian fishing. We were out for a couple of hours when we were swept up by tropical storm Sidney. It hurled us over two hundred miles out to sea and all our supplies were destroyed. Now I can imagine a tropical storm named Brutus doing that to us, but not a tropical storm named Sidney. The name just doesn't suggest that. A storm named Sidney wouldn't have enough energy to put out a match, let alone send us to the middle of the ocean. Anyway, we drifted for over three days and we were ready to meet our maker. Suddenly we saw something drift past us and we paddled with our hands until we brought the tiny little object aboard. It was a little lamp or something and when we tried to wipe it off, a genie appeared. He told us that for rescuing him we could each have one wish and one wish only. I told the genie that I wished that I was home in front of my TV set watching the super-bowl and, poof, I disappeared. My second friend told the genie that he wanted to be in his neighborhood bar with a keg of beer in front of him and, poof, he disappeared. My other friend, Horace, who isn't too bright, looked at the genie and said," Gee, I really don't know what my wish should be. That's a rough decision to make by myself. I wish my friends were here to help me. Poof!" Steve stops reading and looks at Rick to see his reaction.

"I don't believe what I just heard!" he states incredulously.

"Does that you mean you like it?" Steve asks as he antici-pates Rick's approval.

"What the hell's there to like? That doesn't fit in with what we're supposed to be doing and there's nothing Hawaiian about it. That's just another way to use the joke about the three guys lost in the Sahara Desert."

"My folks don't agree with you."

"Look Steve," Rick says forcefully. "I don't give a shit about what your parents think. I know they're big time writer-producers, but this is something we have to do on our own without anyone's help but our own. And as far as I'm concerned, just take that third page and put it in the round file and we'll figure out some new material and I mean new material!"

Steve swallows hard hoping that Rick won't chew off his head for what he's about to say. "I already sent the three pages to the producers."

Rick is thoroughly disgusted. "Shit Steve! We'll never get that job with that garbage for a third page. You should have told me what you wrote before you sent it in. We're supposed to work together, remember? We're partners, even if you don't bother to show up when we have work to do."

"Don't worry about it," he says convincingly. "My parents

wouldn't let us use stuff out of their file if they didn't think it would help us."

Rick doesn't believe his ears. "Did I just hear you right? Did you just tell me that the third page wasn't written by you and that you stole material from your parents' joke file?"

Steve doesn't understand why Rick's so upset. "What are you so worried about? My parents said it would be all right. We'll probably get the job thanks to me."

"Not after I tell them the third page isn't our work."

"C'mon Rick. You wouldn't do that."

"Don't you give a shit about anything? I thought you at least had a little integrity, but I guess now I know different. If you wanted to fool them with old material, you could have at least picked out some good Hawaiian jokes instead of that stuff you read me, and if we get the job you can go it alone because I couldn't stand any more of your tricky bullshit. I have enough problems trying to get you to work at all and I guess the next time you show me something I'll have to ask if you're the one who wrote it or did your parents write it for you."

"They were just trying to help us get that job. I don't see what's so terrible about that."

Steve stands up and heads for the door. "And that's exactly why I'm leaving."

Steve is enraged. He doesn't like anyone to have the last word. "Wait a second, damn it! You know fucking well that the only reason you wanted to write with me is because of my parents. You knew they'd help us get assignments that you couldn't get alone and if you keep this up with all your bullshit, we might as well split up." Steve is confident that Rick will back down.

Rick smiles at the prospect. "That's fine with me."

"We still have an assignment and they're expecting you to write it with me."

"Don't you mean write it I for you? Look Steve, as long as we're exchanging words and spewing forth venom you might as well know right now, and I'm sure it won't come as a surprise, that I can't stand your guts. I've never liked you as a person or as a writer. I don't see how you can even call yourself a writer when the only thing you've ever written is your mother's name on her residual checks you steal out of her mail box. As far as us working together because of your parents, you're absolutely right. I teamed up with you so they could get us assignments and I hoped that you'd become a writer and eventually we wouldn't need your parents contacts. But as it stands now. I'm getting an ulcer because of you and I'd better get rid of you before I kill you."

Steve looks at Rick bewildered. He never thought Rick would say such terrible things to him.

"In case you haven't figured it out yet, I'm dissolving our partnership and I never want to see your fucking face again. I want to wish you all the luck and prosperity that goes along with it, but I can't. I hate your fucking guts with a passion and I suggest that as long as you're here, you might admit yourself to the psychiatric department for a Lithium holiday because that seems to be the only thing in this world that's free. Maybe they can solve your problems for you because I certainly can't." Rick gets up and storms out of the room, but Charlie is blocking his path.

"What's the matter Rick?" Charlie asks in a concerned tone as he raises his arm, preparing to slap Rick on his back.

Rick is beside himself with rage and he instinctively blocks Charlie's arm only to retaliate with his fist in Charlie's stomach. Charlie buckles from the pain as Rick heads for the door.

"Get the fuck out of my way!" Rick shouts as everyone within earshot looks on.

Rick kicks the doors open, then pauses to light a cigarette.

"No smoking in the corridors," George yells from his position outside the therapy room.

"Go fuck yourself George!" snaps Rick as he flicks his cigarette in George's direction.

Rick heads back to the comfortable confines of his unit, confident that he'll feel better when he gets back to his own room. He doesn't know whether he did the right thing concerning his partner, but he knows that it's something he's wanted to do for a long time. Maybe when he gets back to his own room, they'll give him something to calm his nerves.

CHAPTER TWELVE

Rick is still unable to perform his bathroom duties. He knows that the medication nurse outside his door is growing impatient, but he just wants to try his best for another couple of minutes and if anything happens, it will. have been worth the wait.

"I can give you your medication in the bathroom if you like," the nurse suggests, hoping that Rick will comply.

"I'll be out in another minute," Rick calls out from inside.

"Don't hurry on my account," she tells him as she pushes her cart towards the door. "I'll come back at the end of my rounds."

"No! Wait! Rick shrieks as he bolts out of the bathroom, pulling up his pants as he approaches the medication cart.

"If you're constipated, I can have your doctor prescribe an enema."

Rick is terrified at the prospect. "No! I mean I'm not having a hard time or anything. I like to spend a lot of time in there."

"Sounds to me like you've never had an enema before. Have you?"

"No. But if I needed one, I'd get it and I'd be the first to ask for it."

The nurse seems appeased, knowing full well that Rick would never consent to an enema despite his obvious need for one.

Rick takes the cup of pills from the nurse as she pours him some orange juice. Rick looks into the cup and sees his three pills as the nurse hands him his juice.

"Do you think I could get some prune juice instead?" he asks sheepishly, handing her back the orange juice.

The nurse looks at him askance. "I see." She hands him back his juice. "Why don't you wash down your medication with this and I'll see about getting your prune juice."

"Never mind." Rick takes his medication.

Rick returns to his bed as the nurse heads out of his room. He's glad he changed his mind about the prune juice because the thought of drinking something so abhorrent to his taste buds isn't worth the price of being successful in the bathroom. At any rate, he's confident that he won't perish from his terrible constipation. He knows that sooner or later, he'll be able to perform. It's just a matter of time and a lot of discomfort. Anyway, the thought of an enema is too frightening to even think of. He can't imagine consenting to such a terrible endeavor, knowing full well that it would hurt him to no end. The only people who probably like such things are homosexuals, he thinks to himself. After all, they're used to having things shoved up their ass and when they go into the hospital for even a minor illness they probably demand an enema. And why shouldn't they, Rick jokingly thinks, with an obvious smirk on his face, it makes them feel like they never left home.

Rick gets himself comfortable in bed and maneuvers his television into position. He turns it on and is pleased to find one of his favorite shows, *Hogan's Heroes*, is on. He's probably seen this episode at least five times, but he's amused anyway.

As Rick laughs at the same jokes he's heard many times before, he hears a familiar pounding emanating from Jose's side of the room. Rick knows that Jose wants him for something, but he simply doesn't feel like getting out of his bed and tending to Jose no matter what his complaint might be.

Rick turns up the volume on his television, hoping that Jose will get the message and stop his incessant pounding. Nevertheless, Rick's plan doesn't work and Jose continues to pound on his table even louder. Rick doesn't wish to respond to Jose, so he simply depresses the nurse call button hoping that someone will come in and get Jose what he wants. Rick's tired of taking care of Jose. He feels that Jose's taking advantage of him, not realizing that Rick is in the hospital because he has problems of his own.

Minutes later, the nurse still hasn't appeared. Rick pushes his television away in disgust as he raises the head of his bed and stares across the room.

"What do you want Jose?" Rick asks with an air of contempt.

Jose seems pleased that Rick has finally answered his summons and he motions for Rick to come over to his bedside.

"C'mon Jose, I just got comfortable and I don't feel like getting out of bed till I absolutely have to."

Jose isn't interested in hearing any excuses and he again beckons Rick to come over to his bedside.

"Give me a break. Huh!"

Jose pays no attention to Rick's remark and he begins pointing to his mouth simulating a person smoking a cigarette. Rick catches on.

"Shit Jose. Can't you wait till I get up? I don't feel like smoking with you right now."

Undaunted, Jose continues pointing to his mouth. He tries speaking, but as before, he finds the task impossible.

Rick turns away from Jose and lights a cigarette for himself. Rick decides to simply ignore his roommate figuring that he'll eventually grow tired and leave him alone.

Jose begins pounding on his table. Rick is fit to be tied

as he takes another puff on his cigarette before turning his attentions back to Jose.

"Damn it Jose!" Rick says under his breath as he gets out of bed and heads across the room. "You can just have one hit, then I'm going back to bed and don't ask me for a cigarette of your own cause it won't work." Rick puts his cigarette up to Jose's mouth, but Jose turns his head away.

"Now what's the matter?"

Jose motions for Rick to hand him his pencil and he begins writing a message on his pad. Rick waits patiently as Jose scribbles on the pad. A few minutes later, Jose finishes and hands the pad to Rick. As Rick prepares to read Jose's message, Jose motions for Rick to place his cigarette in between his lips. Rick seems perturbed, but he complies with Jose's request.

Jose inhales the smoke deep into his lungs, savoring the experience as Rick extinguishes the cigarette in the ashtray. Rick stares at the paper for a moment before reading it to himself.

WHEN YOU WERE NOT HERE BEFORE A GIRL CAME IN TO ROOM AND LOOK AT EVERYTHING THERE WAS. SHE SAID SOMETHING TO ME BUT I DID NOT ANSWER HER BECAUSE I DID NOT LIKE HER AND I DID NOT KNOW IF SHE WAS SUPPOSE TO BE IN HERE SO I PRETEND THAT I WAS SLEEPING. I THINK SHE WANTED TO LOOK THROUGH MY THINGS BUT I THINK SHE WAS SCARED OF ME BECAUSE I AM A BIG MAN AND SHE THOUGHT I WOULD BEAT HER UP IF I WOKE UP AND SHE SAW THAT I WAS LOOKING AT HER SO SHE WENT OVER TO YOUR BED AND LOOK AROUND OVER THERE BECAUSE YOU WERE NOT HERE TO STOP HER. I THOUGHT SHE WAS PRETTY BUT I THINK SHE WAS FAT

AND I THINK SHE EATS TO MUCH BECAUSE SHE LOOKS LIKE SHE IS FAT. SHE WAS NOT AFRAID OF ALEXANDER EITHER BECAUSE HE LOOK AT HER WHEN SHE WAS IN TO YOUR LITTLE SUITCASE: AND SHE DID NOT CARE THAT ALEXANDER WAS LOOKING AT HER. I THINK SHE TOOK SOMETHING OUT OF YOUR SUITCASE BECAUSE SHE HAD YOUR CIGARETTES IN HER HAND WHEN SHE LEFT BECAUSE I SAW HER HOLDING YOUR CARTON OF CIGARETTES IN HER HAND BUT SHE DID NOT KNOW THAT I WAS WATCHING HER BECAUSE I LIKE GIRLS WITH BLOND HAIR EVEN THOUGH HER HAIR REALLY WAS NOT THAT BLOND LIKE IT WOULD BE IF SHE PUT BLOND PAINT ON IT LIKE A GIRL I KNOW DOES. I DO NOT TRUST HER BECAUSE I THINK THAT SHE TOOK YOUR CIGARETTES AND I DO NOT LIKE PEOPLE WHO TAKE THINGS WHEN THEY ARE NOT SUPPOSE TO BE STEALING BECAUSE I THINK SHE CAN BE PUT INTO A JAIL FOR THAT. BUT DO NOT TELL HER THAT I TOLD YOU BECAUSE SHE MIGHT COME IN AND HIT ME AND HURT ME.

Rick sets down the paper on Jose's table. "You mean you saw her going through my things?"

Jose nods his head as Rick returns to his side of the room and picks up his grip. Rick reaches inside and retrieves his carton of cigarettes.

"That bitch took two packs!" Rick slams his grip onto the floor, then returns to Jose's bedside. "What else do you remember besides her blond hair? Was she kind of plump with a roll of fat around her stomach and did her hair need washing?"

Jose again nods his head up and down.

"Sounds like Carla. I'll bet she knew exactly where my cigarettes were from the last time she came in."

Rick can see that Jos doesn't comprehend his statement. "That happened before you got here. I'm sure it's her though. I don't know anyone else who looks like that and from the way she gobbled up my cigarettes before, I'm sure she's the one."

Jose grabs the pad of paper and scribbles another message. He hands it to Rick.

PLEASE DO NOT TELL HER THAT I TOID YOU THAT'SAW HER TAKE YOUR CIGARETTES BECAUSE SHE WILL GET MAD AT ME AND BEAT ME UP AND I CAN NOT DO ANYTHING BECAUSE I CAN NOT GET OUT OF MY BED AND I AM NOT SUPPOSE TO HIT A GIRL BECAUSE IT IS NOT RIGHT.

Rick smiles as he sets down Jose's paper. "Don't worry about it. I'll take care of her in my own way and she'll never know who told me."

Jose seems content with Rick's reply as he begins pointing towards his mouth again. Rick recognizes what Jose wants.

"All right, I guess I owe you a cigarette." Rick lights a cigarette and places it into Jose's mouth.

As Rick continues helping Jose smoke, an attendant enters the room and places a covered tray on Jose's table. Then the attendant goes out into the corridor only to return a moment later with Rick's tray which he sets on Rick's table.

"Excuse me," Rick calls out. "Is there any way I could get a Coke or something?"

"Well, there's a machine in the lobby, but I'm not allowed to get anything like that for patients." The attendant looks around making sure that he's not being observed by other hospital personnel. "I guess I can take a run down there if you give me the money, it's sixty cents."

Rick seems let down. "Thanks anyway, but I won't have any money until later. I thought maybe you could get it from the kitchen or something."

Hearing this, Jose taps Rick and points towards his dresser drawer.

Rick opens the drawer and sees assorted change inside.

"Thanks Jose." Rick counts out sixty cents which he hands the attendant. "I'll pay you back tomorrow," Rick tells his roommate.

Rick gives Jose another drag off his cigarette as he closes the drawer. However, Jose spots something in his drawer and indicates that Rick should open it again. Rick complies as Jose points to a picture of a nurse which is next to Jose's personal phone book. Jose motions for Rick to bring out the picture and the book as he props the head of his bed up. Then Jose takes both articles from Rick and he plants a kiss on the picture of the young, black haired nurse. Jose sets the picture on his stomach then picks up his pad of paper and his pencil. He begins writing as Rick leans over to read his latest message.

THIS IS MY GIRLFRIEND ON THE PICTURE AND I THINK SHE IS VERY PRETTY AND SHE LIKES. ME A LOT AND SHE LIKES TO TAKE CARE OF ME AND I WANT YOU TO LOOK IN MY PHONE BOOK BECAUSE THE FIRST TELEPHONE NUMBER IN IT IS HER TELEPHONE NUMBER AND I WANT YOU TO DIAL HER NUMBER ON MY PHONE SO I CAN CALL HER AND TELL HER WHERE I AM AND WHAT HAPPENED TO ME BECAUSE SHE WILL WANT TO KNOW WHY I AM IN HERE BECAUSE SHE IS MY GIRLFRIEND AND I THINK THAT WE WILL GET MARRIED ONE DAY BECAUSE I REALLY LIKE HER AND SHE TAKES GOOD CARE OF ME BECAUSE SHE IS A NURSE.

Rick grabs the pencil from Jose's hand. "You don't have to write anymore. I think I get the message."

Jose looks at his roommate and smiles affectionately as Rick finds the number in the phone book and begins dialing. Jose's obvious excitement at the prospect of talking to his girlfriend manifests itself 'by his heavy and erratic breathing. After a few moments, Rick sets down the phone.

"I'm sorry. I got a recording that says her number's no longer working. She either moved or her phone's just broken down. "Rick sees the pain in Jose's eyes. "We'll try again later."

Jose's eyes begin to water as he stares at his supposed girlfriend's picture.

Rick hands him a Kleenex as the attendant returns with a can of Coke which he hands to Rick.

"If anybody asks where you got it, tell 'em you got it yourself. Okay?"

Rick nods. "Thanks." Rick opens the can and takes a sip as Jose retrieves his baby bottle from the side of his bed, holding it up.

"You want some?" Rick asks noticing that Jose is beaming with delight in anticipation.

"All right," Rick says as he removes the top of Jose's bottle and pours in some Coke. "But I don't know whether you're supposed to be drinking this stuff or not and I don't feel like asking because I don't know if this will still be fresh by the time they decide to answer the buzzer."

Jose smiles as he takes his bottle from Rick. He promptly places it. between his lips and begins sucking on the nipple. Then Jose takes the nipple away from his mouth and tries speaking. At first, Rick detects a faint audible sound.

"Wait a second," he says excitedly. "Say that again, but slow down,"

Jose repeats his message as Rick leans down so that his ear

is only a few inches from Jose's mouth.

Rick is ecstatic. "Did you say, thank you?"

Jose excitedly nods his head up and down as he breaks out with a large smile stretching from ear to ear.

"That's great! You're getting your voice back. But don't try and extend yourself because it probably takes a long time and you shouldn't force it."

Rick spots the lunch tray near his bed. "I'd better go eat my lunch before it gets cold and rigor mortis sets in."

Jose smiles at his little joke. Rick knows that Jose probably doesn't understand what he just said and he appreciates Jose for humoring him even if the joke wasn't very funny.

As Rick heads back to his side of the room, he stops by Jose's table and lifts the cover off Jose's lunch tray. "Let's see what magnificent repast they've prepared for you." Rick is surprised to find a chicken dinner, a roll, and a piece of corn on his plate. "What the hell's the matter with those idiots?" he says disgustedly. "Don't they know you can't eat this shit?"

Jose knows what Rick's leading up to and he doesn't want to cause anyone extra work. Jose waves his arms around hoping to get Rick's attention.

"Don't worry Jose. I'll get 'em to take this back and bring you something you can eat."

Jose tries speaking, but he can't make himself understood. However, he does get Rick's attention so he begins scribbling another message on his pad of paper. Rick leans over and looks at Jose's message as he writes.

I DO NOT HAVE TO EAT MY LUNCH NOW BECAUSE I AM NOT HUNGRY AND YOU CAN HAVE IT IF YOU WANT IT BECAUSE YOU KNOW THAT I CANNOT EAT THAT BECAUSE I CANNOT SWALLOW IT AND I WANT YOU TO CALL MY GIRLFRIEND AGAIN BECAUSE I KNOW THAT

SHE MISSES ME BECAUSE SHE LIKES ME AND SHE LIKES TO TAKE CARE OF ME.

Rick feels uncomfortable leaning over Jose's bed and he stands erect. He's read enough. "I already told you her line's out of order and it's probably not even her phone anymore."

Jose sets down his pencil and points to the phone as he tries to say! "Please."

Rick knows that if he doesn't at least try to get a hold of Jose's girlfriend, he'll probably start crying and Rick doesn't want to see that happen.

Rick picks up Jose's phone book and tries the number again, but as before, the line is out of order. Rick hangs up the phone and looks at Jose through the corner of his eye. He can easily tell that Jose is on the verge of tears. Then, Jose begins to cry.

"It's still out of order," Rick says, picking up a tissue to wipe Jose's steady stream of tears. "Don't cry," Rick pleads as he turns his head in the opposite direction. For the first time, Jose's plight affects Rick. Before coming to this hospital, Rick never knew that people like Jose existed. Oh sure, Rick thought, he was aware like anyone else about the horrible tricks played on some people by nature, but since you don't normally come into day to d contact with these people, it's easy to convince yourself that these people simply don't exist. Like most people, Rick sees a selected few of these handicapped people and he stares at them like anyone else because it's an odd sight to see someone without an arm or a leg. It's always been a hideous sight in Rick's mind, partly stemming from the fear that it's just possible he might end up that way as a result of a car accident or from something bizarre.

Therefore, he feels, if you pretend that it's not there, it seems unrealistic that something like that can befall a normal individual.

There were a number of retarded students attending the same high school where Rick went and everyone adjusted to the fact that from time to time they would run into these people. Whenever Rick or his friends saw these handicapped people, they frequently joked about them not realizing how callous their behavior was. He made more jokes than any of his friends until he was involved in an incident he'll never forget. He was on his way to his next class when he turned a corner and bumped into one of the female students. Rick fumed as his books were knocked onto the ground. "Why don't you look where you're going!" he snapped, are you blind?"

"Yes," the girl replied. "As a matter of fact, I am."

Even though that incident happened long ago, Rick still remembers it like it happened yesterday. And now, he's taking care of someone who'd gladly be blind in exchange for the full use of his body. In his wildest dreams, Rick never thought he'd be tending to someone who's not only paralyzed and wears diapers, but someone who's also an epileptic.

As Rick wipes Jose's tears, he wishes to himself that he were in some other room where he wouldn't have to tend to someone as pathetic as Jose. He's ashamed of himself for feeling this way, but he can't hide his true feelings from himself.

Jose silently stares at the picture of his supposed girlfriend. Rick can't help noticing that his eyes are continuing to water as he looks longingly at the picture.

"How long has she been your girlfriend?" Rick asks hoping that he can get Jose's mind off the fact that her number's no longer working.

Jose sets the picture on his stomach and holds up two fingers.

"Two years?"

Jose shakes his head negatively as he beckons Rick closer. Rick leans down as Jose tries speaking. Jose takes a moment to concentrate before working himself up to the point where he believes that he can make his words understood. Rick positions himself immediately next to Jose's mouth as Jose speaks.

Rick smiles. "Did you say two months?"

Jose nods his head up and down. He smiles with delight knowing that he finally made himself understood.

"That's terrific. but I think you should stick to writing your thoughts on paper so your vocal cords won't be strained."

Jose's pained expression conveys to Rick that he doesn't want to remain silent any longer.

"Just hang in there for a few days and then you can talk up a storm and we can yell across the room at each other, okay?"

Jose beams with delight at the prospect and extends his hand grabbing Rick's hand. He shakes Rick's hand with his weak grip as he continues smiling.

Sherri enters the room pushing in a hospital wash cart. "How ya doing Rick?" she calls out as she positions the cart next to the closed partition surrounding Alexander's bed.

"What are you doing with that thing?" Rick curiously replies as Sherri opens the partition.

"It's time for Alexander's bath and I didn't want to leave this unit till he gets it."

Rick applauds Sherri's noble gesture as a nurse enters and approaches Alexander.

Alexander's attention is riveted to his television set. He's still watching reports on the Pope's visit.

"Time for your bath Alexander."

"Oh, go away," he insipidly replies, in his usual nasal tone.

"You can watch the Pope later, Alexander." Sherri reaches over and shuts off his television. "This nurse is very busy and she has a lot of patients to attend to after she washes you, so you'd better do what she says and stop wasting her time."

"Leave me alone," Alexander answers as he turns on his

side and covers his face with his blanket.

"It's only a sponge bath Alexander," the nurse informs him. "It'll be over before you know it and you'll feel a whole lot better," she tells him in a soothing manner. "I'm sure you don't like being a stinker."

"I don't care, go away!" Alexander replies from underneath his blanket. "I don't want a bath and you can't make me."

Sherri heads for the door. "Sorry I can't stay around for the fun."

"Thanks a lot," the nurse quips as she turns her attention back to Alexander. "C'mon Alexander. You're just making matters worse. I'm sure you don't like your smell any more than your roommates do."

"Go away!" he yells in a firm tone as he lashes out blindly with his arm hoping to intimidate her.

Then the nurse grabs Alexander's blanket and pulls it off his body and onto the floor. Alexander quickly turns over and shoots her a nasty look.

"I'm not taking a bath and I want my blanket back. It's cold in here."

The nurse ignores his request and prepares his wash cloth. "Forget it Alexander. Don't expect any favors from me until I finish washing you off." The nurse approaches Alexander and grabs onto his arm preparing to scrub it with her wash cloth.

Alexander grabs the wash cloth away from the nurse and flings it across the room. The nurse is visibly shaken as she walks across the room and retrieves the wash cloth. She returns to her position next to Alexander's bed, but instead of pursuing the matter, she drops the wash cloth on her cart and pushes it out towards the door.

"You can't just give up like that," Rick calls out. "I really don't blame you for giving up, but you don't realize how difficult it is to breathe in here."

"Don't worry about it because as soon as I finish with my rounds, I'll be back with a couple of attendants who'll hold him down, if necessary, while I bathe him." She heads out of the room as Alexander calls out.

"Nurse."

The nurse pokes her head into the room, figuring that Alexander changed his mind.

"What is it Alexander?"

"Could I have two bananas from the kitchen?"

The nurse doesn't answer, but she does shoot Alexander a confused look as she shakes her head in disgust before disappearing out of the doorway.

"I think Alexander won the first round with the nurse," Rick tells Jose, who now seems to have forgotten about his own problems.

Jose points to his nose and then indicates Alexander.

"Yeah, he does smell pretty bad doesn't he,"

Rick races to his side of the room to answer his phone. Rick is surprised to hear Mark's voice on the other end. He thought that after he left the hospital the other day, he'd never hear from him again. That would be fine with Rick because he didn't care for Mark much anyway and he knows that Mark feels the same way about him, so why is he calling?

"I'm doing really shitty Rick and I kind of need your help if I'm gonna nail those bastards to the wall."

Rick has no idea what Mark's talking about. "Huh?"

"I couldn't wait to get myself out of that place and get away from those incompetents and now I'm suffering because of them and I'm not gonna let them get away with it because they really screwed me up!"

Rick is more confused than ever and he has a hard time making any sense out of what Mark's telling him in his rapid-fire way of speaking. "Wait a second," Rick interrupts.

"Slowdown and tell me what you're talking about, will ya?"

Mark is obviously perturbed. "C'mon Rick, you know what I'm talking about. Those assholes got me addicted to pills and now I'm going through terrible withdrawal because of those bastards and I'm gonna get even with 'em."

Rick remains silent, preferring to let Mark continue.

"Well are you going to back me up, or aren't you?" he asks impatiently.

"What do you mean?" Rick innocently replies.

"Don't give me that shit! You're not blind! You know damn well that they got me hooked on pills because you saw them giving me that stuff and you know that they always had me doped up. I only went there because I was depressed and I ended up breaking my leg and getting hooked on heavy narcotics because of those incompetents and I'm going to sue them for everything they have."

"So what do you want me to do?"

"You're my witness that they got me hooked and made me take their narcotics and that they wanted to keep me in so they could get more money from my insurance company."

"Listen Mark, I really don't know what to tell ya because I was pretty loaded myself when you were here and I really don't remember anything except that you kept asking them for more powerful pills because the ones they kept giving you weren't working."

Mark is enraged. "That's a lie. You know they forced me to take all those pills!"

"Not really. Like I said, I was too out of it to pay attention to anyone else's problems but my own."

Hearing this, Mark hangs up the phone without saying good bye. Rick slams down the phone.

"That guy's really a jerk," Rick mumbles to himself as he sits down on his bed. "No, I take that back. He's not a jerk, he's an asshole!"

As Rick makes himself comfortable in his bed, he hears Jose pounding once again. Rick looks across the room and sees that Jose wants him to come back to his bedside.

"What do you want Jose?"

Jose motions towards his mouth indicating that he wants Rick to help him smoke a cigarette.

"Give me a break, will ya? Just let me relax for a while before you have another cigarette and stop that damn pounding on your table. It's giving me a headache." Rick expects Jose to relent as he turns his attention back to his own affairs Jose resumes his pounding.

"Damn it Jose! What is it?"

Jose again indicates that he wants a cigarette.

"Didn't you just hear me tell you I'll help you smoke a cigarette later, now leave me alone!" Rick turns on his television and turns up the volume control in case Jose begins pounding on his table again.

As Rick flips through the channels, he feels guilty about the harsh way he just spoke to his roommate. Rick pushes his television out of the way and sits up in bed facing Jose. "I'm sorry Jose, but it's just that I'm real tired and I need some time to myself. But if you really want a cigarette, I guess I can come over and help you smoke one, okay?"

Jose doesn't respond to Rick's proposition. Then Rick realizes that Jose is in the midst of a seizure. Rick immediately springs out of his bed, racing over to Jose's bedside. He rips a tongue depressor off the wall and jams it into Jose's mouth, making sure that he puts it in the proper place. Then Rick presses the nurses call button as he stares at his roommate.

"Someone help!" Rick calls out as the seizure progresses, but no one comes. Rick holds down Jose's arms fearing that Jose might hurt himself if his arms crash into the guardrails as they did before. Rick never realized that Jose was as strong as he is, as he presses with all his might trying to keep Jose's arms pinned to his side. Suddenly, Jose's legs begin moving. It doesn't faze Rick in the least, until he remembers that Jose is paralyzed from the waist down and couldn't possibly be moving his lower extremities. Rick thinks that he was just seeing things, but Jose's legs move again and again. "Help somebody!" He's having a seizure! Help!" Rick cries out as he anticipates everyone's reaction when he tells them that Jose was moving his legs around so he probably isn't paralyzed anymore. "C'mon Jose, snap out of it. Your legs aren't paralyzed anymore. Rick is ecstatic. He can't wait to spring the news on Jose.

Suddenly, Jose's body stops shaking and his eyes open. He looks up and sees Rick standing over him like a guardian angel. Jose smiles.

"Are you all right?"

Jose nods his head up and down and he tries speaking.

"Don't do that Jose. We have an understanding, remember? You won't try talking until you're stronger and I intend on keeping that bargain, okay?"

Jose shakes his head from side to side as he shrugs his shoulders.

"Well this is the seizure to remember Because I've got some great news for you and all I ask is that after I tell you, I don't want you to get out of your bed and kiss me okay?

Jose is understandably puzzled, and for a good reason. He knows he'd never be able to perform such a feat.

"Now I don't know how it happened, but while you were having that seizure, something happened to your body and your legs started working again."

Much to Rick's surprise, Jose doesn't seem the least bit moved with the bombshell he just got.

"Didn't you understand what I just said? I said your legs

are all better. You're not paralyzed anymore."

Jose still doesn't react like Rick expected he would. Instead, Jose stares blankly at his friend.

"Go on, move your legs," Rick removes the sheets covering Jose Is legs.

Rick stares at Jose's legs for a few moments, but they fail to oblige. "C'mon Jose, move 'em."

Rick can see that Jose's face shows the pained expression of someone who's trying with all his might, but he's only doing it to show Rick that he's unable to accommodate him.

"I know I saw them move before, but I guess if you could move them, they'd be bouncing up and down."

Nurse Doris Rayburn enters the room and sees Rick standing by Jose's bed. "Get away from him!" she barks.

"Is that how you thank someone for doing your job for you?"

"I don't know what you're talking about and I don't care. All I want from you is to get back to your bed and stay there like you're supposed to be doing. I can't have you running around bothering the other patients and if you continue to exhibit this erratic behavior of yours, I'll have you moved to another unit where they'll keep you under their thumb."

Rick is enraged. "Look lady! If it wasn't for me, this guy could be dead right now, because I was the only one in this damn place who bothered taking care of him while he had his seizure."

Doris Rayburn is dumbfounded. "What are you talking about? When did he have a seizure?"

"It ended just before you bothered showing up. Didn't you hear me screaming for help?"

Doris takes Jose's pulse, preferring not to answer Rick's question.

"And what about the call I put out for a nurse. Didn't you

hear the buzzer or is it out of order?"

Doris answers without thinking. "I thought Alexander was calling for some thing to eat." Doris catches herself. "I mean, well, his seizure's over so there Is no harm done."

"How can you say that?" Rick incredulously inquires. "If I wasn't here to jam that depressor in his mouth, he could have choked on his tongue and died."

"That's not likely to happen," she says coldly. "People like him are constantly having seizures that go unattended.'

"Well what if I'm not here to help him and he has a grand mal? Do you think that Alexander's gonna call for help and even if he did, you'd probably ignore the call anyway."

Doris fumes. "Back to your bed!"

Doris and Rick stare at each other as Jose taps Doris' hand and then indicates towards his mouth.

"He wants a cigarette," Rick informs her.

"No smoking for you Jose. You just had a seizure and I don't think that your doctor would approve of you smoking. Anyway, you should quit that nasty habit. It Is not good for you."

"Yeah Jose and just think, if you quit smoking you could probably start practicing for the Olympics again."

Doris shoots Rick a vitriolic look as he heads back towards his side of the room.

"I'm going, I'm going, but just let me ask you one question."

"As long as it concerns yourself and your treatment."

"What if he has another seizure and no one bothers to show up?"

Doris takes the used tongue depressor from Jose's bed and tapes it back on the wall above his bed as she listens to Rick.

"Do you want me to ignore his seizure and hope that he doesn't choke to death, or do you want me to call someone, in which case, they'll hopefully arrive in time to save him?"

"Look!" she bellows, "I can't have my nurses running back and forth in this room every time he has a mild seizure, so why don't you just keep an eye on him and if he has a seizure that lasts for more than three minutes, press the call button and one of my nurses will come in."

"And what are you gonna do if he chokes to death right away?" Doris heads for the door, ignoring Rick's question.

"Answer the question, damn it!"

Doris whirls around. She's obviously" run out of patience. "You just do what I said and stop expecting the worst to happen."

Rick still isn't satisfied. "But what if he has a seizure while I'm in therapy? Who's gonna know he's having a seizure if no one's going to check on him?"

"I suggest you worry about yourself and stop trying to tell me how to go about my business."

"Why don't you just shoot him and be done with it!" Rick yells out hoping that Doris will hear his remark before she is out of earshot.

Rick knows that Doris resents his behavior. After all, people usually" do whatever doctors and nurses tell them, figuring that they have their best interest in mind. But in Rick's case, he feels that Doris just doesn't care anything about the patients she's supposed to be caring for. Rick feels that Doris and her staff aren't doing their jobs correctly and he's confident that if he's insistent in making his position clear, they just might think twice about their abhorrent behavior and start functioning correctly.

Rick's confrontation with Doris convinces him that he'll have to keep an eye on Jose himself. He's resolved to the fact that it's just possible that Doris and her staff don't expect Jose to make it, and one of the reasons they hesitate to come around on a regular basis is because they're afraid Jose might perish at any moment. At any rate, Rick plans on doing his best to make sure such a fate doesn't befall his roommate.

"How do you feel?" Rick calls out to Jose.

Jose smiles at his friend as he restrains himself from crying.

"I know what'll make you feel better," Rick says as he approaches Jose's bedside with a cigarette in his hand. "How about a cigarette? You look like you could use one. And this time I won't go away till you tell me to. Even if it means smoking the whole pack." Rick places the cigarette between Jose's lips and then lights one for himself as well. "Take your time my friend. I'm not going anywhere."

CHAPTER THIRTEEN

"How you tonight?" a Korean nurse greets Rick as she begins the night shift.

Rick is surprised that this woman came into his room expressly to exchange pleasantries with him. Needless to say, he's bewildered. "I'm fine, thanks. Nice of you to ask."

"I be better in eight hours. That when I go home and go sleep I no get enough sleep this morning and I still tired. "She yawns.

"Well, I won't call you unless it's something urgent." Rick indicates the empty bed opposite Alexander's. "You can lie down over there if you want, but don't expect to be treated like a patient."

"You funny man," she says giggling as she heads for the door. "You be good boy and I see you later." She exits.

Peace and quiet seem almost impossible to attain. Every time Rick tries getting some rest someone always interrupts him.

It's either Jose pounding on his table, the screaming man from down the corridor, an unexpected visitor or the phone ringing that keeps Rick from getting a quiet moment to himself. Rick desperately wants at least a few moments without interruptions and it seems as though he'll finally succeed. He sits up in bed, noticing that Jose's resting quietly. Then Rick turns his attention to Alexander and sees him sleeping, or at least pretending to be asleep. Everything seems conducive to what Rick wants. Then Rick remembers that the phone might possibly awaken him in the event he does get the rest he needs, so he simply takes the receiver off the hook and places it under his pillow.

Rick finally closes his eyes in confidence. He's certain that he's covered all bases in his quest for peace and quiet. Then he hears that all too familiar sound of Alexander's television as he changes the channels from one program to the next in search of a program dealing with the Pope's visit.

Rick's immediate reaction is one of hostility, but he catches himself before he spouts off at Alexander. He realizes that Alexander has every right to use his television as he sees fit, but that right doesn't extend to annoying him. "Take it easy with that TV," Rick calls out, but Alexander simply ignores him and continues changing the channels."

"C'mon Alexander, you're giving me a headache."

Alexander continues to ignore Rick as he stops on a channel which reports on the Pope's visit. Then Alexander turns up the up the volume, drowning out Rick's pleas for him to stop making so much noise.

"Turn it down Alex, will ya?"

"The name's Alexander!"

Rick's patience dissipates. "I don't really give a shit! Just turn down the sound. I can't even hear myself think, but you wouldn't know about things like that, would you?"

Alexander turns away from Rick and continues watching his program, failing to lower the volume on his set.

Rick feels that he was more than fair with Alexander and he isn't quite sure how to make his point. His first reaction is to simply go over to Alexander and rip the plug out of the wall. That would certainly solve the problem, but there's no telling how Alexander might react. He might be the type who'll wait until Rick's asleep and slash his throat. Rick decides to think of other things to do to Alexander, but quickly dismisses them figuring that Alexander would have nothing to lose if he did decide to get even.

Rick is intimidated. He knows he'll never be able to get the rest he wants. Then Rick comes up with a plan. He turns on his television, deciding to turn up the volume on his set loud enough to drown out the sounds from Alexander's set. At first, Rick is pleased with himself, but Alexander doesn't react as he expected. Rick shuts off his television, determined to find another way to get even with Alexander.

Rick lies in bed trying to figure out some other way to infuriate Alexander. He wants to devise something that Alexander won't know he planned, but what?

"How many time you move bowels today?" the Korean nurse asks as she enters the room, approaching Rick's bed.

Rick is taken aback, not realizing that this is normal hospital procedure. "I didn't know I was supposed to keep score," he answers glibly.

She ignores his remark. "How many time? You have only one bowel movement or you not have any?"

"Hell, I don't know."

The nurse makes some notes on her chart. "Next time you have bowel movement, you let me know."

"Believe me, if I move my bowels, you'll know. I'll be the only one in here smiling."

The nurse doesn't laugh at Rick's attempt at humor, evidenced by the blank expression on her face.

"You have bowel movement pretty soon or you get enema," she threatens.

"Aren't you gonna say please?"

"You never mind." She heads out of the room, stopping outside the doorway, then she turns around. "I come back later. Maybe you not look so tired and you move bowels for me."

Rick no longer feels like sleeping. He's too worried about what the nurse said about a bowel movement. He doesn't want to think about it, but it's hard for him not to. He desperately wants to perform in the bathroom, fearing that they'll force him to have an enema if he doesn't go soon. He figures that if he must have an enema, they'll probably send George in to give it and he simply couldn't handle that. Rick knows there's no point worrying about it. As far as he's concerned, he'll force himself into going even if it means eating a pound of prunes.

Rick lies in bed deciding to make another trip to the bathroom. When he gets up he hears an all too familiar noise emanating from Jose's side of the room. At first Rick surmises that Jose probably wants him to help him smoke another cigarette. Rick doesn't want to look in Jose's direction hoping that he'll grow tired and stop his incessant pounding.

Suddenly it dawns on Rick that the pounding noise isn't coming from Jose pounding on the table. Against his better judgement, Rick looks across the room and sees Jose's arms flying about crashing into the guardrails of his bed. Jose's having another seizure. Rick's first thought is to race to Jose's aid, but he doesn't feel like having another confrontation with the hospital personnel so he presses the nurses call button.

Minutes pass and no one enters the room. Then the seizure ends and Jose falls into a deep sleep. His body's obviously exhausted from the trying effects of the seizure.

The Korean nurse enters and sees that Rick is the only one awake. "What you call nurse for?" she caustically asks.

Rick resents her vicious attitude. He's at a total loss to explain why any nurse should act this way. "If you came in right away when I called for a nurse, you'd know."

"What you mean?" she snaps. "Jose just had another seizure."

"He always have seizures. That nothing new. Why you so worried about him? He friend of yours?"

"Apparently the only one," he quips.

"How you know he have seizure? You not doctor."

"Believe me, I know. Take my word for it."

"How long seizure"

"What the hell difference does it make if you don't bother showing up till it's over?"

The nurse proceeds to Jose's bedside ignoring Rick's question. She picks up his hand and takes his pulse. "You wake up," she calls out. Then she rips the tongue depressor off the wall and jams it into Jose's mouth.

"What the hell are you doing?" Rick yells across the room. "He's not having a seizure, he's sleeping!"

Even though Jose's sleeping, he attempts to push the depressor out of his mouth. Seeing this, the nurse holds the tongue depressor in place as Jose opens his eyes. Then Jose begins choking on the tongue depressor and the nurse finally removes it.

"How you feel?"

Jose smiles affably as the nurse tapes the depressor back on the wall.

"You be fine," she says heading for the door. Then she turns around to address Rick. "You no call for nurse unless he have seizure for long time."

Alexander sees the nurse by the door. "Nurse, could I have some vanilla ice cream? Two portions."

The nurse stares at Alexander with bitter disapproval. "You no need ice cream."

"But I want vanilla ice cream," he whines. "A double portion."

"I not waitress. I head nurse!" she chides. "You no get ice cream until you take bath. You very dirty."

Alexander doesn't answer back, preferring to swing out his television in front of his face to continue watching shows on the Pope's visit.

Jose gets the nurse's attention by pounding on his table.

"What you want now?" she calls out from her position by the door. "You have seizure?"

Jose shakes his head negatively as he points towards his waist. With his other hand, he motions for her to come over to his bedside.

"If you not have seizure, I send in your nurse. She take care you."

"Why the hell don't you take care of him like you're supposed to?" Rick indignantly asks.

"I send in other nurse. I go on break now," she informs Rick and Jose as she exits.

"What's the matter Jose?" Rick asks his crying roommate.

Jose motions towards his waist as another Korean nurse enters.

"Why you cry? You wet pants?"

"I think he needs to be changed," Rick informs her knowing that it's still an embarrassing thing for Jose to relate to strange people.

The nurse remains silent, but there's an unmistakable expression of disgust on her face. It's obvious that she finds changing a grown man's diaper somewhat distasteful.

The nurse looks around Jose's bed until she finds his box of disposable diapers. She sets the box on Jose's table and then removes his blanket and sheets. She hesitates at first, but finally relents and has a look inside Jose's diaper. "You make mess in diaper," she coldly informs him thinking that he doesn't realize this because he's paralyzed, "just like baby."

Jose begins crying as the nurse reaches into the Pampers box. Jose will never get used to the fact that he's condemned to a lifetime of diapers. It's a hard fact of reality that he'll never fully adjust to. If only the nurses would realize that he doesn't like wearing a diaper any more than they like changing one, but this hasn't happened thus far.

"You no have no diapers in box," she informs Jose. "I go storeroom and see if have more," she tells him as she undoes his soiled diaper. "You try and not go more because your diaper no have room," she yells out as she exits.

Rick desperately wants to say something to Jose, but he doesn't know what he could possibly say to make his predicament more comfortable. Instead, Rick flips on his television and positions it in front of his face so he doesn't have to look in Jose's direction.

When Rick's program ends, he notices that thirty minutes have passed and Jose's nurse hasn't returned with a new supply of diapers. Rick presses the call button and for the first time, a nurse responds immediately.

"Who press button?"

"I did. I want to know why the nurse didn't come back with Jose's diapers. He's been laying in that stuff for forty-five minutes and she promised to get him a new supply and change him."

"She on break now."

Rick is enraged. "What the hell is he supposed to do in the meantime? He can't go anymore because there isn't any more room from what the nurse told him. You don't have to go over and see it for yourself. You can smell how bad it is."

"You no need get mad. I just in storeroom and we no have no diaper."

"What do you mean you don't have any more? What's he supposed to do?"

"We get diaper Monday."

"This is Saturday! What are you gonna do for two days, stick a cork up his ass and hope no one gets hurt when it shoots out or are you people just gonna stay away from this room until your precious shipment comes in."

The nurse looks away from Rick and focuses her attention on Jose. "You call family. They bring diaper."

Hearing this, Rick bolts out of his bed and ushers the nurse to the corner of the room. Rick knows Jose will try and listen to what he has to say so he whispers.

"Don't you know he doesn't have any family whatsoever and how the hell can you people be so god damn uncaring! He is not some fucking animal who can be humiliated for a couple of days! You can't make up to him for something like this!"

"You no worry about him. He be fine."

"Well, the least you could do is send one of the nurses over to the store for a box of diapers and if you can't do that you can certainly take some hospital sheets or even a towel until you get a hold of some diapers."

"When man from store come, you give him money and he buy diapers."

"Since when did I become the procurement officer around here? Not only don't I have any money for myself, but now you're putting me in charge of buying him diapers." Rick pauses for a moment trying to capture a small bit of his lost composure. "I'm a patient for Christ sakes!"

"You no act like patient. I hear about you. You always get mad at nurse and tell how treat patient who have seizure."

"Look! You weren't here before when one of your nurses shoved a tongue depressor in his mouth because she thought he was having a seizure." Rick raises his voice unaware that Jose is listening to his every word. "The poor guy was just sleeping and they don't even know how to tell the difference."

Rick is interrupted by Jose's pounding on the table. Rick looks at his roommate who's motioning towards his mouth indicating that he wants a cigarette.

"Shit Jose!" Rick says, ready to bite off Jose's head as well. Then Rick catches himself staring at his unfortunate roommate who's wearing a full diaper which is unfastened and extremely unpleasant to look at. Rick lights up a cigarette and places it between Jose's lips. Jose takes in a long drag and smiles as he savors the smoke in his lungs.

"He no allowed to smoke," the nurse informs Rick.

"Why don't you call his doctor and ask him. And while he's on the line you might ask him what to do about the diapers."

The nurse takes the cigarette out of Rick's hand and extinguishes it. "I no need call doctor. I head nurse."

Rick heads back to his side of the room and lights up a fresh cigarette. He returns to Jose's bedside and places the cigarette into Jose's eager mouth. The nurse resents Rick's obstinate behavior.

"He no smoke!" she fumes as she takes the cigarette out of Jose's mouth and extinguishes it. Then she heads for the door.

"What about his diaper?" Rick calls out.

The nurse whirls around, disgusted with the past few minutes. "He be fine. He wait for morning nurse to change diaper." satisfied that she answered Rick's question, she exits.

Rick is fit to be tied. He looks at his roommate who's now in tears.

Rick covers Jose with his blankets as he tries figuring a way to take care of his problem. Rick returns to his table where he lights up a cigarette. He walks back to Jose's bed and puts the cigarette between Jose's lips. As soon as Jose realizes that he can start smoking again, his crying ceases.

"Don't worry my friend. I'll get you some fresh diapers."

Rick stands quietly for a moment, then gets an idea. Rick picks up Jose's phone and dials.

Valerie is delighted that Rick called her even though he doesn't wish to talk about himself or her. Rick's only interest right now is getting Jose some fresh diapers and the logical choice seems to be Valerie. Rick asks her to bring some of their baby's diapers to the hospital. He explains Jose's predicament to his wife, who is understandably shaken to hear how Jose's being treated by the hospital staff. Valerie promises to bring a box of diapers down to the hospital immediately.

§

Rick sleeps comfortably until the screaming from down the corridor awakens him. His immediate reaction is fright, but it dissipates as Rick realizes what the sound is. Rick looks around the room and sees Jose sleeping. Rick spots a new box of diapers on Jose's table and figures that the hospital probably broke down and supplied him with some diapers after all.

Rick remembers asking Valerie to bring some diapers down to the hospital and theorizes that Valerie hasn't arrived yet. Hoping to save her the trip, Rick phones his wife and is surprised to find her still home. Much to his dismay, Valerie informs him that she had in fact been to see him and deliver the diapers, but she was stopped by the nursing staff from seeing him due to the fact that visiting hours were over. Rick is appalled, but he doesn't blame his wife for not forcing the issue. After all, she was on a mission of mercy, more or less and he least they could have done was let Valerie visit him for a few fleeting moments.

Rick hangs up the phone and presses the call button. Ten minutes later, the head Korean nurse enters. The nurse notices that Jose is fast asleep and that Alexander is drenched in the light of his television, his eyes riveted to the screen. She quickly surmises that Rick summoned her and approaches his bed, shutting off his call button.

"What you want?" she asks indignantly. "Why not you sleep?"

Rick is already upset and he doesn't feel like submitting to her stupid questions when he's the one who wanted her there in the first place. "And what makes you think I'm not asleep?" Rick asks slyly hoping to throw her off guard. "Maybe I'm really sleeping and I'm just having a nightmare and you're the star."

"What you mean?" She displays a confused look. "You have nightmare?"

The nurse's comment causes Rick to shake his head in utter amazement.

"Never mind that. Just what do you know about telling my wife that she couldn't visit me when she was here before?"

"She only brings diaper for him," she indicates Jose, "not come to visit you."

Rick is aghast. "C'mon lady! You don't honestly expect me to believe that, do you? I just talked to my wife and she said you wouldn't let her visit me because visiting hours were over."

"She know when to visit you. She not allowed to visit after eight. You tell her."

"Look! In the first place, she only came here because you wouldn't get Jose some clean diapers like you're supposed to do, and as long as she was here doing your job for you, the least you could have done was let her in for a couple of minutes."

"All hospital have rules."

Rick can no longer hold back his frustration.

"Fuck the rules lady! And while you're at it, fuck yourself and your whole damn fucking staff!"

The nurse is obviously upset at Rick's tone and language.

"You no need talk like that," she cautions, shaking her finger at him.

"If the shoe fits," Rick yells out as the nurse turns around and walks out of his room ignoring his final comment.

Rick feels relieved that he unloaded on her. He's not sure if swearing was the proper tactic, but it sure felt good at the time. He's certain that repercussions are likely to follow, but right now he really doesn't care. If he has to swear and scream to get his point across and possibly get some action out of them then it will be worth it.

In spite of his exhaustion, Rick finds it impossible to sleep. He tosses and turns in bed for over three. hours, unable to keep his eyes shut for more than a few moments. He keeps thinking that someone in his room and he's not about to go to sleep if he suspects that someone's watching him. The screaming man seems to be in good voice tonight, Rick thinks, as the man yells out every few minutes making it harder and harder for him to rest.

After several fruitless hours, Rick finally decides that since he can't go to sleep, he might as well see what's on television. Much to his dismay, there isn't anything he cares to watch so he shuts off his set.

Rick stares around his room for a few minutes, but finds this task as boring as the current crop of programs on television. It would be different if there was a show on that he worked on or was going to work on, but because of his problem with Placidyls, he could hardly spell his name let alone write a good script for television. Rick realizes that his thoughts wandered back to his writing profession and he finds this distasteful. It depresses him to think of such things and he doesn't want to think about anything to do with writing because he would then begin thinking about his former partner, and that's the last thing he wants to think about. Besides, even the thought of Steve makes Rick's stomach churn with pain. Rick rubs his stomach, hoping that the sensation will subside. He thought this unpleasant feeling left forever when he told Steve to go his own way, but he knows that Steve will only have to go to his parent's side to get work. This infuriates Rick even though he knew this would happen as soon as he got rid of Steve.

The discomfort in his gut dissipates as Rick concentrates on the activities outside his door. Several nurses have congregated at the nurse's station to chatter incessantly in their native tongue. Every few moments, one or more of the nurses begin giggling and this disturbs Rick. How is he supposed to get some rest if the nurses make more noise than the patients, he wonders as he sits up in bed.

After debating the issue with himself for several minutes, Rick decides to see if the nurses will possibly let him sit out in the corridor. He feels that for right now, he'd be more comfortable out there even if he couldn't communicate with them. He knows they'll probably reject his idea due to the way he's treated them, but he's so bored right now, he's willing to try anything to break the monotony.

Rick puts on his bathrobe and heads out the door. several nurses spot him in his doorway, but they turn their attention back to their own affairs. Rick looks off to his left and sees two chairs against the wall. He slowly walks over to one of the chairs and plops himself down.

"Why not you in bed?" the head nurse asks.

Rick's first reaction is hostile, but because her attitude seems most affable, Rick manages to suppress his first remark. "I just couldn't sleep so I thought I could come out here for a while until I got tired enough to go back to bed."

"That okay if you no make no noise," she tells him as she joins the conversation with the other nurses.

Rick never heard Korean before coming to this hospital

and he tries listening, thinking that he'll be able to pick out at least a few key words. Unfortunately, one word sounds like another and Rick can't understand a thing.

The man down the corridor cries out, but the nurses fail to respond, almost as if they didn't hear a thing. Rick stares at the nurses thinking that they'll at least look down the corridor, but not one of them seems interested in the screaming man's plight.

Rick forgets about the man's cries as his own problem surfaces. As far as Rick's concerned, it's now or never and he makes a hasty retreat to the confines of his bathroom. This time, he's sure he'll perform even though he's gone through false alarms before.

After several exhausting minutes, Rick exits his bathroom a failure. He was sure he'd have some good news for the nurse when she came in to check his bodily functions. He tried as hard as humanly possible and now the only solution seems to be an enema. He'll probably consider it tomorrow if he doesn't blow up first.

Rick heads back to the chair in the corridor when he spots a familiar face sitting in the chair next to his. Carla's hands cover her face which is buried on her lap. Apparently, she is nauseous.

Rick is concerned with "Carla' s apparent illness. He's aware that she stole from him, but doesn't really blame her figuring that she probably has a lot of problems to contend with and isn't her normal self. After all, they're both in the same strange environment, subject to the same harsh conditions, so why should they exhibit normal behavior in such a place. "Are you all right?"

Carla is shocked to hear a man's voice so close to her. Her hands fall away from her face as she looks up and sees Rick. "Oh hi," she sluggishly greets him. "I didn't think anyone was here. How long you been sitting there?"

"I was here a while ago and I just came back. I couldn't sleep so I thought I'd break the monotony and come out here."

"I know what you mean. It's boring in my room and it smells."

Rick laughs as he thinks about Alexander's stench. He could easily top Carla's complaint using Alexander as proof, but that topic's too distasteful to discuss. "What are you doing in this unit? I thought you had a room in three."

"They're always moving me around to make room for a new addict or psycho. I don't really care though, because I get to meet all sorts of people and some of 'em help me along."

Rick displays his usual puzzled look.

"That way I get to find out who's all right and who isn't."

"How do you classify me?"

"You'd be okay if you weren't married." Carla laughs as she pats Rick's leg. "I'm just kidding."

Rick smiles knowingly. He remembers her first reaction when she found out he was married and she's not likely to treat him like he is single.

Their talk of drugs and hospital life lasts until sunrise. Rick still can't get over the fact that Carla checked in the hospital to get Placidyls instead of getting help for her problem.

"I'll quit taking drugs as soon as I'm ready," she says confidently, "but that won't happen for a while and I won't have to check into a hospital to do it either."

"I said the same thing a couple of weeks ago, and look where I am now."

"Everyone's different," she says smugly.

"Not to change the subject or anything, but I heard you were in my room today and you sort of borrowed a couple packs of cigarettes."

"Who told you that?"

"I don't see that it makes any difference and I don't really care to press the issue, but I would appreciate it if it didn't happen again."

"You accusing me of stealing your stupid smokes?" she asks indignantly.

"Look Carla, I don't want to make a big stink about it, but all I know is that ever since I've been here, you've been borrowing cigarettes from everyone in this place because you didn't have any money to buy your own," Rick indicates the pack of Marlboro cigarettes in Carla's hand," and now you've got a pack of Marlboros in your hand. Doesn't that strike you odd?"

"So what! I borrowed some money from a friend and bought the cigarettes from the machine in the admitting room."

"C'mon Carla, let's not argue about it."

"You really have a fucked attitude! I told you where I got I 'em and I don't give a shit whether or not you believe me!"

"Look, just forget it, but I want you to know that I don't appreciate people who go around looking through other people's things. Now I just want to drop it, okay?"

"Oh sure, just like that. You accuse me of stealing and now you just want to forget it, right? Well, I don't wanna drop it till you apologize."

"I'd gladly say I'm sorry if I thought I was wrong, but I don't think I am." Rick takes the pack of cigarettes from Carla's hand and shows her the bottom of the pack. "Now you claim you got these from a machine."

"That's right and I borrowed the money from a friend of mine."

"Yeah, but cigarettes that come from a machine always have a tax stamp on the bottom and I don't see anything like that, do you?" Rick holds the pack in front of Carla's face.

Carla becomes defensive. "I don't know what the hell

you're talking about and I don't care."

"It's pretty obvious this pack didn't come from a machine. It came out of my carton."

Carla stands up ready to leave as the man from down the corridor screams out.

"*Et me ot ah ere!*" the man cries out.

Carla seems concerned as she fastens her bathrobe closed.

"You know anything about that guy?"

"Not really, and from the sound of him, I don't think I want to."

"You interested in finding out?" Rick asks with a gleam in his eyes. He can tell Carla is still pretty upset with their previous conversation. "Listen, I'm sorry about what I said before and I'd just like to forget it okay?"

Carla looks at Rick harshly, then smiles. "Sure, why not." She offers Rick a cigarette out of her pack.

Rick takes a cigarette and lights it. Then he stares at the cigarette. "A Marlboro," he says glibly. "My favorite brand."

"*Et me ot ah ere!*" the man cries out again.

Rick and Carla exchange curious looks, then focus their attention on the nursing staff who seem interested only in their private conversation.

As Rick and Carla decide whether or not to investigate the man's room, Rick spots a blinking light above one of the doors in the unit.

"What's that light for?"

"It signals the nurses. It's connected to the button next to your bed."

"No wonder they never come when I call for them. They're too small to see up that far."

Carla laughs as Rick stares at the group of giggling nurses, waiting for them to spot the blinking light.

"Excuse me," Rick calls out interrupting their conversation,"

I think someone's calling you."

The nurses turn around and look at Rick, very annoyed that he interrupted them. Then one of the nurses, upset that she has to leave her friends, walks slowly into the patient's room.

"I hope that guy's not on the critical list."

Carla snickers at Rick's remark. "I hope I don't have to call them for something serious. I know you get more privacy here, but you could wind up dead before they bother answering your call. At least it's not like that on unit three."

"*Et me ot ah ere!*"

"Shall we have a look?" Rick suggests.

Carla motions towards the group of nurses huddled up by their station, giggling.

"Don't worry about them. If they say anything just ignore 'em. All they can do is tell us to go back to our rooms and if that happens we can get even with them and drive 'em crazy by pressing the call button and then when they come in, pretend that we weren't the ones who called." Rick smiles. He's pleased he finally came up with something to disturb the nurses.

Rick and Carla inch their way down the corridor as the man cries out. Rick's heart races as they approach the open door to the man's room. Carla attempts to step in front of Rick, but he holds her back thinking that he should be the first one to see what lies in the room. After all, Rick's been subjected to the strange cries ever since he's been there and it's only fair that he should be the first one to see just exactly who the man is and why he keeps pleading for help.

Rick cautiously takes a step into the room and sees a black man lying in his bed, bedsheets restraining his arms and legs.

"*Et me ot ah ere!*"

Rick instinctively jumps back, bumping into Carla. He doesn't know what to make of this strange man tied to his bed.

He looks to be in his late twenties or early thirties. His frail body seems out of proportion with his large hands and feet. Rick guesses that this six-foot man probably weighs about one hundred pounds, that is of course if you include his bushy head of jet black hair which makes Alexander's hair look like it was just shampooed.

The man begins pulling on his bonds and he sways his body back and forth in an attempt to break free. At first Rick suspects that the man's having a seizure because of his incredible strength, but he quickly dismisses this thought when he sees that the man is very much awake.

"I wan go ome!"

Rick and Carla exchange confused looks as they wonder what the man's doing in this place with his hands and feet tied to his bed. They talk silently to each other as the strange man throws his body from side to side, causing the bed to bounce up and down.

"Et me ot ah ere!"

"I wonder why he can't talk right?"

"Did you ever know a wounded animal that could speak English? "Rick comments as he notices the screaming man's roommate sitting quietly on the edge of his own bed. "Excuse me sir, but do you know what's the matter with this guy?"

Rick and Carla watch the man as he inhales on his cigarette, apparently choosing to ignore Rick's question.

"He looks like death warmed over," Carla tells Rick as they both stare at the elderly man who resembles a corpse.

"I'll bet he can't even hear us. That's probably why they stuck him in here with this screaming banshee."

"Yeah," Carla says laughing. "I'll bet he was fine before they put him in here with this guy."

Rick and Carla continue to speculate on both men's conditions as the head Korean nurse enters the room and stands behind them with her hands planted firmly on her tiny hips.

"What you do here?"

Rick and Carla are startled.

"Why ah, we just came in because we heard him screaming and we thought he needed help."

Carla nods her head in agreement.

"You not allowed in room except own."

"What's wrong with him anyway? Why is he tied down to his bed and how come that other guy won't answer me?"

"You no need know. It our business not yours," she tells Rick as she pushes Rick and Carla out into the corridor.

"Is it all right if we go back to our chairs for a while?"

"That okay, but you no go in patient's room or you get trouble."

Rick and Carla return to their chairs opposite the nurse's station.

"I'd still like to know what's the matter with that guy. I don't know why they just don't tell me.

"I wouldn't worry about him if I were you. Personally, the only person I give a shit about is myself and my friends."

"Where does that leave me?"

"I'll let you know later, provided you don't talk about your wife."

Rick doesn't particularly care for Carla's attitude and he doesn't like being told what he can talk about. However, he's aware that Carla's giving him a choice. She'll be his friend provided that he doesn't mention Valerie, a prospect which Rick finds distasteful. After all, why shouldn't he talk about the woman he loves. Nevertheless, after a few moments of silent pondering, Rick decides to go along with Carla's request figuring that he should make an effort to get along with as many patients as possible.

"That's not the fairest proposition I've heard, but I guess I'll go along with you. If you want, I'll even call her and tell her not to visit me anymore." Rick smirks letting Carla know that her demands are a bit ridiculous.

Carla gets the message. "You don't have to go that far. I guess if I was married to you, I'd break my ass to come see you no matter what anyone else says. So just forget what I said, okay?" She smiles.

"Forget what?" Rick asks facetiously.

"Very funny," Carla replies sarcastically as she watches one of the nurses changing the calendar on the wall. "Shit! This month's almost half over."

Rick looks at the calendar noticing that today is the twelfth.

"What's the matter?" Carla asks noticing that Rick's deep in thought.

"Shit! Today's Valerie's birthday and I totally forgot about it!"

"You mean you didn't get her a present or even a card?"

"I would have, but I forgot because I'm so hung up on my own problems. I never forgot before and I don't think being here is a good enough excuse."

"I don't know why you're so upset. If your wife doesn't understand that you don't have time to worry about her birthday, then I think there's something wrong with her."

"Yeah, well she'll pretend that it doesn't matter, but somewhere down the line when we're arguing about some shit, she'll bring it up for added ammunition. That's just the way she is. Besides, I don't know why I'm working myself up like this. She obviously doesn't expect me to get her a present while I'm in here or even a card for that matter. I just wish there was something I could do besides wish her happy birthday over the phone."

"How about a pass?"

"Huh! What kind of pass?"

"You know, a pass to go home for a few hours. I don't know what kind of condition you're in or what stuff they're giving you, but I don't see how it would hurt if you asked."

"Who do I ask?"

"Ask your doctor and tell him why you want a pass and if he says no, keep after him till he changes his mind."

"That's fine, but I don't know who to ask."

Carla reaches for Rick's hand and examines his hospital band. "You've got Dr. Berger too," she says holding out her hospital band for him to see.

"Yeah, I haven't seen him yet, but I still feel like we're going steady." Rick's aware he already used this joke and is happy to see that Carla is amused.

"I know what you mean. I don't think we'll ever see him unless we croak or something."

"In that case, I hope I never see him."

"Have you seen any doctor more than once?"

"Sure," Rick says indicating inside his room. "My roommate's doctor's been in to see him a few times."

"Talk to him and try and get a pass."

"What if he isn't my doctor?"

"It doesn't matter. Every doctor who comes to this place can do anything for the inmates even though he's not taking care of them."

Rick's spirits are lifted. "I've got nothing to lose," he says philosophically.

"And while you're out, maybe you can look around your place for some extra Placidyls for me"

Rick looks at Carla suspiciously.

"C'mon Rick, if it wasn't for me, you'd never know about the pass and the least you could do is bring me back anything you find. You know, like a reward." Carla gets up and heads towards her room. "I'll even pay you for it."

"I thought you didn't have any money."

"Who said anything about money," she says working up a sexy smile.

Rick heads back into his room and plops himself on his bed. He closes his eyes, confident that he'll be able to get a couple hours of sleep before breakfast arrives.

Rick's thoughts wander through everything that's happened to him in the hospital. He remembers how scared he was about admitting himself, but he's glad he did despite the screw up with his medication. He's even looking forward to the therapy sessions, deciding that he kind of likes participating and learning about other people's problems. Suddenly, it dawns on him that he really likes being in this hospital. He feels comfortable here even though he still has to contend with the incompetent nurses, a smelly roommate and another roommate who might very well be deceased if he wasn't there.

Just as Rick begins to doze off, he hears an ominous sound coming from across the room. Rick doesn't recognize the sound at first and doesn't catch on that the familiar sound is Jose. Rick finally realizes that Jose is choking and he instinctively springs up and sees his roommate gagging. Rick bolts out of bed and races over to Jose's side of the room. Unfortunately, Rick fails to negotiate around Jose's table and he accidently wraps his leg around it. He cries out in pain as he falls onto the floor next to Jose's bed. Despite Rick's own agony, he manages to prop himself up, rip the tongue depressor off the wall and jam it into his roommate's mouth. Rick watches Jose's seizure for a moment before pressing the nurse call button and heading back towards his own bed.

As Rick reaches his bed, he collapses and falls onto the floor.

Hours later, one of the nurses from the new shift finds

Rick on the floor. She awakens Rick and helps him back into his bed.

"My leg's killing me!" Rick informs the nurse as she covers him with a blanket.

"I shouldn't wonder after spending the night on the hard floor," she tells him as she heads for the door.

"Wait a second," Rick calls out causing the nurse to return to his bedside.

"You don't understand. I hurt my leg when I went over to jam a tongue depressor in his mouth because he was having a seizure. I slammed it into his table really hard and it really hurts bad." Rick uncovers his leg and tries lifting it, but stops as the pain overtakes him. "Ouch!"

The nurse removes Rick's hand from his leg and covers it up. "If it hurts I don't think you should be lifting it up like that."

"Can you give me something for the pain?"

"Not unless pain medication is on your chart," she says coldly as she walks over to Jose's bed and picks up a tongue depressor lying next to Jose's head. "Why did you take it upon yourself to use this instead of calling in one of the nurses?"

"There wasn't time. He was choking to death and I had to do something, but after I put it into his mouth I pressed the button for the nurses to come."

"Well, there's no record of his supposed seizure on his chart." She picks up the call button and depresses it. Then she exits the room and stands outside the doorway staring up at the light.

"Is it blinking?" Rick calls out.

The nurse walks out of sight without answering.

"Shit!" Rick comments to himself in disgust as he gets out of bed, presses the call button and heads out of his room stopping outside his doorway. He looks up and sees that the light above his door isn't working. "Excuse me please," Rick yells out to the nurse sitting at the nurse's station.

"Yes, what is it?"

Her concerned attitude throws Rick for a loop due to the fact that he expected her to be hostile like everyone else. "Well, I really hurt my leg when I helped my roommate with his seizure last night and I need some medication for the pain."

"Aren't you the one who's being treated for Placidyl addiction?"

"Yes."

"I'm afraid we can only treat you for that problem. If you need further medical attention, I suggest you talk to your doctor when he makes his rounds."

"But I haven't seen one doctor since I've been here and I don't think I can wait for one to show up."

"You just go back to bed and I'll send your doctor in when he arrives."

"But I just told you don't know who my doctor is."

"Which doctor's name is on your wrist band?"

"Dr. Berger, but I haven't seen—"

The nurse interrupts," When Dr. Berger gets here I'll send him in okay? Now get back to bed and try not to think about any pain medication or your injury. Your mind can act as a powerful pain pill if you'll let it."

Rick heads back to his bed disgusted with the whole incident. "What the fuck's the matter with everybody in this place," Rick asks himself as he cautiously climbs back into bed. Then Rick gets an idea and picks up his telephone.

As the phone rings, Rick decides that he won't say anything to Valerie about her birthday. He prefers thinking that when he gets his pass, he'll surprise her and she won't care that he failed to wish her a happy birthday.

Anyway, wishing his wife a nice birthday is the last thing

on his mind right now. All he's concerned with is the agonizing pain in his leg and he needs relief as soon as possible.

"Hi honey, it's me. Yeah, yeah, listen. You know that bottle in my desk with one pill in it, well bring it to me as soon as you can. Yeah, it's a Percodan, so what? I know I've had it for over six months, but I need it Because I really screwed up my leg last night when I was trying to help Jose and they won't give me anything for the pain and they said I'd have to ask my doctor, but so far, I haven't seen him and my leg's killing me. "Rick listens to Valerie's harsh words concerning his abstention from pills, but he doesn't care for her words of wisdom. "Look!" he shouts into the phone, "just bring it to me and I promise I'll only take it if I absolutely have to. I just want it here as a sort of security blanket. Just bring it, okay? Good bye," he says in a now cheerful tone, happy with the fact that in a couple of hours, he'll be able to get relief from the pain and hopefully his doctor, whoever he is, will prescribe some more pain medication for his leg.

Rick can hardly wait for Valerie to arrive. He keeps looking at his open door expecting her to enter even though he knows she won't be there for a couple of hours. He catches himself doing it again and realizes he's doing it due to his excitement at the prospect of taking his emergency Percodan which he's been saving for over six months. He'll be fine as soon as he takes the pill, he thinks to himself as he stares at his open door hoping that Valerie will show up any minute.

Rick turns his attention towards Jose and thinks to himself that if it wasn't for his seizure, he wouldn't be in such terrible pain now, and he wouldn't need to take a Percodan. "Damn you Jose," Rick mumbles under his breath, "it's all your fault!"

CHAPTER FOURTEEN

Rick awakens as the meal attendant enters his room and distributes three breakfast trays. Rick's disappointed to see the meal attendant, thinking at first that Va1erie had arrived with his emergency Percodan. However, Rick forgets about the pain in his leg when he sees the rotten banana and corn flakes on his tray. He pushes his tray aside in disgust deciding to wait for lunch. Rick looks across the room and spots an identical breakfast on Jose's tray.

"Wait a second," Rick calls out stopping the attendant by the door. "He can't eat that stuff."

"I only, work here man. Everybody gets the same food around here unless they're a diabetic or something."

"Yeah, but he's not allowed to eat solids."

"Well, that's what they gave him so he'd better eat it or starve," he states on his way out the door.

"Don't worry Jose," Rick yells across the room to his wide-eyed friend, "I'll call the nurse and have her bring you the right breakfast."

Jose shakes his head negatively as he tries to speak, and for the first time he is able to make himself understood despite his weakened vocal cords. "I'm not hungry," Jose says in a wheezing tone.

Rick is astonished that Jose's finally able to speak even though he sounds like someone who's choking to death as his words kind of squeak out.

"Save your voice," Rick cautions as Jose takes a drink of juice from his baby bottle.

As Rick stares at Jose, the only sound he hears is Jose sucking on his bottle. It saddens Rick as he listens to Jose drinking in this manner. He can't possibly, fathom being forced to wear diapers and having to rely on a baby bottle and liquid meals in order to survive.

The sound of Alexander changing his television from one channel to another interrupts Rick's train of thought. He turns his attention to Alexander and then back to Jose. Even though Rick's aware Alexander has problems too, he still holds him in contempt. It's as if both men have what the other wants. Jose would love to trade bodies with Alexander, and Alexander probably wouldn't mind. After all, he seems content to stay in bed the rest of his life and not do anything for himself except for an occasional trip to the bathroom. If this were at all possible, both men would have what they want. Rick simply can't understand why anyone would want to give up on himself. Oh sure, there have been times when he wanted to throw in the towel himself, but he never did. It's too easy to give up altogether, but that's apparently what Alexander has decided for himself and it's obvious he's not willing to let anyone help him.

"How long you think you'll be here?" Rick asks Alexander.

"I hope they let me out today," Alexander comments in his usual sotto voice.

Rick gets the impression that Alexander's even too lazy to talk, but as long as he answered his first question, Rick will try and coax more information from him. "Are you looking forward to going home?"

"I'm not going home. I'm going to a convalescent hospital. I don't want to go home."

"Why not? Don't you wanna get better?"

"I just want to go to the convalescent home and let them take care of me." Alexander's tone changes. "Now leave me alone!" he pleads.

Rick's not ready to give up. "I never knew anybody like you. All you want to do is stay in a hospital for the rest of your life and let everyone take care of you and the only thing you'll have to do is breathe." Rick pauses for a moment expecting Alexander to reply.

Alexander ignores Rick and turns over in his bed preferring to face the wall.

Rick doesn't like being ignored and his reaction is anything but pleasant. "I bet you wouldn't even care if you died," Rick yells harshly. "It'd be a real shame to waste a perfectly good body when there's someone in this room who'd give anything to trade places with you. With his brain and your body there's no telling what he could do, but at least he'd have that chance. And even you'd be happy. You wouldn't mind being paralyzed because you act like you are anyway and it would match your mind. Just think of it, you could be the happiest vegetable in the whole world and you could get into the Guinness Book of Records as the only person whose sole goal in life is two scoops of ice cream."

"Leave me alone," Alexander moans as he continues facing the wall.

"I'll leave you alone, as soon as you let them wash your smelly body."

"Don't talk to me," Alexander says in a threatening tone.

"And what are you gonna do about it?" Rick says hoping to get a rise out of him.

"Just leave me alone!"

"You heard my deal," Rick tells him as Dr. Wang enters the room and approaches Jose's bed.

Dr. Wang sees Jose asleep deciding not to awaken him.

"How are you, doctor?" Rick calls out.

Dr. Wang looks at Rick and silently acknowledges him.

"He hasn't been sleeping too long, but I'll bet he's pretty exhausted. He's had a couple of seizures."

"I'll come back and see him later." Dr. Wang heads for the door.

"Excuse me, but could I talk with you for a minute?"

Dr. Wang approaches Rick's bed and takes a seat in the hospital chair. "How you feeling today?"

"Much better thanks, but I was wondering if you could do me a favor. See, I just remembered that today's my wife's birthday and I thought maybe I could leave for a while so I could take her out to dinner or something."

"You can't stay out all night, but I don't see why you can't have a nice time with her for a few hours. But no more than three hours and I want you back before ten."

Rick beams with delight. "That's great! We'll just go out to dinner and then I'll come right back."

Dr. Wang stands up and heads for the door. "You just let the nurse know one hour before you leave."

"Thank you," Rick calls out as Dr. Wang exits the room. Then Rick remembers another matter he wishes to discuss and he shouts out his name.

Dr. Wang reappears in the doorway. "You forget to ask me something?"

"Yes, I did. There are a couple of things. First, they keep giving Jose whole food to eat when he can only eat through a straw or his bottle. And secondly, the light's broken outside the door, but I don't think it matters because they never answer us when we call."

"I'll go to the kitchen right now and see about his meals and don't worry about the light. I'll tell the maintenance man after I go to the kitchen."

"Thank you. I really appreciate it."

Dr. Wang smiles affably. "Don't thank me. I'm the one who should be thanking you for taking care of Jose and being his friend."

Rick knows he should be humble concerning his magnanimous gestures, so he doesn't respond like someone who wants to be patted on the back. "I'm sure he'd do the same for me if situations were reversed."

Dr. Wang smiles and exits as Valerie walks into the room. From the sour look on her face, Rick knows that something's bothering her and he wants to find out what it is before she goes to pieces.

"Hi honey, what's wrong?"

"They almost didn't let me in because they said you weren't allowed visitors."

Rick is infuriated. "Who said that?"

"I don't know except that one of the nurses left a memo in your chart and if it wasn't for that Hawaiian guy in the admitting office, I'd be on my way home. Valerie takes a tissue from her purse and wipes her eyes dry before kissing Rick.

"I bet Doris wrote that note."

"Who's she?"

"She's the head nurse who looks like a dried-up prune. I bet she remembers the Great Depression of the twenties as the time she started collecting social security for her old age."

"Always with the jokes," she says sarcastically. "You must be feeling pretty good." Then Valerie decides to drop a hint about her birthday. "I wonder how many years before I start collecting social security."

Rick realizes that Valerie's trying to hint about today being her birthday. He doesn't want to let on that he knows what she's talking about no matter how upset she gets. he's positive she'll forget all about his temporary loss of memory when he surprises her later that night. Rick decides to change the subject to the Percodan he asked her to bring.

"Did you bring the Percodan?"

Valerie reaches into her purse and removes his prescription bottle, handing it to Rick. "Yes, I did," she says insipidly," but I think you should try and get along without it."

Rick drops the bottle into his grip. "I'll only take it if I absolutely have to, but I just want it here as sort of a security blanket. And if I do end up taking it, I don't want any flak from you because I won't take it unless I really have to, okay?"

Valerie remains silent, preferring to think carefully about her answer knowing she'll probably start an argument if she says what she's thinking.

Jose interrupts Valerie's silent pondering by balling Rick's name. Valerie hears Jose's strange wheezing sound and hesitates turning around.

"Turn around honey and meet Jose."

Valerie forces a smile as she turns and spots Jose lying in his bed sporting a broad smile and waving at her. Then Jose looks at Rick as he indicates towards his mouth.

"What does he want?" Valerie inquires.

Rick lowers his voice. "He wants me to go over and help him smoke." Rick directs his attention at Jose. "C'mon Jose, you can wait till my wife leaves."

Hearing this, Jose's smile turns sour.

"I'll help him have a cigarette Rick," Valerie says as she heads for Jose's bed and lights one of his cigarettes which she places between his lips. Valerie sees Jose's breakfast tray on the table and removes the lid discovering his uneaten meal. "Do you need help with your breakfast?" she asks as Jose takes another puff on the cigarette.

Jose shakes his head from side to side.

"They keep giving him the wrong food, honey. He can't eat anything solid and the hospital hasn't gotten used to liquefying his meals yet."

Valerie seems annoyed as she helps Jose with the cigarette. "What's he supposed to do in the meantime?"

"Hey don't get mad at me! I'm on your side. I even filled his bottle with Coke."

"Huh?"

Jose realizes that Valerie doesn't fully realize his plight and he holds up his baby bottle for her to see. Then Jose sticks the nipple in his mouth and he begins sucking out the fluid.

Valerie is stunned. She doesn't know just how to react as she watches Jose sucking on the nipple between puffs on the cigarette. She's mesmerized by this strange sight as Rick surreptitiously motions that she shouldn't stare at Jose.

Valerie helps Jose take one last puff on his cigarette as Jose writes a message on his pad of paper. Then he hands the pad to her. Valerie reads to herself.

THANK YOU FOR LETTING ME HAVING ONE CIGARETTE BECAUSE I NEED HELP SMOKING A CIGARETTE BECAUSE MY HANDS DO NOT WORK SO GOOD AND I MIGHT START MY BED ON FIRE BECAUSE I NEED YOU TO HELP ME SMOKE A CIGARETTE.

Valerie sets the pad down and smiles at Jose affectionately. "My pleasure Jose."

Jose smiles back as he holds up his empty bottle.

"Would you like something else to drink?"

Jose nods as he indicates the carton of milk on his breakfast tray.

"No problem." Valerie fills the bottle with milk and hands it back to Jose.

Jose positions the bottle on the side of his pillow and then rests his head next to it.

Valerie heads back to her husband's side of the room as Maggie enters.

"Hi folks," she says, approaching. Rick's bed. "Why Rick, you didn't tell me you had such a lovely wife."

Rick introduces Valerie to Maggi, informing his wife that Maggie's the only truly professional nurse in the entire hospital.

"Don't believe him honey," Maggie tells Valerie. "Your husband's probably done more for Jose over there than anyone else has for the past couple of years."

"Well, I can't very well ignore him."

"Why not? Everyone else seems to be doing a good job, especially your roommate over there." Maggie points towards Alexander.

"That reminds me. He had a seizure a while ago and I could have sworn his legs moved and I know he's paralyzed and all that, but I'm sure of what I saw even though I know I must have been imagining things."

"Sounds like you were in the throngs of a dilemma."

Rick is more than anxious to hear Maggie's opinion. He knows she can set him straight. "Well, did he move them, or didn't he?"

"Oh, he moved them all right, but that doesn't mean he isn't paralyzed anymore. It happens to a lot of people like Jose when they're having a seizure. We're not exactly sure what causes it except that we know the brain sends out orders to his paralyzed nerves and for some reason it's like his body temporarily forgets that it's paralyzed. And don't ask me to repeat what I just said because I'm not really sure of it myself."

"Well, at least now I know I wasn't hallucinating and I really saw his legs moving."

Maggie decides to change the subject. After all, she's tired of hospital talk. "You two started a family yet?"

"One little boy so far, and as soon as Rick's all better. we're planning on another."

"We are?" Rick's reaction is one of astonishment, but his words are hardly convincing.

"Very funny!" Valerie comments sarcastically as she sits down on her husband's bed.

"When do you think Rick will be able to go home Maggie?"

"You'll have to ask his doctor. Personally, I hope he stays for a few more days so I can take it easy around here."

"No chance," Rick tells her adamantly, "I'll be on my way home as soon as they'll let me."

"I know I'll be sorry to see you go, but Jose will miss you more and so will the nurses who are supposed to be taking care of him." Maggie directs her words at Valerie. "I don't know how we'd ever contend with Jose without your husband being here. He's practically Jose's personal physician, always checking on him to see if he's all right or if he needs anything. It's a totally magnanimous gesture on his part and I can't think or anyone we'd rather have in the same room with Jose."

Valerie fakes her surprise. "You can't be talking about my Rick!"

Maggie laughs. "I know it's hard to believe, but Jose thinks of Rick like you and I think of our gynecologists."

"I think I've been insulted," Rick says good naturedly.

"Does Jose have a lot of visitors?" Valerie whispers.

"As far as I know, no one has ever called him. I don't think he knows too many people. I think his only friend is your husband."

"And Rick needs all the friends he can get."

"Hey, wait a second. Did you come here to visit me or insult me?" Valerie pinches Rick's cheek. "It's just a little joke darling."

"Don't be so harsh on him Valerie. Why yesterday I heard

him yelling at a friend of his who came to visit him."

"Believe me, that was no friend."

"I kind of gathered that judging from the tone of the conversation."

"Who came to see you?" Valerie curiously asks.

"Steve."

"Don't tell me you finally told him off?" Valerie asks with an obvious sense that she's hit it on the nose.

"Wait a second honey, let me start at the beginning before you blow the ending. I think Maggie would like to hear about it too."

"I have a feeling this is gonna be good," Maggie comments as she picks up Rick's pack of cigarettes. "May I have one?"

"Be my guest." Rick lights the cigarette for Maggie.

"Anyway, it started a few years ago, I decided that I wanted to write television, but no one would buy my scripts. They didn't care how good they were and they didn't even want to read them. It was a Catch-22 situation.

They kept telling me they only use writers who had sold scripts and they didn't bother with new writers who hadn't sold anything. Anyway, I had a friend whose parents were producers and they kept telling me they really liked my scripts, but they wouldn't help me sell them to anyone until I convinced their idiot son to become my partner. I never liked Steve because he was one of those frustrated football jocks who was too fat and stupid to play football or for that matter, he was even too dumb to watch a game. But now he was my partner and suddenly his parents started getting us connected and we sold scripts to different shows. Steve never really helped me write the scripts, but I put his name on them anyway and our partnership flourished. But it got to a point where I really hated to see his lousy fat face and I started getting an ulcer which I guess got aggravated every time I saw him or when I talked to him on the phone. He was one of those guys who'd go to a restaurant with a legal pad hoping that people would ask him what he was doing and he could say he was a writer working on a television script. That's where he did his only writing and I just got tired of writing scripts by myself and putting his name on them and when he showed up here, he didn't come to see how I was doing, he only came here because we were supposed to write a script and I told him I couldn't work on it in here, but he didn't care. He only came here hoping I'd help him write it because he couldn't do it by himself. And that's it. I told him where to go and I broke off our partnership." Rick takes in a deep breath. "I'm out of breath," he gasps.

"That's quite a story," Maggie comments," but aren't you gonna have problems when you try and go it alone?"

"I thought about that, but I don't really care. Steve's parents will probably do their best to blacklist me, but they can't keep me off every television show even though they know an awful lot of people who'll do whatever they tell them."

Valerie seems relieved to hear this, but she's concerned nevertheless. "I know you've thought about getting rid of Steve for a long time and I hope it's worth it and they don't screw up your career."

Rick displays an air of confidence. "Well, it may set me back for a couple of years, but they can't keep me out of the business forever. And if Steve tries to go out on his own, the guys in power won't be fooled and they'll figure out who the real writer of the team was. Besides, I knew when I teamed up with him that I'd only stay with him for as long as humanly possible and I think I went beyond that."

Maggie puts out her cigarette and heads for the door. "Well if I don't see your name on TV for a couple of years, at least I'll know what happened. Nice meeting you Valerie."

"Same here."

Maggie smiles as Valerie and Rick hold hands. "I'll never understand how a guy like you got hold of such an attractive lady," Maggie facetiously comments as she exits.

"I'm exhausted!" Valerie says as she lies down next to her husband as Doris Rayburn enters.

"Get off that bed this instant!" she barks.

"She is not hurting anything," Rick replies defensively.

"That's all right honey," Valerie says as she gets off the bed and sits down in the chair.

Doris watches Valerie, displaying her usual sour expression. "You'" have to leave now and the next time you visit, you'll have to confine your activities to the visitor's room like everyone else. This patient needs his rest and having you around keeps him from getting it."

Valerie gets up and picks up her purse. "I'll talk to you later." Valerie kisses Rick.

Doris doesn't like what she sees. "Here, here! Let's have none of that."

Rick is appalled. "What the hell's the matter with you? She wasn't doing anything and as long as I'm following what I'm supposed to be doing, it's none of your business who sits on my bed or who comes to visit me."

"I see I'll have to get an attendant," Doris threatens as she heads into the corridor, standing within view. "Nurse," she calls out," would you send an attendant in and clear the room of all visitors."

"I'd better go honey before the wicked witch decides to hit me with her broom"

"Sorry honey. I'll call you later, all right?"

"Don't call for an hour. I'm stopping at my mother's first." Valerie approaches the door and turns around to face her husband.

"I love you Valerie."

"I love you too." Valerie heads out the door. She walks past Doris, who's standing near the doorway with her hands on her hips and her nose up in the air. Doris gives Valerie a vitriolic look as she passes.

Then Valerie stops and stares directly at Doris. "No wonder so many people in here are sick. One look at you and they need medical attention!" Valerie heads down the corridor delighted that she had the last word with Doris.

Doris is dumbfounded. She never expected that such a pretty lady would spew forth such venom.

Rick's eyes are. riveted on the door hoping Doris will come back so he can properly tell her where to go. Then Sherri enters the room, sporting her usual cheerful expression.

"Therapy starts in a few minutes Rick." She turns to leave.

Rick forgets about the events of the past few minutes, focusing his attention on Sherri's statement. "Aren't you gonna walk over there with me?"

"I don't think you need me anymore for that."

"You're right," 'Rick says getting out of bed," I don't."

Rick gets dressed in a hurry and heads for the door. Then he remembers something and returns to his bedside for his grip. He reaches inside and removes the pill bottle containing his last Percodan. Rick examines the pill and prepares to take it, but he has second thoughts and drops the pill back into the bottle before throwing it back into his grip. The pain in Rick's leg isn't as bad as before and he decides to save the pill in case he needs it later. After all, if he takes it now, he'll have nothing to take later if another unfortunate accident should befall him. It's not as if he doesn't need a pain pill right now, it's just that for now, he can go without it.

Rick heads for unit three sporting a broad smile. He's proud of himself for not taking the Percodan, figuring that he must be getting better.

Anyway, he'll be able to test himself again when therapy's over and he returns to his room. He's positive he won't need it, but just in case he does, at least it will still be there.

CHAPTER FIFTEEN

Rick walks down the corridor approaching unit three. He's curious how therapy will be today. Will it be interesting with a lot of weird problems being aired, or will it just be a boring session where no one will want to open themselves up to public criticism. At any rate, Rick's looking forward to it, hoping for the best.

As Rick nears unit three's doors, a nurse from unit two exits and sees Rick coming her way.

"Excuse me, but you're Rick Brown, aren't you?"

"Ever since I've been here. Why?"

The nurse looks at her clipboard and then focuses her attention back on Rick. "My records indicate that you haven't had a bowel movement yet. Is that still true?"

Rick has the distinct feeling that if doesn't reply with the right answer, she'll schedule him for an enema. "It used to be true, but not anymore."

The nurse looks at him askance "Is that a yes or a no?"

"Look, I'm not gonna lie to you, but I will tell you that I know I'll be able to go today and if I don't I'll tell you and you can give me an enema. All right?"

The nurse begins writing on her chart. "I'll just make a notation here and if you should become successful, I don't want you to flush your toilet until one of the nurses confirms that you indeed had a bowel movement."

The idea of not flushing the toilet until he lets one of the nurses check his success disturbs Rick. At least he was able to buy himself some time. "Anything you say," he tells her as he walks through the doors and into unit three.

Rick stands by the doorway and looks around. He focuses his attention on the therapy room, noticing that people are just now entering. Rick looks at the clock above the nurse's station and sees that he has a few minutes before therapy is due to start. Then he spots the pay phone on the wall and he decides to make a call. Unfortunately, Rick's pockets are empty and he realizes he'll have to borrow some phone change. Otherwise, he'll have to go back to his room to make the call and by the time he gets back, he won't be allowed in the therapy room.

Rick borrows a dime from one of the nurses after explaining that he'll just call the operator and make his call collect. This way he can return the money in just a few minutes.

Rick telephones his sister and explains his situation. At first Marsha is hesitant to comply, figuring that Rick shouldn't leave the hospital until he's cured. But Rick persists and Marsha finally agrees with his plan.

Rick wants Marsha to pick him up at the hospital and take him to a Marina restaurant where Valerie will be with her girlfriend. After Rick and Valerie celebrate her birthday, Rick will have Valerie take him back to the hospital before his three hours are up.

Rick hangs up the phone, delighted with the prospect of leaving the hospital to be with his wife.

Group therapy is crowded. Dr. Iris Whitehead is happy with the turnout, but she's particularly delighted to see several new faces in the group.

Neil and Carla enter the room holding hands. Everyone stares at the couple as they wonder out loud what the two have been up to in Neil's room with the door closed. Neil and Carla look around the room, but can't find two vacant chairs next to each other.

"Just sit down anywhere," Dr. Whitehead shouts.

Neil and Carla take their seats on the table next to Rick's chair.

Dr. Whitehead directs the attendant to close the door before she starts the session.

"For those of you new to the group, I'm Dr. Whitehead. If I don't speak to you during the course of this session, I'll probably see you later. And if you have any problems or questions regarding your stay here, don't hesitate to seek me out and if you can't find me, feel free to talk with any one of the qualified people you see here. Now I know the rest of you are tired of hearing the same ground rules over and over, but for the sake of our new arrivals I'd like to go over them once again. "Dr. Whitehead notices that Neil and Carla are on the verge of exchanging their tongues. "Neil and Carla! Please restrain your extracurricular activities till you're discharged!"

Neil and Carla disengage and stare innocently at Dr. Whitehead.

Dr. Whitehead shoots them a harsh glance, then returns to her speech. "As I was saying, the purpose of this group is to talk about our feelings openly and if anyone thinks they can offer some encouraging words that might help benefit someone else, they are encouraged to speak up. Now I know It's a pretty scary experience, but we've all gone through it and no one's out to get you."

"I'm not sayin' nothin'!" the new black patient interrupts.

Dr. Whitehead gives the black man a stern look. "If you have something to say, I suggest you wait until It's your turn to speak. Then you can say whatever you want."

"Don't be askin' me no questions because I ain't sayin'nothin'!" he says indignantly.

Dr. Whitehead doesn't wish to exchange words with the black man. Instead she directs her attention across the room where Sue is sitting. Sue looks like she's mad at something or someone and she refuses to look in Dr. Whitehead's direction. Sue prefers staring blankly at the cast on her hand.

"Why don't we start with you Sue," Dr. Whitehead says in an upbeat tone. "How: are you feeling today? I notice you have a cast on your arm. Would you mind sharing with the rest of us how that came to be? "Dr. Whitehead's manner of speech borders on the subservient.

"Leave me alone!" Sue pleads, looking down at the floor.

Dr. Whitehead pursues the matter undaunted. "C'mon Sue. I can't let you stew in your own pot of resentment forever. Why not tell the group how you broke your hand and, who knows, maybe you'll feel better?"

A couple of patients try coaxing Sue to let loose with an explanation. Finally, she relents.

"My hand got broken Because I punched the wall."

"Did you want to break your hand? "Dr. Whitehead asks, hoping sue will open up.

"That's right I wanted it busted!"

"You know Sue, yesterday you said you wanted to break your hand by hitting it into the wall, but what I want to know now is, do you feel better now that your hand is broken?"

"No I don't t I feel worse."

"What do you feel like doing now?"

"I feel like punching the wall with my good hand till It's all bloody and broken."

"Why on earth would you want to do that to yourself?"

"1 because I don't like myself! Now leave me alone!"

Rick decides to join in. "Sue, you're obviously very upset by something and maybe if you open up you'll see we're here to help and maybe someone's been where you are right now and they might have the right words to help you."

"You don't know anything about how I feel. No one does, so just shut up your fuckin' face and leave me alone!" Sue looks at everyone in the room. "All of you, just leave me alone!"

"C'mon Sue, don't shut us out," Neil says compassionately. "I don't know about the rest of the people in here, but I've been where you are and I know where you 're coming from."

"You don't know anything about me. My problems are my own and I don't want to tell a bunch of sick people about them!"

Neil doesn't take offense at Sue's belligerence. "You're not gonna shut us out by insulting us. The purpose of these sessions is so we can help each other, but if you won't let us help you then I don't think we should waste so much time with you. If you'll look around, you'll see that everyone seems interested in helping and if they weren't, they'd stay in their rooms where they could stare at the walls."

"I don't want anyone's help, especially yours!"

Dr. Whitehead interrupts. "That's enough Neil. I think we should move along to someone else while we still have time and if sue feels like sharing her problems and trusting us, then we can deal with her again. But for now, let's move on.

As Dr. Whitehead studies her notes preparing to go on to the next patient, Sue stands up and walks towards the door. Dr. Whitehead looks up, surprised to see Sue racing past her.

"The session's not over Sue," she says calmly.

"I don't care. I'm going! I'm not gonna stay another second and I'm never coming back to this room!"

"Why do you feel the need to take out your hostilities on these people? You're not the only one with problems, but you seem to be the only one who prefers running away from them."

Sue looks at Dr. Whitehead caustically. "I refuse to stay in the same room as him," she says pointing at Charlie, who is sitting next to Dr. Whitehead," and if he comes near me and tries hugging me again I'll kill him dead!"

Dr. Whitehead is shocked with Sue's latest burst of hostility. "What have you got against Charlie?" she asks, noticing that Charlie is staring at Sue displaying one of his grins.

"If he looks at me or comes near me again and touches me, I'll kill him!" sue raises her fist and waves it with a threatening motion in front of Charlie's face.

Charlie doesn't know how to react, but he says the first thing that pops into his head. "You're really crazy, you know that? All I did was hug you because I thought you liked me. I like hugging people because that's just the way I am. I thought you liked me," he adds innocently.

"Well, I don't like you and don't you ever come near me again!"

"I guess I won't hug you anymore unless you ask me to," Charlie replies obsequiously.

Dr. Whitehead decides to take charge. "All right Sue, now please go and sit down so we can continue with the group."

"Go to hell lady!" Sue barks as she heads out the door slamming it shut.

The group begins. chatting amongst themselves concerning Sue's anti-social behavior.

"All right everyone, let's settle down and continue."

The group grows quiet as Dr. Whitehead straightens out her notes.

"Now we have a couple of new people in here today and I'd like to get to them before we run out of time."

One of the new patients stands up. "But what about me Dr. Whitehead? You said we'd talk about my problem today."

"Don't worry Fredrick. I'll get to you as time permits, and if we don't discuss your problem today I'll be happy to talk with you about it in my office."

Fredrick sits down, appeased, even though he's not altogether happy with Dr. Whitehead's solution.

Dr. Whitehead focuses her attention on the black girl in the corner of the room. Shirley is a twenty-year-old beauty with large eyes and a perfect bone structure. Her white hospital gown hides her voluptuous figure, but at this point in her life she's not interested in her appearance. Shirley's problem is angel dust (PCP). Even though she's extremely intelligent she succumbed to peer pressure and on two occasions she smoked the dangerous chemical. She had no idea that such limited use could cause such drastic effects, but now she knows all too well. She's constantly reliving the experience with frequent flashbacks and the very thought of this contributed to her ruined mental state.

Dr. Whitehead informs the group that this is the first-time Shirley has been out of her room in five days. Dr. Whitehead doesn't press Shirley to talk about her problems, preferring to explain them to the group and hopefully stir up some intelligent comments from the group.

Rick decides to break the silence. "Could I ask the group a question and whoever wants to answer it could.?"

Dr. Whitehead seems pleased that her plan seems to be working. "Certainly Rick, but please restrain your comments to the issue at hand."

"Sure. Anyway, I don't really know much about angel dust except what I hear on the news and stuff, but I just don't get it. Now don't get me wrong, because I'm not a prude or anything."

Several patients begin laughing and snickering at Rick's comment.

"What I mean is, well, I've smoked a lot of grass and I've taken just about every dangerous pill there is to take, but no way would I touch angel dust. That's just crazy and stupid.

None of my friends ever took it and I don't see how anyone would even be curious about something like that. It's an animal tranquilizer and I just don't see why anyone would wanna fool around with something like that, especially when they know what could happen to them." Rick pauses to catch his breath, knowing that his demonstrative manner irritates a few people, especially Neil.

"Could I say something?" Neil interrupts.

"Sure," Rick says affably.

"You're full of shit!"

Dr. Whitehead is shocked. "Really Neil! I think you can say something a bit more constructive."

"Sorry Dr. Whitehead, but he doesn't know what he's talking about."

"I think you owe him time enough to finish before you decide he's full of it, to use another expression. "Dr. Whitehead turns back towards Rick. "Continue please."

"I think I said this already, but I still don't understand why anybody would take anything as lethal as an animal tranquilizer knowing they could be ruined for life. Why, it's like putting one bullet in a gun and spinning the chamber around before putting the barrel against your head and pulling the trigger."

"A very interesting analogy." Dr. Whitehead is impressed with Rick's speech. "Would anyone here like to comment on Rick's observation?"

Everyone focuses their attention on Neil. waiting for him to react. Neil sees what's happening and he seems pleased." He lights up a cigarette before commenting. Then he looks directly at Rick.

"You obviously don't know much about the psychology of someone who is experimenting with drugs, because if you did you wouldn't say such stupid things about dust."

Rick is thrown off balance by Neil's callous remark.

However, because he's genuinely curious about people who use angel dust. he beckons Neil to continue. "I know I seem ignorant, but I really want to know because it doesn't make any sense to me."

"Did you ever take a pill that was given to you even though you didn't know what it was or did you just follow your doctor's orders like a good little addict?"

"Sure! If you're talking about taking LSD or some other mind altering drugs, I guess the answer is yes, but there's a big difference between taking stuff that's meant for people and taking stuff that's only for animals. As far as I'm concerned, taking dust is the same idiotic thing as sniffing glue."

Neil takes offense. "So, you're calling me an idiot Because I've smoked dust, right?"

"Look, all I'm saying is anyone who messes around with that stuff is, well, let's just say they're going through a temporary mental breakdown because no sane person would play Russian roulette like that."

"C'mon man, you mean to tell us you never took a couple of extra pills just so you could get high?"

"Sure, I did. That's why I'm here."

Several patients laugh.

"What the fuck do you think I'm talking about? You're no different than the rest of us except you choose to get loaded in your own way. Smoking dust is just another way to get a great high."

Another patient joins in, taking Neil's side. "Yeah man. You probably don't need to take no dust because you've got a doctor giving you all the pills you want, but for people like us, dust is the only thing we can get our hands on because it doesn't cost that much."

"Aren't you afraid you'll screw yourself up for life?"

"I take it to get loaded!" he says indignantly. "The same

way you swallow pills. You don't think you'll get hooked on your pills, and dust smokers don't think anything bad will happen to them. The difference between you and me is that you can afford pills and I can't, so the only thing left that's cheap is dust."

Dr. Whitehead feels that a relative point has been brought out. "I think the important thing is that angel dust is easy to obtain, whereas pills and other drugs are expensive and hard to come by." Dr. Whitehead aims her statement at Rick. "I think you'll find just about everyone in here has tried angel dust at least once, and unfortunately, you can see for yourself what smoking it once or twice can do. Isn't that right Shirley?"

Shirley doesn't respond to Dr. Whitehead's question. She seems to be in a catatonic state.

"Let's move on now," Dr. Whitehead suggests," but please feel free, Rick, to discuss your feelings about angel dust with the patients in this unit. You may learn to understand why they seek out such a dangerous drug."

Rick nods his head as Dr. Whitehead looks through her notes. Then she directs her next comment to the twenty-year-old black man who spoke up earlier. "All right JB. Now we'd like to hear from you. Suppose you tell us something about yourself."

Everyone in the group focuses their attention on the seven-foot giant, waiting for him to speak. JB peers at each person in the room, displaying his eerie stone faced expression which he hopes will intimidate everyone. JB snickers at a couple of people and looks at Rick long and hard hoping he'll say something to him which he can argue about.

"We're waiting JB."

JB faces Dr. Whitehead and shoots her his most venomous look. Then, "I don't have nothing to say to you and don't try and make me talk because I won't be here very long."

Dr. Whitehead is surprised at JB's remark. "Where do you plan on going?"

JB feels he's being gamed by Dr. Whitehead, figuring she's playing a head trip on him so he'll open up to the group. "Oh no! he says omnisciently. "I see what you're tryin' to do. You're tryin' to get me to talk, but it ain't gonna do you no good coz I ain't gonna say nothin'"'!

"I'd just like to know where you plan on going when you leave. You just can't make a statement to this group without an explanation. We'd all like to know where you' re going."

"I'll tell you, but after that, you're not gonna trick me into talkin' because I ain't gonna be here much longer."

"Where are you going?"

"I'm going to the state hospital as soon as they have a bed for me."

"Why don't you just stay here and let us help you?"

"I ain't gonna stay here. This is a crazy place and I ain't crazy. Hey, wait a minute! I ain't gonna say no more Because I told you I wouldn't." JB looks around the room displaying a menacing look.

Rick decides to ask one of his many questions. After all, a nut like this is too good to pass up. "I don't understand why you'd want to go to a state hospital when you could stay here. What's so good about a state hospital anyway?"

"Because I can get me some women there!" JB blurts out. "Now don't be talking to me no more. I don 't like you!"

Rick proceeds undaunted. "Why do you have to go there to get women? What's the matter with the women on the outside?"

"They're crazy that's why. They're against me! Anyway, I don't need them. I got me one woman at the state hospital who I get in the bushes. She likes me to stick it to her in the bushes, I got a really big one and they all go crazy over me.

They all love me." JB rubs his groin for all to see. "And they all love what's in my pants Because I know how to use it."

Dr. Whitehead decides she'd better join the discussion and dissuade JB from his current activity. "That's very interesting JB, but why did you come here instead of the state hospital?"

"They don't got no beds right now, but as soon as someone dies, I'll get his bed and they'll let me back in."

"Don't you want to get better so you won't have to spend the rest of your life in and out of institutions?" Neil asks.

"I ain't talkin' to you. All you is a drug addict and I ain't talkin' to no drug addict! You just leave me alone else I hurt you bad!"

Neil finds JB's statement humorous. "Oh yeah, what are you gonna do?"

"I got me a black belt in karate," he informs Neil as he stands up and demonstrates a karate chop on an invisible target. "I'm also a master at kung fu and judo!" JB jumps in the air and shoots his leg out trying to hit another invisible target. Unfortunately, JB loses his balance and he falls onto the floor.

Everyone laughs as JB gets up. He's infuriated that everyone is amused at his antics and he assumes the standard karate stance. He pivots around for everyone to see that he's a man to be reckoned.

"Sit down JB!" Dr. Whitehead instructs.

JB returns to his seat, staring ominously at the group. "I ain't afraid of nobody and I'll fight any one of you." JB points at Rick. "You wanna go against a master karate expert?"

Rick pretends to be scared, but he breaks out laughing. "I'd hate to see you fall on the floor again and hurt yourself." Rick continues laughing.

JB ignores Rick's comment and he points at Neil who's also laughing. "How 'bout you? You wanna go up against a master karate man and watch me take you apart?"

"Do you think you're up to it?" Neil tries controlling his giddiness, but finds JB's antics too humorous.

JB stands up and assumes another karate stance. Then he strikes at the air while making a loud karate sound, "Hah!"

JB looks at Neil squarely in the face. "I could really hurt you if I want so don't be messin' around with me and don't be talkin' to me!"

Dr. Whitehead's had enough. "Sit down JB! Now!"

JB stares at Dr. Whitehead and then takes his seat. Then JB points at Dr. Whitehead. "And I don't want you talkin' to me no more either! I don't wanna talk to no more people Because I won't be here pretty soon. This is a crazy place and I ain't stayin'."

"Could I just say one thing Dr. Whitehead?"

"Certainly Rick, but just make sure it pertains to this group."

Rick nods his head. "Listen JB, before we all give you the silent treatment, I just want to know if you want to get better. And if you do, then I think you ought to let us try and help you as long as you're here because we all know how lonely it can be by yourself. You've probably noticed we're not all impressed with your behavior and I'm here to tell you your obtrusive behavior is really unbecoming."

JB looks at Rick curiously.

"Let me rephrase that," Rick says laughing to himself in embarrassment. He realizes he's probably the only one who understood what he just said, save Dr. Whitehead. "What I mean is, we're all in this place together and we've all got serious problems. The reason for these sessions is to try and help each other with our problems. What you don't realize is some of us have already gone through what you're experiencing now and maybe you can find out how that person solved his problem and it just might help you solve yours. Look! It's too easy to kick back and keep moving from one hospital to another, but you've got it lucky. You've stumbled into a situation where you might find the answer to your problem and all you have to do is listen and talk to the people around you instead of threatening them and hoping they'll keep their distance. If you do that, you might as well give up on yourself. Look around you. Every person wants to get better and get the hell out of this place. We can't do it alone and we can't do it by hiding in our rooms or another hospital. We've either got to get better here or we might as well forget it. So, don't keep pushing us away. Especially when we want to help."

There's a moment of silence as everyone waits for JB to react. Dr. Whitehead and Rick exchange glances.

"I hope you're through because I didn't listen to your stupid jive. All I want is to be left alone and I'll be outta here before you know it so just leave me alone!"

Rick feels let down even though he knows he scored some points with Dr. Whitehead and the group.

"Maybe the state hospital is just the place for you JB," Dr. Whitehead tells him, "but as long as you're in this hospital you'll abide by the rules and if you choose not to, I can have you confined to one of our special rooms."

"I ain't botherin' nobody and don't be talkin' at me no more, because if you do, I ain't gonna stay."

Dr. Whitehead decides to move on. "All right JB. I think we've taken enough time with you."

JB interrupts. "That's good!" he says hoping to make everyone laugh, but no one does.

Dr. Whitehead looks through her notes then directs her attention to a very disillusioned looking Carmen who's sitting next to JB with her head buried in her lap.

"How are you feeling today Carmen? I heard your husband came to see you last night. Did anything get accomplished?"

Carmen slowly picks per head up as she wipes her eyes dry with a tissue. "He came to see me all right. He said he wanted me to take him back and that I shouldn't stay here anymore because he needs me."

"What did you say?"

"I told him I'd have to think about It."

Neil decides to add to this discussion. After all, he's spoken to Carmen at length about her problem and he really does care about her "Excuse me Carmen, but what was all that yelling and screaming about? You had the door closed, but we all heard the screaming and it didn't sound like you really want to go back to him."

Carol decides to voice her opinion also," I saw your husband when he came in and he didn't impress me as the kind of guy who really wanted his wife back,"

Dr. Whitehead's glad that more people have joined the discussion. "In what way Carol?"

"Well, if situations were reversed and I was trying to get my husband to leave this place and come home, I'd at least try and make myself look presentable when I came here, He didn't strike me as looking that way. He was kind of sloppy looking and I think he could have at least gotten a little dressed up for his wife."

"Do you agree Carmen?" Dr. Whitehead inquires.

"Gee, I don't know," she says glumly. "He's always dressed like that."

Rick decides it's time he spoke out. "I think we're kind of getting off the track here." Rick looks at Carmen. "Didn't you say he wants you to take him back?"

"He said that a couple of times and he was crying."

"Don't take offense, but I thought when the wife ran out on her husband, she's supposed to be the one who asks if her husband will take her back."

"Good point Rick," Dr. Whitehead comments. "I think you've pointed out a situation where each partner feels equally guilty."

"I think her husband should be here too," Neil comments facetiously.

"You know, joking around is often a device to get at the truth and what Neil just said may in fact point out something very significant here."

Neil is taken aback He had no idea his comment was so profound.

Dr. Whitehead continues. "You see Carmen, oftentimes when there are problems in a marriage, both partners frequently blame themselves and they retreat into their own space excluding their partner. In your case, you found it awfully lonely in there and you subsequently got more and more depressed and you found out that running away from the problem was easier than coping with it. I suspect your husband also backed away from the problem and retreated into his own space. This is a common problem between husbands and wives and I know you probably feel that no one's experienced what you're going through right now."

Carmen stares attentively at Dr. Whitehead, trying to understand what she's saying. "I don't know what was going on with him because he never bothered coming home and talking to me.

The only time I saw him was when his clothes got dirty and he needed me to wash them."

"Do you feel he was treating you more as a cleaning lady than as a wife?"

"Sometimes I felt like that, but then he'd show up and we'd make love and I thought things would be all right again."

A couple of patients laugh, but Dr. Whitehead ignores them.

"Looking back on that, do you think you were fooling yourself or did you really believe everything was going to be the way it was?"

Carmen is reluctant at first, but relents. "Well, uh, I guess I was fooling myself, but he kept telling me he was going through a bunch of changes and I just had to be patient if I loved him."

Neil interrupts. "He was just trying to lay a guilt trip on you so he could screw around and do whatever he wanted and you couldn't come back at him and if you did, then that meant you didn't love him."

Carmen is getting ready to crawl back into her shell. "Yeah I know. Sometimes I feel like just picking up my kids and leaving him tor good."

"Why don't you?" Carol asks.

"Because I know he'd find me and he'd beat me up." Carmen is just about ready to cry as she relates to everyone what she's had on her mind for a long time. "He has friends all over and they'd find me and my kids where ever we went. I know they would. That's why I'm scared to leave him. He won't let me run away and he won't let me get a divorce." Carmen buries her head in her lap and she begins to cry.

"C'mon Carmen," Carol says," don't cry. You know, in all the times I've talked to you, you never even mentioned divorcing him and now that you've said it for the first time, I think you're finally getting your act together. Do you really mean it when you say he won't let you divorce him? You don't need his permission. All you have to do is make up your mind that that's what you want and find yourself a good lawyer."

Carmen looks up as she wipes her eyes dry. "But you don't understand. If he finds out I want a divorce and that I've got a lawyer, he'll beat me up bad and then who would take care of my kids?"

Dr. Whitehead listens intently while making some notes. Then she decides to speak. "I don't know if you just heard yourself Carmen, but you're always referring to your children as 'your' kids. You've never once mentioned that they're also a product of your husband. Do you feel he acts independently, like a person who doesn't take on the responsibilities of children?"

"If you mean is he a good father, I guess so, but I don't have anything to compare him with. My dad always beat my mom when I was young and then one day he didn't come home."

"Sounds like you married a guy just like your father," Charlie comments as he chuckles nervously."

Dr. Whitehead is delighted that Charlie has contributed to the discussion. "That's a very astute observation Charlie. Do you have anything else to contribute which might benefit Carmen?"

Charlie chortles as he thinks of something else to tell Carmen. Then, "You know, I saw your husband when he came in and I said 'hi' to him and he gave me a dirty look. That made me really mad because he smiled at Norma when he passed her so I thought he'd be nice to me too, but he wasn't. I think he asked her if she wanted to sneak out of the hospital and go someplace with him."

Everyone looks at Norma who's sitting quietly. Carmen shoots her a menacing look.

Norma looks around and notices everyone staring at her. She feels like she's in the hot seat. "He said something to me, but I don't remember what it was."

"Do you think your husband propositioned Norma?"

"I don't think so, Dr. Whitehead. I know he loves me and he wouldn't do anything like that."

"Well, I know that's what he said," states Charlie, "because I was standing by the nurse's station waiting for my Lithium and he was standing right next to me. I thought that maybe he could be my friend, but he wouldn't smile at me like I was smiling at him and I don't think it's right for him to yell and scream at Carmen like he did. If I was married to her," he chuckles," I'd only scream at her if she didn't like me."

Carmen looks at Charlie affectionately. "Right now, I like you more than I like my husband."

Charlie chortles uncontrollably.

Dr. Whitehead tries calming Charlie down and hopefully she can get the discussion focused back on Carmen's problem.

Rick gets the discussion back on the track. "Listen Carmen. Can you honestly tell everyone in this room that you love your husband?"

"I think I love him. Anyway, I used to."

"Well, do you, or don't you?" Neil asks.

Carmen clenches her fists. "I don't know. I know he loves me, but I just wish things were like they used to be and that he wouldn't keep making fun of me Because I'm fat."

"That's because you're Mexican," Charlie interrupts, hoping to get the other patients to laugh with him, but no one does.

Dr. Whitehead decides to take over. "If you've been listening to yourself Carmen, I think you've been having trouble admitting that you really don't have the same feelings for your husband you once cherished. I think you're in love with the way you and your husband used to be."

"You shouldn't go back with him unless it's what you want to do, and I wouldn't advise you to do it unless you're absolutely sure," Rick interjects.

Norma raises her hand instead of talking out. Dr. Whitehead points to her.

"I saw Carmen's husband when he was leaving and he was kind of smiling about something. How come?"

"Well, he said he needs me to come home and be with him and my kids and that he'd be good if I gave him one more chance."

"Don't tell me you believe that shit!" Neil comments.

"I don't know. I guess I'll go home when I get out of here, but I just Don't know."

"All right everybody," Dr. Whitehead says loudly. "I'm glad to see everyone contributing to this discussion and I'm sure Carmen appreciates our concern, but we haven't really done anything concrete here. What I'd like to do is try something different with Carmen. Role playing. Is that all right with you Carmen?"

"Gee, I don't know if I can handle that."

"If it becomes too uncomfortable then we'll just stop, but I think you might learn something by it and that's maybe what you need to help you make a decision by yourself."

"I'll try it," Carmen says reluctantly.

"How about you Rick? Would you like to be Carmen's husband?"

"If you don't tell my wife," Rick says causing everyone to laugh including Dr. Whitehead.

"All right Rick. Why don't you and Carmen bring your chairs to the center of the room and we'll assume that you've been out all night and it's three in the morning."

Rick and Carmen take their positions in the center of the room and face each other. Rick laughs nervously as he waits for Carmen to begin.

"Where have you been all night?" Carmen snaps. "Do you know it's three in the morning and you promised you'd be home for dinner?"

Rick pretends to look at his watch. "It's only a quarter to three," he says facetiously.

Carmen is perturbed. "There you go again. Why don't you

just answer my question instead of trying to make a joke out of it. Now tell me where you were?" she demands.

"I was out looking for a job! Why don't you just leave me alone?

It's bad enough I can't find work and then I have to come home and you give me a bunch of shit! Stay off my case!"

"You were in some bar with that damn gang of yours, weren't you?"

"What if I was?" he snaps defensively. "After all the shit I put up with today, I don't see what's wrong with having a beer with my friends."

"One beer doesn't make you drunk Carlos. Why didn't you at least call me? You know I didn't even have dinner because I was waiting for you to come home so we could eat together."

"You could have fooled me. You look like you've already eaten."

"Wow! Carla mumbles to herself as she looks over at Dr. Whitehead. "I feel like I'm really fighting with my husband."

"Good Carmen, but don't stop now," Dr. Whitehead instructs.

Rick decides to pick up where he left off, hoping Carmen will get back to role playing. But before Rick can continue, Carmen looks at him squarely.

"You sound so much like my husband, I'm really beginning to hate you!"

"Wait a minute Carmen. I'm only pretending to be Carlos."

"Get back on the track, you guys," Dr. Whitehead commands.

Rick nods his head in agreement and he continues playing his role. "I don't know why I even bothered coming home. The guys got mad at me because I had to leave and it was my turn to buy the beers."

"You care more about your damn gang than you do about

me and the kids. I was even supposed to go to the doctor today so he could check my infection that you claim you didn't give me, but I had to call and cancel because you didn't come home to watch the kids like you said you would."

Rick becomes enraged. "Don't you say anything bad about my friends. I was hanging around with them when I met you and you didn't say anything bad about them then. I think you're just jealous because I hang around with my friends and you're mad because you don't have any friends to hang around with."

"I don't have time to hang around bars and do nothing. I have two kids to take care of by myself while you're out cruising and getting drunk. That's all you ever do is get drunk with your friends."

Rick is fed up. "I'm tired and I'm going to bed and if you don't stop this shit I'll leave. You got that?"

"What about dinner? Aren't you going to eat something?"

"What's in the refrigerator? I feel like a beer." Rick looks at Dr. Whitehead, hoping that she'll tell him to stop.

"That was very good Rick."

"I'll say," Carmen comments as she blows her nose and wipes the perspiration off her face. "For a while, I really saw Carlos sitting there and he even sounded like Carlos and he said the same things that Carlos says."

Dr. Whitehead seems very pleased. "That's very good Carmen, but this wasn't just a game you were playing. I hope you learned something by what was said. Did you notice that you backed down at the end and appeared to forget the whole incident?"

"I guess so, but I was just so mad and frustrated that I knew if I didn't stop, he'd leave because he's done that before and sometimes he doesn't come back for days."

"Where does he go and what does he say when he comes back?"

"I think he stays with his gang friends and when I ask him where he's been, he gets mad and tells me that if I don't leave him alone, he'll leave again."

"I'd divorce the bastard," Neil says. "I wouldn't take that kind of shit from anybody. You'd be better off by yourself."

Carol decides to speak out and voice her opinion also. "I don't think he cares about your kids either. He just cares about himself and he sounds like he really wants to be free. It's obvious that he can't handle the responsibilities of a family."

"I'd like to have the last word on this matter," Dr. Whitehead informs the group," and then we can move on to someone else before we run out of time."

"But I still don't know what to do," Carmen says dejectedly. "I've been here for a long time and I'm more depressed now than I ever was." Carmen drops her head and she begins crying.

Dr. Whitehead makes some notes on Carmen's chart. "Well, I think we'll change your medication and put you on something stronger. We can talk about what you've said today in private. Can you wait until tomorrow Carmen?"

Carmen prefers not to look up. She doesn't want everyone to see her crying even though they all know she is. "I guess so," she says obsequiously. The room is silent as Dr. Whitehead continues writing on Carmen's chart. Rick looks around the room noticing that Neil's hand has invaded the privacy of Carla's blouse. As Neil's hand moves across Carla's chest. Rick looks on hoping to get a glimpse of Carla's breasts. Unfortunately, Neil only unfastened one button and her blouse won't open up to any great degree. Rick looks around the room at the rest of the group to see if anyone else has spotted Neil and Carla. Then Rick's eyes meet up with Judy's. Rick didn't know that Judy was present in the room, but now he can't help noticing. Judy smiles at Rick and he quickly discovers the reason why. Rick can't help looking as he spots Judy's legs spread for his eyes only. He takes in an eyeful and then looks back up at Judy and sees her licking her lips, hoping to entice him to take another look. Rick's first reaction is to lower his eyes once again, but he decides against it, seeing that Dr. Whitehead has stopped writing.

Dr. Whitehead spots Neil with his hand in Carla's blouse and she makes a throat clearing noise until Neil realizes that he's been caught. Neil doesn't seem the least bit embarrassed as he slowly removes his hand from Carla's blouse taking one last feel.

"Does anyone have a thought they'd care to discuss today?"

"I have something to say," Neil informs the group.

"As long as it pertains to the people in this group," Dr. Whitehead informs him.

"Yeah, it does, It's about Rick."

Rick smiles nervously as he awaits Neil's statement.

"You know Rick, I've seen you walking around here for a few days and I've talked to you and stuff and I've seen you talking to other people in here and I have to say that you seem like a really nice guy.

Rick is optimistically cautious. He has a feeling that Neil is leading up to something that he doesn't care to hear.

"You even seem really intelligent, like someone who shouldn't even be here, but what I don't understand is," Neil hesitates, choosing his words carefully, "what are you hiding?"

Rick smiles nervously as he decides if he should try answering Neil's question. He doesn't know quite how to respond to his question, let alone say anything at all.

"You've told us why you're here and I don't really remember, but you just strike me as someone who's not telling us what's really going on inside your head and I'd like to know what it is because you're kind of spooky."

Rick decides that the only thing he can do is explain his

problem and hopefully that will satisfy Neil. "Well, I don't know if I should really start at the beginning."

Neil is anxious to hear Rick's response. "Just tell us what's going on inside your head right now."

"There's not much to tell," Rick says reluctantly as he decides just what he should divulge. "I got addicted to a sleeping pill and when I couldn't handle quitting by myself, I checked in here. That's really about it." Rick hopes that Neil will be happy with his response and not try to coax anything else out of him. As far as Rick is concerned, he doesn't care to repeat the whole story leading up to the hospital and he kind of resents Neil for his prying.

Dr. Whitehead decides to intervene after seeing Rick squirm nervously in his chair. "I think Rick answered your question Neil, and now I think we'd like to hear you speak for a change. I'm sure we'd all like to know how you're doing now, compared to how you were when you checked in."

Neil seems delighted with the prospect of addressing the group. He winks at Carla as he lights up a cigarette. Then Neil inhales and blows out the smoke before speaking. "Well. I think most of you have seen me around and if you haven't seen me around or talked to me then you must have been hiding because I'm all over this place and I try talking to everyone. As most of you know. I'm here for heroin addiction. I've been sticking myself with the needle for over three years and I just got to the point in my life where I want to pull myself together and get out there and make a bunch of money. It's hard to do when you're on something, and believe me, I've been on just about everything there is to be on. Now I'm not putting down Rick's problem or anything, but I got to the point where I was using more stuff in a day than he probably used in a month."

"I doubt it," Rick mumbles to himself, unaware that he spoke loud enough for Neil to hear.

"Okay Rick, how much were you taking and what was it?"

"Four Placidyl seven hundred and fifties."

Neil seems delighted. "Pickles! My favorites. I used to shoot five of them at a time and then I'd shoot another five or six two hours later."

Rick looks at Neil skeptically.

Neil takes offense. "Hey man, don't look at me like that. You're not a real dope addict until you start shooting stuff other people swallow and I stopped taking pills a long time ago because you get a better high when you're shooting the stuff. You're strictly in the minor leagues compared to me."

Dr. Whitehead doesn't care to hear Neil and Rick verbally squaring off. "Would you boys mind comparing notes some other time."

"Sure. Anyway, I got to the point where I was shooting anything and every thing and I didn't care about anything else except my dope. But I'm here to tell you that I haven't taken so much as an aspirin for over four weeks and I'll never go back to the way I used to be because I've got to get on with my life and it's a life without any drugs whatsoever."

A couple of patients begin to applaud. and in a matter of moments everyone in the room joins in including Rick and Dr. Whitehead.

As the clapping stops, Dr. Whitehead decides to speak. "You've made great progress Neil, but I wouldn't say that you're completely cured yet."

"Oh, I know. I've still got a lot of head problems. But now that I've got a job lined up when I leave here I think I'll be ready to leave before you know it and you'll never hear from me again. The way I feel now, I wouldn't even take so much as a vitamin pill."

Dr. Whitehead smiles good naturedly. "Well, I don't think you have to go that far. You're always welcome to come back and visit the group sessions, but I don't think that now is the time to be discussing this."

As the session continues, Dr. Whitehead spots a man who is wearing street clothes. "I see we have a former patient here today who's visiting. Louis, would you raise your hand please so we can all see who you are."

Louis, a frail man in his early forties, raises his hand as he smiles nervously. Louis is probably one of the few people in the world who thinks that a crew cut is still in style. His sideburns are almost nonexistent and his pale complexion is an indication that he spends all of his time indoors. Even though he's been around for many years, Louis is only now out on his own. He's an extremely quiet and shy man who fell to pieces when his mother passed away. He's only been out of the hospital for two weeks, after being treated for severe depression. Dr. Whitehead is very pleased he came back for a visit.

Louis raise his hand as he speaks. "I wasn't doing anything today and I thought that I might like to come over and visit everybody."

"We're glad to see you again Louis. What have you been doing since you left us!"

"Well, I haven't been doing too much. I spend a lot of time in my mother's garden. You know she's not here anymore."

"Yes, I know Louis. That's why you were here before."

"I'm better now though. I still miss her and I think about her all the time."

"You're not mad at her anymore for dying, are you?"

"I don't think so."

"Excuse me, Dr. Whitehead," Charlie interrupts," but could I say something about taking drugs because that's what we were talking about before and I never got a chance to say anything."

"Go ahead Charlie."

"Well, I just want to say that drugs are bad and you shouldn't take anything that could hurt you. "Charlie laughs nervously. He's proud of himself for speaking up.

"Does anyone care to add to what Charlie has just said?"

"I do," Carol blurts out. "I just wanted to add to what Charlie said. "It's a lot harder to get off drugs than it is to take them and I think we all know that we're lucky to have a place like this where they care about us and want to help us get off drugs."

Several patients vocally agree with Carol's statement. When everyone's finished, Carmen decides to add her own thoughts as well.

"I used to be pretty fucked up on drugs and stuff, but then I really didn't know how bad they were. My husband used to come home in the middle of the night with a bunch of drugs and we'd just sit around and get loaded. I don't know why I did it, I just did. But when I get out of here, I'm never gonna take drugs again no matter who gives them to me, because I know how they can fuck you up and it's just not worth it."

Rick decides to get back into the discussion. "Excuse me, but I think it's great that everyone agrees that drugs are bad and I applaud everyone for saying they'll never take any more drugs, but I feel we've skirted over an important issue and I think it should be brought out in the open."

Everyone's eyes focus on Rick as they await one of his profound statements. Even Dr. Whitehead's stopped writing.

"Now I think we can all agree that one of the reasons we take drugs is because we want to forget about some kind of problem in our life. Whether we use a needle, our lungs, or just swallow something, our main purpose is to get loaded for a few hours so we can forget about why we wanted to take the drug in the first place. The only problem with that is when the two hours have passed and we're not loaded anymore, the problems we wanted to forget are still there. And they won't go away until we solve them ourselves without using a drug because drugs don't solve anything. I should know. Whenever I got pissed off because someone stole a script from me or something, I'd take a couple of extra pills to get loaded and my mind turned to Jello for a few hours, but when the stuff wore off, I'd remember why I took the stuff in the first place and I'd be pissed off all over again."

"I agree with what you're saying," Neil comments," but everybody's different."

"Sure, everybody's different and what I said mainly applies to me, but I think we all get the message. Look! Let me equate it to you another way. I have a bad back and there are times when the pain becomes unbearable. If I take a pain pill, the pain goes away, but that doesn't mean I won't have discomfort when the pill wears off. All I'm doing is getting artificial relief, which is only temporary. If I keep taking pills every time I feel the least little pain, I suddenly face drug addiction and a possible fatal overdose."

Dr. Whitehead sees that everyone is quite taken with Rick's remarks, and no one feels like continuing the discussion.

The door to the therapy room opens and the medication nurse takes one step inside. "It's medication time," she informs the group.

"Well, I guess that's all the time we have for now," Dr. Whitehead says as everyone races for the door trying to be the first one in line at the medication window.

Rick looks on incredulously. He finds it quite amusing that a few minutes ago, everyone was discussing the evils of drugs and how several patients adamantly said they'd never take any more drugs. But when the nurse came in and informed them they can get their free drugs, everyone took off for their dope like they were giving away money.

Rick is the last one to exit the therapy room, He walks through the television room and finds it empty, He soon discovers the reason why as he enters the corridor and sees all the patients standing in line next to the nurse's station waiting patiently as the medication nurse hands them their pills and other medications.

Rick starts for the exit, but stops short of the doors. Why should he go all the way back to his unit for his medicine when all he's getting are vitamins and anti-itch pills? Needless to say, Rick decides to remain in unit three and forgo his own medication.

Charlie sees Rick standing by the exit and greets him with a slap on the back. Rick whirls around with fists clenched, but relaxes when he discovers that Charlie is the one who touched him, Charlie just stands there with a big wide grin on his face.

"I just took my Lithium," he says with a chuckle," They're giving me twice as much as they did yesterday and I think they finally figured out that I need the stronger dosage. It takes them awhile before they figure out what to give because everybody's different."

"You're certainly different all right," Rick quips.

"I know," he chortles. "I think I'll go in the television room. You want to come with me and we can watch the same program together?"

"No thanks, I'm going back to my unit." Rick takes a few steps towards the exit.

Charlie enters the television room as Rick looks back over his shoulder. Then Rick sneaks by the TV room hoping Charlie won't see that he didn't leave the unit.

Rick wanders down unit three's main corridor and stops at an open doorway. He takes a peak into the room and is shocked to see Judy lying on her bed with her legs spread. Rick does a double take as he sees Judy masturbating. Judy spots

Rick and continues undaunted with a smile on her face which she lets subside long enough to lick her lips hoping to entice Rick to enter.

"C'mon in sugar, the party's just beginning."

Rick's first thought is to accommodate her request, but he quickly comes to his senses. "I've got things to do," he says nervously, his heartbeat accelerating. "See you later maybe." Rick races away from Judy's room and down the corridor.

Rick stops at the open door of the arts and crafts room and peers inside. He spots various art projects adorning the walls next to an old piano, and in the small room nearby he sees a ping pong table where two patients are playing.

"Three hundred and thirteen to two hundred and ninety-one," one of the players announces as he serves the ball."

Rick looks on in astonishment as the player hits the serve in the air and it bounces into the next room only to stop when it hits the side of the open door where Rick is standing. The patient who served the ball comes over to retrieve the ball. Rick bends down and picks up the ping pong ball which he hands to the patient.

"You wanna play the winner?" the patient asks.

"I don't know. How much are you playing to?"

"Twenty-two hundred and fifteen, why?"

Rick says the first thing that pops into his head. "What are you crazy?"

The patient doesn't take offense. "That's why we're here," he casually replies.

"I'll come back tomorrow."

"I can't save your place in line for you. If you wanna be the next one to play, you'll have to wait."

"That's all right."

"Suit yourself," he tells Rick as he heads back to the ping pong room to continue his game.

Rick spots several people sitting at a table in the center of the arts and crafts room. From the silence in the room and the frozen expressions on everyone's faces. Rick surmises they're probably catatonics. After all, he's never seen any of these patients before.

Rick proceeds down the corridor, stopping at a room near the exit sign. He looks inside and notices the pool table in the room. Rick enters and begins playing a game by himself. He's surprised he's still able to play well even though it's been years since he's tried. Rick uses combination shots to achieve his goal and he sends three balls into the side pocket using only two shots. However, this soon becomes boring and Rick sets up a couple of trick shots, which he messes up due to his inexperience. Rick tries one last shot, deciding that he'll find something else to occupy his time as soon as he finishes. Unfortunately, he misses on his first attempt to get two balls into the same pocket and he's forced to prop himself onto the table in order to take another shot.

As Rick prepares to shoot, he detects another presence in the room. He cocks his head back as a hand grabs onto his groin and begins squeezing ever so gently. Rick is startled and he jerks himself free of the wandering hand. He hops off the table and sees Judy standing inches away licking her lips.

"I saw you playing with the balls on the table and I just thought I'd like to play with some balls also. I like the real ones better anyway." Judy stands by the doorway hoping Rick won't dart out of the room.

Rick doesn't know quite how to act or what to say. Perhaps if Judy was more discrete about her activities, he might go along with her. "Do you want to play a game with me?" Rick nervously asks as he racks up the balls.

"Can I use your stick to play with?"

"Sure," Rick says holding out his pool cue.

Judy reaches for the cue, but suddenly grabs for Rick's groin. "I'd rather use your stick."

Rick backs away and throws the cue on the table. "You can break," he tells her as he takes a seat in the corner of the room.

Judy picks up the cue and shoots the cue ball into the freshly racked balls.

Rick stand up and takes another cue stick off the wall. "Good break, but you didn't get any balls into the pockets."

Judy moves to the other side of the table preparing to take another shot. "I'm not through yet."

"I thought we were playing a game."

Judy's shot misses and she moves to the other side of the table where she'll make her next shot. "This is how I play pool," she says as she stands in front of Rick.

Judy takes her position for the next shot. She stands a couple of feet away from the table so that she's only inches away from Rick's chair. She maneuvers herself enabling Rick to get a glimpse of her bare bottom. Then she takes a step back so that her flesh is only a couple of inches from Rick's face. In a moment of sexual weakness, Rick leans forward and slides his hand between Judy's eager cheeks. He's delighted at the touch of another as his hand caresses Judy's moisture. Judy moves her hips rhythmically as she moans with delight. Then Judy hikes her dress up to her waist and sits on Rick's lap trapping his hand between her legs. Judy squirms about hoping to give Rick the chance to guide his hand inside her, but as soon as she does this, Rick hears voices coming from the corridor. Not wanting to get caught, Rick slides his hand out from underneath Judy and he stands up. Judy falls against the pool table and looks at Rick contemptuously.

"Don't leave me now. I was just getting ready to come."

Rick flings the door open and looks back at Judy. "Be back in a minute. I'm just going to get some rubbers," Rick scurries out of the room, hoping Judy won't follow.

"Do you want me to wait for you here or do you want to go to my room?"

Rick doesn't respond causing Judy to exercise her lungs. "I'll wait for you in here," she calls out as she props herself up onto the pool table and begins removing what little clothes she has on.

Rick leaves the corridor via the exit next to the pool room and is surprised to find several patients playing volleyball in the large fenced-in parking lot. Rick recognizes several players in the game, but there are at least ten people he's never seen before. He figures they're probably from the alcoholic unit and they just came by to participate in the outdoor activities.

"C'mon Rick. We need you on our team," Sherri calls out from the court.

"I'd love to Sherri, but I don't think my back could handle it."

Rick looks away from the game and sees Dr. Whitehead and Charlie playing cards. "Who's winning?"

Charlie looks up and is delighted to see Rick. "I think I am," he says chuckling nervously," but I think she's helping me."

"Do you want to play the next game?" Dr. Whitehead asks.

"Thanks anyway, I'd rather watch."

Suddenly, everyone hears a terrible scream coming from somewhere inside unit three. Rick is the first one to rush into the unit, but the screaming abruptly stops. Rick opens the door to the pool room and sees Judy sitting on the pool table wearing her birthday suit."

"I thought you'd never come back sugar."

"Don't go away," Rick tells her as he slams the door shut.

Rick scampers down the corridor as JB runs out of one of the rooms.

"JB! I know that's you. Come back here!" Rick shouts as he stops at the room where JB exited. Rick looks into the room as the screaming starts up again. Rick doesn't see anyone in the room and he enters approaching the open bathroom door.

Norma is lying on the floor pulling up her pants as the tears roll off her face and onto the tile floor. She continues screaming as several patients gather in her room. Dr. Whitehead pushes everyone aside. She bends down to comfort Norma.

"It's all right Norma, we're here now," Dr. Whitehead pulls Norma close to her and she begins caressing her head, hoping to calm her down.

"He tried to rape me!"

"Who did?"

"He tried to rape me!"

"Who did Norma? Tell me who?"

"He tried to rape me!"

"I can't help you if I don't know who you're talking about."

Dr. Whitehead tries comforting Norma as JB enters the room and stands in the doorway behind several patients. Norma spots JB and screams out again,

"That's him! "Norma wails as she points an accusing finger at JB.

"She's crazy!" JB responds defensively. "I just came in to use the bathroom. I didn't know she was in there." JB smiles innocently.

"He's lying! He was following me and saying things to me and I went to my room to get away from him. He knew I was in the bathroom and he came in and took his thing out of his pants and pushed it into my face." Norma's eyes begin tearing once again.

Neil enters the room in time to learn what transpired. "You're really sick man!" he tells JB.

"Is all this true JB?" Dr. Whitehead inquires.

"You wouldn't be believin' her if I wasn't black! I told you what happened, but I guess you'll believe her because she's white."

JB pushes his way through several patients and he storms out of the room. "You white people always stick together! If I wasn't here, you'd find some other nigger to blame!"

"I'll get you something to make you feel better," Dr. Whitehead tells Norma. "All right everybody, return to your own business. It's almost time for lunch."

Everyone files out of Norma's room as Dr. Whitehead orders an attendant to bring Norma some medication to ease her stress.

Dr. Whitehead helps Norma get into her bed, assuring her that she'll stop shaking as soon as her medication arrives.

The meal cart is wheeled into unit three and everyone tries to be the first to get their tray.

"You want to share my lunch with me?" Charlie asks Rick as he removes his tray from the cart.

"Thanks anyway Charlie, but you might go into the pool room and tell the girl in there that they brought the lunches in." Rick smiles to himself as he thinks how Charlie will react when he discovers a naked girl in the pool room.

"Maybe she'll even want to be my friend," Charlie tells Rick as he walks down the corridor towards the pool room.

Rick would dearly love to wait around and see Charlie's reaction, but decides against it, figuring he'd better get back to his unit before his lunch gets cold.

Rick exits unit three and heads down the corridor. He can hardly wait to get back to his own room, eat lunch and come back to unit three. Maybe he really belongs there after all.

CHAPTER SIXTEEN

"You'd never catch me using any kind of drugs. I don't care what it is," Neil informs the afternoon therapy session under the direction of Dr. Schwartz. "Why do you think they call it dope?" Neil adds hoping that no one, especially Dr. Schwartz, has ever heard this old and tired advertising statement which was shown on television in the seventies.

"We all applaud your anti-drug attitude Neil, but I think it's time to let someone else have the floor." Dr. Schwartz turns his attentions toward Carol. "How about you Carol. You seem to be the most well-adjusted and sapid person in this room. How are you feeling about your parents today? Especially your father."

Carol displays a confused look. "What's sapid?"

Several patients laugh.

Dr. Schwartz doesn't appreciate the laughter. "I don't know why you find Carol's question so amusing. I'm sure you probably don't know what the word means yourself, do you Neil?"

Neil stops laughing and looks coldly at Dr. Schwartz. "No I don't."

"Well then, I'll tell you. A sapid person is one who displays a particular zest for life. I'd say that describes Carol, wouldn't you?"

"Yes sir, Dr. Schwartz," Neil replies obsequiously.

Dr. Schwartz seems pleased with the way he handled the situation. "As I was saying Carol, I'd like to know how you're feeling today about yourself?"

"If you don't mind Dr. Schwartz, I'm not feeling too sapid today and I'd really like to just listen to someone else today."

"Certainly Carol. We all know how you've contributed in the past so I think you can just be a spectator today."

Dr. Schwartz turns his attentions to the person next to Carol and is surprised to see it's Louis. "Well, I see you've decided to stay a while and visit with us Louis."

Louis rolls up his sleeve and displays the hospital band around his wrist. "I'm not a visitor anymore Dr. Schwartz. I thought that maybe I should check back in because I don't think I'm ready for the outside yet."

"I'm sorry to hear that Louis, but I'm confident we can make you feel like a part of society again."

"Excuse me Dr. Schwartz," Rick interrupts," but isn't one of the purposes of these sessions to discuss problems we've been having in here as well as on the outside?"

"Something on your mind, Rick?"

Rick nods his head in agreement as the other patients wait for him to speak. "I sure do. It's about what happened earlier to one of the girls in this unit. Now I don't have positive proof because I didn't actually witness what JB did, so from now on I'll just refer to him as the culprit."

JB stands up, shaking his fists at Rick. "Is that it! Am I guilty cos I'm the only black man in here? You're just prejudiced against me!"

Dr. Schwartz decides he'd better intervene. "Take it easy JB and as for you Mr. Brown, I'd like to caution you that no one's on trial. And as you just stated, you didn't see what happened and I don't think you should be pointing an accusing finger at anyone unless you have some kind of proof."

JB shakes his fists at the entire group. "This whole group's against me and I'm not gonna talk to none of you no more and I'm not gonna come to none of these stupid group things. "JB heads for the door.

"Wait a second JB. You can't just run away from your problems like this. You can't very well stay here and ignore everyone in this place."

"Yes, I can. I'm goin' to the state hospital, as soon as they call and don't be talkin' to me no more cos I know you're against me too!"

"Why on earth would you want to go there?" Dr. Schwartz inquires.

JB ignores Dr. Schwartz's question, preferring to give the entire group his venomous stare. "You all think I tried to rape that ugly girl, but I didn't. I told you I just made a mistake because I wanted to use the bathroom, but because I'm black you think I did it and it wasn't me because all the girls in here is too ugly for me to poke and I don't want to touch any of 'em because I can get me all the women I want at the state hospital. They all love me and they like me to poke 'em in the bushes." JB continues shaking his fists at the group.

"And don't none of you talk to me no more because I don't like none of you," he points at Rick, "especially you," he points at Neil," and you!"

Rick is kind of scared and he looks at Neil to see his reaction. Neil just stares at JB ominously.

"And don't none of you talk about me either!" JB warns the group as he exits the therapy room, slamming the door behind him.

Dr. Schwartz is visibly shaken, and he suspends further discussions, informing the group that he forgot about a previous commitment. He promptly dismisses the group, promising them that tomorrow he'll extend the group's time.

Rick decides to return to his room for a fresh pack of cigarettes. As he walks down the many corridors leading to his unit, he reflects on the time he's spent the hospital. He's glad he chose this place for his cure. He's feeling much better and he's made a lot of friends. He's really having a good time. Up until the afternoon session, Rick figured that when he is discharged, he'd probably come back for frequent visits, but the thought of how Louis came to visit and ended up checking back in disturbs Rick deeply. Maybe it wouldn't be such a good idea to come back here for visits after all, Rick thinks to himself as he approaches his room.

Rick removes a fresh pack of cigarettes from his grip as Maggie enters his room.

"Going somewhere Rick?"

"I thought I'd go back to three. There's more going on there and the time goes by much quicker."

"From what I've heard, it sounds anything but boring."

"I guess you heard about that girl who almost got raped?"

"I thank God she wasn't really hurt. That JB sounds like a keg of dynamite ready to explode."

"Why don't they do something about him then?"

"I heard they're trying to transfer him out as fast as they can."

"That's fine," Rick says sarcastically. "What are the women supposed to do in the meantime while he prowls the halls when he should be locked away?"

"If I was in that unit, he'd be locked in isolation and put in a strait jacket, but I don't have any jurisdiction over there and I'm not supposed to butt in."

"Why don't they just put him away somewhere? Those women are pretty scared and to tell you the truth, I'm a bit nervous myself."

"I guess he'll just have to get caught in the act before they do something. Personally, I hope they get rid of him before he has that chance."

Rick nods his head in agreement as he lights up a cigarette.

"Oh, I almost forgot why I came in here in the first place. I understand you and Nurse Rayburn exchanged words this morning."

"That bitch! You know what she did?"

"She came over to me right after she left your room and said she kicked out your girlfriend for sitting on your bed. I set her straight though and told her that was your wife and the mother of your child." Maggie laughs as she reflects on Nurse Rayburn's reaction. "I thought she'd fall out of her chair when I told her."

"She's got a lot of nerve for such an old biddy. You shouldn't have been so polite about it."

"Don't worry about it. I had a talk with the head administrator about her and he promised he'd speak to her."

"At least that's something."

"I thought that would cheer you up," Maggie heads for the door.

"Thanks Maggie. You're still the only ray of sunshine in this place," Maggie looks over her shoulder and winks at Rick. "Don't expect her to be nice to you. That's too big a miracle to hope for."

Rick reaches into his grip and takes a second pack of cigarettes just in case he runs out while he's in unit three. After all, everyone keeps asking him for a cigarette and as long as he has them, he doesn't mind sharing.

Rick heads out of his room as Jose is pounding on his table trying to get Rick's attention. Rick's first thought is to simply ignore Jose's incessant pounding and leave the room. But that would make him feel pretty guilty, especially if Jose wanted something important like a nurse to change his diaper.

Rick walks over to Jose's bedside and looks down at his unfortunate roommate. Jose points towards his mouth.

"C'mon Jose, give me a break and ask one of the nurses to help you smoke." Jose shakes his head from side to side as he points towards the corner of the room. Rick looks over to Alexander's bed and notices that it's been made up and Alexander's nowhere in sight.

"Where's Alexander?"

Jose tries speaking, but Rick is only able to understand a few words. "Save your voice," Rick says as he hands Jose a pad of paper and a pencil.

Jose smiles at Rick as he picks up the pad of paper, but he again motions towards his mouth.

"All right. I'll help you smoke while you're writing."

Jose practically smokes the entire cigarette as he writes down his message. Rick takes the pad away from Jose and reads to himself.

WHEN YOU WERE NOT IN HERE, TWO NURSES CAME IN AND PUT ALEXANDER IN A WHEELCHAIR AND TOOK HIM OUT BECAUSE HE WAS GOING TO GO TO A NURSING HOME. I THINK HE WILL BE HAPPY THERE BECAUSE IN A NURSING HOME THEY TAKE CARE OF YOU ALL OF THE TIME AND YOU DO NOT HAVE TO DO ANYTHING. I THINK THEY ARE GOING TO PUT ME IN A NURSING HOME TOO AND I DO NOT WANT TO GO BECAUSE I WAS IN ONE ONCE AND THEY TREAT YOU LIKE YOU HAVE A DISEASE AND THEY DO NOT COME TO SEE YOU ALL THE TIME BECAUSE MOST OF THE PEOPLE IN THERE ARE VERY OLD AND THE YOUNG PEOPLE IN THERE ARE ALWAYS DYING OR SOMETHJNG AND I THINK THAT THEY ARE

AFRAID OF PEOPLE WHO ARE DYING AND I AM NOT DYING SO I DO NOT WANT TO GO THERE. I THINK ALEXANDER DID NOT WANT TO LEAVE BECAUSE HE DID NOT WANT TO GET OUT OF BED BUT HE DID. BEFORE YOU CAME BACK A NURSE CAME IN WITH A MAN WHO IS GOING TO SLEEP IN ALEXANDER'S BED AND I THINK THAT I LIKE HIM BECAUSE HE SAID HELLO TO ME AND THEN HE WENT SOMEWHERE. I THINK HE HAS BEEN HERE BEFORE BECAUSE HE ASKED THE NURSE IF HE COULD GO OVER TO UNIT THREE AND SHE SAID HE COULD AND! THEN HE LEFT. I THINK HE IS A DRUG ADDICT BECAUSE THE NURSE LOOKED AT HIS ARMS AND I THINK THAT HE HAD NEEDLE MARKS ON THEM.

Rick finishes reading as Jose motions him to bend down so he can tell him something.

"It still smells in here," Jose tells Rick in his squeaky voice.

Rick can't help laughing and Jose joins in.

"At least Alexander left us something to remember him by. "Rick heads for the door, deciding to return to unit three and maybe locate his new roommate. He's sure he'll have to be better than Alexander and maybe he can help Jose too, thus taking some of Rick's responsibilities.

Rick enters unit three and goes directly into the television room. He takes a seat next to Charlie and Carmen and tries listening to their conversation. Charlie and Carmen are so engrossed with their discussion they fail to notice Rick's presence.

"Well, personally I think you should divorce him because I don't like to see you so unhappy and I think when you finally leave here you shouldn't go home because he'll just make you mad again and I should know what it's like to be mad and I don't like to feel this way and you shouldn't either." Charlie's air of confidence abruptly fades. "I hope you're not mad at me because of what I just said because if you are I promise I won't say anything anymore."

Carmen looks at Charlie lovingly. She hugs him. "Don't be silly Charlie. I love you for what you just said. If I knew you cared this much, I would have been nicer to you when I first came in."

Charlie chuckles nervously as he looks around the room hoping to see someone watching him. Then he looks to his side and is delighted to see Rick. Charlie chortles nervously. "We're just good friends."

Charlie and Carmen end their embrace. Carmen offers Charlie one of her cigarettes.

"No thanks," Charlie says wav1ng his hand "I think I'd better go because I think my Lithium is wearing off and I wanna see if I can get them to give me some more."

Carmen doesn't see Rick until Charlie gets up and leaves. However, as soon as she does, she leans over and throws her arms around Rick.

"I didn't get a chance before to tell you how much I appreciate what you said to me. I'm glad you're one of the people who cares about me."

Before Rick can respond, Carmen plants a passionate kiss on his lips. Rick can tell Carmen wants to exchange tongues, but he restrains himself and keeps his mouth closed even though there's a compelling force trying to get the best of him. The hell with it, Rick thinks to himself as he lets Carmen's eager tongue slide into his mouth. Rick revels in the moment as Carmen's tongue explores his mouth and toyfully plays with his tongue. Rick decides to reciprocate and lets his tongue escape only to be met by Carmen's cavernous mouth as she sucks on his tongue much to their mutual delight.

As their tongues intertwine, Rick can't help feeling the delightful pressure trapped in his pants. He pulls Carmen closer leaving just enough room for her hand to maneuver. Much to Rick's astonishment, Carmen surreptitiously moves her hand slowly down his chest and past his waist. Sudden, it dawns on Rick that he could easily be caught by anyone who happens by and he immediately withdraws his tongue from Carmen's mouth as he backs off.

Carmen seems hurt. "What's the matter Rick?"

"Nothing. I shouldn't have let this happen in the first place and I shouldn't be leading you on like this. I don't know why I let myself do this, but I'm glad it was you." Rick feels embarrassed that he let himself get this involved, but feels he got out of it the best way he could think of. He hopes Carmen's feelings weren't bruised. "I guess we just needed some comfort and we found it the best way we could. I don't know about you, but I feel one hell of a lot better even though I feel kind of guilty about it, because I really love my wife and I'd never do anything that would upset her."

Carmen regains her composure. We'll, I don't care what Carlos would say because I've sort of made up my mind and as soon as I get out of here I think I might even see a lawyer."

Rick is elated. "That's great! Do you think you'll really go through with it?"

Carmen's jubilance turns to depression. "I don't know, but I think I felt good about saying it. If you don't mind, maybe we can talk about it later and I promise I'll try and keep myself from kissing you again."

"It'll be harder on me," Rick tells her, hoping to lift her spirits.

Charlie enters the TV room and sees Rick and Carmen talking "They said I had to wait for medication time before they'd give me my Lithium. I wish the clock would move faster," he says chortling.

Rick stands up and wipes the sweat off his face. He hopes Charlie won't notice that both he and Carmen are sweating profusely. Maybe if he changes the subject, Charlie won't bother to ask why they're perspiring.

"Did you see a new guy in here today in the past couple of hours?"

Charlie shakes his head in confusion. "I don't know Rick, Maybe I did, but I really don't remember."

"What's he look like?" Carmen asks.

"I don't know. He checked into my room while I was in here and just about the only thing I know about him is that he's on heroin or something."

"I think I know who it might be," Charlie interrupts. "I saw this new guy with Neil in the hallway and they were talking. I think they were talking about me, because when I walked by they stopped talking. Maybe they're in Neil's room."

"Where's that?"

"You know where the room is with the pool table?"

Rick nods his head.

"I know where it is too," Charlie jokes.

Carmen chooses to ignore Charlie's remark. "Neil's in the room right before you get to the pool room. If you don't see him around, he's usually in there sleeping."

Rick thanks Carmen and he exits the TV room heading down the corridor towards Neil's room.

Rick opens Neil's door and enters without knocking. Rick spots Neil sitting on his bed with a syringe poised above a small spoon. Neil hears his door opening and he looks up. He is immediately frightened, so much so that he drops the spoon on the floor and its contents spill out.

"Close the door Rick!" Neil shouts as he reaches for his

spoon, finding it empty. "Shit! That was good stuff down the tubes."

"Is it all right if I stay awhile?" Rick asks as he curiously stares at Neil's syringe on the bed.

"I guess so, but just stand against the door so no one comes in until I'm finished." Neil goes into his guitar case and removes a little plastic bag of brown powder.

Rick is astonished. "Is that what I think it is?" Rick's voice cracks nervously.

"It ain't brown sugar," Neil retorts as he sprinkles a tiny portion of the powder into the spoon.

"I've never seen heroin. before, let alone watch someone shoot it. Can I stay and watch you do it?"

"Sure, but just don't move away from that door."

"I thought you quit that stuff. You had me convinced you did."

Neil seems pleased to hear Rick's remark. "Look Rick. Everything I said in therapy is true. It's just that it doesn't apply to me and as long as I say those things, no one would ever suspect me of getting high in here."

"I don't understand what you're doing here if you're planning on staying on the stuff."

Neil walks over to his sink and lets a couple of drops of water fall into his spoon. "It's not hard to understand. My parents kicked me out of the house for shooting and when my money ran out I came back here. I was here six months ago, and I left when I got my head straight and as soon as I can find a good job, I'll leave again. I've still got another week on Medi-Cal anyway. "Neil sits down on his bed and removes the cotton from a cotton swab which he rolls into a tiny ball before dropping it into the spoon.

"I thought you already had a job lined up. At least that's what you said in group."

"That's just a line to keep that idiot doctor off my back."

"Could you tell me what you're doing? Like I said before, I've never seen heroin before let alone watch somebody shooting."

Neil looks up and smiles. He's amused at Rick's naivete. "Sure. Well, first you put the stuff in a spoon, but not too much. Then you put a couple of drops of water in. "Neil approaches Rick to show him what he's talking about. Neil points into the spoon. "You see that wad of cotton in there?"

"Yeah."

Neil lights a match and holds it under the spoon. Well, when I hold this match underneath the spoon, it makes the cotton absorb all the shit they cut the heroin with. It's sort of like a magnet because the only stuff that's left on top of the water is the pure heroin." Neil blows the match out and throws it onto the floor. Then he removes the syringe from his pocket and he uses it to suck the brown powder off the water in the spoon. "Then you draw the stuff into the needle and hold it in the air like this and tap it as you slightly force the air out using a little thumb pressure."

Rick watches in astonishment as Neil holds the needle up and flicks it with his finger while pushing on the plunger ever so slightly. A few minute drops of water fly out of the needle in a stream as Neil continues flicking the syringe. Then Neil hands the syringe to Rick. "Hold it a minute will ya?"

Rick takes the needle and holds it as he watches Neil tying a rubber strip around his upper arm. Then Neil folds his arm back like he's going to show off his muscle.

"Let me have it," he says as he takes the needle back. "You don't have to watch if you don't want to. There's really nothing to see."

"I can always turn away if I start feeling squeamish."

Neil studies his arm until he decides which vein he'll inject.

Then he tenses as he plunges the needle into his vein. Neil makes a horrible face as he injects himself. Rick finds himself staring around the room hoping that Neil won't notice that he really doesn't have such a strong stomach.

"That's it!" Neil announces as he removes the needle from his vein. and undoes the rubber strip around his arm.

"How long does it take before it hits you?"

Neil goes over to his guitar case and throws the syringe inside. "I'll clean it up later. Now, what'd you say?"

"I just wanted to know how long it takes to start working."

"Are you kidding?" Neil rubs the spot on his arm where he injected himself. "I'm already on a high. It works right away."

"You don't seem loaded to me. How can you maintain? Especially on heroin."

"The stuffs not really that good, but it does its job pretty good for being a cheap high."

Rick looks at Neil askance. "Didn't you tell me you were broke when you came in here?"

"I was, but I have a talent for making money to buy things wherever I go."

Rick is more confused than ever. "I still don't understand. Even if you could get hold of some money in here, how could you turn it into a syringe and some heroin?"

Neil looks at Rick and begins laughing. "I'm really surprised at you Rick. For such an intelligent guy, you've been here long enough to figure out a few things, but I think you've been walking around with your eyes closed. I know they screwed you up when you first came in because I heard the nurses talking about it, but I guess they fucked you up worse than you thought."

"What are you talking about?"

Neil thinks long and hard, finally deciding to clear Rick's confusion. "You might as well hear it from me instead of finding it out on the streets," Neil laughs. "Guess you might even want to thank me."

Rick is more confused than ever. "I feel pretty stupid Neil because I still don't know what you're talking about!"

"Look man, when you came in here you had two bucks in your wallet."

"Had is right." Rick suddenly catches on. "Hey wait a second! How'd you know that?"

Neil laughs. "Now you're getting it! I heard you wanted a Pickle so I accommodated you at a fair price. Normally, I charge more for a Pickle, but I knew you couldn't afford it."

Rick can't believe his ears. "You mean you came into my room and traded a Placidyl for my two bucks?"

"It was worth it, wasn't it? I mean you were in a pretty bad way."

"I didn't even take it."

Neil looks at Rick skeptically. "Why not? It wasn't defective, was it?"

Rick is perturbed. "Look Neil, it may interest you to know I came in here to get off that stuff and not to get more! I'm aware a lot of people in here are only trying to score drugs for free and I really don't care, even though it's a sad commentary on the goings on with the system, but I don't think you should be going around playing Johnny Appleseed with pills unless someone specifically asks you to." Rick catches himself speaking. "What am I saying? I'm condoning what you're doing when I should be punching you in the mouth."

Neil backs away. He suddenly realizes that he should have kept his mouth shut. "Sorry Rick. I hope I didn't screw you up. You want your two bucks back?"

"Forget the money and you don't have to worry because I'm not gonna hit you." Rick shakes his head like he's trying to get the rocks out. "You're a real Dr. Jeckle and Mr. Hyde, you know that? One minute you're lecturing everyone on the evils of drugs and the next minute you're shooting yourself with heroin. Don't you think you've got a serious problem?"

"I've been shooting the stuff for years. I can handle it."

"I wouldn't be so sure about that. Look where you are."

Neil drops his head, not knowing quite what to say. It's obvious he feels ashamed.

"I'm not gonna blow the whistle on you if that's what you're worried about, but just try and understand that there are people in here who are really trying to get better. Now I know it's a hard thing to do, especially in this place, because I think it's run as a business and not as a hospital and that's a shame Because the only reason I'm ever gonna get better is because I want to."

I hope you make it Rick," Neil says sincerely.

"I hope so too."

Paul walks into Neil's room as Rick and Neil hit a lull in their conversation. Paul is a good looking, thirty-year-old with jet black hair and a tan complexion. Paul has everything going for him, except for his only physical flaw which bothers him to no end. He's only five feet five inches tall.

Paul walks over to Neil and whispers something to him.

"No problem Paul. Rick's all right."

"Hearing this, Paul reaches into his pocket and removes a handful of pills which he gives to Neil.

Neil goes over to his guitar case and opens it, tossing in the pills.

Rick walks over to Paul and extends his hand. "I'm Rick Brown from unit two."

Paul and Rick shake hands.

"I'm Paul. I'm in two also, maybe you're my roommate. You are if there's a guy in the room who they say always has seizures."

"That's the room all right. The guy's name is Jose. What's with all those pills anyway?"

"I made a deal with Neil's connection. You know she's one of the nurses."

Neil hears this and shakes his head. "I guess you know everything now."

Paul is a bit confused. "I thought you said he was all right."

Rick wants to put their fears to rest. After all, he has to live there too.

"I hope he is," Neil tells Paul nervously as he stares at Rick.

"Don't worry about it. I already forgot what I heard."

Neil's obviously relieved. "That's good."

"Listen Neil, Bessy wants to know when you're gonna get her medication changed."

"It's already been taken care of so just make sure she gives you two pills starting tomorrow."

"No problem," Paul replies as Rick listens intently. "I'll see you guys later. I've got to call my wife and tell her I checked in."

"How does your wife feel about you admitting yourself in here?"

"Well, the way she put it to me, I'd either have to check in and get the heroin out of my system or I could look forward to being a bachelor again."

"I know what you mean, except I don't think I reached that point yet with my wife."

Rick and Paul head back to unit two together. Rick's glad that Paul is his roommate. After all, anyone's better than Alexander and at least this way, he and Paul might help each other get cured forever. At any rate, Rick's certainly going to try even if the odds are against him.

CHAPTER SEVENTEEN

The cold sea breeze hits Rick as he exits his sister's car in the parking lot of the Marina restaurant. Rick isn't exactly dressed for cold weather, evidenced by his short-sleeved shirt. If he had known he was going to surprise his wife for her birthday, he could have had her bring his jacket to the hospital under false pretenses. At any rate, there's nothing he can do about it now except to race for the restaurant's door. Hopefully it will be warmer inside.

Gullivers is Rick and Valerie's favorite restaurant. They always ate there whenever they decided to go to the Marina. This is the first time, Rick has ever been there without his wife, but in a few minutes they'll be together again.

Rick checks with the reservations clerk and is delighted to learn that Valerie hasn't arrived. Rick takes his place in the corner of the waiting room where he has a perfect vantage point to see everyone coming and going. He borrows a menu from one of the cocktail waitresses which he holds in front of his face. Every few seconds, his eyes rise up over the top of the menu, enabling him to see whoever enters.

"Would you like something from the bar while you're waiting?" a waitress asks.

"No thanks," Rick responds as he holds the menu in front of his face.

"Can I help you read the menu? Looks to me like you're

having problems. It's really quite easy, we only serve prime rib here."

Rick keeps the menu planted in front of his face as he answers. "I know this looks a little funny, but I'm just hiding my face so my wife doesn't see me when she comes in. I'm gonna surprise her for her birthday."

"Good luck."

Rick lowers his menu slightly, enabling him to watch the waitress as she walks away. He is surprised to discover that her sexy voice in no way matches her figure. She's gotta weigh at least a hundred and eighty pounds, Rick thinks to himself as she slowly negotiates the stairway which leads into the dining room.

Rick looks at the clock above the reservations desk and figures he only has two hours to get back to the hospital. "I wish she'd hurry up and get here," Rick mumbles under his breath as he positions the menu in front of his face.

After thirty minutes pass, Rick wonders if Valerie and her girlfriend are ever going to come. Then the two women enter the restaurant and check with the reservations clerk. Rick hears the clerk inform them that their table will be ready in a few minutes. Valerie tells the clerk they'll go into the bar until they're called.

Rick's eyes peer over his menu as he watches Valerie and her girlfriend enter the bar area. A few minutes later, Valerie's girlfriend approaches Rick.

"Valerie thinks I'm going to the bathroom."

"Think she saw me?"

"Well, you were the only person in this room with a menu for a face." She laughs. Valerie's girlfriend heads for the exit. "She's pretty down in the dumps right now. All she keeps talking about is you and how she wishes she didn't have to spend her birthday without you. My ride's waiting. Good luck." Valerie's girlfriend exits.

Rick sets his menu down and heads into the bar. He spots Valerie sitting in a booth near the fireplace sipping on her drink. She looks anything but happy as Rick approaches.

"You ready to order another drink lady?"

"Not yet," Valerie casually remarks, preferring to stare at her drink. "Can you come back in a few minutes?"

"Valerie!"

Valerie looks up and sees Rick smiling affectionately. Valerie immediately vaults out of the booth and throws her arms around her husband. Their loving embrace draws stares from the other people in the bar.

"Why didn't you tell me they were letting you out? I would have picked you up."

Rick holds out his arm for Valerie to inspect. Valerie spots the hospital band around his wrist.

"Don't tell me you have to go back!"

"They only gave me three hours. If I don't get back in time, I'll be AWOL and they'll send the MPs after me. By the way, happy birthday."

Valerie smiles as Rick takes her in his arms and kisses her passionately.

"Don't you think we'd better sit down?" she says as their kissing subsides.

"What for? We're the biggest thing happening here."

C'mon Rick. This is embarrassing."

"No problem," he says as he sits down in the booth with Valerie. "I can kiss you just as well in the booth."

"You'd better move over so Janet will have a place to sit."

"What for? She's on her way home."

"You mean she was part of your little plot?"

"Yep!" Rick proudly states. "Remind me to send her my emergency Percodan."

"You mean you didn't take it?"

"That's right. I told you I just wanted it handy as sort of an insurance policy."

"When do you get out for good?" she anxiously asks.

"Shouldn't be much longer. As far as I'm concerned I'm already cured."

"So why can't you come home now? I miss you and I don't like sleeping alone."

"I don't know. I guess they'll let me go in a couple of days. I'll see if I can't find out something when I get back."

After they're seated in the dining room, the waitress comes over to take their order, but she stops short when she spots Rick's wristband.

"Is that a hospital band?"

"I wouldn't say that. It's more like a looney hatch wristband. I just escaped and if anybody in a white coat comes around. don't tell 'em you saw me."

The waitress looks at Rick askance then directs her stare at Valerie. "Is he kidding?" she hesitantly asks.

Rick can sense that the waitress is becoming unnerved. "Yeah, I'm kidding. They let me out of the hospital so I could take my wife out for dinner, so could you hurry up and take our order because I have to get back pretty soon."

"Sure, what would you like?"

When their dinner arrives, Rick and Valerie eat fast so they'll still have plenty of time before Rick has to return to the hospital.

"How's Jose doing?" Valerie asks as she takes her last bite of prime rib.

Rick hesitates before answering. He doesn't want to let on about the strange happenings he's been a part of. Instead, he tells her Jose's doing okay and that nothing unusual is going on at the hospital. He knows Valerie would be horrified if she knew the real truth, especially the part about Neil shooting heroin and being a drug supplier for his fellow patients.

The staff of waitresses sings 'Happy Birthday' to Valerie and present her with a small birthday cupcake. Valerie's face is red with embarrassment as she blows out the candles.

As Rick and Valerie share the cupcake, Valerie quizzes her husband on his drug recovery program.

"It's pretty routine. After breakfast, I go to group therapy and then I come back to my room for lunch before the next session."

Valerie seems interested. "What do you do when you're not in with the group?"

"Nothing special. Just hang around a lot and talk to the other patients or I go outside and watch 'em play volleyball."

"It doesn't sound so terrible. Are you sure you want to come home?"

"What's that supposed to mean?"

"Well, from the way you talk about that place, it sounds like you're having a great time."

"Don't be silly honey," he tells her as he wonders to himself how she guessed his true feelings about the hospital. He had no idea he painted such a rosy picture of hospital life there. Even as he's sitting there contemplating his next statement, he can't help wondering what's going on at the hospital while he's with his wife.

"Rick, it's just that I love you so much and I miss you because you're not home with me." Valerie's eyes become glassy.

Rick knows that at any moment Valerie will burst out crying. He hopes she doesn't because that infuriates him. That's the one thing about his wife he's never been able to cope with. He'll do anything to keep her from crying even if that includes lying to her. "C'mon Valerie. You don't think I like being in that place with all those addicts and alcoholics.

Not to mention all those depressed nuts who walk around like zombies. Look, I went there to get help and I'm not gonna leave until they're convinced I'm cured. I wouldn't want to come home until I'm better and I know you wouldn't want me to come home unless I was."

"I know Rick," she says wiping her eyes. "I know you have to stay there until you get better, but it's just that I miss you so much and I'd rather have you with me. I'm not used to living in the house when you 're not there."

"Well, I'll ask the doctor when he thinks I can come home."

"Will you let me know as soon as you find out?"

"How 'bout if I just surprise you by knocking on our front door," Rick says facetiously.

Valerie works up a smile. "No thanks. This surprise was plenty."

As Valerie drives Rick back to the hospital, she informs him he'll arrive about fifteen minutes early, explaining that she could come into the waiting room and they could talk for a while.

"Think I'd better get back to my room. If they know I came back early this time, they might give me another pass if I need one. "Rick knows this isn't exactly true. He just wants to get back as soon as possible and find out what transpired while he was away. After all, he feels like an integral part of the hospital and he really hated to leave even though it was only for three hours.

"I sure hope nothing good happened," Rick tells himself as he enters the hospital and races down the corridor for his room. "I hope Jose did all right without me."

CHAPTER EIGHTEEN

Rick returns to his room discovering Jose quietly sleeping with his television set still on. Rick walks over to Jose's bedside and flips off his TV which he swings back against the wall. Rick hears a strange sucking sound and notices that even though Jose's fast asleep, he still has the baby bottle pressed up against his mouth and he's sucking vigorously on the nipple. Rick adjusts Jose's blanket before returning to his own side of the room.

Rick decides to try one last time in the bathroom before turning in.

After only a few minutes in the bathroom, Rick finally manages to relieve his pressure. Rick is ecstatic and he pulls the nurse emergency cord next to the toilet. Several minutes later, one of the Korean nurses opens up the bathroom door and spots Rick sitting on the toilet, beaming.

"You no look like you need help. Why you bother me?" "I was told to let you know when I moved my bowels."

"That very good," She backs out of the doorway.

"Don't you want to see?"

"I no need see in toilet. I smell it." She closes the bathroom door.

Rick returns to his bed in an elevated state. He figures that all that moving around while he was with his wife loosened up his system, allowing his normal bodily functions to commence.

Rick relaxes on his bed when he realizes that Paul's bed is empty. Rick figures that Paul's probably in unit three and he decides to go over there and see what transpired during his absence.

"Where you go?" a Korean nurse asks as she spots Rick heading down unit two's corridor.

Rick doesn't turn around, thinking she won't stop him if he doesn't face her. "I have to go to unit three for a few minutes," he yells out as he rounds the corridor and disappears out of sight.

Rick enters unit three and is immediately confronted by Charlie, Neil and Paul. From the look of things, it seems as though they were waiting for him to walk into their unit.

"Don't tell me you guys have nothing better to do than wait for me so you could hear how my dinner was?"

"We thought you'd like to hear what happened while you were gone," Neil says with a sense of urgency in his voice.

"What do you mean? What happened?"

Charlie chortles. "It's about that black guy."

"JB? What'd he do?"

Paul takes over the conversation as he puts his hand over Charlie's mouth hoping to drown out his obnoxious sounds. "You know that black girl on PCP who always has flashbacks and they have to lock her up in restraints at night?"

Rick nods his head. He has a feeling he knows what Paul's about to relate.

"While she was tied down, JB snuck in her room and raped her. If Charlie didn't happen by, there's no telling what he would have done after that."

"They couldn't get her to stop screaming so they knocked her out. Now, she's really gonna be fucked up!" Neil reaches into Rick's pocket and removes one of his cigarettes. "It's obvious this staff isn't gonna do anything about JB, so I think that puts the ball in our court.

"Wait a minute Neil. if we're going to take care of him, I want to make sure of what really happened. "Rick looks directly at Charlie." Tell me exactly what you saw without speculating."

Charlie chortles nervously, obviously intimidated with all the attention he's getting. "Why don't you tell Rick, Paul?"

"You're the one who saw what happened Charlie."

"But if JB finds out I told on him then he'll be mad at me and he might hurt me with his karat and judo."

"C'mon Charlie. JB doesn't know any of that stuff. And even if he did, one punch in his mouth would take care of him."

"Well, all right," Charlie says obsequiously," but promise me you won't tell him that I told you."

Rick wants to ease Charlie's fears. "Don't worry about him."

Charlie relents. "Oh, all right." Charlie takes in a deep breath. "I was going to Neil's room because the nurse told me I couldn't have any more Lithium because the medication room was locked up until the morning and she said that Neil might give me some."

Neil is shocked to hear this. "Which nurse?"

"The one who's always going to your room when you're there."

Neil seems relieved. "Charlie, the next time you want more dope, don't go to a nurse and Don't ever mention my name!"

Rick doesn't like the way the conversation is going and he decides to interrupt. "Excuse me guys, but can we get back to the matter at hand. Now Charlie you said you were on your way to Neil's room, so tell me what happened and don't leave out a thing."

Charlie nods his head as he tries remembering. "I was

going to Neil's room like I said before and I passed by a room and I looked inside to see if any of my friends were in there so I could say 'hi'. I didn't know it was the Negro girl's room until I looked in and saw her all tied up to her bed and JB was lying on her and he had his pants almost off and it looked like he was doing one of those funny black dances on her." He chuckles. "I never saw anyone dancing on a bed before."

"C'mon Charlie. Never mind the dancing."

"Well, I can't help it! That's what it looked like, but the Negro girl didn't look like she was having a good time Because she was trying to scream. I thought it was part of the dance, but I never saw anyone dancing on top of another person before and I never heard of a dance where your penis is supposed to stick out like his did." Charlie chortles loudly. "I didn't like to hear her screaming, but I got to see her with her legs spread for JB. I wasn't going to say anything, but I thought he was hurting her and she couldn't tell him because he had his hand over her mouth, so I told him I thought he shouldn't be doing that."

"Did JB say anything to you?" Rick asks as the others listen intently.

"He started screaming at me too, and he came after me with his penis hanging out of his pants, so I ran to Neil's room and hid in his bathroom."

Neil decides to contribute what he knows. "I was in the pool room when I saw Charlie running into my room. I went into the corridor and I saw JB running out of Shirley's room and I heard her screaming."

"I heard her screaming too," Paul says, "and I saw JB go into his room and slam the door."

"How's Shirley doing?"

"She's all right now. They sedated her."

"They catch JB?" Rick asks, figuring that their answer will be affirmative.

"That's the part I can't figure out," Paul tells him. "I told the head guy what happened and he took care of Shirley, but he didn't give me the impression he really gave a damn about JB and what he did. He just told me that I shouldn't worry about him because JB was going to a state hospital pretty soon."

"You've got to be kidding!" Rick incredulously states. "You mean to tell me they just plan on letting him run around here unchecked? For all we know, he could be raping someone else right now!"

"If there's one thing I won't tolerate, it's rape" Neil blurts out.

"In every hospital I've ever been in, I always got as much pussy as I wanted, but I'd never force anyone to do it. I don't have to." he adds proudly.

"Got any ideas?" Paul asks Rick.

"It's not much of an idea, but as long as we have to live in this place, I really don't feel that comfortable about closing my eyes to sleep even though I'm in another unit. If they're not willing to take some sort of measures against JB for the protection of everyone in this place, then I think it's up to us to do something about him."

"I could just lock myself in my room and you could come get me in the morning," Charlie interrupts.

Rick, Paul and Neil stare bewildered at Charlie. "We're in this together Charlie," Paul informs him.

"Yeah, but, maybe if we tell them again about JB, they'll do something," Charlie theorizes hoping his friends will adopt his suggestion.

Rick feels that nothing's getting accomplished and decides to take over the discussion. "It's obvious they don't give a damn about what JB does in here as long as they're not affected, so that only leaves one thing. Us!"

"What do you suggest?"

"I think we'd better have a talk with Mr. JB and set him straight about a few things. You know, tell him it's for his own good and all that shit."

Paul seems a bit confused. "What if he just ignores us?"

Neil smashes his fist into his hand. "Then we'll just have to persuade him to see things our way."

The four patients scour unit three looking for JB. As they approach the exit, George walks into the unit. As soon as George sees Rick, he smiles slyly. "What's happening I fellas?"

Rick decides to take charge, fearing that someone, especially Charlie, might tell him too much. Well George, since no one cares to handle JB's actions by locking him away, we've decided to have a talk with him and straighten him out."

"Sounds a bit drastic to me for such a petty thing. Why I bet that girl was so loaded, she won't remember a thing except she had a wonderful time."

Rick is enraged. "You're really sick George, you know that?"

"Well Ricky, some people like butter and others like margarine."

"I should expect a warped remark like that from someone as twisted as you!"

George is delighted. "Keep talkin' Ricky. You're giving me goose bumps."

"Take a hike George."

George smiles and heads for the exit. "Anything you say Ricky, but I'll be back later."

"I hate that fucking fag!" Rick tells his comrades.

"Forget about him, we've got work to do."

"Maybe JB' s not even here."

"Unless he's hiding under someone's bed, he's either in the TV room or the therapy room."

"What if he's not there either?"

"Why don't we first check the therapy room before we

leave the unit."

The four men walk into the therapy room and spot JB sitting in the corner talking with Judy. JB has his hand between Judy's legs as she leans back to allow his probing fingers room to explore.

"What the fuck you doing JB?" Rick calls out as he approaches with his three friends following close behind.

JB removes his hand as Judy sits up smiling. "Do you want a turn too sugar?" Judy asks.

Rick ignores her question as he stares vitriolically at JB.

"Why you guys followin' me? All I want is to be left alone. I ain't botherin' nothin'. You keep wantin' to cause me trouble because you're jealous that all the chicks love me and not you. I can't give 'em enough of my love."

"Look JB, you'd better cool it and get back to your room if you know what's good for you!" Rick warns.

"Leave me alone," JB says defensively. "I didn't do nothin'! You're just out to get me because you're prejudiced against all brothers."

Rick turns around expecting one of his friends to say something, but they just look at Rick hoping he'll continue.

"We know what you did to Shirley, JB, and we're here to tell you you'd better watch your step from now on because we'll be watching you and if you screw up again, we'll fix it so you won't have another chance. You got that?"

JB shakes his fists at Rick. "I told you don't want you talkin' to me."

"I don't give a shit about what you say! I'd be happy to just ignore you, but I have to live in this place too and I'm not about to sit by while you terrorize and rape the patients."

"I don't gotta rape nobody. They all want me to stick it in 'em. Can I help it if they want my manhood inside of 'em?"

Neil decides to speak up. "You'd better do like Rick says or you won't wake up for breakfast!"

JB shakes his fists at Neil. "I 'specially don't want you talking to me. You're whiter than they are and I don't like you either. I don't like no dope addicts telling me what to do, 'specially you!"

Neil is determined to get his point across. We're telling you for your own good. I suggest you listen good because this is the only warning you're gonna get."

"He wasn't doing anything wrong." Judy informs the group. Rick picks up Judy's arm and leads her towards the door. "Are we going to your room Rick?"

Rick shakes his head negatively. "No we're not," he replies adamantly. "I think you'd better leave now."

"I'll wait for you in my room in case you change your mind." Judy licks her lips hoping to influence Rick's decision.

"You're awfully tempting Judy, but I won't change my mind. "Rick closes the door.

"Why'd you make her go?" JB protests.

"Because we don't want any witnesses," Paul cautions.

JB gets up and heads for the door, shaking his fists. "I'm leavin' too! You're all crazy people!"

"You'd better do what we said JB or suffer the consequences," Neil reminds him.

"You're just jealous because you ain't gettin' it like I am," JB calls out as he leaves the room, closing the door behind him.

"I think I'm kind of scared of him," Charlie tells his three friends.

"Don't be ridiculous Charlie," Rick tells him. "You have to realize a guy like JB is really a sick individual who wouldn't hurt anyone unless he was sure he wouldn't get any resistance. And believe me, he'd be the last one to challenge you." Rick face his friends. "I know you'll think I'm probably a chicken or something, but I feel we have to take control of the situation even though I'm going back to my own unit. They'll probably send somebody over from my unit anyway, so I might as well get back as soon as I can, but not before we figure out how to handle JB."

"Don't tell us you've got an idea from one of your scripts that fits in this place," Neil chides.

"Nothing that comes to mind, but it's something that makes sense. Look, JB wouldn't think of repeating his behavior unless he thought no one was watching him, so I think we should divide up our time and sort of keep a surveillance on him. He'll probably try and lose you, but at least he won't be molesting anyone."

Charlie yawns. "I just wanna go to sleep. I'm tired."

"Go to sleep if you want," Paul tells him," but if I were you, I'd be afraid to close my eyes while JB's roaming around."

Charlie looks around nervously. "I'm gonna stay in here till morning and I'm gonna lock the door so he can't come in here," he states, his voice trembling.

"As long as you're willing to stay in here, you might as well prop a chair next to the window so you can see down the corridor. And if JB decides to go prowling around, he'll spot you watching him and he'll think twice before trying any of his shit."

Charlie chortles nervously.

"C 'mon Charlie," Neil says in a soothing voice. "He's too chicken to challenge you. Just let him see you and if you need me, just stick your head out the door and yell. I'll be sitting in my doorway watching the other corridor."

"Well all right, but if you want to come in here tonight, knock three times on the door fast and then knock twice slow. I'll know it's you."

"Sure Charlie," Neil replies as he tries to hold in his

laughter," but what if I want to come in and forget the code?"

"When I ask who's there, you say your name and I'll let you in."

Rick seems pleased, but he's glad he doesn't have to stay in unit three. He knows he'll even be uncomfortable in his own bed, figuring that if JB sneaks out of unit three, he's just crazy enough to find another unit where he can prowl around undisturbed.

Rick heads for the door. "I'm glad you guys have tonight worked out so I'll head back to my unit. Want to walk back with me Paul?" Rick says pretending to be scared.

"Think I'll hang around awhile."

"See you back in the room," Rick states as he heads out of the therapy room. He's confident his friends will take care of JB.

Rick approaches the exit when he hears his name being called out. Rick stops in his tracks and sees Judy standing out in the corridor outside her room.

"What do you want Judy? If you want me to come into your room you can forget it." Rick tells her in a determined voice.

Judy does her best to look sympathetic. "Please Rick. My sink's leaking and I can't clean up unless you can fix it."

"Don't give me that. Ask one of the attendants."

"I did, but they said I have to wait for the maintenance man in the morning and I can't wait that long. Please."

Rick is still skeptical. "Are you sure?"

"I swear. Just come in and take a look at it. I'm sure you can figure it out. Please, it'll just take a minute and I won't attack you or anything. I promise."

Rick doesn't know whether or not to believe her, but he does know that if she did ask for help, she was probably fluffed off by one of the staff who probably felt that fixing a sink was beneath his dignity.

As Rick debates the issue with himself, he spots one of the staff sitting behind the desk staring at him."

"I'm just gonna go take a look at her faucet and that's it," Rick says with conviction as he heads down the corridor towards Judy's room.

"Thanks Rick," Judy says as she leads Rick into her bathroom. "I promise I won't touch you unless you want me to."

Rick becomes slightly apprehensive when he notices that the door leading into the next room is shut. Rick prepares to open the door, but Judy stops him.

"They don't like their door open except when my door's closed." "Look Judy, your sink better be busted or I'm gonna split." Judy indicates the sink. "See for yourself."

"I will as soon as you get out of here so I can have room to maneuver." Rick stares at her with a look of determination and she backs out of the room.

Rick checks the hot water faucet and is surprised to discover that Judy was telling the truth. After a few feats of strength, Rick fixes the faucet and prepares to check the connection beneath the sink when he feels the presence of someone else in the bathroom. Rick turns his head and sees Judy standing behind him. Her hospital gown is hiked up to her waist enabling her to masturbate openly while she stares upward in ecstasy as she works on herself. Rick can't help staring as he watches her fingers sliding in and out while she rubs her buttocks against the bathroom wall moving ever so rhythmically as she experiences the tiny self-induced climaxes caused by her probing fingers.

The unmistakable odor of Judy's womanhood permeates the bathroom as Rick takes delight at the beautiful vision before him. Then Judy opens her eyes and spots Rick gaping at her.

"See something you like?" she asks sensually as she

continues undaunted, moving her fingers even faster as she moans with delight. "Do it to me Rick!" she demands.

Rick finds himself hard pressed to look away and in a moment of sexual weakness finally relents, pushing her hands out of his way. enabling him to accommodate Judy with his own probing fingers.

"Taste me!" Judy begs as she tries guiding Rick's head towards her.

Rick fights the impulse deciding he'd better check the doorway making sure he's not being observed, but when he looks to the open doorway he sees JB standing there staring ominously. Rick immediately pushes Judy out of his way, then races out of the room past a smiling JB. Rick sees JB entering Judy's bathroom as he exits the room and makes his way down the corridor.

Rick approaches the exit as Neil spots him.

"I thought you went back to two."

Rick regains his composure before speaking. "I just wanted to see if Carol was all right before I left."

"Did you see JB down there?"

"I have not seen him, Rick retorts, trying to sound blasé. "I think maybe he's down the other corridor," Rick tells Neil as he exits unit three hoping that Neil won't find out where he really was and what he was doing.

CHAPTER NINETEEN

Rick awakens from the sound of the breakfast cart being wheeled down the corridor of unit two. He sit's up in bed and looks towards his doorway expecting the cart to be wheeled in at any moment. Paul also wakes up and sees Rick staring at the door.

"What are you looking at? Paul asks as he rubs the sleep out of his eyes.

"I'm just waiting for 'em to bring in our breakfast."

"If the food's anything like it was last time I was here, you're wasting your time."

"I know it's pretty bad, but what can I say, I'm starving."

Paul grins. "You've probably been here a long time."

"I know what you mean. I think my taste buds are dead from all the slop they give us."

"Think I'll skip breakfast and wait till that guy comes in and I'll have him bring me a roast beef sandwich from down the street."

"What time did you come back to the room last night?"

"A few minutes after you left. JB didn't seem like he was planning anything so I left."

As Rick and Paul continue to converse, Jose wakes up and begins pounding on his table hoping to get Rick's attention. Rick surreptitiously glances over to Jose's side of the room, but he quickly looks away.

"I think that guy wants you for something."

"I'm tired of him bugging me," Rick says callously hoping Jose will hear him and stop his incessant pounding. "If he wants something he ought to just press his button and wait for the nurse like everyone el se."

"Maybe his button's broken."

Rick doesn't want Paul to think he doesn't care about his fellow roommate, so he decides to see what Jose wants.

"What's the matter Jose?"

Jose points towards his mouth.

"You know what he wants?"

"He wants me to help him smoke a cigarette, but I don't feel like getting out of bed yet."

"No problem," Paul tells Rick as he gets out of his bed and approaches Jose. He lights up a cigarette and sticks it between Jose's lips. "I hate smokin' alone."

Rick is delighted that Paul's taking an interest in Jose. After all, Rick feels that Jose abused him by always treating him as if he were his personal nurse or something. Rick didn't mind at first and he even felt good about helping Jose, but as far as he's concerned, Jose took advantage of him and he doesn't feel obligated to keep helping him for the rest of his hospital stay. Rick has to concentrate on his own problems if he's going to get better.

Rick's breakfast is brought in and placed on his table. Rick moves his table in front of him and he maneuvers his television set blocking out Jose's side of the room. As Rick consumes his meal, he hears Jose pounding for attention and calling out his name, but Rick simply ignores his unfortunate roommate, hoping he'll get the message and leave him alone."

After breakfast, Rick and Paul head for unit three. They walk past unit one as Nick approaches, still confined to his wheelchair.

"You guys wouldn't have an extra cigarette on you, would you?"

The two men turn around. Rick instantly recognizes Nick. If Rick had known it was Nick, he would have just kept walking.

Paul smiles affably as he removes a cigarette from his pocket and hands it to Nick. "No problem." Paul looks at Rick expecting him to also give Nick a cigarette.

"I thought you went home Nick."

"Well man," Nick looks up, his eyes drooping and his mouth hanging open, "you can see I'm still here so I guess I didn't."

"Give the poor guy one of your smokes, Rick."

Rick gives Nick a stern look. "No thanks. He's had enough of my cigarettes!" Rick gives Paul a gentle push down the corridor. "Let's go."

As Rick and Paul approach unit three, they notice the open door leading into the admitting room. Rick peers in and sees a few policemen walking around near the pharmacy. One of the officer's spots Rick and he walks over to close the door.

"What happened officer?"

"You fellas didn't happen to see anyone hanging around in the lobby last night, did you?"

Paul steps in front of Rick where he has a better vantage point into the room. He sees the damaged door to the pharmacy. "Somebody break in and steal drugs?"

"Did either of you see anything last night?"

"No sir," Rick replies as the officer closes. the door.

"I wonder if it was anybody from here?" Paul wonders as they enter unit three.

Dr. Whitehead follows Rick and Paul into the therapy room. She waits for everyone to be seated before beginning.

"Excuse me Dr. Whitehead, but I think we ought to discuss

something that isn't really part of our normal discussion, but is in fact germane to everyone in this place."

"Well, if it affects everyone like you say, I'm sure we'd all like to hear what it is. Just try and make it brief so we can get on with the purpose of these sessions."

Rick looks around the room, focusing his attention on JB. "I don't know if you're aware of it or not, but during the last twenty-four hours, one of the people in this room attempted rape twice and was successful once. I don't think we have to mention who the victims are, but I think we ought to point out the guilty party to let him know we aren't gonna put up with it anymore."

Dr. Whitehead decides to interrupt Rick before he forces a confrontation. Before she speaks, she notices that JB's ignoring everyone, preferring to practice his karate moves hoping to intimidate the other patients. "We're aware of the problem Rick, and as soon as our group is finished I'm having a staff meeting to work out a solution."

Carol decides to speak up. "Well, I think the staffs waiting too long.

They know what should be done and I don't see why he gets to roam around in the meantime."

"Hey! I never touched your lily-white ass, so don't you be talkin' to me either!" JB yells out shaking his fists at Carol.

"See how unstable he is Dr. Whitehead? I'm scared to be in the same room with him!"

JB stares ominously at Carol. "You're just mad because I don't want to stick it in you. You probably got VD you ugly syphilis face!"

"That will be enough JB!" Dr. Whitehead cautions.

"You wouldn't come down on me if you didn't hate niggers!"

Dr. Whitehead tries keeping her composure. "If you'll look

around you JB, you'll notice you're not the only black person in the room." She indicates a fat black man who's in the hospital for alcoholism.

"He's no nigger! He's just black on the outside and I's black through and through. This is a white man's hospital anyway and I ain't stayin' so you just leave me alone!" JB shakes his fists at Dr. Whitehead, then demonstrates a few karate moves in the air, complete with sound effects.

"I don't think JB belongs here," Charlie comments nervously, his voice trembling.

Hearing this, JB stands up and approaches Charlie. He spits on Charlie's shoes. then assumes a karate stance. C'mon big man, let's see if you wanna go up against my fast moves!" JB slices the air with another intimidating karate, chop.

"Sit down JB!" Dr. Whitehead commands.

"I'll take on all of you!" JB threatens as he demonstrates his karate once again. "I ain't afraid of nothing'! you's all prejudiced against black men because we's better lovers than you white folks."

"Sit down, now! Dr. Whitehead orders.

"I don't have to be listenin' to you! I don't have to listen to none of you!" JB races out of the room shaking his fists at the entire group.

The room is silent as Dr. Whitehead contemplates her next move.

"I think he ought to be locked in a padded room," Carol mumbles under her breath.

"I hope you can help him get better," Carmen tells Dr. Whitehead.

"I'm sure we all share your feelings Carmen, and I think I'd better initiate some action for his own good. "Dr. Whitehead begins writing on her chart.

Most of the group begin discussing JB's problem, but

Neil refrains from commenting, preferring to sit motionless displaying an ominous smile.

"Can I have everybody's attention please." Dr. Whitehead stands up.

"I'll expect to see all of you back here in half an hour and we'll pick up our discussion then."

Dr. Whitehead exits the room followed by several patients. Carmen and Norma are surprised to see Carol heading for the door.

"Stay here with us Carol," Carmen calls out. "We've got to stick together until they take care of JB."

"I guess you're right," Carol informs her friends as she approaches, "I didn't even know where I was going."

Rick and Paul decide to head outside to the recreation area, hoping to watch a volleyball game. Several other patients apparently have the same idea.

"Did Neil look okay to you in there?"

"I didn't notice, why?"

"Either he's loaded on heroin or he's super depressed. He's always talking in group, but he didn't say one word. I didn't think he could resist the temptation after what JB said. He knows JB's full of shit."

"I wouldn't worry about him," Paul comments in a reassuring tone. "I know Neil from the time I was here. One second he'd be talking up a storm and the next thing I knew, he was in another world. He's one of those thinkers, you know?"

Rick and Paul are the last to enter the therapy room as Dr. Whitehead prepares to start. Neil and Carla take their seats in the corner of the room as Dr. Whitehead finished making notes on one of the charts on her lap.

Then she. looks up, seemingly pleased about something until she notices Sue with a cast on both her hands.

"Nice of you to join us again Sue. I see you've kept your

word and broken your other hand as well."

Sue looks at Dr. Whitehead with tears streaming down her face. "Leave me alone!" she pleads.

"You're obviously not here with the rest of us because you wish to be ignored, are you?"

"I said, Leave me alone!"

"Now that both of your hands are broken, you must feel better. Do you?"

"No! And stop talking to me!"

"I know you don't want me to ignore you any more than you want to go on punishing yourself by inflicting pain on yourself."

"Yeah Sue, open up. I know what you're going through because I was where you are and it didn't do any good keeping it inside. I was only fooling myself and I kept sticking myself with. needles so I could keep my distance from anyone who wanted to help and it didn't get better until I opened up in ground just like this." Neil looks around the room, hoping that another patient will add to what he's said.

Sue is infuriated that anyone, especially Neil, would dare suggest she needs help. "You don't know what it's like! My problems are my own and if I feel like breaking both my arms and legs, it's none of anyone' s business except my own."

"Then why didn't you just stay in your room instead of coming here? You knew when you sat down we wouldn't leave you alone. No one in here gets special treatment, especially when there's an obvious problem to be discussed."

Sue gets up and runs for the door.

"Don't go Sue," Rick pleads as she opens the door.

Dr. Whitehead decides to intervene. "Let her go Rick! It's obvious she won't let us help her. I'm afraid that in her condition she can only be treated privately and we can't reach her until she's ready."

Sue stands by the door listening to Dr. Whitehead. The

she slams the door shut as the paging system switches on and an alarm bell begins to sound. Everyone listens to the voice coming out of the speaker.

"Code blue, unit three, fifteen. Code blue, unit three, fifteen. Code blue, unit three, fifteen."

The message continues as several hospital personnel race into unit three and head down the corridor.

"Remain. Seated!" Dr. Whitehead shouts as several patients approach the window and look out into the corridor as more hospital personnel race into room fifteen located at the end of the corridor.

Dr. Whitehead sees what's going on, deciding that her assistance might be imperative to whatever's going on. Then she hastily exits the room, cautioning the group not to leave until she returns. Everyone stands by the window wondering what's going on as several doctors enter the unit heading for room fifteen.

"Anyone know whose room that is?" Rick asks aloud.

"I think that's my room," one of the male patients informs Rick. "JB's my roommate."

Hearing this, Rick and Paul head for the door.

"I don't think you're supposed to leave here," Charlie reminds them as they head for the door.   .   !

Rick and Paul prefer not to answer Charlie's remark and they exit the room, moving cautiously down the corridor followed by several patients from the therapy room.

Several minutes pass while the. entire therapy group congregates near room fifteen. Then several doctors exit displaying placid expressions. Rick overhears two doctors discussing the patient inside. Apparently JB injected a toxic substance into his system. Paul is anxious to hear what Rick overheard, but shudders when Rick tells him.

A few nurses exit room fifteen shaking their heads in

disbelief as they try to restore order in the unit telling the people standing in the corridor to clear a path. Then two attendants wheel out a gurney with a white sheet covering a human body. As the gurney passes by the curious onlookers, Neil leans forward and peaks underneath the sheet. Two nurses watch in disgust, deciding not to reprimand his activity. Neil stares at the motionless figure, then lets the sheet drop back on the body.

Neil half smiles. "I guess you's ain't so dangerous after all. You's sure ain't gonna be messin' with me no more!" Neil mumbles under his breath, so no one can hear.

"I sure couldn't look under there," Rick tells Neil as they watch the gurney travelling down the corridor and out of the unit.

"It goes with the territory," Neil says casually.

Rick doesn't wish to discuss the matter further, but he wants his curiosity satisfied. "Was it who I think it was?"

"Would you be happy if I told you that we won't have any more trouble from JB?" Neil asks, smirking.

Rick isn't too distressed to hear that JB was under that sheet. "I guess if anybody had to knock off it might as well be him, but he didn't impress me as the type who shoots."

"You only, have to screw up once before your lights go out!"

"I don't understand you Neil. You act like you're glad JB killed himself."

"Aren't you?"

"I can't honestly say I'll cry for him, but he is a human being."

"Well, I don't think those girls he raped will agree with you and neither will the rest of the people in this unit. Why don't you go and ask Carla if she's glad he's dead? Did you know that this morning, JB pried off the doorknob to the shower room and almost attacked Carla? The staff didn't do shit about it, because they didn't see it happen, but I did!" he adds boastfully.

Dr. Whitehead orders everyone to quiet down as Rick stares curiously at Neil trying to figure out the hidden meaning behind his words.

"Would everyone please return to their own room, and all those people from units one and two please return to your rooms also. We'll let you know when we'll continue with group."

"A few patients slowly file throughout unit three as Carla walks up to Dr. Whitehead.

"I'm scared Dr. Whitehead. What happened to JB might happen to someone else next, even me!"

Dr. Whitehead puts her arm around Carla comforting her. "There's nothing to worry about Carla."

"What'd he die from?"

"I' afraid we won't know till the autopsy. In the meantime, why don't you go back to your room and I'll have something sent in to help you rest, okay?"

Carla looks around nervously as if she's afraid to let go of Dr. Whitehead. "Will you come back to my room with me?"

Dr. Whitehead nods her head as she leads Carla away from JB's room.

"I can't wait to get back to our room," Paul informs Rick as they head out of unit three.

"I had no idea your taste buds gave out on you so soon that You'd be anxious to get back for lunch."

"Shit Rick I ain't gonna eat that slop. I've got to make a phone call so I can keep myself together."

"You know Paul, ever since I've been here, everybody keeps telling me one thing when they really mean another. If a guy tells me he likes it when it snows, I think he's talking about the stuff snowmen are made of instead of cocaine. I must be stupid or something because I still can't get with the language that's spoken around here."

"Let's not go into that now," he says kiddingly as they enter their room.

Rick lies down on his bed as Paul picks up the phone and begins dialing.

"I hate to ask another ridiculous question, but what exactly are you doing here? I mean, I thought you were here to get off drugs and now you're trying to get more. Correct me if I'm wrong, but isn't this a drug rehabilitation hospital?"

Paul holds up his hand indicating he wants Rick to be quiet while he talks on the phone. Rick turns on his television, pretending to be occupied as he eavesdrops on Paul's conversation. Rick is astonished to listen to his roommate as he arranges to buy some heroin. Unfortunately, Paul has to go out of the hospital to pick it up.

Paul finishes his conversation and looks across the room at Rick. "Could you do me a favor Rick?

Rick shuts off his TV and faces Paul. "First tell me what you're doing here if you're not quitting the stuff?"

"Hey man, don't come down on me like that! It was either check in here for two weeks or my old lady was gonna split on me."

"As long as you're here, why don't you at least give it a try and quit?"

"That was my plan when I checked in, but I didn't know they stopped treating heroin withdrawal with Methadone and that's the only way I'd even give quitting a shot. They expect me to just go cold-turkey after I've been using for five years. No way I could handle that!"

"How long you think you can fool your wife? She'll know you didn't kick it the first day you get home."

"I don't see how she can split on me after I've been here for two weeks. I'll even stay longer if Medi-Cal extends me."

"You've got a definite problem my friend."

"That mean you won't help me? because if you turn me down, I can always ask someone else."

Rick decides not to answer for a few moments as he ponders the situation. He knows that if he turns down Paul's request, no matter how unreasonable, he stands to create an uncomfortable climate between his roommate and himself. And as long as he's condemned to this hospital, he'd better make as many allies as possible. "What kind of favor?" he asks hesitantly.

Just cover for me for couple hours and if you want I'll split some heroin with you."

"I don't know Paul. If you get busted, they might find out I helped cover for you and they'd kick me out before I'm ready. Besides, I don't even want you to share your heroin with me."

"You worry too much man. It's no sweat. If someone comes around looking for me, you just; tell 'em you don't know where I am. Even if they: catch me, I wouldn't let anyone hang with me." Be a good guy, huh?"

"I don't know Paul."

"C'mon Rick."

"All right," Rick says reluctantly," but you'd better be back in two hours."

Paul gets up and heads for the door. "Thanks a lot man. Let's go."

"Go where?"

I need you to watch out for me while I hop the fence."

Reluctantly, Rick follows Paul out onto the empty Volleyball court. Paul takes his position against the fence.

"Don't just stand there doing nothing," Paul calls out. Pick up the ball over there and just start bouncing it so you don't look so damn suspicious."

Rick leers at Paul letting him know he's not happy about the situation. Then he picks up the ball and begins bouncing it as he looks around, hoping that no one's watching him.

Minutes later, and old car pulls into the alley next to the fence and Paul exchanges a few words with its occupants.

Paul looks away from his friends in the car focusing his attention on Rick. "It's time," he calls out.

"Go ahead," Rick tells him.

Paul climbs up the fence, but his pocket rips open spilling its contents on Rick's side of the fence. Seeing this, Rick casually strolls over and picks them up as Paul drops to the other side.

"Let me have them!" Paul demands.

Rick studies the pill bottles that fell out of Paul's pocket. "Where'd you get all this shit?"

What do you care? I'm trading this for the heroin," Paul nastily retorts as he reaches through the fence and grabs the bottles from Rick.

"Was this stuff ripped off from the pharmacy?"

"How the fuck should I know!" Paul replies indignantly as he stuffs the bottles into his pocket. "I didn't ark Neil where he got the stuff and you shouldn't either."

Rick digests what he's heard as Paul gets into his friend's car. Rick watches the car drive out of the alley as Dr. Whitehead approaches from behind.

"See anything interesting?"

Rick jerks his head around, surprised to hear anyone's voice, especially Dr. Whitehead's. You scared me!"

"I didn't mean to. What are you doing out here?"

"Oh, I just came out here to get some fresh air. That wasn't an easy thing to see before."

"I know what you mean. I never get used to it either. We're

supposed to expect that sort of thing and let it pass without letting it affect us, but I don't think I can ever just let it pass through me like nothing happened."

Rick looks away hoping she'll change the subject.

I know it's a hard thing to get out of your head, so if you like I can prescribe something to make you feel relaxed that won't interfere with your treatment.

"No thanks, I think I'll just go back to my room and lie down awhile."

"Glad to hear you say that," she tells Rick as they head back to their respective units.

As Rick retreats back to his unit, he wonders just how long Dr. Whitehead was standing behind him. Did she see him watching out while Paul vaulted over the fence? Rick has his doubts, figuring that if she saw what he was doing, she'd probably tell him and not make a game out of it. At any rate, Rick is glad he didn't get caught. Now he only hopes Paul will return undetected.

Jose pounds on his table hoping to get Rick's attention, but instead of responding, Rick simply whirls his television around, obstructing his view of Jose. Then Rick turns up the sound on his TV drowning out Jose's pounding.

"How's my favorite patient doing today?" Maggie asks as she enters the room, noticing Paul's empty bed.

Rick's delighted to see Maggie. "I'm fine, but I think Jose's the one who needs your attention."

Maggie looks over at Jose. She notices that his bottle has fallen to the floor. She bends down to pick it up and places it next to Jose's mouth. "Here you go Jose." Maggie turns around to address Rick. "By the way, have you seen Paul around? His wife is in the waiting room."

"Uh, I think I saw him in unit three before I left."

"All right dear, I'll go tell him he has a visitor."

Rick watches Maggie leave his room as he decides on a course of action. He knows that if Maggie doesn't find Paul in unit three, she'll probably assume he went back to his room. Unfortunately, Rick knows that unless he can somehow fool Maggie, and anyone else who joins her search, it won't take them long to figure out that Paul's left the hospital. If this happens, they'll probably await Paul's return and check him for drugs. At any rate, Rick knows he'd better do something and do it posthaste.

Rick races down the maze of corridors until he enters unit three.

Rick takes his place in the television room a few moments before Maggie pokes her head inside. She spots Rick sitting in front of the TV. Rick casually looks up and displays a pleased look upon Maggie. "Did you see Paul?"

Maggie shake her head indicating that she hasn't

"He just left here a minute ago. I tried telling him he has a visitor, but I guess he didn't hear me. I think he went back to our room for cigarettes or something." Rick hopes his answer will appease her.

I promised his wife I'd send him in before she has to go to work."

"I'll find him for you, Rick spouts hoping Maggie will agree.

"Don't worry about it honey. I have to head back to that unit anyway. You stay here and watch your program."

Rick looks on as Maggie exits the room and walks out of unit three. Then Rick gets up and races down the corridor and through the open emergency doors which lead to unit two. Rick closes the door quietly so as not to arouse suspicion as to his behavior. He casually walks down the corridor towards his room as the medication nurse enters pushing in her cart.

"If you're looking for Paul he'll be back in about ten

minutes."

The medication nurse checks her watch. "Well, if he's in another room, I can still give him his medication."

"I think he's in unit one. That's where he said he was going, but he said he'd be back in about ten minutes."

"That's okay. I'll come back when I finish my rounds."

Rick breathes a sigh of relief until he hears Maggie's voice coming closer to his room. He takes his medication from the nurse and swallows it quickly on his way to the bathroom. He slams the door and presses his ear up against it as he hears Maggie enter.

"Hi Flora," Maggie greets the nurse.

Maggie indicates Paul's bed. "You seen that patient? I've been looking for him all over to tell him his wife's here for a visit."

"He's in unit one. I'm heading that way pretty soon. I'll tell him he has a visitor if you like."

"Thanks anyway, Flora, but I'll tell him, myself before his wife has to leave."

When he's sure Maggie is gone, Rick exits the bathroom and continues roaming around to the different units for the next couple of hours leading Maggie on a wild goose chase.

"It's a good thing Maggie has a lot of stuff on her mind besides Paul," Ri.ck mumbles. to himself as he runs from unit three back to unit two, "otherwise she'd figure out what I was doing in no time."

During the course of Maggie's search, Rick enlists the effort of other patients who tell Maggie that they just saw Paul a minute ago heading for another part of the hospital.

"I'm gonna get to the bottom of this right now!" Maggie informs the staff of unit three as Rick listens from down the corridor.

Rick knows he can't fool Maggie any longer and he doesn't

want to come out and just lie to her, figuring she could make his stay even; harder on him. So he decides to take refuge in Neil's room. This way if Maggie does come in and confronts him, he can have Neil back up his story. Neil's fooled everybody into thinking that he's a perfect angel so Maggie would believe him in an instant.

Rick enters Neil's room untrounced hoping to find Paul inside. He stands in the middle of the room for a moment before speaking as Paul enters and closes the door.

"Nice of you to come back," Rick quips.

"It took me longer than I thought, but at least I got the stuff." Paul reaches into his pocket and removes a small packet which he tosses to Neil. "How'd it go, Rick?"

"Are you kidding!" Rick chides. "Everyone in this place was looking for your ass! You're lucky you didn't get busted when you walked in."

"No sweat man," he comments casually. "I already talked to Maggie and she told me about my wife coming to visit. She looked surprised to see me, but she didn't say anything. You worry too much man. I'm back ain't I?"

"That's the best news I've heard all day and don't expect me to do it again Because I don't like lying to them and I especially don't like, running around this place covering for you."

"Well, I got enough stuff so there won't have to be a next time."

Rick informs Paul exactly what transpired while he was gone as Neil checks the contents of the packet.

"Hey Paul," Neil interrupts. "Where the hell's the syringe? I can't shoot this stuff without a needle. You were supposed to bring me one remember?"

"I know man, but they didn't have any and I couldn't afford to stay away from here any longer while I looked."

Neil is visibly upset. "Fuck man! What the fuck am I supposed to do with a bunch of horse and no needle? I need the stuff right now and my connection isn't even working tonight or there'd be no problem."

As Rick listens to Neil's rage, he remembers that he watched Neil shoot heroin earlier and when he finished he threw the needle into his guitar case.

"What happened to that needle you threw into your stash before?" Rick inquires.

Neil reacts nervously looking around the room in an attempt to avoid Rick's question. "I don't know man, I guess I lost it or something."

Hearing this, Rick suddenly gets an uneasy feeling about Neil. Is it possible Neil's needle was the one JB supposedly used to kill himself, Rick wonders as he makes a conscious effort to avoid Neil's piercing eyes. Could Neil actually do something crazy like that to another human being? Then Rick remembers how Neil acted in group therapy as he watched JB's raving in silence, almost like a man who was at peace with himself having made a decision. At any rate, Rick decides to keep his suspicions to himself fearing what Neil might do if in fact he is responsible for the demise of a fellow patient, even someone as despicable as JB.

Rick declines further comment on the issue, deciding that the less he says the better. After all, he wants to stay on Neil's good side, figuring that the life he saves might very well be his own.

CHAPTER TWENTY

Rick loathes staying in his room. It's the only place in the entire hospital where he can't get any rest thanks to his roommate, Jose. Rick continually ignores Jose's cries for assistance hoping he'll simply just call for a nurse like every other patient.

Dr. Whitehead enters the room as Rick blasts the volume on his TV, drowning out Jose's pounding. Dr. Whitehead walks over to Rick's TV and turns down the volume as she spots Jose trying to get her attention.

"Can I get you something?"

"Can you help me smoke a cigarette please?" Jose cries out barely making himself understood.

Dr. Whitehead obliges his request, but after she places the cigarette into his mouth, she returns to Rick's side of the room.

"You're not gonna lie in bed all day, are you?"

"To tell the truth, I'm kind of tired and I'd like to take it easy for a while."

"You know Rick, you've been here for over a week and I think that while you're here, you ought to have a few sessions in private."

"You mean with a psychiatrist?"

"That bother you?"

"Does it cost extra?"

"No. It's part of your treatment. I'm surprised you haven't taken advantage of our services."

"You know this is the third time since I've been here that someone suggested I should have private therapy, but no one seems to know who I'm supposed to see or when I'm supposed to go. Are you the one I should have the session with?"

"No, I'm not. I only take care of patients with severe depression problems. I'm not fully acquainted with the technique of treating a drug addiction."

"That's fine, but since you know that I should see one of the shrinks, are you planning to set me up with someone or are you just going to assume, like everyone else has done, that I'm supposed to know where to go and who to see."

"I'm surprised at you Rick," she says smiling. "I thought you'd give me a hard time about spending time in private therapy."

"Hey, it's free isn't it and I don't see how it could hurt. I know I'm a long way from being perfect and I've got problems like everyone else, but as long as I'm here and it doesn't cost extra, I don't see why I shouldn't take advantage of the situation. Who know, I might even get over a few of my hang-ups if there's someone there to help me overcome them."

"That's a very healthy attitude."

"Anyway. it would be just my luck that they wouldn't let me go on time because someone forgot to have me talk to a therapist. I'd just as soon get it over with."

"Well, I'll bring up your name at the staff meeting this afternoon."

"I hate to sound like I don't believe you or anything. but that's exactly what the other doctors said they'd do and so far, they haven't done shit! They like hearing themselves talk."

"You won't have any reason to be cynical after I get you that appointment."

Dr. Whitehead heads for the door, ignoring Jose's cry for help.

Rick looks across the room at his unfortunate roommate, noticing Jose's panicked expression as an unpleasant odor permeates the room.

"Fire!" Jose calls out as his voice begins to fail.

Rick vaults out of bed and races over to Jose's bedside noticing that his pillow is smoldering from the cigarette that dropped onto it. Rick picks up Jose's pitcher of water and dumps it on the pillow, extinguishing it.

"What's that smell?" one of the nurses asks suspiciously as she stands in the doorway sniffing the air. "Are you trying to burn this hospital down? What's the matter with you?"

Rick shoves the empty plastic container in her hands. "You take care of him from now on!" Rick's finally decided he'll no longer do her job. "I'm not supposed to be his nurse, you are!"

The nurse stares at Rick in bewilderment as he storms out of the room.

Jose tries speaking to the nurse, but she can't understand a word. Jose is disappointed that his voice is all but gone, so he indicates that he needs his diaper changed.

"I'll tell your nurse to come change you as soon as she comes back from lunch." The nurse sets down the empty pitcher on Jose's table and hurriedly exits before the head nurse enters and orders her to perform the distasteful task of changing a grown man's dirty diaper.

Rick walks through the maze of corridors, stopping outside unit one. Rick isn't in too big of a hurry to return to unit three, figuring that Neil just might confront him about JB's death. Rick's gut feeling is that Neil killed JB, but he's not about to point an accusing finger at him, especially when Neil might do something to him if he suspected that Rick is the only one who figured it out. Rick doesn't want to go on hiding from Neil, but he'll make every effort to avoid him while he's still there.

Rick is still curious about the goings on in unit one and he'd just like to go in for one last time to see what really goes on.

Rick enters the alcoholic unit and spots Nick wheeling himself down the corridor. Rick's first reaction is to leave, but he doesn't. He waits silently by the exit until Nick disappears inside one of the rooms at the end of the corridor.

Rick strolls down the corridor unnoticed until the medication nurse pushes her cart past him. She greets Rick as she maneuvers her cart into the room directly ahead.

Rick stops dead in his tracks as he tries remembering where he saw this nurse before. Suddenly it dawns on him that this nurse is the one he suspected of filching his medication. As he approaches the room and peers in, Rick theorizes that maybe she's the one who supplies Neil with drugs.

Rick watches in amazement as the nurse takes a few dollars from her patient which she changes for drugs. Then the patient spots Rick and quickly throws his pills underneath his sheets. The nurse sees he's acting awfully strange and she turns around spotting Rick.

"He's one of the good guys," the nurse tells her patient as she smiles at Rick.

Rick smiles back nervously, deciding to continue his tour of unit one.

Rick succumbs to the temptation of another open door. He remembers this room from his earlier visit as the one where a man, he guesses is a patient, asked him for money. Afraid that the man's probably in the room, Rick takes a fleeting glance inside. Rick is surprised to see that there is only one person in the room, Judy. She is sprawled out on the bed completely nude. Judy wiggles and squirms on the bed as she caresses herself staring an invitation at Rick.

"You didn't have to come all the way over here just to taste my delights. You can have me whenever you want, but c'mon in anyway and stick it in me."

Rick looks at her askance trying to figure out what she meant by her remarks concerning his trek into unit one. Rick yields to the temptation, but just as he takes one step into the room, a hand firmly lands on his shoulder holding him back. Rick whirls around nervously and confronts the same man he saw near the room earlier.

"Pay up first man!" he demands.

Rick is totally perplexed. "What?"

"Don't be giving me any of your shit! You didn't pay me no money before, but now you owe ten bucks and you ain't gonna leave until you pay."

Rick thinks fast, hoping to overcome this idiot with his brains because he certainly couldn't handle him physically. "She's a friend of mine from unit three. They sent me to find her for her psychiatric evaluation testing. They're interested in her sapid behavior late, especially concerning the obsequious nature exhibited by her fellow patients who up until the past few hours have been attributing their obtrusive behavior to the repartee between themselves and Judy." Rick studies the man's face hoping he was able ta flim-flam the man into letting him leave safely.

The man looks at Rick with a glazed expression. However, his perplexed state quickly fades. "Don't think you're gonna get out of here unless you pay me the money! Now dig in those pockets and let loose with the green stuff!"

Hearing this, Rick nervously tries thinking of some other way to peacefully remove himself from the clutches of this pimp.

"C'mon man, time is money and you owe me and I want it else I'll take it out of you and I ain't gonna say please."

"Look man, Rick tells him harshly as he surreptitiously

reaches into his cigarette pack removing a cigarette. Then Rick puts the cigarette behind him while he tries fashioning it into a facsimile of marijuana cigarette. "I just came over to find Judy and tell her she has to get back to her unit. I didn't do anything with her and I don't owe you any money."

"You looked at her didn't you, and that's not for free." The man backs up and clenches his fists.

Rick takes a step backwards into the room she hurriedly empties the tobacco out of his cigarette and then twists the ends. The man takes a few steps into the room hoping to back Rick up into the corner.

"You gonna pay me the money?" He shakes his fists in Rick's face.

Rick smiles confidently as he brings out his hand and offers the fake marijuana to the pimp. "All I have is my last joint of Hawaiian. I've been saving it for an emergency."

The man grabs the fake joint from Rick and slips it into his pocket. "I should be chargin' you more for taking up my time, but I'll take this for now for what you got to see and if you come back you'd better bring back at least ten more of these or I'll bust your head! You got that?"

"Yes sir," Rick says obsequiously as he makes his way past the man and out of the room as Judy looks on disappointed.

Rick heads down the wrong end of the corridor, and instead of winding up where he came in, he ends up at the end of the corridor. Rick sees the pimp staring at him from his position outside Judy's room and Rick stares back. Hoping to scare Rick, the pimp takes a few steps toward Rick until a customer approaches looking to procure Judy's services. Rick is stunned when he recognizes that the man entering the room is Zulu.

"What the hell's Zulu gonna do with Judy?" Rick mumbles under his breath as the pimp closes the door and stands outside the room counting the money Zulu paid him.

Rick desperately wants to get the hell out of unit one, but he doesn't know how Judy's a pimp will act when he sees him passing. It's just possible he may have discovered that his supposed marijuana is only tobacco, in which case Rick doesn't want to go anywhere near him.

Rick instinctively takes a few steps down the corridor while watching the pimp. Unfortunately, Rick isn't watching where he's going and he accidently walks into the open door of a large room. Rick quickly recovers and notices that this room is much larger than the other rooms in this unit. He spots six beds, each occupied by a female patient. None of the women pay any attention to Rick as he glares in at them. However, Rick spots one woman who, for some reason unknown to him, seems to strike a familiar cord in his mind. The woman sees Rick staring at her and she turns her head only to look at Rick a moment later with the same curious look. Then she gets off her bed and approaches as Rick studies her face trying to figure out why he thinks he's met her before.

"You name isn't Rick, Ricky Brown, is it?"

Rick is aghast. "How'd you know that? I think I know you too, but I can't place you. Do I know you?"

"Well, it was a long time ago, but you still look kind of the same."

Suddenly it dawns on Rick just who this familiar face belongs to. "It's Kim, right?"

Kim smiles affably. "I'm surprised you recognizes me," she says reluctantly as she looks down at her beer belly. "I guess you know why I'm here." Kim doesn't wish to talk about anything dealing with her stay in the hospital and quickly changes the subject. "What have you been doing with your life?"

"Well," Rick smiles," do you want me to start with elementary school and work my way up to this hospital?"

Kim giggles, like the little girl she'd like to be again. "No, silly. I don't think I'll be here that long."

For the next few minutes Rick and Kim converse about their lives including the unfortunate circumstances that led them both to the same hospital some twenty years down the line.

Kim's conversation leads her to talk about her alcohol history. "If you remember me in high school, you probably saw me fucked up all the time on booze. I started drinking with the guys I ran around with and I even had a bottle in my locker. I started just drinking beer and shit, but after a while, when I could legally buy the hard stuff instead of stealing it from my parent's liquor cabinet, I went on to about a quart or vodka a day. I know I'm an alcoholic and I want to get better." Kim notices Rick's eyes. They're riveted on her belly which resembles a keg of beer.

"I don't like not being able to look at my feet because my stomach's so fat!"

Rick is aware that Kim caught him staring at her stomach and he casually pretends to remove something from his eye, hoping she won't comment.

"You don't have to look away. I know it's there too. God, I wish it wasn't!" Kim laughs nervously. "I remember how I used to make fun of all my friends who had stomachs like mine and now I'm just as disgusting to look at as they were."

Rick wishes he hadn't entered the room and met up with his former elementary school classmate. After all, he had fond memories of her up until now. He finds it distasteful to even look at her with her large beer belly obscuring what might otherwise be her nicely formed tiny breasts. Instead, her stomach looks almost as if it's part of her chest as well.

Kim continues complaining about her sorry state as Rick listens with a forced look of interest. He studies her carefully trying to picture that little girl he once thought was so cute. He can't help noticing her long spaghetti-like blonde hair which desperately cries out for a good shampooing. Her hair keeps falling on her face as she continues talking. She continually blows the hair away from her mouth and shakes her head hoping it will fall back into place. As she does this, Rick can't help thinking that if she used at least a little make-up she might look slightly better.

"I' d probably be in my favorite bar with the guys if my liver didn't give out on me last week. My doctor said I'm lucky to be alive. I wish I could believe that, but right now I really need a drink. If I could just have one more drink, I know I'd feel better. Then I'd let 'em cure me."

Rick interrupts Kim's pathetic speech deciding he'd rather talk about his problems than listen to hers. Anyway, he feels that her story is no different than any other alcoholic, whereas his experience is unique. After all, it involves him.

As Rick indulges himself, explaining his problem with Placidyls, he notices that Kim doesn't seem the least bit interested. She keeps turning her head so she can see everything that's going on in her unit. Rick decides to see if she's paying any attention to him by throwing a few non-sequiturs into his dissertation on drugs.

"So, he came over to me and he took all my pills and he died right there in front of me. Then he got up and I told him to buy Texaco because it's really cheap and they make great tacos."

"I know what you mean," she answers back as she looks at Rick for a moment before looking down the hall.

Rick stops talking, preferring to stare at. Kim giving her the once over. He can't get over how they both started out as innocents and now their only thing in common is this hospital.

Rick finds this encounter distasteful and politely excuses

himself, telling Kim that he'll look her up when they're both discharged. They both know Rick has no intention of fulfilling his words, but it seems like the logical thing to say.

Rick heads out of unit one delighted to find Judy's pimp nowhere in sight. He's still disturbed that he found one of his childhood classmates in the same hospital. He feels embarrassed that he had to meet her under such circumstances and he's sure she feels the same way. After all, she seemed more surprised to see him than delighted, and he should know because that's exactly the way he felt.

Dr. Schwartz approaches Rick as he enters unit three.

"Could I have a word with you Mr. Brown?"

"Sure," Rick answers nervously, figuring that Dr. Schwartz somehow found out that he helped Paul sneak out of the hospital.

Dr. Schwartz checks his records before speaking. "I don't seem to see on your record where you were counseled in private either by me or anyone else. I get the impression you're deliberately avoiding talking to a psychiatrist. Am I right in this regard? Are you in fact afraid to have private therapy?"

"Course not" Rick replies demonstratively. "I just saw Dr. Whitehead and she said she'd set up an appointment for me as soon as she could."

"I'll be the one who gets your case, so if you want, we could start in with your therapy right away. Do you object?"

"Why should I? I'm not afraid of anything. Besides, I don't see how it could hurt me. As long as it's part of my treatment and it doesn't cost extra, I'm all for it."

Dr. Schwartz checks his watch. "Are you doing anything now?"

"Not really."

"Good," he replies as he starts down the corridor. "Let's

spend a few minutes in my office and see if we can't accomplish something."

Rick follows Dr. Schwartz into the arts and crafts room and then into his tiny office located next to the ping pong room.

"Just have a seat anywhere, Mr. Brown," Dr. Schwartz says as he takes his place behind his small desk adorned with various bowling trophies. Then he takes a pipe out of his pocket and jams it between his teeth.

Rick spots the customary couch against the wall, but opts for the Hepplewhite chair in the corner of the room. Rick makes himself comfortable, pressing his back against the back of the chair. Then Rick removes an ashtray from the small table next to the couch and gets ready to light up a cigarette. Dr. Schwartz looks away from his notes noticing that Rick is going to smoke.

"I'd appreciate you not smoking until your session's over. You see, this room doesn't have very good ventilation and I hate the smell of cigarette smoke. It Is very bad for the health you know. I think you can wait."

Rick reluctantly takes the cigarette out of his mouth and places it back into the pack. He doesn't like the idea of not smoking while he's in therapy. After all, he always smokes in situations of stress, particularly when it involves bearing his soul to a stranger. "How about if I just have this one cigarette?"

"I'd prefer you didn't. You can smoke when you leave. I just don't like people who smoke around me. We all have our little quirks Mr. Brown. I'm sure you have your own also, like people who smoke pipes or cigars. If you'll notice my pipe. I never smoke it, but I just like having it around. Some people fidget with pencils and such and I use a pipe."

"I think you're comparing apples and oranges." Rick stands up and opens the door. "I'll just blow my smoke out the door."

"Close the door Mr. Brown and let's get to work. You can smoke all you want, but not in here."

Rick closes the door and returns to his chair. He doesn't like being intimidated, especially when he feels that Dr. Schwartz should bend over backwards in order to make him feel at ease. And if smoking helps him get to this state, he should encourage it instead of making it an issue. As it stands right now, Rick feels anything but comfortable thanks to Dr. Schwartz' negative attitude towards patients who smoke. What kind of nut is he, Rick thinks to himself as he watches Dr. Schwartz looking through his file. You'd think he'd know better than to make me uncomfortable when he should be doing everything he could to make me feel like he's my friend.

Dr. Schwartz studies Rick's chart for a few minutes before beginning. "As I see it, you were doing fine until you had that back injury of yours, at which point you suffered a few setbacks in. your recovery phase which kept you on assorted pain and sleeping drugs. Is that right?"

"Yeah, well, I don't know whether or not the surgery worked because I got in a car accident and then I…"

Dr. Schwartz interrupts. "Yes, yes I know all that, just let me finish. As I was saying, you took some twenty or so different controlled substances one of which you became addicted to. From the history you gave on the admitting forms, I see you innocently started with small doses and gradually increased to larger doses. You realize, of course, that someone in the field of television like yourself is more frequently put into positions of stress due to the unemployment picture which you face more times than the average worker. I'm sure this led to your addiction. It Is a very competitive field, isn't it?"

"I don't think that has any bearing on my addiction," Rick replies indignantly.

Dr. Schwartz is too busy making notes on Rick's chart

to pay attention to his remarks. Then he looks up and stares blankly at Rick. "Would you care to add anything? For instance, is anything in particular bothering you now?"

Rick instinctively reaches for a cigarette, but Dr. Schwartz stops him, reminding him that he can wait for their session to end before smoking. Rick resents Dr. Schwartz for this, but decides to continue anyway, hoping his resentment for the doctor won't preclude him from bearing his soul.

"Well, I guess one of the things bothering me is my former partner. Before we teamed up I was writing scripts and I couldn't get anybody to read them except my family. Everybody always told me how good they were, and they were right but I couldn't get the people in the business to read them. Anyway, I had this friend, well, I really didn't like him, but he hung around with my other friends so I guess I had to be friendly to him. His folks were big writers in the business and I got them to read my stuff even though I had this feeling they wouldn't help me even if they thought I was good. I was really shocked when Steve, that's my partner, I mean my ex-partner, wanted to write a script for the show his parents were working on. He knew he didn't have any talent so he asked me if I'd help him. When his mother found out, she agreed to read the scripts I wrote and one day she came out and said, 'Did you write this script Rick?' and I remember I was really nervous and I said, 'yes, why' and she said, 'it's really good!' I felt great after that, but she didn't pursue the matter with me and I knew she'd never help me unless there was something in it for her. I didn't think she wanted me to succeed when her son was such a failure. See, Steve wasn't much of anything, especially as far as his father was concerned. All Steve's father ever did was complain about what a bum Steve was and how he never does anything constructive. Then, Steve's father would always go back into his bedroom and watch the football games on television. His father always yelled at him comparing him to me. He'd say, 'why don't you be like Rick and try and do something with your life. Steve knew how to handle his father. He was on the football team at school and he really tried hard to be a jock, but he was too fat and he was always getting yelled at by the coach until he invited him over to meet his parents and then they sent the coach on a trip so he wouldn't kick their kid off the team. Steve was a big gambler too and whenever he'd lose, he'd get his dad to give him money telling him he broke a window when he was playing football or something and his dad always gave him money to pay for it. I think he knew Steve was lying, but he didn't want to admit that his son was anything but a future All-American." Rick pauses to catch his breath hoping Dr. Schwartz will comment, but he doesn't.

Dr. Schwartz remains silent as he stares at Rick waiting for him to continue.

"I knew I wanted to be a writer and I decided that Steve's parents would help us get connections if their son was involved so I convinced Steve that we should write together. I told him that he didn't have to write a word and I'd do all the work and put his name on the script. At that time, Steve liked the idea and said he'd try and write with me, but after we started working together, I think he got kind of embarrassed because he couldn't write a single word of dialogue without calling his mom on the phone and check his joke with her first. That really pissed me off and we fought about it so he stopped showing up altogether and I'd just write the whole script and put his name on it. I didn't like doing it but I figured that when I got established enough, I'd drop Steve and go it alone. I remember one time, Steve said he had same good material for our script, but he told me he couldn't work in my office. He said I should go to the race track and meet him there so he could work. I don't know why I fell for that shit, but I went to the track and got to watch him lose a bunch of money while he yelled stupid jokes at me while the horses were running. He didn't want me there to write. He just wanted me there so he could have someone to talk to between races, I guess I was kind of insecure because I didn't want to test the waters alone so I only have myself to blame," Rick pauses and stares at Dr. Schwartz hoping he'll offer his views, but, as before, he remains silent.

"I was ready to break off the partnership a couple of months ago, but I decided to wait. See, we were supposed to write a Hawaiian monologue for a new show and Steve showed up at my house three hours after we were supposed to start working on it. When he came over, I had already written the monologue and Steve really liked it, but he said he wanted to take it home and type it on his mother's typewriter for good luck, then he showed up here and showed me that he added a third page to the monologue and said that his parents said it was okay to use material out of their Hawaiian joke file. I was really pissed and told him that I wouldn't turn his parent's work in as our own, but he insisted. He said something to the effect that I shouldn't care so long as it got us the job, I hope we don't get the assignment because I told Steve to go fuck himself. Even when I had my back operation, Steve tried to get me to postpone it so he could write one of our scripts together, He was afraid he couldn't do it alone, so he didn't even try," Rick stops again, hoping that Dr. Schwartz will at least say something to show that he's listening, but as before, he's says nothing,

"Steve even came here because we're supposed to be working on a script, I told him to go to hell and I didn't want to see him anymore. He didn't care much for what I had to say. He didn't even care about what I was doing in here. He just wanted me to help him write the script because he knew he couldn't even spell his name right unless I did it for him and I just got fed. up with all that shit and told him to go find someone else to write his scripts for him," Rick catches himself. "Oh, I'm sorry. I already said that. "Anyway, I knew I was cutting my own throat, but I couldn't take it anymore. I know his parents will get even with me for getting rid of their little boy, but I don't care. I'm just glad it's over. I think I was getting an ulcer from him. I remember when I'd hear his car pulling into the driveway, I'd get a pain in my stomach that wouldn't go away until he did. Even when my phone rang and I thought it was him, I'd still get that pain in my stomach and I'd tell my wife to tell him I wasn't home. Do you think I did the right thing getting rid of Steve?"

Dr. Schwartz doesn't respond. Instead, he stares at Rick blankly.

Rick feels slightly relieved that he's unloading his pent up feelings, but he wishes Dr. Schwartz would at least interject a few words to show that he is in fact listening.

Dr. Schwartz looks away from Rick to make some notes on his chart. Much to Rick's surprise, Dr. Schwartz finally speaks, even though it's brief.

"Continue please."

"I have a feeling his parents will get even with me for dumping their little boy, but I'm prepared for that. I don't think they can really blacklist me and even if they could, I don't think it will last for more than a couple of years. That's the trouble with this business. Everybody knows everybody and if one person gets pissed off at you, they tell their friends in the business that you're no good and pretty soon the word gets around. You know it's really weird. When I came in here I had two problems, Placidyls and Steve. Now, when I leave, those problems will be gone, but I'll probably have a new problem to worry about, I'll be blacklisted. That might be a good time to sit down for two years and write a book about my Hollywood experiences. What do you think?"

Finally, Dr. Schwartz decides to speak. "I think you're a depressed person with a lot of problems that are only now coming to the surface. He pauses hoping Rick will be impressed with his evaluation. "What do you think?"

Rick is puzzled. "Aren't you going to tell me? I mean, aren't you supposed to listen and find out what's buggin' me and then come up with some solution?"

"That would make my job awfully easy, but I'm afraid it doesn't work that way. You see, you need a lot of time in therapy before I can even begin to help. It takes at least three hours before I can even get to know my patient to see if he is indeed in trouble. You'd be surprised at all the patients who come in for the first time and relate things to me that aren't relevant to their real problem. They get over it though," he adds confidently. "and that's when we can get together and help each other."

"But the things I told you about are what's buggin' me."

Dr. Schwartz sits back in his chair as if he's going to say something profound. "I'm sure you feel that way now, but you'll see that as we spend more and more time together, you'll find out things about yourself that are the true causes of your manifestations. This is just the beginning. "He takes out a small prescription pad and begins writing.

Dr. Schwartz finishes with one piece of paper and rips it off, enabling him to write another prescription. "Here you go," he says as he hands both papers to Rick. "Take these to the medication nurse on your unit."

"What are they for?" Rick asks as he tries reading Dr. Schwartz's writing.

"Just something to help you relax."

"What are they exactly?"

"Mellaril and Ativan," he retorts matter-of-factly.

"Harmless tranquilizers which I believe might be the very thing you need in your condition."

Rick throws the slips of paper onto Dr. Schwartz's desk, noticing that there's an ashtray on his desk with a couple of butts in it. "I thought you said no one's allowed to smoke in here." He indicates the ashtray.

Dr. Schwartz takes the ashtray and empties it into the trash. "That was from an earlier meeting with the administrator of this hospital," he informs Rick believing he won't pursue the matter.

"Then how come you wouldn't let—

Dr. Schwartz interrupts. "We must make some allowances and exceptions throughout life." He picks up the prescriptions and hands them back to Rick. "As a rule, I like my patients to take the medication I prescribe them."

"How can I make you understand that I don't need or want any more pills, especially tranquilizers! I came to this place to get off them and now you want to give me more. Isn't there a better way?"

"Just take the medication Rick and I'll evaluate you at our next session to see if there's any improvement. You know you can't get better unless you first decide you want to help yourself and you can only do that if you take my advice and your medication."

"You sure I can't get by on my own?"

Dr. Schwartz shakes his head in disgust. He's tired of discussing the matter. "Yes, I'm sure!" he replies holding up Rick's hospital file. "All the reports on you since you checked in seem to indicate that you've been extremely tense and that you've been anything but obliging as far as the staff is concerned. You haven't let yourself relax for one minute and I think it's time for you to let us treat you the way we know how."

Rick gets up and heads for the door with a forced smile emblazoned on his face. He realizes he'd better not say anything more, deciding that if Dr. Schwartz gets any madder, his next step is liable to be putting him in restraints.

"Now take the medication I prescribed and I'll see you later"

Rick leaves unit three as the medication nurse announces to the unit that all patients should report to the medication window for their drugs. As Rick closes the doors of unit three, he looks over his shoulder and notices the mad rush of patients as they try to form a line in front of the window so they can get their pills and shots as soon as possible.

Rick's attitude changes as he nears his own unit. "Maybe these new pills will help after all," he mumbles to himself as he nears the nurses station. "I wonder if these pills will get me loaded like I used to be," he says, as he hands the prescriptions to the medication nurse.

Rick watches the nurse as she drops several pills into a cup and hands it to him. Rick looks into the cup noticing his usual dose of vitamin pills, anti-itch pill and now two new pills.

"Doctor knows best," Rick says as he washes down his pills with some orange juice.

"I think you'd better go lie down in bed," the nurse tells him.

"You're the boss," Rick replies as he turns and heads into his room ignoring Jose's plea for a cigarette.

Rick plops down on his bed as Jose tries getting his attention.

"Maybe I do need to be more relaxed," Rick says softly as he waits for the tranquilizers to begin working.

CHAPTER TWENTY-ONE

"Excuse me nurse, but I think it's been more than three hours and I haven't gotten my medication yet," Rick yells to a passing nurse as his tenth day at the hospital approaches the noon hour.

The nurse stops in Rick's doorway, looks at her watch and then stares at Rick. "I'm afraid it's only been two hours. I think you can hold out for another hour."

Rick didn't think he could con the nurse. After all, he knew it wasn't time for his Mellaril and Ativan supply to be replenished but he certainly couldn't be faulted tor trying to obtain another dosage before the pills he had already taken wore off. There's nothing worse than coming down from good dope, Rick tells himself as he tries relaxing in bed hoping the hour will pass quickly.

"Aren't you coming to group today?" Sherri inquires as she approaches Rick's bed.

Rick looks up dazed. "As soon as I get my medication I'll be there. If I don't get there on time, tell 'em to start without me." Rick grins, hoping that Sherri will burst forth with laughter, but she doesn't.

"Are you feeling all right Rick? You look kind of woozy."

"I'm fine. Really!"

Sherri studies him carefully and isn't happy with what she sees. "You're sure about that?"

"Course I am he replies indignantly. "I'm just waiting for my medication, then I'll go over to group, okay?"

Sherri leaves the room as a nurse enters and removes Jose's untouched breakfast tray.

"What time is it please?" Rick asks.

The nurse checks her watch before replying. "It's fifty-five minutes before you get your medication."

"Is it possible I could get one of my tranquilizers now instead of having to wait for both pills later?"

The nurse shakes her head negatively. "Afraid not. You have to wait for your medication like anyone else. Besides, there's a reason why you should wait for the proper time before taking medication, especially the kind of pills you're taking."

Rick decides not to press the issue figuring he's just wasting his time.

He'll just have to get through the next fifty-five minutes by himself. "I hope she gets here on time," Rick mutters softly.

"I'm sorry. Were you talking to me?" the nurse asks as she takes Jose's tray and starts for the door.

"No I wasn't. I was just wondering why I can't just go home and take my medication there. I could come back for the group and for the sessions with my doctor and it'd be just like I was still here, only I wouldn't have to stay here."

"Sounds reasonable to me. You've been here long enough anyway. If it were up to me, I think I'd let you go home and come back every day as an out-patient.

Why don't you bring that up to your doctor and see what he says?"

"I will."

As the minutes slowly pass, Rick lies in bed wondering why he never heard of Mellaril or Ativan pills before he arrived there. Surely, they must be new drugs, he thought. If they weren't he probably would have taken them while he was being treated for his bad back. After all, he tried at least every other pill.

"Is it time yet?" Rick calls out to a passing nurse. "Almost," she replies smiling.

Rick wishes there were some way of speeding up the medication nurse's watch. He doesn't feel that elevated anymore and he knows he won't feel better until he is given his Mellaril and Atiman. He only hopes his body hasn't grown immune to these wonder drugs which create such a state of ecstasy.

Rick doesn't know which drug makes him feel so care free, but he misses the feeling. He wishes he knew about these drugs earlier. If he had, he would have taken them whenever he had to see Steve. He probably wouldn't have gotten that pain in his stomach like he always did and maybe Steve would have come around in time and developed into a real television writer and hold up his end of their partnership.

"Sorry I'm late," the medication nurse tells Rick as she wheels in her cart. She hastily prepares Rick's medication and hands him his usual cup of pills.

Rick looks into the cup and recognizes every pill except one. He removes

the pill and shows it to the nurse." What kind's this one?"

"Mellaril."

"This doesn't look like a Mellaril. You've made a mistake," he says cautiously, trying not to ruffle her feathers.

"It's the same pill you've been taking, only a stronger dosage."

Rick's suspicious attitude changes as his eyes practically pop out of his head and his mouth drops wide open. "You mean this isn't fifty milligrams?"

"Try one hundred milligrams. You doctor changed it this morning."

Hearing this, Rick drops the pill into the cup and empties the contents into his mouth, washing them all down with orange juice. "See you in three hours," he tells her as he flies out of his room and down the corridor heading for unit three.

Rick rounds another corridor passing unit one. He thinks about entering the alcoholic wing, but changes his mind, then decides to enter and tell Kim that he might be released soon.

Rick walks into the unit and heads for the end of the corridor where Kim's room is located. He stops in the doorway and looks in, only to discover that her bed is without sheets and her belongings are nowhere in sight."

"You want something?" one of the female patients inquires.

"Do you know where Kim is?"

"Probably in the bar down the street," she says smirking. "Don't count on seeing her again. She left AMA."

Rick is distressed to hear about Kim deciding to just leave unit one. He'll go over to unit three and hopefully find something to elevate his spirits.

"*Et me ot ah ere!*" a familiar voice cries out from behind one of unit one's closed doors.

Rick hears the strange plea again and decides to investigate. He makes his way to the room and peers inside, spotting the same man from his unit tied down to his bed in this padded room. The man sees Rick looking in and he cries out again. As Rick stares in, he catches a glimpse of an attendant approaching and decides to leave unit one before he's mistaken for a member of this unit and forced to remain.

Approaching unit three, Rick looks through the open door of the admitting room. and sees Nick sitting in his wheelchair, apparently checking out. Nick spots Rick and calls out,

"You got an extra cigarette man?"

"You checking out Nick?"

"Yeah man, they're sending me home."

Rick heads into unit three delighted to hear that Nick's leaving. As Rick pushes open the doors he hears Nick calling out to him for one last cigarette. Rick ignores Nick's request as he lets the doors slam closed.

Rick takes a seat in Dr. Schwartz's office as the doctor ignores his presence, preferring to sift through the massive pile of papers on his desk. After a few minutes, Dr. Schwartz looks up.

"How you feeling today Rick? Are you relaxed or do you still feel tense?"

"You're the doctor, you tell me."

Dr. Schwartz smiles slyly. "I think your brain is too tense Rick." He pauses for dramatic effect. "Two tenths, the size of a normal brain." He begins laughing at his obvious attempt at humor.

Rick appreciates Dr. Schwartz's levity, but he liked the joke better when Abbott and Costello performed it.

"Now, let's see if we can't get down to business." Dr. Schwartz skims through his notes. "The staff reports on you are very favorable of late."

"I had a feeling they would be. I don't think I've argued with any of the nurses since B.T."

"B.T. What's B.T.?"

Before Tranquilizers."

He ignores Rick's joke. "I see. Why don't you tell me again how it came to be that you got addicted to all those pills?"

Rick is perturbed to hear Dr. Schwartz infer that he was addicted to more than one pill. "I was just hooked on one pill remember?"

Dr. Schwartz sheepishly drops the file he was looking at into an open drawer. Then he picks up another file from his desk. "I'm sorry. I must have been looking at someone else's file. Please ago on and tell me, about. whatever it was you were addicted to and try not to leave anything out no matter how irrelevant you might think it is."

"Like I told you before, it started out really easy when my doctor told me to take one Placidyl to help me sleep through the night. See, he said I had to sleep on my back, but I never did, so he figured the pills would knock me out and I could go to sleep on my back anyway. It worked great for a few weeks, but then one pill wasn't doing the trick so I went to two pills, then three pills and when I started taking four pills, I knew I needed help and that's when I came here." Rick sits back in his chair, signifying that he's finished.

Dr. Schwartz stares at Rick expecting him to continue. The room's silent for a few moments when Dr. Schwartz decides it's his turn to say something.

"How did your wife react to all those pills you were taking?"

"Excuse me doctor, but I don't see the relevance of repeating all those things we've already discussed."

"I can't, help you if you won't cooperate. Now, I don't care if this is old hat to you. All I'm concerned with is, getting to the root of your problems and I can't see how we're going to accomplish anything if you're insistent about arguing with my techniques which I've been using for many years. Now please continue."

Rick sits in his chair stewing. He doesn't care for Dr. Schwartz's attitude, deciding that he's really bored with these counterproductive sessions. After all, Dr. Schwartz never says anything of value and never offers an opinion as to how Rick should cope with his problems. Instead, he just nods his head up and down, hardly uttering a word unless he's forced to by Rick's silence. Rick only agreed to the therapy because he thought he'd just have to go a couple of times. He had no idea that once they latched on to him, they'd never let go. It strikes him odd that they'd give him more drugs when they must surely know he can't handle anything addictive. If he could, he wouldn't be there in the first place.

Rick would like to just pick up and leave Dr. Schwartz's office but he doesn't want to because any friction between himself and the doctor. He might as well cut his own throat and be done with it.

Rick would like to discontinue the sessions altogether, but he's afraid to mention it figuring that Dr. Schwartz might construe that as another sign of mental imbalance.

After serious consideration, Rick decides to simply continue and comply with Dr. Schwartz's request. "Well, Valerie didn't say much to me while I took all that stuff, but I knew she wanted to. I finally got her to say what was on her mind. She said she was afraid that if there was a fire or something, she wouldn't be able to wake me up because I was so loaded and she said she was scared because she thought I'd eventually take an overdose and die. I think she was, right about that though because at the rate I was going I wasn't getting better and would have eventual taken too much. She never really said much beyond that because she was kind of afraid of what I might do. I know I changed a lot and I guess I was a real bastard because I had a really short temper and I was always ready to explode."

Dr. Schwartz files Rick's chart in his desk and stands up. "I think we can continue this tomorrow Rick."

Rick is aghast. Apparently, Dr. Schwartz wasn't even listening to him.

Dr. Schwartz holds the door open for Rick. "You might want to repeat some of the things we've discussed in your group session."

"But I wasn't finished telling you about my wife," Rick angrily reminds him.

"No need for that," he says callously," I already know how

she reacted. I'll see you here the same time tomorrow okay?"

Rick takes out a cigarette and begins to light it.

"Wait until you're in the corridor before you light that."

Rick smiles affably as he puts his cigarette back into his pocket.

"You'd better get back to your room for your medication before group starts."

Rick heads for the door in silence, then turns around deciding to ask Dr. Schwartz one more question. "When do you think I'll be able to go home?"

"Don't worry about that now. I'll tell you when I think you're ready."

"But I feel ready now! Rick insists. "If you still want to see me, I can come back for the group sessions and I can even come back and keep my appointments with you."

"I don't think so Rick. Not at this point anyway. I'll tell you when I think it's in your best interest to function as an out-patient. I know you wouldn't want to leave AMA."

"I've been here ten days already!"

"You knew when you asked us for help that you might be here for two weeks, even longer if necessary. The important thing for you to do is not worry about how long you've been here. You should concentrate on getting better and letting us help you the best way we know how. I wish it could be done overnight, but we haven It progressed that far. Maybe we'll have a miracle cure in ten years, but not now. I can see from our sessions you're showing marked improvement, but by no stretch of the imagination are you ready to leave here now and that's the last word I have on the matter."

"Do you think I could have another pass to go home and spend some time with my wife and little boy?"

"I don't think that would be wise at this point of your recovery process. You'll be home before you know it anyway.

Now I think you'd better get back to your unit for your medication before you end up missing the group session" Dr. Schwartz heads back into his office and shuts the door.

Rick exits the arts and crafts room more depressed than he's been in a long time. He was sure Dr. Schwartz would at least give him some indication when he'd be released. Unfortunately, he didn't and now Rick feels like he'll never be able to go home. Maybe that guy was right when he told Rick that once they get a hold of somebody with private insurance, they never let him go. At any rate, Rick feels ready to leave the hospital no matter what Dr. Schwartz thinks.

Rick walks slowly back to his unit as a familiar figure approaches.

"I went to your room looking for you," Charlie says laughing nervously, "but you weren't there. I wanted to ask if you had a script I could look at because I've never seen a real television script before and I thought maybe if you had one with you I could look at it or something and pretend that I was one of the actors in the show."

"I don't have any scripts with me, but I can have my wife bring one down for you."

"I just want to look at it for a few minutes. I won't get it dirty or anything."

"Tell you what Charlie, I'll call Valerie and have her bring one of my shows down as soon as she visits me again. You can keep the script for yourself and you can take your time looking at it."

Charlie is aghast. "Really! You mean I can keep it for myself?"

"Hey, don't get so excited. It's only a script. I've got lots of 'em and I'd be happy to let you have one."

"Thanks Rick," Charlie chortles as he starts his journey back to unit three. Rick approaches his room and spots Dr.

Wang coming his way.

"Excuse me Dr. Wang, but could I talk to you for a minute?"

"Sure Rick. What can I do for you?"

"Well, I've been here for ten days now and I think I'm ready to go home. I know I'm not totally cured, but I can make arrangements not to miss any group sessions and I can even keep my appointments with Dr. Schwartz for private therapy. I know I can handle it and if I think I need to come back here, I won't hesitate to check myself back in, but I know that won't happen because. I've got my addiction problem licked."

"I see," Dr. Wang comments as he looks through his charts. "You have made a marked improvement the last week. I don't see why you can't go home, if you keep coming to group and Dr. Schwartz."

Rick is ecstatic. "You mean I can leave?"

"I'll stop by the office in a few minutes and tell them I think you're ready to be discharged. You can pick up the medication you'll need at the pharmacy on your way out." Dr. Wang smiles affably as he closes up his chart and heads down the corridor.

Rick can't believe his ears as he stands rigid in the corridor, overcome with joy. He never fathomed that he could leave, especially since Dr. Schwartz rejected the idea.

Rick spots the medication nurse pushing her cart into his room and he races in behind her. First, he'll get his medication and then he'll call Valerie with the good news.

Rick sits on his bed, patiently waiting as the nurse prepares his medication. She hands him his cup of pills and he gulps them down in a hurry without the benefit of a liquid.

"Thank you very much," Rick tells the nurse as he picks up his phone and dials. "Hi Valerie, it's me. Listen, I was wondering if you'd do me a favor. I want you to get in the car and come down to the hospital right away. No nothing's wrong. I just want you to come pick me up" Rick pauses for a moment collecting his thoughts. "I'm coming home!"

CHAPTER TWENTY-TWO

It's great to be home, Rick thinks to himself as he relaxes on his own bed, two hours after coming back from the hospital. He only has to share his bed with Valerie and best of all, he knows everything that's likely to happen. No Strangers will come in and take his blood or order him to therapy and there's no one else to take care of. Rick wonders what will become of Jose without him being there to care for him, but he figures that Jose got along without him before and he's confident Jose will continue to forge ahead. At any rate, Rick plans on seeing just how Jose is doing when he returns to the hospital for his private sessions with Dr. Schwartz.

Rick had no idea he'd truly miss the hospital. After all, he made many friends and his whole life revolved around the happenings there. Only now, he no longer belongs after being cured of his Placidyl addiction which nearly cost him his life. Rick wonders how his friends are doing without him there to help guide them along. He's even curious what therapy sessions will be like without his input.

"How does it feel to finally lie in your own bed?" Valerie asks as she brings Rick a glass of milk to help wash down the medication he's been prescribed.

Rick pops the tranquilizers in his mouth and washes them down with the milk. "Great I'd probably be there another week if I hadn't bumped into Dr. Wang."

Valerie climbs onto the bed and cuddles with her husband. "I love you for what you did," she tells him as her eyes swell and tears begin to form. "I was so scared being home alone without you. I don't know how I made it through these past two weeks."

I wasn't gone two weeks!"

"You're only counting the time you spent in the hospital. I'm counting the few days before you made up your mind to go there. I hardly even knew you and I was scared you wouldn't wake up in the morning and then I'd be alone." Tears begin rolling down Valerie's face and she buries her head under Rick's caressing arm.

"It's over honey," he tells her in a reassuring tone. "I know how scared you must have been, but now it's over and I'm okay. Really! I'm sorry for what I put you through, but at that time I really wasn't myself. Those damn pills took me over and I really didn't care about anything except plopping them into my mouth, but that's history and we have our lives to lead." Rick lifts Valerie's head in front of his and kisses her passionately as her tears roll onto Rick's face. They laugh.

"I thought you never cry."

Rick smiles. "These are your tears." Rick wipes his face dry. "How long do you have to take those pills?"

"I guess until Dr. Schwartz feel I don't need them anymore. As far as I'm concerned, I don't think I need 'em at all."

"At least they're not sleeping pills."

"Oh, I don't know. If I took a triple dose, I'd fall asleep."

Valerie doesn't appreciate his remark.

"I'm only kidding," he says pulling Valerie against him. "After Schwartz releases me, I'll think twice about taking so much as one aspirin for a headache. You have no idea what dope does to you unless you actually have the experience yourself. I didn't know what was going on until it was too late."

Valerie sits up and looks at Rick with a seriousness emblazoned on her face. "Can't we just forget what happened and never mention that place again or the people in there? You're home with me now and that's all that counts."

"That's a tall order honey. I lived with those people for ten days and I'm not likely' to forget about it."

Valerie picks up Rick's hand and places it against her warm stomach indicating her need to be touched. "Please Rick. Do it for met" she pleads as she guides his hand in a sensual motion. "Let's forget what happened and just love each other."

Rick reaches up and shuts off the lights as Valerie snuggles up next to him and begins caressing her lover. Rick's glad to be home, but more importantly, he's glad Valerie was waiting for him to return. Now he can go on with his life and love his wife again and again even more passionately. He only realizes now, that she truly loves him more than he ever thought possible. He just hopes the tranquilizers don't inhibit his lovemaking and if they do, Valerie will just have to be patient until he's allowed to quit taking them altogether.

Rick is anxious to return to the hospital for his first visit. as an out-patient. He races through the admitting room and proceeds directly towards unit three, but stops dead in his tracks as he thinks about Jose. After a moment or in indecision, Rick decides to go back to his old room and see how Jose's getting along without him.

As Rick strolls down the corridors heading for unit two, he hears an all too familiar screaming emanating from unit one.

"*Et me ot ah ere!*"

George exits unit one and brightens immediately upon seeing Rick standing a few feet away. "I'm glad to see you've come back Ricky. I was hurt you left without saying goodbye to me."

Rick isn't too crazy about seeing George, but decides to

ask him a question that's been haunting him ever since he was admitted. "C'mon George, I wouldn't leave here permanently without telling you goodbye. By the way, maybe you could tell me what's the matter with that guy who's always screaming. He was in my unit for a while and he drove me crazy and I never found out what his problem is."

George looks at Rick slyly as he tilts his head. "And what'll you give me if I tell you?"

"Don't give me that shit George! Just tell me, please!"

"Well okay," George says relenting. "That guy's been here longer than me and I've been here two years. They'll never make him better because he's what you might call permanently retarded and his folks pay a lot of money to keep him here. Shit man! They don't even come to visit him like you think they would. You'd think their guilty consciences would at least make them come visit their kid at Christmas time. I feel sorry for the guy, but there's nothing me or nobody else can do except just pump him with IVs and make sure he doesn't get loose and hurt himself." George begins laughing. "Boy oh boy! You should see him sometime when he gets himself loose and runs down the halls. He's got more soulful moves than a rooster with his balls cut off."

"You mean he's only in here because he retarded?"

"He's more than retarded my man. He has about five seizures every day and he needs to be in a place like this. I wish they'd transfer him to another hospital because I'm the nigger they call to clean up his ass."

"I don't envy you."

"Hey man, just be glad you are who you are and you don't have to have someone like me come in every time you wet your pants. He might as well be some god damn animal because he sure don't seem like no person."

"I think I liked it better when I didn't know what was

wrong with him." Rick heads down the corridor. "I'll see you later George and thanks for the information."

"Hey man, any time you want something or just want to talk, you know where you can find me," George calls out as Rick disappears into another corridor.

As Rick approaches his old room on unit two. Doris Rayburn sees him coming and gets up to intercept him.

"Where do you think you're going?" she asks caustically.

Rick is taken aback at. her chiding tone. "I'm just going to my old room to see how Jose's doing. That's not a crime, is it?"

Doris isn't amused with Rick's levity. "Former patients are forbidden from visiting other patients. That's strict hospital policy and one to which I highly subscribe. You I'll have to leave."

Rick can't fathom why Doris' attitude is so harsh. "I just want to see if he needs anything."

"He doesn't need anything from you we can't give him ourselves. That's why we're here. Now you'll have to leave or do you want to be escorted from this unit?"

Rick takes a step away from Doris then whirls around staring at her vitriolically. "You know Doris, the kindest thing I can say about knowing you is that you fit the textbook definition of a bitch!" Rick quickly turns around and heads down the corridor making sure Doris can't get in the last word.

Rick heads back towards unit three as Maggie exits the admitting room and sees him coming her way.

"Back so soon?"

"Don't worry, I'm just visiting. At least that's one of the reasons I'm here. Did you know I'm not allowed to go visit Jose?"

Maggie nods omnisciently. "Doris cut you off at the pass huh?"

"I'll say she did. She's got me tuned in like radar."

"We'll, she is following hospital policy and they don't

generally bend the rules around here unless you have someone backing you up."

"That mean you'll do something?"

"I don't see why not. I'll have a talk with the administrator and see if you can't be the exception to the rule. If anyone should be allowed to visit Jose, I think it should be you. You took better care of him than anyone around here. I know he'd appreciate seeing you. As soon as he found out you were gone he had another one of his seizures."

"I've been thinking about that and it seems that whenever he gets upset or mad about something the next thing you know, he has a seizure. Think there's any relationship?"

"You tell me. You've 'Spent more time with him than anyone else." Maggie checks her watch. "I'd better get back to the unit and relieve one of my nurses." Maggie heads down the corridor walking backwards enabling her to keep talking to Rick. "Check with the administrator later before you leave and I'll see if I can't get her to let you visit Jose."

"Thanks," Rick yells down the corridor as Maggie heads for unit two.

Rick approaches unit three's doors, then remembers he left one of his television scripts in his car which he brought for Charlie. Rick leaves through the admitting room and returns to his car.

Script in hand, Rick enters unit three and begins looking for Charlie. Rick checks both corridors and even goes outside where several new patients are playing volleyball, but Charlie's nowhere in sight.

Rick heads for the nurse's station when he spots Charlie sitting in the television room.

"How ya doing Charlie?"

Charlie looks up exhibiting his dazed state. "I'm okay now, but I didn't feel so good so they gave me more Lithium. Think they figured out how much to give me this time."

Rick drops the script on Charlie's lap. Charlie picks it up and curiously looks it over.

"I autographed the front page for you," Rick informs him, hoping that Charlie will value the script even more.

"Thanks a lot. I'll try and read it and give it back to you before you leave."

"But I'm not a patient here anymore. I'm back at home and I come here for groups and private sessions now."

"Does that mean you're not going to be my friend anymore?" he asks, giggling nervously.

"Don't be silly. I wrote my phone number on the script and if you ever feel lonely or just want to give me a call, I'd like to talk with you."

Charlie doesn't react to Rick's statement as he gets up and heads for the door. "I think I'll go back to my room," he says sluggishly.

"Aren't you coming to group?"

"Dr. Schwartz called it off because he had to go somewhere I think." Charlie continues walking down the corridor towards his room.

"That's great!" Rick sarcastically mumbles to himself as he stands in the TV room alone. "I came all this way for group and my session with that inconsiderate asshole and he decides to take the day off. I'll bet he didn't even call Valerie to cancel my appointment!"

Rick exits unit three. He decides to return home until the next day when he'd be expected to keep his next appointment with Dr. Schwartz.

The next morning, Rick takes his two tranquilizers before breakfast and leaves for the. hospital an hour early.

He plans on visiting his friends before his session with Dr. Schwartz.

As he nears the hospital, Rick almost causes a traffic accident, but he reacts in time and proceeds normally to the hospital. When he walks through the doors, he begins feeling agitated due to the accident which he narrowly escaped. He automatically reaches for a cigarette to calm his jumbled nerves, then remembers that he brought along his medicine in case he stayed at the hospital more than three hours. Rick's certain his nervousness will dissipate once he fortifies himself with an Ativan and Mellaril.

Rick walks through the admitting doors making a right turn into the first open door. Rick walks into the room and spots the hospital administrator sitting behind her desk.

"Excuse me, but I used to be a patient here and I wanted to find out—

"I know who you are Mr. Brown," she interrupts. "Maggie told me to expect you."

"I don't know whether you know it or not, but Doris has it in for me."

"Tell you what I am aware of Mr. Brown. I know for a fact that if it wasn't for your caring attitude, we'd have had an impossible time caring for Jose. Thanks to you, my staff was free to handle their routine duties with good conscience knowing you were keeping an eye on our star patient."

Rick didn't come here to hear a long speech. "Did you tell Doris it's all right for me to visit him?"

The administrator looks away as if she's afraid to confront Rick directly. "As far as I'm concerned, rules are made to be broken and if you like, you can have the run of the entire hospital, but as to your request to visit with Jose," she pauses," I'm afraid he left us sometime this morning and we don't know where he could have gone."

Rick is aghast. "You mean he ran away? Don't you have any

idea where he went? Did he take his medication with him?"

"I was hoping you could shed some light on his whereabouts, but I can see you don't know any more than we do. Most of my people are out right now looking for him. I didn't think he could have gone far. He's in one of our wheelchairs. How he managed to get himself in one of those things I'll never know. You think there Is any chance he's trying to find you?"

Rick shakes his head. "I doubt it. He doesn't know where I live and he doesn't even know my last name so I doubt he's trying to call me up."

"If he decides to show himself on your doorstep, I'd appreciate hearing from you."

"Don't worry. The last thing my wife and I need is another mouth to feed." Rick heads for the door, but turns back for a second. "Thanks for setting Doris straight."

"My pleasure, only the next time you bump heads with her try and restrain yourself from calling her names. That only makes her harder to work with and no matter how she treated you, she is one of the best in her profession."

Rick grins. "I don't know about being the best, but I'm sure she was the first."

Rick enters unit three and sees Sherri coming his way. He can easily see that something is troubling her.

"Where you headed Sherri?"

"I'm taking the rest of the day off and going home," she tells him avoiding his curious glance.

"What's the matter? You feel all right?"

"No I don't feel all right. I feel stupid and I should know better than to get involved like I did."

Rick doesn't know what she's referring to. "Slow down and tell me about it."

"I knew I'd run into something like this in my profession, but I never thought I could lose my perspective, but I did."

Rick doesn't say a word, hoping Sherri will continue without his prompting.

"I just feel stupid that's all. I thought he cared the same way about me as I did him, but I guess he didn't because he's not even here anymore and he didn't even say goodbye or leave so much as a note. He just left."

"Who are you talking about? Is it someone I know?" Rick anxiously inquires.

"It's Neil. I feel like I let myself down because I really thought we had something real between us, but I guess I called that wrong. He promised we'd see each other when he got his head together and left here, but I guess that was just a line. He was the only one in here who wasn't on something and I thought he was telling it to me straight, but I guess that's his way of getting what he wants and I fell for it all the way."

"Don't take this wrong," Rick interrupts," but I think you forgot why Neil was here in the first place."

"You don't have to say 'I told you so' because I already know that. I just can't believe I let my guard down and actually convinced myself that I could have something real with someone in this place. I know other people in here who fell for one of the patients, but they got their heads together in a hurry. I just can't believe I let that happen. I guess I just thought Neil was different."

"I'd just forget about him if I were you. Anyway, you've got lots of company. He had just about everybody in here fooled pretty good, including me." Sherri looks at Rick curiously. "How do you mean?"

Rick doesn't want to relate everything he knows and suspects about Neil, but he feels that a little information can't hurt. "Let's just say he was a master con artist and if he said 'apples' he was really saying 'oranges'. When I first met him, I thought he was a real nice guy too, but the longer I stayed around him, the less I trusted him."

"I have a feeling there's something you're deliberately' not telling me."

Rick smiles slyly. "Like I said, he fooled all of us."

Sherri heads for the door. "I appreciate your words of wisdom, but I'm still going home."

"You're coming back, aren't you?"

"Right after lunch." Sherri smiles at Rick as she exits.

Rick checks his watch, figuring he still has about twenty minutes before his private session with Dr. Schwartz. In that time, he decides to wander through the corridors and visit with his old friends of unit three.

Rick heads down one corridor and is surprised at the number of new faces he sees. As each patient approaches, Rick instinctively smiles thinking that it's someone he knows, but so far, every face is strange.

Rick continues down the corridor heading for Charlie's room. He's confident that Charlie didn't leave due to his long-term state of depression.

Rick enters Charlie's room and is surprised to see a new patient asleep on Charlie's bed. The patient on the next bed informs Rick that Charlie was discharged early that morning, adding that he doesn't know where he went.

As Rick exits the room, he spots the script he gave Charlie abandoned in the trash can. Rick reaches down and picks it up, putting it under his arm before deciding to throw it back into the trash.

Rick heads down the other corridor, distressed to see more unfamiliar faces passing him. For the first time, Rick feels out of place and very uncomfortable in a unit where he once felt so secure and at home. Only now, he no longer belongs.

Rick hears the sounds of an active volleyball game and heads outside, figuring his friends are probably playing.

Unfortunately, as before, all the participants are new patients and Rick doesn't recognize even one face on either side of the net.

Rick heads back inside, deciding to play a solitary game of pool like he used to when he was a part of the hospital. Upon entering the room, Rick is delighted to see Carol practicing her trick shots. Rick stands in the doorway beaming, but Carol just looks up at him for a moment and then resumes her game. Rick's first thought is that Carol is probably under the influence of her medication, otherwise she'd throw her arms around him.

"You're the best thing I've seen all day," he happily announces.

Carol makes another shot, ignoring Rick's remark as well as his presence.

"Where'd everybody go?"

Carol ignores Rick's question and pushes him aside to make another shot.

"Are you feeling all right?"

Carol sets her pool cue against the table and looks at Rick venomously. "What are you doing back here anyway? I thought you went home to your wife and kid to live happily ever after!"

Rick is stunned at Carol's tone. "What'd I do?" he asks innocently.

"Who do you think you are? Huh! You think you can just come in here whenever you feel like it arid ask a bunch of questions like you're one of the doctors or something?"

"Carol, it's me, Rick."

"I really don't care. You're just a visitor now and you don't belong here anymore. Did you come back just to look at the freaks in the hospital or something? Why don't you go home and stay away because that's what I'd do if they'd let me leave. I'd never come back. You just can't come back and pretend you belong with the rest of the gang. You're better now and you don't belong here so why don't you leave?" Carol angrily picks up her pool cue and misses the next shot.

Dejected, Rick heads out of the room. Then he turns around and sees Carol staring at him caustically.

"Is Carla still here?"

"She left when Neil did. They left together just like you left me here! I'm the only one left out of the whole gang mid I thought I'd be the first to get out."

"Hey Carol, I'm sorry. You'll be getting out pretty soon."

"Just leave me alone and don't ever come back because you don't belong here no more!" Carol throws her cue against the wall. "You should be in here, not me!"

Rick hastily retreats down the corridor and into the arts and crafts room five minutes before his appointment with Dr. Schwartz.

As Rick sits in the outer office, he reflects on what Carol told him about not belonging anymore. "Maybe I don't belong here anymore," Rick mutters under his breath as Dr. Schwartz's secretary informs him that the doctor will be a few minutes late. Rick is relieved to hear this, deciding he doesn't need his sessions with Dr. Schwartz anymore. As far as he's concerned, he no longer requires the services of Dr. Schwartz.

"Could you please tell Dr. Schwartz I had to leave." Rick tells the secretary as he gets up and exits the arts and crafts room.

"What should I tell the doctor?" the secretary calls out.

"Tell him I'll come back when he allows his patients to smoke," Rick replies glibly.

The secretary stares at Rick blankly. "Huh?"

"Tell him I got better without him!" Rick joyfully informs her as he heads down the corridor for the exit.

As Rick approaches the doors, he stops to peer into the

therapy room where a group is in session. Rick's first thought is to join the patients and liven up the activities, but he changes his mind when he fails to recognize even one face. Even the therapist in charge is a stranger to Rick. As far as he's concerned, this is the last time he'll ever see a therapy group, and for that matter, it's the last time he'll ever visit this hospital.

§

Rick Brown is cured. It's been two weeks since he last visited the hospital and he no longer misses seeing his fellow patients or, for that matter, anything dealing with the hospital. He can't even remember what a Placidyl does or what it tastes like and in his mind that means he's cured. The only thing about his hospital ordeal which still leaves a bad taste in his mouth are all those uncomfortable sessions with Dr. Schwartz. Rick feels cheated that he spent so much time with Dr. Schwartz and he never once said anything to benefit Rick's problems. Instead, he listened in silence and only spoke when Rick demanded his opinion. Even then, he didn't say anything constructive.

Rick has faithfully' stayed on his Mellaril and Ativan pills ever since Dr. Schwartz prescribed them. He has grown accustomed to the feeling he attains from the medication and looks forward to taking them every three hours. Rick likes the idea of having all tension relieved, especially when he's having such a hard time trying to make contacts which might lead to a script assignment without his former partner. Unfortunate, all the connections he made with the help of Steve and his parents no longer exist. Rick soon realizes that when he made an enemy of Steve's parents by dropping their no talent son, he also made enemies with all their friends in the business. Rick is distressed with this revelation, but figures it's only a minor setback which he'll be able to overcome in a short time.

"What's the matter? You look depressed," Valerie tells her husband as she watches him slam down the phone in his office.

"I don't know what's going on. I just talked to Frank Sanders over at Fox and he told me He couldn't use me like he said he would last month."

"Did he say why?"

"He inferred that I wasn't exactly wanted in this town because of what I did to Steve.

He didn't come right out and say it in so many words, but I got the feeling that Steve's parents have more friends than I thought and he's one of them."

"What are you gonna do?" Maybe you should have a talk with Steve's folks."

"No way! I've been looking for an excuse to start on my book and it looks like I have a couple of years to do it, now that I'm apparently ostracized from television. I must have talked to everybody I know in the business and they treat me like poison or something. Guess I'll just work on my book for a while and maybe I can get something sold in the meantime till this whole mess blows over."

"I don It like to say I told you so but you knew when you dumped Steve that you'd be set back for a time."

"I know but I really didn't think it would happen like this. I had no idea his parents had so many friends who'd bend over backwards to keep their son's ex-partner from showing him up."

"It's too late to change it now."

"Like I said, I'll start on my book till all those assholes realize that all they're doing is blacklisting me for no damn good reason. Then they'll call me back and ask me to write for them. You'll see."

"When are you gonna start your book?"

"Right now," Rick announces proudly as he picks up the

phone. "Right after I call the hospital and cancel all future appointments with Dr. Schwartz and tell his damn secretary to stop calling me about coming in. I told her I wasn't coming back, but I'll tell her again."

"Can I get you anything before you start, like some coffee or something?"

Rick looks lovingly at his accommodating spouse and proudly tells her, "The first thing you can do is go into the medicine cabinet and take out all my pills. All of them!"

Valerie is distressed to hear Rick asking for his pills. "I thought you stopped taking them yesterday when you said they kept you from thinking straight and you couldn't sit at the typewriter," she interrupts.

Rick smiles slyly. "I meant it too. I want you to take those pills and flush 'em down the toilet.

Valerie beams with delight. "Really?"

"Really," he assures her. "Then I'll take that coffee."

Valerie proudly marches into the master bathroom. She empties Rick's pill bottles into the toilet and flushes it. Minutes later, Valerie returns to her husband's office carrying a new legal pad and a fresh pot of coffee. She sets them on his desk.

"I just called Schwartz's office and told his secretary to settle up with the insurance company because I'm not coming back," he proudly announces as he positions the legal pad in front of him. Then Rick faces his typewriter, noticing how clean it is. Even the ribbon's been changed.

"I just wanted everything to be perfect when you started working again."

Rick could easily break down and cry, but he's not one to do that, even though it would ease the pressure he's forcing himself to endure. "It's gonna be rough with no money coming in."

"I can always get a job until you sell something."

"I swear Valerie, I'm the luckiest person in the world."

Valerie smiles at her husband lovingly. "I don't know about that." Valerie pauses. "Maybe the second."

Rick gets up to hold his wife for a few moments. Then they kiss passionately, but Valerie breaks it off.

"If you're gonna start working on that book, I think I'd better leave you alone or you might not want to work on it till tomorrow."

Rick pulls Valerie close to him and caresses her bottom. "So, what would be so terrible about that?" he whispers into her ear.

"Never mind. I've got a lot of things to do around here including your laundry and I want to get it done tonight."

"How about getting it done today so we can watch television in our room tonight."

"Television!"

"Yeah. There's a really great movie on at one."

"I'll never make it that late."

"You will if I keep you up." Rick grabs Valerie and playfully kisses her neck, then slowly moves down to her more sensuous areas.

"I don't think I can wait till tonight," she says giggling," unless I leave you to your book right now." Valerie heads for the door, blowing Rick one last kiss.

Rick positions himself in front of his typewriter and assorts his notes. Then Rick slips a piece of paper into his typewriter and types the title page. Rick stares at his three-word title, *The Hollywood Bandits* and decides that this is the best possible title for a book concerning the atrocities of the entertainment business with special emphasis on the people in television he's run across.

For the next two hours, Rick stares at the title page in somewhat of a dazed state. He can't understand why he's not typing, especially when his notes clearly indicate the beginning of his story.

Rick sifts through his notes a fourth and then a fifth time before deciding that he's simply too tired to press on.

Much to Valerie's dismay, Rick declines dinner that night explaining that he's so excited to be home, he simply doesn't have an appetite.

Rick retires early that night, hoping that his splitting headache will subside if he lies down. Unfortunately, the headache doesn't lessen to any degree and Rick finds that even though he's totally exhausted, he still can't go to sleep. He figures he's just going through a period of adjustment and he'll be fine as soon as his body gets used to the routine of being home again.

"Your feet are freezing!" Valerie tells Rick as she snuggles up to him under the sheets. Valerie's hands begin caressing Rick's chest until he gently pushes her hands away.

"I don't feel so good honey," he states in somewhat of a whining tone.

Valerie sits up and places her hand on Rick's forehead. "You don't feel warm. What's bothering you?"

"I don't know exactly. It's not like I'm coming down with something, but I just feel really lousy. How does my tongue look?" Rick sticks out his tongue.

Valerie is startled at the sight of Rick's almost white and shriveled up tongue. She gasps. "What have you been eating? It's all white!"

"Cotton-mouth?" he asks hesitantly.

"Yeah, just like you had when you were on all that stuff. Maybe I should call the doctor."

"No way!" Rick comments shaking his head. "It's just left over withdrawal from the Placidyls. I'll be all right tomorrow. I promise."

"You'd better be," Valerie responds firmly.

A few minutes later, Rick looks at his wife and notices her sleeping peacefully. Unfortunately, he senses that he'll be unable to sleep even though he's very tired.

Valerie awakens early the following morning and discovers that Rick's side of the bed has already been made. Valerie throws on her bathrobe and walks throughout the house until she finds Rick sitting motionless behind his typewriter.

"How long you been working?"

Rick turns around wiping the sweat from his brow. "I don't know. I guess a few hours."

"How much sleep did you get?"

"Not very much. I mean, none at all. I don't know what's wong with me because I'm really tired, but I just can't fall asleep and my headache won't go away." Rick stands up. "Maybe I'll try again I because I really don't feel I can handle the typewriter." Then Rick falls back onto his chair almost knocking it over.

Valerie races across the room hoping to catch her husband before he sustains injury. Rick quickly recovers and decides to sit back in his chair.

"I'm all right, but I think I'd better lie down."

As Valerie looks on, her eyes become glassy as she remembers how Rick behaved on the day he committed himself for Placidyl-addiction. She experiences a Déjà vu as she watches Rick fumbling around trying to get his papers in order. "Maybe you'd better call the hospital or something and tell them what's wrong," she nervously suggests, her voice trembling.

"I'll be all right," Rick tells her, trying to sound sure or himself. "If I could just throw up or something."

"'Do you feel nauseous too?"

"I think so." Rick gets up.

"Honey, please call the hospital.

Rick stares at Valerie caustically, then begins to cry. "I'm sorry honey," he says rubbing his eyes. "I don't know what's happening to me! One second I feel like working and the next thing I know, I can't even see straight or think right."

Valerie picks up the phone and begins dialing. "I'll talk to them if you won't."

Hearing this, Rick snatches the receiver from Valerie's hand and waits for someone at the hospital to answer. The hospital operator transfers Rick to the head of admitting.

"This is Rick Brown. I was in your hospital for Placidyl addiction for about two weeks and now I've been home for two weeks and I think I'm going through withdrawal and I wanted to know if you could tell me what's wrong."

"I think I remember you Mr. Brown. Aren't you the patient who took such marvelous care of the epileptic patient in your room?"

"Damn it! I didn't call to talk about him, I want to know if you can help me!"

"What seems to be the problem?" the voice asks uncaringly.

"I've been experiencing dizziness and headaches and I'm sweating and I feel like throwing up a lot."

"How long have you been feeling this way?"

"Hell! I don't remember. Just tell me what I'm supposed to do! Please!"

"You could come down and we could observe you, but we don't have any room right now. Maybe you should call your own doctor or try another hospital."

"Can't you just look at me and tell me what I'm supposed to do? I feel like I'm coming apart!"

"Tell you what we can do Mr. Brow. Why don't you come down and if I think you should be admitted, you can wait in the admitting room till someone checks out."

"That doesn't make any sense! What if no one checks out? You can't treat me in the admitting room."

"That's the best we can do," the voice answers callously, "and from what I know about insurance companies, they probably wouldn't pay for any additional treatment anyway. If you decide to come here, we need eight hundred dollars until we get verification from your insurance company."

Rick is enraged. "Why didn't you people think of that before you let me go?

It's your fault I'm this way, I didn't do anything your doctors didn't tell me and look where it got me."

"Sorry Mr. Brown. Perhaps you might try another hospital which isn't as crowded."

"Thanks a lot!" Rick slams down the phone.

"What'd they say?" Valerie anxiously asks.

"The truth?"

"Of course, I want the truth! Don't play games."

"They told me to go fuck myself because my insurance ran out." Rick slams his fist against the side of his desk.

Valerie pulls herself together. "We can't just sit back and do nothing. Maybe you should call your own doctor and see what he says."

Rick slowly picks up the phone and begins dialing. "I hope he's not still mad at me for getting addicted to Placidyls."

"C'mon Rick. If anything, he feels bad because he prescribed all those pills. You're no more to blame than he is. It just happened."

Rick is glad to hear his doctor's voice and is delighted that he's really concerned with Rick's plight. He informs Rick that he's going through withdrawal due to the Mellaril and Ativan pills which Dr. Schwartz had no business prescribing. He impresses Rick with the urgency of checking into a proper clinic capable of handling his treatment.

"Should I go back to the same hospital?"

"Hell no! There's a drug rehabilitation clinic about a mile from you.

Vandorf Community I think. Check with information and get your butt over there while I call ahead and make arrangements. Those bastards at that other place did you more harm than good and I'm not gonna stand by and watch you suffer because of them. Now get your butt over there. Pronto!"

Rick hangs up the phone avoiding Valerie's curious glances.

"What'd he say?"

Rick wipes the sweat off his face with his sleeve as he looks at his wife. His voice is shaking. "He wants me to go to Vandorf Community for a while."

Valerie doesn't flinch as Rick expected she would. Instead, she turns to leave Rick's office. "I'll have you packed in five minutes and we can leave in ten."

Rick stares at Valerie with a curious glaze. "How come you're taking this so calm?"

"Because I love you and I want you to get better. Now do what you have to do because we're leaving for the hospital in ten minutes."

§

Valerie has a hard time keeping her eyes and thoughts on the road ahead while Rick squirms in the seat beside her.

"I know you don't want to talk about it and I'll never ask you again, but why in the world would they let you come home if you weren't better and how come they let you come home with two different types of tranquilizers when they knew damn well you could get hooked on them too?" Valerie pauses hoping Rick will answer, but he refrains.

"What went on in that place for two weeks?" Valerie begins crying.

"Don't cry!"

"I can 't help it. You were away from me and our baby for two weeks and now you're going back for who knows how long. I hate being in that house without you. It's scary! I'm sorry Rick. I guess I'm just mad I because I thought you liked being in that place. And just when everything's all right again, I have to take you to some other hospital for the same thing. It's not fair! I just want you to get better and come home for good. Is that such a terrible thing to ask? Is it?"

Rick desperately wants to say the right words but nothing comes to mind. He's too concerned with the treatment he'll be getting and scared about going to a strange hospital.

Vandorf Community Hospital looks more like a hospital than the other one did. Even though it's considerably smaller, it has a homier atmosphere to it which Rick likens to his old college days when he lived in a dormitory.

As explained by the admitting clerk, Vandorf has two units. The first unit treats drug and depression cases while the second unit is reserved for medical cases. Rick inquires about televisions in the rooms and learns that the first unit only has one television for everyone while the second unit has a television set for each patient. Valerie knows what Rick's about to propose and she decides to remain silent as he tells the clerk the reasons why he needs to be in the medical unit.

Rick relates his drug history to the clerk, at which point an attendant enters to escort Rick to the second unit. Rick kisses Valerie goodbye, assuring her that this time he'll get cured. Then Rick heads down the corridor with the attendant on his way to his room.

Rick has his choice of the four empty beds in the room and

opts for the one in the comer. As soon as he gets comfortable and all preliminary tests are completed, the medication nurse arrives for Rick's first dose of his withdrawal medicine.

Rick's first reaction is to ask the nurse about each and every pill, but he doesn't want to be reminded of the way he did things in that other hospital so be refrains from commenting. He takes his medicine like a good patient.

Rick lies in bed watching television as the night shift comes on. Rick listens to the many voices outside his room and is delighted to hear all the nurses conversing in English. At last, Rick thinks to himself, he Is finally in the right place and he's going to get better.

Four hours pass and the medication nurse pushes her cart into Rick's room right on time. The nurse dutifully prepares Rick's medication and hands him a cup containing his pills. As before, Rick simply empties the cup into his mouth and washes down the pills with some orange juice. Then Rick's curiosity gets the best of him and he decides to ask about his medication.

What kind or pills did I take?" he asks matter-of-factly.

"Well let's see," she replies looking at her instructions. "Some Mag Sulfate to help wash out your system, one anti-seizure pill, one anti-itch capsule and something to help you sleep tonight."

"Oh yeah, what kind of sleeping pill?"

The nurse pushes her cart towards the door then turns around to answer. "You've probably never heard of it before. It's called Placidyl."

The End

ABOUT THE AUTHOR

When Ron was at Hanna-Barbera studios, he was the writer for *Scooby-Doo*, as well as *The Smurfs*, the *Snorks* and other well-known cartoon shows. He also worked on *Mork and Mindy* and *The Pink Panther* where he made his reputation! Norman Lear's production company put Ron to work on *Good Times*, *The Jefferson's*, *All in the Family* and *Chips*.

Danny Simon, the brother of Neil Simon later brought Ron onto his staff to write for his ABC Special. Neil Simon reportedly always said that it was his brother that taught him to write.

During his free time from all the busy creations that he worked on in Hollywood, Ron took the time to write the Thriller movie called *Terror in Paradise*. It is still available on Amazon. Also available on DaDons's Rare Laser Discs website and eBay.

Ron often talks about Bud Abbott from the team of *Abbott and Costello*. When Ron was 16 years old and living in Encino, California, he struck up a friendship with Abbott as he sat at the feet of the master, both as a friend and as a student of comedy writing.

Ron also worked with Sherwood Schwartz, the great writer and producer, over the years. With Sherwood, Ron worked on the *Gilligan's Island* series for Metro Media. Ron said that each day was so very exciting for him as he watched the characters delivering his written lines for them.

Ron's beloved characters were Gilligan, The Skipper, Mary Ann, Mrs. Howell and the Professor. Two of Ron's favorite stories include his interaction with John Travolta and Wayne Newton.

Hollywood Friends can be found on www.lostagepublishing.com. Ron is also the author of two other books, *Pickled*, and *Bound 4 Vegas*.

Ron Sellz resides in Chatsworth, CA, is happily married to his wife Teri, and has three sons: Stuart, Scott and Brandon.